ALISON

Her passionate intensity had brought her success. Her elegant beauty had attracted many lovers. Her money had given her freedom. But her heart had so often led her to the wrong kind of man. And now, daring to love again could save her...or destroy her.

HUNTER

His TV fame made him irresistible to women, and his sexual charisma ignited Alison's deepest longings. But why did he want her? For her sweet beauty, for her money and class—or for the part she could play in his shocking fantasy life?

STUART

For years he had put his whole life into building a Florida real estate empire. But he had no one to share it with. Until he met Alison, the only woman he could ever love.

Love Needs No Reason

Shirley Dowling

 AVON
PUBLISHERS OF BARD, CAMELOT, DISCUS AND FLARE BOOKS

AVON BOOKS
A division of
The Hearst Corporation
1790 Broadway
New York, New York 10019

First Avon Printing,.February, 1985

AVON TRADEMARK REG. U.S. PAT. OFF. AND IN OTHER COUNTRIES, MARCA REGISTRADA, HECHO EN U.S.A.

Printed in the U.S.A.

WFH 10 9 8 7 6 5 4 3 2 1

For Papa

Love Needs No Reason

Part I

1

Diana Trask stood at the window with her attention fixed on the parking lot below. The slender young woman had been standing almost like a statue for several minutes, quietly watching something below. The window blinds were tilted against the early-morning sunlight, all but one narrow slat, which she held open with the tip of her forefinger. An isolated beam of light shone through, dancing warm highlights on her short brown hair. Diana listened to Jackie as she wound up a telephone conversation in the next office but didn't turn around even when she felt the other woman's presence in the room with her.

Jackie Aaron bounded across the long office at a frenetic gait, one typical of her constant energy. Diana smiled to herself. Jackie seldom entered a room any other way, particularly first thing in the morning. Suddenly, as spontaneously as she had entered, Jackie stopped dead and straightened the metal nameplate that stood in the center of the ornate desk that dominated the room. On the nameplate the words ALISON AMES—CREATIVE DIRECTOR were spelled in simple, chiseled letters, burnished brass on brass.

All at once somber, Jackie circled to the owner's side of the polished mahogany antique and pulled up to her full five feet two inches of height before perching her fists on her hips. She shook her dark curls,

3

sighing dramatically at the pile of paperwork that lay beside the typewriter. "I can't get over this mess. Look! She didn't even take her briefcase. She never does that."

Diana glanced briefly at the clutter of papers and nodded, then turned back to the window. "I know."

"Any sign of her yet?"

"Yes," Diana answered in a hush. "She pulled into her parking place about five minutes ago. She's just sitting behind the wheel."

"My God. She really made it. Why is she pushing herself so soon?"

"She has an appointment with Mr. Ingalls at ten. She told me on the phone that she's going to ask him to extend her vacation into a leave of absence now— two months, maybe more."

"Her vacation! I'd forgotten all about it. It would have started today, anyhow, wouldn't it? Then *this* had to go and happen. God, what a week for me to be on my cruise." Jackie stepped closer to the window and lifted apart two of the mini blinds to peer outside. "Why is she sitting there in the broiling sun? Look, her car window's open, so the air conditioning can't be on, can it? It's got to be a hundred and ten inside that car. She must be out of her mind."

"My guess is, she's psyching herself up to come in. It's going to be tough on her."

"Why? Did she find out about it here, is that what you mean? Switchboard said they were about half-way into the six o'clock news when she came rushing out through the lobby and . . ."

"Here she comes." Diana let the blind slip closed and took Jackie's elbow. "Come on, let's get out to our desks and look busy. Just pretend nothing has changed. Let Alison do the talking, okay?"

"But I'm dying to know how it happened," Jackie persisted. "There sure is a lot of buzzing around the station. Ron Gallegher's wife is an RN at St.

Vincent's and she told him the police were called in and there was an au—"

"Cool it, Jackie. I only know what I read in the paper, like everyone else." Diana sat down at her desk in the outside office and eyed the open door anxiously. The telephone at her elbow caused both young women to turn with a start. "Good morning, Channel 32 Production. Alison Ames's office. This is Diana, may I help you?"

"Yes, Diana. Stuart Stratton here. May I speak to Alison?"

Diana reacted in surprise. If the person on the telephone hadn't identified himself she would never have recognized him. Stuart's voice, normally so jovial and strong, was soft, cautious-sounding. "She hasn't come in yet, Mr. Stratton. I . . . I don't think she will be returning any business calls today. She's only coming in to keep an appointment before she heads over to the Grove. She's beginning an extended leave this morning."

"What did you say? Alison's what?"

"She's going away for at least two months, maybe more. I'll be handling all of the commercial production for her, so perhaps I—"

"I . . . oh, yes. Yes, that's why I'm calling." Suddenly he cleared his throat and spoke out, sounding serious and quite confident again. "It's about the spot you're going to shoot for me on Wednesday, Diana. Something has changed since I approved the script, something important. It's a change I really want to discuss with Alison before she leaves." After an awkward pause he spoke softly once more, in a way Diana found tenderly appealing. "Please," he said.

"Sure. I'll tell her the minute she gets in."

"Thank you."

"Say, Mr. Stratton, I don't want to interfere, but

you have heard, haven't you? You know, the news about Mr. Ames?"

"Yes, I've heard. Thank you, Diana. Thank you very much."

Quietly Diana replaced the receiver and turned to Jackie with a shrug. "Beats *me* why he's so hot to talk to her, today of all days. He sounded almost frantic. Says he wants a change in his new script."

"Then why couldn't he discuss it with you? You'd have been going on the shoot this week, anyhow, not Alison."

"Yeah. It's weird. I know he knew about her vacation, but he really freaked when I told him she was going on leave. Oh, well. Say, Jackie, let's cut the chatter, okay? Alison's liable to . . ."

Jackie stepped over to Diana's desk and folded her arms across her abdomen. In a whisper she said, "Everybody's going crazy with curiosity about Hunter Ames. I hear—"

"What do you hear, Jackie?" a voice asked sharply. Alison stood just inside the open door, pulled to her full height, her tawny eyes flashing sparks of anger. Even in the emotion of the moment both girls noticed how elegant she looked this morning. As always, Alison was stunning, tall, and regal, her head held high, her golden-red hair twisted in a little bun on its crown. But today there was something more, a sort of commanding presence about her, a quiet, almost arrogant, resolve in the set of her jaw.

Jackie stepped back awkwardly. Her cheeks flushed crimson, and her black eyes sought Diana's only briefly in a plea for help. "I hear—they've cut back the guest list for the preview party this year. To the bone, according to the gossip in the coffee shop."

Alison glanced quickly from Jackie to Diana.

"That's the latest scoop, Alison." Diana nodded.

"They're not even sending the newsies. Only personalities, plus sales and production staffs—and the executives, of course. But everyone else is out. Everybody at Channel 32 is buzzing about it."

"Everyone thinks it's because of our new manager," Jackie added quickly, relieved to be out from under Alison's scowl. "They say Mr. Ingalls did the same thing when they pulled him in to troubleshoot Channel 9 out in Utah. They say he chops expenses to the quick every place he goes."

"Oh." Alison walked into her office and crossed over to her desk. The two assistants followed a few steps and paused awkwardly near her open door. "I see," she said detachedly. She sat and glanced down at the unfinished stack of work and winced, only now remembering that she had left it in her rush to leave last Friday.

Diana broke the silence. "Are you all right, Alison? Aren't you pushing yourself to come in so soon?"

"I needed to pick up some papers I'll be working on at the Grove now that I'll be away so much longer than I'd planned." She glanced at her watch. "And I want a few minutes to myself before I'm due in Mr. Ingalls's office."

Jackie began to edge through the door. "There was one message a few minutes ago," Diana said quietly. "Stuart Stratton called. I told him you were going on leave. I tried to get him to let me help, but he seemed upset that he might not get to talk to you personally."

"Thank you," Alison said coolly. "I'll take care of it."

"Is there anything—"

"No, thank you. I'll be fine." Alison began to rummage in the bottom desk drawer, her signal for them to leave. Once alone she fell back in her chair and sat for a long moment, deep in thought. She looked sadly at the half-typed storyboard in her typewriter, the script she was working on when she'd gotten Hunter's call late Friday afternoon. She stared sightlessly at the words on the page, then ripped out the sheet and put it with the other papers. Diana would take care of it.

She closed her eyes for a few moments. How could she leave this room? This had become her home, her refuge in the last couple of years—the only place she could manage to be happy anymore, except, of course, for the Grove. She could always be happy at the Grove. It was home—her security, her heart.

Then slowly she allowed her eyes to travel around the office. Her surroundings spelled success. Three fine Oriental rugs were carefully placed around the room on top of champagne wall-to-wall carpeting. The exquisite rugs were a subtle compliment to rich, dark antique pieces, and especially to her enormous mahogany desk, the desk that had belonged to her grandmother. It had been her father's treasure, and because it was, it meant even more to her now that it was hers. The room was narrow, but Alison had made it seem wider with delicate choices of furniture, careful positioning of one rather large mirror, and paintings of varying sizes. The paintings were originals, and they were good. No company budget would have allowed such an expenditure, so she had bought them on her own, splurging from her inheritance after McIver died.

She sat daydreaming for a moment, staring at the extraordinarily fine works of art and thinking of her father, wondering if he would have liked them. She smiled, McIver Watson would have liked anything in the world she liked. Should she take them down today—take them with her to the Grove? No, that was silly. She wasn't resigning, she was just going on leave. "I'm not ready to give up what I've built—not yet," she said to herself.

Her eyes fell on the telephone, and a deep shudder racked her body. The last conversation she'd had on that ugly cold instrument was the wretched dialogue with Hunter Friday evening. Was it only last Friday? So much had happened so quickly since then. She leaned forward and covered both ears with her cupped palms, trying to block the sound of her husband's voice. His words were still so clear: "Listen to me, Alison. Let's just have fun with each other this one last time. Let's check out of this marriage with class. I'll be out of your life after tonight, out of it forever—you'll see. Trust me. Get ready to start a new page. By your birthday, I promise. On your birthday you'll have a whole new start. This party's a big celebration. Three's my lucky number. Now you'll be my little double-three. My child bride is growing up at last." He laughed. "Oh, excuse me, my soon to be *ex*-child bride. But just laugh with me one more time, that's all I ask. Don't be nervous about it, darling. Relax. I'll never sleep under your roof again, that's a promise. But get ready for a birthday party you'll never forget!"

She leaned forward and laid her cheek on her forearms, eyes still closed. Inside she felt a strange hollowness, a dull, empty ache. Yesterday, July 29, 1984—thirty-three! Suddenly she felt old. "I *am* thirty-three, and I *am* starting all over again," she said aloud. Abruptly she sat bolt upright and began fumbling angrily through her top desk drawer. She threw a few of her personal belongings into her briefcase, then pulled out the flat file containing papers she'd been collecting for this year's income tax. She stuffed them hurriedly into the outer pocket of the case, stifling angry tears, then sat back for a moment in reflection. She forced herself to gain control. She couldn't lose it now.

She checked her watch. Still fifteen minutes until time to meet Ingalls, so there was time to make the call. But what if it were the wrong thing to do? Maybe her emotions were too close to the surface to talk to him today. She closed her eyes again and laid her head back, trying to gain composure. Then, taking a deep breath, she picked up the receiver.

"Good morning, Stratton and Associates."

"Hello, this is Alison Ames returning Mr. Stratton's call."

"Certainly, Mrs. Ames."

Instantly she could hear his voice. "Alison, thank God! Are you all right?"

"Oh, Stuart, your voice sounds so good."

"I don't know how I've lived through the last three days without hearing yours. But I didn't try to call. I didn't think I should."

"You were right. Besides, you didn't need to. I knew you were thinking of me."

"Meet me, Alison, for lunch. Please don't say no. I want to make up for the time we missed together Saturday. You promised me time to celebrate your birthday. I've *got* to see you, Alison." Stuart waited patiently through the long silence. Finally, "Alison?"

She answered, "I heard you, but everything's different now."

"Meet me at the Shrimp Shanty on Oleander, the place we had our first lunch alone together." After a long pause he continued softly, "The day we—"

"Please," she said.

"Do you remember the place?"

"You know I remember."

"No one will be there, I promise. I need to be with you, Alison. I need to see you alone. But you're right, everything *has* changed. That's why I've got to see you before you leave."

"Stuart, I'm scared. It would be worse to be seen today—than it was then."

"I'm telling you, you won't see anyone you know there. It's a place I discovered years ago."

"Stuart, I . . ." Her voice trailed away. Then urgently she sat forward and spoke emphatically, gesturing to no one with her empty hand. "I've got to get away, Stuart. I'm going ahead with my plans to go home to the Grove, but I'll stay longer than a month now. I'm staying until it's time to enroll the children in school in the fall, maybe longer. Gordie and Margaret are paying the servants and closing up my house in town for me. I really don't see how I—"

"Please, darling. It doesn't have to be for long, I promise. There are some things I need to hear myself saying aloud. Meet me."

After a long hesitation she sighed deeply then said, "All right, but not in a public place. I'll be leaving here by ten-thirty or so. I'm on my way out to lock up the beach house. We cleared out all of—" Her voice caught, then she said softly, "The cleaning lady should be gone by now. I was going to send you the key, anyhow. I'm putting the place up for sale." She paused, then said, "Yes, meet me at Sunfish Key at eleven-thirty."

"Do you mean it?"

"You know I want to see you, Stuart." After a long pause she said, "Stuart?"

"Yes?"

"Oh, nothing."

"I love you very much, Alison."

She took another measured breath. "I'll see you soon," she promised. The instant she hung up, the interoffice buzzer sounded. "Yes?"

"Mr. Ingalls has asked if you're in yet," said Diana's voice.

Quickly Alison checked her watch. "But I have another five minutes. Oh, no matter. Please tell his secretary I'm on my way."

She rose and walked quickly to the oval mirror that hung above her mahogany credenza. She straightened the gold chains around her neck and adjusted the tiny gold lion's head that hung from an amulet on the longest golden thread, then eyed herself appraisingly.

Alison's beauty had so long been an established fact that she thought little of it. All of her life she had been told she was a beautiful girl. She supposed it must be true but showed no real signs of vanity except for immaculate grooming and for indulging in an exquisite wardrobe that was extravagant beyond belief. In a ritual that had begun in her mid-twenties she flew to New York twice each year and every spring to Atlanta just to shop for clothes. Always her choices were very simple, elegantly tailored, only the best. Any shades in the beige spectrum, from palest cream to tan, were her favorites, though once in a rare while she would select something in a vibrant color or stark black. And every now and then she would purchase a garment in peach or apricot to compliment her hair.

Alison was a redhead. Her hair was a light, tawny shade of red that in any exposure to the sun turned into a genuine strawberry blond. She wore it in a simple bun on the crown on her head most of the time; but down, it was shoulder-length, brushed back and falling from a center part into a natural pageboy. In her leisure hours she generally combed it into a high ponytail, the way she'd worn it as a child back home at the Grove.

Her eyes were enormous and wide set, and on most days were a yellowish brown, an amber, catlike color. And, like a cat's, they could turn as chartreuse as budding leaves in early springtime. The lashes that framed them were thick, but they were light in color, and long before Lady Di discovered the trick, Alison had been having her lashes dyed a very dark brown, aware that her eyes were her best feature. When she was little, Gordie, her oldest brother, teased her about them constantly. "You're going to grow up to be a hypnotist with those big yellow eyes of yours, Alison," he'd warn, "or maybe a gypsy fortune-teller." It was true that there was a mesmerizing quality about them. Her keen intelligence was mirrored there. Still, because she was so clever, they exposed her quick perceptiveness only when she wanted them to. At other times her eyes masked all show of emotion. According to her will, they could be as cool and murky as two shaded moss-green ponds on a still summer's day.

Her facial features were even, and her skin flawless, except for a tiny smattering of pale, light brown freckles she took great care never to expose to the open sun, even greater care to conceal with makeup discreetly applied. But she'd never been able to cover up the generous splash of freckles that peppered the pale skin embracing her shoulders, arms, and legs.

Her body was slim, elegant-looking, with small, firm breasts and a good waist and hip line that lent proof of proper diet and disciplined daily exercise. There were fully equipped exercise rooms and Jacuzzis in both the beach and town houses, and it was her routine to spend at least forty-five minutes every day in strenuous exercise and dance. Actually she engaged in very few excesses. Her only real passion for anything fattening was homemade mayonnaise. Almost anything tasted better to her if it were mixed up in a salad made with mayonnaise, the kind she'd watched Minnie make from the time she was able to peek on tiptoe over the top of the kitchen counter at the big house at the Grove. "Stop that child from lickin' the bowl, Minerva!" McIver used to command the servant as he passed through the big kitchen, usually stopping for a pat on Alison's little bottom and a shake of his great dark head. "She'll grow up to be fat as a butterball!"

But in spite of Minnie, who still made big jars of the stuff, Alison seldom succumbed to the temptation, and managed to hold her weight at a constant one hundred twenty-three pounds, lean for her five-foot-eight-inch frame. Her belly was flat, but her ass was deliciously round, her upper thighs were rounded and full, offering a sexy allure to the men who noticed her skirts and the way they fell against them when she walked. Actually she was, to a man's eye, the sexiest of women, possessing a maddening appeal, made somehow more tantalizing by the aloof, unattainable cover-up she rarely let down. To all strangers she remained friendly, yet coolly untouchable, careful to avoid sending out body signals that might indicate her being aware of her own sensuality. But the real Alison, the hidden Alison, was precisely the highly sexual lady each admirer's sixth sense perceived her to be.

Now she leaned closer to the mirror to scrutinize her makeup. Satisfied, she hurried down the hall to Mr. Ingalls's office. His secretary was missing, and his door was closed. That was odd. She struggled with an uncontrollable bout of anxiety. Pausing a moment, she gazed at the small, recently installed nameplate on the cold-looking door. FRED INGALLS—MANAGER. It seemed wrong to see this stranger's name in place of Sam's. Everything was still new to her, unfamiliar and insecure, with it now only just over two weeks since Sam Abrahmson's last day as station manager. If only she knew Ingalls a little better. There had to be something likable about him, but up to now she hadn't been able to discern what it could be. Oh, well, he couldn't be too big a bear at a time like this—could he?

She took a deep breath and lifted her chin high. Oh, Sam, why did you have to go and retire? It was always fun to walk through this door when you were behind that desk in there. I need you, Sam. She rapped lightly on the door. "No screw-ups," she said to herself. "You're on your own now, Alison, totally on your own."

2

Stuart Stratton hurried through the outer office of the small modern building that was set back among shade trees in one of Sarasota's oldest sections. Inside there were three small offices and a large outer room, not nearly enough space for the recent boom in his business. A large extension was already in progress in the spacious back lot, and the sound of hammering and sawing was music to his ears.

He nodded a detached good-bye to his surprised secretary as he loped through the reception area. "Mr. Stratton!" she called out after him. "What shall I tell anyone who calls? When may I expect . . ."

Stopping, he turned and paused for a minute. "Sorry, Sally, I wasn't thinking. I'm late for my client. I'm on my way to show the old Mansonhurst estate on Sunfish Key. It's a full hour's drive each way, so I won't be back until after lunch. At least two o'clock, maybe later."

"But—"

"See you then," he called back over his shoulder.

Stuart had built his business from scratch and had planned things very well. There was no question that he was one of the most respected young independent real estate brokers in the city. He dealt in all types of listings but had made his biggest killings in commercial real estate and land deals over near

Disney World in Orlando. Yep, good ol' Lake Buena Vista and the areas surrounding it was where it was *at,* as his little sister would say. But here on the west coast of Florida was where the money was, too, no question about it. It was exciting, electrifying, the lucrative area in the Florida real estate market, and he could project nothing but more of the same as the country rolled into the mid-eighties. He felt a tingle of excitement, aware that if his carefully placed investments continued to do as he anticipated he would have assets of close to a million dollars before he reached his thirty-fifth birthday. Yes, by 1986 it was conceivable that Stuart Stratton would be what people called a millionaire. And when it happened, he'd have done it on his own.

He lifted a tape from the caddy in the console between the bucket seats, then tried to relax to the sounds that filled his car. But relaxation was impossible. He was anxious to clear traffic and hit the highway. It was fifty minutes from here to Sunfish Key, even when traffic conditions were at their best, and he didn't plan on missing one minute of being together with Alison today.

Stuart was not strikingly handsome, feature by feature, but when all of them were thrown together, his looks were enormously appealing. He was tall— six feet, four and a half—and his hair was salt-and-pepper gray, even though he wouldn't reach his thirty-second birthday until November. He'd begun graying in college, and now there was a full shock of it, thick and straight, which he wore short. He had a boyish look but for the gray hair and was always expensively, splendidly dressed. In truth he managed to look dressed up, even in jeans.

He was thin and lanky, yet muscular. He was an avid tennis player, and, looking back, must have run over a thousand miles on basketball courts from junior high clear on through college. His eyes were light blue and crystal clear, framed by brows that were almost black. His most outstanding feature was his smile, a dazzling, wide-open smile that exposed straight white teeth.

Stuart pulled down the visor as he left the shaded boulevard behind, then turned south onto the highway, driving mechanically, hardly noticing where he was going, his mind a light-year away. He thought about the deal he'd closed yesterday afternoon and smiled. Big bucks—big. The fact was, until Alison Ames walked into his life five months ago, Stuart had thought of little else *except* making money, but now most thoughts that kept pushing themselves to the front of his brain seemed to be of her. What's more, he always seemed to be running out of time. He hadn't budgeted any time for emotional involvements, not until Alison Ames took him by surprise. But he'd known from the instant he first laid eyes on her at a sales and marketing seminar in March that he had to see her again. And from the day he walked into her office to commission his first commercial, he was driven to be near her from then on, whatever the stakes.

So he'd seen to it that they'd been thrown together ever since. It was easy. Just as soon as they finished making one commercial, he'd commissioned another, then another. And to top it off, the damned things had paid off like crazy. He'd had to take on two new salesmen and a full-time bookkeeper in the last couple of months. He chuckled. He'd never have considered advertising his real estate company on television if it hadn't been the only way to get close to Alison Ames.

For the first time in his life Stuart Stratton was in love. Today his only thoughts were of his need to be with Alison, absolutely refusing to think back over her words that she was going to go away, to leave him until fall. Beautiful Alison. He hadn't dared hope she'd see him for a while, possibly for months after what had happened Friday. Well, he wasn't going to let her leave him; he'd figure a way to coax her to stay.

Friday. What a difference one little day had made in the complexion of things. He shook his head in disbelief. On Friday Hunter Ames died. Alison was free now. The barrier that had stood between them was suddenly gone. Dead at fifty-two, poor guy. Christ, you never know, do you? Died suddenly, they said on the eleven o'clock news, then both Saturday newspapers reported a massive stroke but no details, none at all. That seemed odd to him. Just long obituaries detailing his career accomplishments, each with a huge picture that must have been taken when he was about forty, right around the time he was a prime acting lead in that soap opera of his. God, what a handsome rascal he was! Stuart had been surprised at just how prominent a part Hunter had played in *In Seasons of Change.* He'd never watched a soap opera in his life, but, boy, this one must be a biggie, and it was Hunter's baby. He'd conceived the idea, been the head writer all these years—nineteen since its opening telecast, the paper said—and until just a few seasons ago had been cast as one of the continuing leads. He'd played the bad guy, the man you loved to hate, and had millions of fans who adored his character, the write-up said. Funny. Alison had never mentioned a word of that to him.

Actually Alison had told Stuart little about Hunter, only that he was an actor and writer who was living in New York when they met. But she refused to move to New York, so when they got married, he agreed to live in Sarasota, and a few years after that, he decided to write his character out of the drama. She said it was because he'd become sick of making the occasional commute to New York when he had a part in the series, and besides, the main thrust of

Hunter's career was in creating the story line, and he could do that in Florida as easily as in New York. Stuart could certainly relate to such a move. Why would anyone want to work up there if he could bring his career down here with him?

So how about that! Hunter Ames had just up and moved the entire kit and kaboodle down to Florida when Alison announced she'd never live in New York. Stuart grinned. He didn't blame Hunter; he'd move locations, too, if it were the only way he could get her to marry him. He had to admire the guy, though. He must have had a lot of clout with the network to pull off the move. The writers, whole teams of them Alison said, had to fly down to work at their house on Sunfish Key when each new segment of the drama was being planned. She'd told him they stayed holed up out there for weeks at a time when they were really into it, that she rarely saw Hunter when the New York writers were down.

Hunter Ames. Must have been quite a guy. Stuart guessed that if he'd known all of the things he now knew after reading those obituary notices and had realized how good-looking he was, he'd have been jealous as hell these last few months. Boy, here one day, active as hell—dynamic, no two ways about it— then gone. He wondered if Alison had found him already dead when she got home Friday night. Stuart thought back on their telephone conversation as she was winding up to leave Friday, and their plans for lunch at his place Saturday on her way to the Grove. It was close to six o'clock when they'd talked. Stuart shuddered. Was Hunter Ames already dead when he and Alison had been making their Saturday plans to celebrate her birthday? What a grizzly thought. Still, it was true: the obstacle between them really was gone now. Now they were free to talk about their future.

Stuart squirmed and brushed back an imaginary

lock of hair from his forehead. Why was he so uneasy? He thought it through; it was because the last thing Alison might be thinking today was that she was now free to share a life with him. God knows she'd never really let him know she was feeling it, too, the magnetic lure that was there between them. Except for that one other time he had been to the house on Sunfish Key, the day they had first made love together. On that one special day *she* had come to him and had seemed, however briefly, to belong to him.

But that was the end of May and here it was almost August, and all that had really happened in between were the stolen hours together in the silent coolness of his apartment, moments of escape, just a vigorous sexual fling, hardly the sort of relationship lifetime dreams are made of.

He allowed his mind to go back over it all again as he absently tossed a quarter in the toll basket leading onto the Key. Infatuation. That's how it all began. They met in March and felt instant infatuation, both of them; he was positive of that. Then friendship. A nice, sensible working friendship that had caught fire one lazy afternoon in May right here on Sunfish Key. Who said anything about love? Friends turned into lovers, that's all in the world they really were. It happened all the time in the movies. Nothing to get excited about—and, for sure, nothing to build a future on.

All well and good except for one little thing: He had gone and taken it all very seriously. Stuart shifted in his seat, antsy now to get there. Just a few minutes more. But wait a minute. There *was* that possibility that Alison had taken it all very seriously, too. If that were so, did he have what it would take to hold her? Hell, he just didn't know. He could damned sure try. He did have one thing that he knew appealed to her: He knew how to make people laugh, to look at the light side of life. Alison went for that, seemed to need it desperately. When they were alone, everything they did seemed to take on a mood of gaiety, became a romp, a marvelous game— however short the time they were able to steal. Although he'd been careful as hell never to breathe the words that he loved her, never once—not until this morning when he'd heard himself saying them for the first time over the telephone.

So it was done. He had told her he loved her—loved her very much. What's more, he'd figured out over the weekend that if he could only get her alone he was going to tell her everything that was in his heart. Even if it meant immediate rejection, he intended to lay it out in front of her. From the instant he heard Hunter's death reported on "Friday Late Night" he knew he was tired of simply working out his commercials with her every couple of weeks with never a minute to be with her alone; tired of the brief moments they'd managed to steal over the summer; tired of having her only long enough to make love with her and watch her disappear. Now was the time to tell her he wanted her, wanted her every night, *all* night, for the rest of his life.

Wasn't it?

He concentrated for a long time, driving mechanically, slowly, on the almost deserted road. Timing. He was aware that timing was the single absolute ingredient that could make or break a business deal. Then he smiled. His sense of timing had always been his greatest strength. He would know. He'd know when he saw her today if the time was right.

Stuart entered the finger of land slowly, glancing casually around to see if any of Alison's neighbors were outdoors. The small cul-de-sac roadway was totally deserted. All six houses that dotted the circle were closed tight against the late-morning heat, but their quiet air conditioning systems hummed proof that someone was indeed home—and perhaps watching. Could there be extra interest focused on 437 Sunfish Key Cove today? he wondered, knowing this was the retreat where Hunter Ames came to do his writing. Well, so what? Alison must not be worried about it. It was her suggestion to meet here. He decided not to worry about anything right now.

He took a final swift glance around the circle before turning into the garage. He smiled. The big door yawned open wide; Alison's sleek, golden Corvette was parked on the right side. He pulled in beside it and strode quickly over to the switch, then listened for the sound of the great double door as it swung securely shut behind him.

He stepped from the stifling heat into the silent coolness of the house and glanced quickly all around, noticing the silence, engulfed by a feeling of desertion. The kitchen was immaculately tidy, almost as though no one lived here. Its lonely emptiness was contradicted only by the quiet hum of the built-in copper-colored refrigerator and the slow circle of the second hand of the clock on the range. He looked out and was impressed, as he had been that one time before, by the view of the green Gulf of Mexico lying beyond the mounds of white sand and sea oats that sloped down to the water's edge. It was all here: gulf, sand, and horizon, framed like a beautiful painting by an enormous paned window. No drapery or blind screened the window. Its only decoration was a row of rough Mexican tiles that circled the perimeter, and baskets—a dozen or more natural straw baskets in different sizes and shapes—hanging from the cypress beam that lay closest to the floor-to-ceiling window. Black one-way glass filled the window frame, lending an even cooler dimension to the gray cypress paneling of the kitchen walls.

Beyond the kitchen was a sunken dining room, then the wide central hall, which spanned the breadth of the cypress A-frame house from entry to beach side. Beyond that Stuart could see the sprawling living room with its free-standing fireplace in the far corner. Something caught his eye, struck him as odd. What was it? Suddenly it hit him. It was that the room was so completely tidy. The other time Alison had brought him here he'd been impressed by the incongruity of that one room inside this magnificent place. Then it was littered with manuscripts and books and piles of file folders spilling over with papers. There had been pillows scattered over the floor and wastebaskets crammed to overflowing. Filled ashtrays and half-full glasses were everywhere. "We're not allowed to enter that room," Alison had explained, "not the servants, or the children, or I. Not until Hunter announces he's taking a break. It's where he writes."

Today the room was immaculate. The only reminder of its former clutter was an enormous IBM typewriter centered on a fine antique desk under the picture window facing the Gulf. The modern machine looked hideously out of place on the Chippendale desk. Stuart hadn't even noticed the desk the other time because of all the disorder, but now it jumped out at him. In a setting so designed for beach life-style, it didn't seem to fit in this room, either; it was the only antique among cypress and glass and driftwood mixed with fine, simple, overstuffed furniture. Must have been a special pet of Hunter's, Stuart thought. Man, oh man, but did that desk look valuable.

Then he noticed something and winced. There was a sheet of paper half-filled with dialogue still in the typewriter. Whoever had cleaned up must have missed it—or didn't want to touch it. No wonder. He wouldn't have wanted to touch anything of Hunter's, either. He didn't even want to think about the man right now. He stepped into the two-storied center hall and looked around for some sign of Alison.

"Stuart," she called out from above.

He glanced up to see her standing on the balcony overlooking the hall, leaning with both forearms on the cypress railing, her graceful hands dangling in beautiful relaxation. His heart stopped, then pounded so fiercely that he felt it would jump right into his throat. She was incredibly lovely. She looked different to him, more beautiful than ever before. There was a certain tenderness about her, a vulnerability. What was it? She was dressed as he usually saw her at work, in a tailored linen skirt, a simple silk blouse of matching eggshell color, and sandals with slim little straps across her toes in the exact same shade—almost no color at all. Always Alison's hallmark: simple, expensive clothes and tailored gold jewelry around her neck and wrists. He noticed the square smoky topaz ring she always wore on the index finger of her left hand, and as he did, he spotted something unusual, something missing from the third finger of that same hand. Her wide gold wedding band was gone.

Slowly his eyes traveled back up to her face. Something about her was different. She had a casual look, a look of abandon. But there was more, something physical. Then he realized. Her hair. Her hair was down and around her shoulders, not up in the little knot she usually wore it in during business hours. He loved to see it down. He'd first seen it that way on that day they'd spent here alone together, then afterward only when she came to him at his apartment to make love. But for everyone else's eyes she wore it in a plain, almost severe fashion. Her hair, her magnificent hair, a mane splashed in copper by the noontime sunlight that filtered through the glass doors behind her, the same light that now cast a rim of gold along one side of her exquisite face.

"What took you so long?" she asked softly.

"I thought I was on time." His voice was husky.

She grinned. "So you are. I was just thinking about you. Made it seem like a long time . . . your getting here."

He ducked his head, a little embarrassed. "Are you coming down?"

"I've been out on the upstairs deck. There's a delicious breeze off the water. Why don't we talk out there?"

He turned and sprinted the first six steps to the landing, then paused to look at her again. He encountered the very same heart-hammering sensation he had felt when they first met, tantalized again by her eyes—tawny, hazel, golden, green? No matter. He only knew they fascinated him. They'd been so powerful that he hadn't been able to discover the wonders of the rest of her face until later. But now he knew all of her features by heart. Her nose was straight and slim, her chin strong. Her mouth was full, sensuous, pouting its invitation for him to taste it. Yet at times it could look set, determined, businesslike. Or when he least expected, it could break into a full, open grin showing a row of white teeth, flawless except for a tiny crisscrossing of her two middle upper teeth, a small imperfection that made her smile more alluring to him, her beauty more real.

But she wasn't smiling today. As he moved closer he could see weariness in her face. For the first time all of her cool defenses were down. He saw sadness and hurt and defeat in her magnificent eyes. He wanted to hold her, to protect her forever. But he paused at the top of the stairs, standing several feet away from her, waiting to follow her lead.

"Come," she said. "Come see my beautiful view." She held out her hand to him and he took it; it was as cool and pale as alabaster. He stepped with her through the big double glass doors, glancing for a moment only down toward the loft on the right where he knew a huge bed lay waiting. Not a ray of light filtered from the loft; the storm shutters must already be closed.

"Why don't you take off your jacket?" she asked. "You'll be more comfortable." He followed her over to a round table and chairs drawn under the shelter of a huge beach umbrella. "I can't sit in the direct sun," she apologized with a grin. "I turn into one enormous freckle."

"Freckles couldn't be anything but beautiful on you." He smiled, then released her hand to slip out of his coat. Before he tossed it on the chair beside him, he fumbled in the inside breast pocket, feeling her eyes on him as he produced the gift, a tiny gift-wrapped box and birthday card. He'd picked the craziest card he could find, one he was sure would make her laugh. Grinning his widest, he placed them both on the table in front of her. "Happy birthday, my friend," he said tenderly.

She returned his grin, saying nothing, and began by opening her card. He'd been right. She laughed out loud. Then she looked up, eyeing him suspiciously as she undid the ribbon from the little box. "I'm afraid you've done something extravagant. This box is too tiny not to contain something special."

He smiled and watched in anticipation as she opened the small velvet box. In it was an exquisite golden necklace. Hanging from the delicate, almost invisible chain was a triple golden heart, three slim open hearts, crafted three-dimensionally, one on top of the other. Centering the topmost heart, in a little vertical row, were three flawless, precisely matched diamonds.

She faced him with tears in her eyes. "It's incredibly lovely, Stuart. Thank you."

"I hope you'll wear it."

"Of course I will." She undid the tiny catch and fastened it around her neck. It looked gorgeous to him, circling her beautiful neck; the hearts rested just where he'd pictured they would, in the dimpled place where her collarbones met. The diamonds sparked in the noonday sunlight; the golden hearts seemed to pick color from her hair. She smiled over at him, looking beautiful, childlike. "There. How does it look?"

"Like it belongs there. When I saw it, I had to have it for you. It's like you, Alison. There seem to be three of you. There's the Alison you've given to me. Then there's the Alison you always keep hidden." He noticed tears welling in her eyes. "And there's the Alison that's out there somewhere in the future, the real Alison I want to know someday."

"Stuart, I . . ." Her voice broke, and she began to cry.

"Alison, darling," he said, reaching for her hand again.

"No, don't," she said, pulling away. "I can't." She shook her head. "I can't let you touch me today. I'm not strong enough. I can't give in to my emotions. I . . ."

"I only want to console you," he said gently. He sat back and eyed her tenderly. "That's all."

"Don't you see?" she said. "It's *me* I don't trust."

"Do you mean that?"

"Stuart, I've got to tell you something. You must try to understand why I'm going away." When he shook his head and reached for her again, she cried out, "No! I mean it. I'm going, and I really don't know when I'll be back." Then she added softly, "Or if. Mr. Ingalls agreed to at least two months' leave of absence until I make my decision."

"Two months! I'll die if I can't be around you for two months. Please come back sooner, Alison. I won't try to see you alone, I promise. You can name the time, whenever you think it's proper. Just don't put yourself where I can't at least be near you."

"Stuart, I—"

"Work is the best thing for you, don't you see that? Everything I've read about grief says that work—"

"Stop talking about grief!" Her voice was brittle. Then, after a long pause, "Don't you see? I'm not grieving. I haven't been in love with Hunter for a long time—maybe for years." Stuart sat back, silent, waiting. Finally she sighed. "I guess I've shocked you."

"No," he said gently, "as a matter of fact I knew the love had to be gone. You could never have turned to me if you still loved your husband. It wouldn't be your style. But I am a little shocked that you're saying it out loud, saying it so—" He caught himself short.

"So soon?" She smiled sarcastically. "Yes, I'm shocked, too." She gazed directly into his eyes. "And I couldn't have confessed those words to another living soul."

"I'm glad you can talk to me."

She nodded. "So I'll shock you even more. Not only am I not grieving him, I *hate* him for what he did."

"What do you mean?"

"His death was a suicide. An overdose of Seconal."

Stuart took a deep breath. "My God."

"Yes," she breathed.

"How did you keep it out of the news?"

"Even from his grave McIver still has pull all over the state."

Stuart lifted her hand, kissed her fingertips. "I'm so sorry," he said. She made no move to pull away.

"It's got to be kept a secret, don't you see?" she said emphatically. "Can't you just imagine the scandal the truth would cause? I simply cannot allow my children to be haunted the rest of their lives with the specter of this nightmare. I'll *never* forgive Hunter for not considering them before he did such a cowardly thing." She burst into tears and wept quietly for a few minutes with her face in her hands. Stuart sat, helplessly looking on, yearning to hold her in his arms.

He waited until she had wiped her eyes, then took both of her hands. "Easy, darling. Do you want to talk about it?"

Slowly she opened her eyes and smiled tenderly at him. "Not now. Sometime. Sometime down the road we'll talk. Does it hurt you that I can't just now?"

"No."

"It's all so horrible, Stuart. It's why I've got to take Carrie and Wattie home for a while. I need time to think, to wait for it to die down. The children are totally at home on the Grove. We have their horses there, and they enjoy sailing on the lake. But mainly they just love being around their cousins. The boys are wonderful with my kids." Stuart watched her as she fought tears again. "It's an isolated world there on the Grove. If this thing breaks and there's a scandal, at least I can keep it from Carrie and Wattie until school starts again."

"May I come to see you at the Grove?"

She smiled and took her time before speaking. "I'm afraid we might start a scandal of our own. Don't forget how everyone hovers over me. I've told you that. It will be worse now than ever. Besides, I really do have to be by myself for a while, to sort out my thoughts."

He hesitated, then asked quietly, "Am I in any of your thoughts?"

She waited for what seemed to him an eternity. Then, in measured words, she answered, "You're the best friend I've ever had in the world."

"Do you mean that?"

"Yes."

Stuart left her gaze and turned to scan the water, thinking things through, wrestling with his decision whether to say more. Finally he spoke. "I can settle for that—for now."

She searched his face silently, then glanced down at her watch. "It's time, darling."

Darling! She had never called him that before. She stood and said, "Come on, I need your help. Just a few things left to batten down." Together they lowered the beach umbrella and moved the outdoor furniture into the upper hall before locking the storm shutters securely behind them. Alison smiled gratefully at him, then turned away. "That's everything upstairs now." Without looking back she skipped quickly down the stairs. "Just a couple of jobs downstairs now, okay?" She grinned over her shoulder and added, "Then you can pick up your paycheck and go home."

Laughing with her, he followed closely behind, observing her tall, agile body as she moved beautifully, gracefully. When they stepped through the French doors onto the downstairs terrace, Stuart noticed that all of the furniture had already been lifted in. "Only the shutters to see about down here?" he asked.

She nodded, then walked slowly over to lean for a moment against the cypress railing. He stood back, silently watching her, then he stepped closer and took her shoulders in his hands. She reached around and laid her hand over one of his, saying nothing. Then she turned to face him. "I mustn't linger too long," she said. She moved away from him toward the picture window that separated them from the living room.

"Here, I'll do it," he said. He swiftly secured the shutters over the window, noticing again the typewriter through the glass. Then he walked down and closed off the great expanse of glass that spanned the dining room and kitchen walls.

Alison watched him as he worked, feeling such emotion, loving him for all of the wonderful things he had come to mean to her. He looked funny and awkward, down on his haunches struggling with the bolt on the bottom of the final shutter. It was the sort of nasty little task Hunter would never have done cheerfully, would have told her to hire a handyman to do. Choked with gratitude, she walked back over to the dock's edge, not wanting Stuart to see her cry again.

When Stuart looked around, Alison was leaning against the railing, facing the wind off the surf. He joined her, and together they gazed a moment longer at the rolling waves. She seemed to be telling it goodbye. "Don't," he said firmly.

She faced him and eyed him in surprise. "Don't what?"

. "Don't put this place on the market. Don't give it up yet. You belong here, Alison."

"I was going to give you the key today. I'd almost decided to get rid of the house on the mainland, too."

"Don't make those decisions yet. Please don't. It's too soon."

Wearily she turned and waited inside the hall as he pulled the big shutters in behind the French doors and fastened the double bolts. Then, smiling, he said, "Well, my friend, I'd hate to be the hurricane that thought it was going to blow this place down. Have you forgotten anything?"

"I only have to come back in and pull the master switch when our cars are out of the garage."

He waited while she paused inside the darkened living room to look back one more time. She stared for a long moment at the desk where Hunter had spent so much of his time, then crossed over and smiled wryly at the script in the typewriter. She ripped it out and stood near a crack of light that spilled through the shutter. Squinting, she read it, then crushed it in her fist and tossed it in the fireplace. She spun around, eyes flashing in anger, and said, "Loaded as usual. Hunter's dialogue was always loaded. Kept all the poor dreary listeners out there glued to their sets." She glared at the typewriter, not able to mask her emotions now. "Did I ever tell you how he wrote himself out of *In Seasons of Change* five years ago?" Stuart shook a silent no. "With a suicide. He had his character commit suicide! An overdose of Seconal," she said sarcastically. "It made for a blockbuster of a month at the network, let me tell you. The funeral went on for days."

Stuart said nothing, only gazed at her compassionately, waiting for her venom to pass, to be done with.

"Prophetic, huh?" she said, her voice rising. Her eyes glistened with anger and pain.

He walked over and closed the draperies behind the desk, then turned to her and took her hand. "Come on. You mustn't make them worry." He guided her into the big hall, now dark and silent. The only sounds were the waves on the beach and the distant call of a sea gull. Tenderly he pulled her into his arms.

Every floodgate opened; Alison wept as though she would never stop. She clung to him, arms tight around his neck. He held her, stroking her back, kissing her hair, whispering words of comfort. Finally gaining control, she said against his shoulder, "I want you to love me now." She lifted her face up to his. "Will you love me before I go away?"

Silently, swiftly, he guided her to the stairs, then took her elbow as they mounted, stopping at the top of the darkened hallway to look around for a light switch. She took his hand and said, "Come, I like the darkness. I'll lead the way."

Beside the great bed he gathered her again in his

arms, kissing her, devouring her, tasting the salt still on her cheeks, hungrily kissing away her tears. By a crack of sunlight through the covered window he could watch her as she began to undress, first carefully removing her jewelry, all but the necklace he'd just given her. The diamonds sparked in the semidarkness as she moved. Then she undid the buttons of her blouse and pulled her silky bra free from her breasts. Her nipples were hard, as hard and exquisite as precious pink gems. Her hair fell loosely around her pale shoulders. Then, motionless, he watched her step out of her skirt and hose, staring at her flat white belly and the tantalizing curve of her thighs. "Jesus God," he said.

From across the darkened room Alison felt his eyes on her. A wonderful sensation pricked slowly across her body in response. In an instant she was beside him, touching his shoulders, lifting her lips to his. "I want to undress you," she whispered. Deftly she undid the knot of his tie, then tossed it on the chair where she had laid her own clothes. Next she unbuttoned his shirt and slipped it across his back; it fell to the floor. She ran her cool hands across his chest. "I love your crazy gray hair," she said. "It's even gray here," she murmured as she leaned in to kiss his nipple, then slid her lips across his chest to kiss the other. Then, taking his hand, she guided him over to the enormous bed. "Come with me, Stuart," she said. "Come to my bed."

She allowed the mood of total sensuality to envelop her as she felt the same breathless emotion she had known that first time Stuart ever took her in his arms. Now as then, he loved her with all of the strength, yet gentleness, she yearned for. He was wonderful, wonderful! Again she experienced it, that feeling of being transported as he kissed her breasts, her back, her neck, cupping each curve of her ass in both of his hands. In her ear she heard him say, "Oh, my God, you are so exciting to me!"

When he kissed the place where the little golden hearts lay, she responded wildly, ecstatically, crying out as his mouth moved to the curve of her shoulder, her chin, her lips—again and again her lips.

"I want you," she cried out. "Only you. Love me, darling."

He called out her name and kicked free of his pants and was on her, in her, wildly inside her. She lifted herself to him, hot, tight, welcoming him, wanting him. She could feel his hands cool under her back, then around her shoulders, stroking her, moving, caressing. In harmony with the rhythm of his ass locked tight underneath her ankles, she rose with him, fell back with him, clung tightly to him as he uttered breathless little sounds of ecstasy. She lost all sense of time, knew only that she wanted this moment to last forever. It was—it must be—a dream, an incredible, heavenly dream.

From somewhere in the distance she heard him say her name. "Alison." Then again he said it, "Alison. I . . . I'll have to stop."

Rising higher to meet him, she said, "Don't stop! Oh, darling, don't stop!" Breathlessly she cried, "Oh, God, Stuart, yes! Now!" Then she sighed deeply, "Oh, yes. Yes, darling, yes."

She clung tightly to him as he cried out in his own passion, then said her name as together their heartbeats began to slow. He nestled against her hair, then said again, "Oh, Alison, Alison." Sighing deeply now, "I do love you so."

He rolled over on his side, pulling her with him. They lay quietly for what seemed to her a very long time. Then she moved her lips against his ear and said, "Thank you for loving me. Thank you for being my friend."

He raised up on his elbow and gazed deeply into

her eyes. "I do love you, Alison. I'll always be your friend."

She drew back and looked earnestly into his eyes, searching them in the partial darkness. An expression of hope flooded over her face. "I guess I've never really had that before." She stared away into space for a moment, then looked back at him and smiled. "Friend. I like the sound of it."

"Promise me you'll remember that."

"I'll remember."

"And I want you to remember something else, Alison, something important," Stuart said tenderly. He pulled her tighter against his body, memorizing her every curve, breathing deeply of her elusive fragrance. He hung for a moment on the brink of telling her everything. No, not now. He knew the time wasn't right; he would have to wait awhile. But he would tell her someday. And someday he would hear her declare the words he was longing to hear. Instead he said simply, "Remember that I'll still be here when you come back. Just don't make me wait too long."

He could wait. Yes, he'd wait awhile, but one day he would hear her say she loved him, too. Yes, one day he would have her for his own; he promised himself that.

Part II

1

The day that Alison Carrington Watson was born was hot and humid. She arrived at exactly three o'clock on a cloudless Sunday afternoon, after a long labor and exhausting delivery. It had been nearly thirteen years since Alliene Watson had delivered her last baby, a second fine boy for McIver, another raven-haired Scot like himself. But Alliene was twenty-seven years old at that time, and as soon as she held little Todd on her arms, the agony of the labor and delivery were forgotten, and in no time she had back her strength, at least as much as her body dictated she could have.

Alliene wasn't particularly strong; rather, she was quite fragile-looking, with golden red hair and skin so fair she dared never stay out long in the strong Florida sun. But in spite of her delicate appearance she displayed an inner strength, a sort of elegant command in the body signals she expressed, and there was calm, cool assurance present in her lovely blue eyes. To McIver she was, from the first instant he laid eyes on her, the most beautiful girl he had ever met. In appearance they were a total contrast. McIver was big, a tall and rugged man with hair so raven-black it shone blue in the light, and the ruddy sort of complexion that is typical of so many Scotsmen. He towered almost six feet three inches, with huge, athletic shoulders that gave him a husky, though never fat, presence when he entered a room. Beside him Alliene seemed almost as small as a little girl, a child he could easily carry in his arms.

Alliene's first pregnancy was so difficult that it really should have been her last, but she desperately wanted more than one baby and was determined to have a big family for her husband, four children at least. From the start she knew McIver wanted several children. As an only child he had yearned for brothers and sisters, and soon after Alliene presented him with Gordie, their first son, he openly expressed his wish to have a daughter. But after Todd's arrival it seemed out of the question to put his wife through a third pregnancy. The entire business of childbearing was difficult for Alliene. It took over five years of trying and a miserable pregnancy to bring Gordie into the world, and it was the same when Alliene carried Todd three years later, only worse. Then she'd been ordered to spend the last six weeks before his arrival in bed, and she was left dangerously thin and listless after the delivery.

So together the couple decided that Gordie and Todd were all the family they would ever try to have. But late in 1950, the weekend after the family's big Thanksgiving feast, Alliene began to suffer from frequent spells of nausea. Soon, in the mornings, she couldn't bear the smell of coffee perking, a symptom reminiscent of both of her other pregnancies. Privately the couple talked about it, assuring each other that it simply couldn't be.

Still, the nausea continued, and next all of the other telltale indications began to happen in their proper sequence, and by the beginning of the new year, the doctor had confirmed the news: another baby was indeed on the way and would probably arrive around the middle of August. Everyone was stunned. Alliene was approaching her fortieth birthday, and McIver would be forty-four years old in

March. They laughed and joked about it to the family, but privately it was no laughing matter. Alliene's health was a definite issue. McIver could hear her in their bathroom in the night, retching and crying out in exhaustion. What's more, the doctor had told them it would be a serious thing for her to carry and deliver another child at her age, particularly with Rh negative blood. In general her state of health was not good, and there could be a certain danger to the child as well.

Still, a baby was on the way. A miracle. An act of God. And from the moment the news was confirmed they did everything they could to avoid a possible miscarriage. Alliene agreed to obey her doctor's orders and spend the entire balance of the pregnancy off her feet, though reluctantly, because of a present household upheaval. Only four months before the news of the new baby was confirmed they had begun a major remodeling of their home. The place was horribly torn up and promised to stay that way at least until the end of spring. For years Alliene had relied on the one full-time servant, Lonnie Wilson, to help her keep clean the sprawling home and keep tidy Grandfather's cottage by the gate, but now things had taken on a new complexion. It was obvious the family would need additional help, someone to live in at least for Alliene's confinement and a few months after the new baby arrived. Lonnie was strong and a hard worker, but the woman was a laundress, not a manager. McIver advertised and began interviews to find the right person to take over the reins of running the two households at the Grove and to be a proper nursemaid for the new baby.

Within minutes into one of the interviews McIver knew he'd found the one for the position. She was a fine-looking nineteen-year-old black girl named Minerva Gass, who had come to Florida to care for her dying grandmother. Now alone, she wanted to stay

on instead of returning to Macon, Georgia. Best of
all, she had outstanding references from day work
she'd done back home. She was a proud-looking
young woman, quite tall, nearly five-ten, and raw-
boned. She wasn't a pound overweight, just big, with
marvelous posture and unusually delicate, Cauca-
sian facial features. Alliene silently studied Minerva
while her husband did all of the questioning. When
Minerva's eyes met hers, she knew this was an intelligent, self-confident person.

That night as they lay together in their bedroom
watching the flames from the open hearth dance and
reflect against the ivory walls, McIver held Alliene
against his strong chest. He stroked her back and
reached up to touch her hair. Bending to kiss the tip
of her slender nose, he softly asked, "Feelin' okay,
pet?"

"I'm feelin' just fine tonight, darlin'. Really."

He smiled into the darkness over her head. Her
soft little southern accent had never ceased to enchant him. All of his life he'd heard only the strong
Scottish brogues his parents had brought over from
the old country with them, and the redneck ex-
changes of the hired hands that drifted in and out
during fruit-picking season. Even in public schools
in Grove Dale he hadn't really encountered a truly
southern gentle-spoken person like the lady he held
in his arms. Maybe that had been a big part of what
had captured him from the start—her soft, elegant
voice. Her very first words to him had made his heart
sing on that spring day when they met, the Saturday
before Easter of his senior year at the university. He
could still see her sitting on the white front porch
swing at her parents' house; he knew the minute he
walked up the steps that he wanted to marry her. To
this day he still felt lucky that he'd accepted Jim
Laskell's invitation to come home to Tampa with
him for the weekend. "There's this redhead that

lives in Hyde Park, Lucy's best friend. She's gorgeous, McIver, no kiddin'. You've got to meet her. And you'd better make it this weekend or you'll have to wait till summer. She's going back to Brenau the day after Easter."

He smiled again and pulled her closer to him. "So you think you'll be comfortable with the new girl in the house?"

"Uh huh." She snuggled in closer and kissed his neck. "I liked her a lot."

"So did I."

"Do you think we'll have a problem with Lonnie?" she asked pensively.

"Lonnie is a fine woman, pet, and I know we depended on her a great deal when the boys were small, but she could never run this place."

"I guess not."

"We need someone just like Minerva. I want her to take over everything for you. Lonnie will have to adjust. But don't worry, I'll have a wee talk with her. I'll give her some special new duties all her own— and a nice raise in salary. She'll understand." He hugged his wife gently and stroked her shoulder. "I'll handle it, you'll see. I'll have her liking Minerva in no time."

"The boys seemed to like her right off."

"It's you that matters."

"It's the baby that matters." She drew back and looked into her husband's eyes. "I want the baby to be okay, that's what I'm prayin' for, darlin'. She's just got to be okay!"

McIver grinned. "She?"

"She."

"So far we've run to boys."

"I have a feelin' in my bones this time. I really do. I never had a feelin' before. I even know what her name's going to be, if you like it, too." Without waiting she went on, "Alison. I loved your mother's middle name, such a beautiful name." She looked over at the fire wistfully. "I miss her, McIver. I miss her terribly."

Gently he pulled her close against his neck again. "I will miss her every day until the day I die."

"Besides, we've already named one boy after your father, and one after mine, just like you say Scottish people do. Seems to me we're all out of boys' names."

He chuckled. "I guess you're right. It will have to be a girl." Pondering, he said, "I love it. Alison. It's soft, like my mother was, and like you." Pulling her closer still, he whispered the name again. "Alison. I like it. For my mother. And like a wee little Alliene."

Within minutes McIver could feel the gentle heaving of his wife's ribs against his hand and knew she had drifted into sleep. More than anything he wanted everything to be right for his Alliene. A girl. So she had already decided the new baby was to be a girl, a little baby daughter they would name for his mother, Mary Alison. He squeezed his eyes tight and thought about his mother. Gone just over a year now, and the pain of loss was still strong.

Even though McIver was only four years old on that day in 1911 when Gordon and Mary Watson lifted their young son from the gangplank of the steamship that brought them down Florida's St. John's River into the mouth of Lake Monroe to dock at the central Florida village of Sanford, he remembered the day in explicit detail. From there they boarded the new Atlantic Coastline Railroad and traveled to Auburndale, the closest hamlet to their new home that boasted a station and platform, traveling the rest of the way to Grove Dale by horse and wagon. He could still picture in his mind the lineman on the platform when he flagged the train to a stop just for them. It was a breathless moment he would never forget.

McIver was a Scot, a true Scot as his mother often reminded him, with "nae other blood in your veins," though he was born in the United States of America. As young immigrants, his parents had first settled in Jacksonville in north Florida, intending to own land in the center of the state eventually. Immediately they began to build the nest egg such a move south would take. Gordon found work as a machinist, and his bride practiced her own skill: dressmaking. Within a year of their marriage Mary Alison Watson presented Gordon with the only child they would ever have, a son. In the Scottish tradition of naming the firstborn son for his paternal grandfather, they named the baby McIver. While her young boy slept or played Mary Alison continued to take in sewing and to save, and in less than four years the couple purchased, sight unseen, fifty acres just south of Grove Dale in Grove County. On May 2, 1911, the young family made the move.

Grove County was situated almost in the dead center of the state, roughly halfway down the four-hundred-mile-long peninsula and about a third of the distance closer to the Gulf of Mexico on Florida's west coast than to its Atlantic eastern shore. The climate there was generally temperate in winter, but, like all of Florida, hot and humid from late April through October. But the young Scots were prepared for the long summers and quite willing to take on this negative side of the area they had chosen for their permanent home.

McIver was too young to remember the hardship of the first two years at their new home—land that would always be known to him simply as the Grove— but he would never forget his mother's tears when they first walked through the door of the tiny one-room cottage that stood on the southern edge of their property. It was so much worse than they'd been led to believe at the real estate closing. But the family had to make do. It would be temporary; they spent only the dollars necessary to make the place clean and livable.

The next two years were spent in ceaseless work. The comfortable nest egg they had accumulated was nearly gone, a good portion of it for the purchase of the land, and the balance was already earmarked for the cost of acreage development and for personal emergencies. What's more, even if all went well, it would still be a full five years before a grove of new sapling fruit trees would mature and be ready for harvest; money had to be earned in the meantime. Gordon got on as a machinist at an Auburndale fruit-packing plant, and Mary Alison quietly began to take in sewing and build a business of her own. The first summer's long evening hours of daylight went into uprooting and burning the old, shriveled trees that were all their property had to offer, and in tilling the land to make ready for the new young trees they would buy. Once the fifty acres were planted with strong Hamlin orange saplings, the couple's energies then turned to laying the foundation of the home they would have near the lake that lay just inside the northern boundary of the land. It was an especially slow process because they did the work themselves.

Even though the original house was small, Gordon had visions of a much bigger place someday and cleared and prepared three acres between the lake and the highway, with an eventual family compound in mind. The new home itself was simple, just one huge room, but the ceiling was fourteen feet high and coved for coolness, with wonderful big oak beams to support it. At one end was an enormous rock fireplace, which was the family's only method of heating for years to come, and in the corner next to it was a shiny new cooking stove for Mary Alison. Adjacent were the dry sink and wooden icebox, and be-

yond, the door that led to the backyard, with its well
and outhouse. McIver's parents' bed was positioned
on the wall opposite one of the two big picture windows that overlooked the lake, and in the far corner
behind a freestanding bookcase partition he had his
own bed, dresser, and desk.

It took over two years to complete the new house,
and in the fall of 1913 they made the move, turning
the cottage over to their first hired hand, a
seventeen-year-old drifter named Ben Hewett. Gordon told Ben he could live there for as long as he
worked for the family.

A month after their move to the new house, Gordon made a down payment on an additional one hundred acres on the southwest boundary of the
property, down near Ben's cottage, acreage filled
with dying orange trees, the shoots of which were excellent for grafting young saplings. Gordon had kept
his ears open at work and around the village and had
been giving some thought for months to entering
this phase of the citrus business as a sideline. From
all he had been able to learn during his hours spent
at the packing plant and his trips to town on weekends, there was good money to be made in the planting and grafting of young citrus saplings for resale.
He already was the owner of the necessary key pos-
session if one were to get into the grafting business:
a lake, with rich, wet lakeside soil at its banks, black
mud in which to plant new shoots. With only Ben
Hewett and an old Negro hired hand to help him,
Gordon planted one entire side of the lake's bank
with shoots grafted from the one hundred acres of dying Valencia trees. Within a few short weeks the
bank of the lake had hundreds of shoots taking root,
the first step of the process before balling the saplings for transplanting. Each night Gordon stopped
by on his way home from the packing plant just to
marvel at the sight of over a thousand shoots stretch-

ing their pale green branches toward the sun. "A bonnie, bonnie sight," he would mutter to himself.

Word swept the country of the young Scot's lakefront experiment, and long before the first crop of saplings had matured enough for transplanting and shipping, Gordon had received orders from landowners all over Polk County for his healthy-looking young Valencia trees. Quite suddenly then, Gordon Watson found himself in a phase of the citrus business he had never originally even dreamed of embracing.

When he began to get orders for Pineapple and Hamlin saplings as well as Valencias, he dispatched Ben to buy cuttings from these other varieties of trees. Then he hired an excavation crew to clear away the foliage on the eastern side of the lake to make room for more planting. Soon hundreds of new rootings found their place over there as well.

In the evenings, with her son tucked into bed and her sewing put away for the night, Mary Alison entered each new transaction in her ledger, and as each new order came, the couple traveled over to First Polk Bank in Lakeland to deposit that day's receipts. Before long it was evident from the bottom-line figure in their ledger that they had forged a highly profitable business, and all within three years of their arrival in Grove Dale, and still with a full two years to go before their own first grove would be ready to bear fruit.

It wasn't until 1916 when the time came to labor over the bountiful harvest of his initial fifty-acre grove that Gordon felt able to give up the job at the packing plant and devote himself to the Grove. Now he literally basked in the heady feeling of being his own boss. To top things, the Hamlin harvest that their first fifty acres yielded was grand beyond his wildest dreams; the fruit was plump and juicy and brought top dollar at market. Gordon and Mary Alison were elated. Ten years into their marriage, five of them here on the Grove, and things were going very well indeed.

Still, they never considered resting for even a wee bit, not now. They endured Florida's annual eight months of heat without complaint. They battled the relentless droves of mosquitoes and other insects and learned to kill snakes with practiced skill. They became part of the community and made loyal friends with their neighbors. They joined the Grove Dale Presbyterian Church and tithed ten percent of every dollar they earned, and could be seen each Sunday morning of the year in their favorite pew with their young son, scrubbed and groomed and dressed like a bandbox, seated between them.

In those early days Lakeland had its first power plant. In every way the town was fast becoming a city and was the hub of Polk County, the county that bordered Grove County to the northwest. When the family was eligible to hook into Lakeland's power supply in 1917, things were going very well for them financially. Gordon installed three overhead paddle fans, two in the big main room and one in last year's new addition, Mary Alison's kitchen. And he announced the best news of all to his excited son: They were going to add on two bedrooms: one on the southwest side of the house—a private room for his parents at last; and a room of his own on the west wall of the kitchen. Such luxury seemed like heaven to McIver. The prospect of a room all to himself only made him want to work harder, to contribute all he could to the family effort.

Even before he was old enough to realize he was doing so, McIver began to learn evey facet of the citrus business. When he was only four years old, he'd been at his father's side to watch the planting of each tree in their first grove, and when he was nine, was one of the hands who shinnied up the trees and twisted the oranges from their branches and tossed them into the baskets below. He was in the fields on winter nights when frost warnings were out to help his father light the smudge pots for the warmth that would save the crops. He tended the vegetable garden, and he learned how to gig and clean frogs, then later watched the frog legs jump in Mary Alison's frying pan for dinner. It was his chore to help his mother with her canning, to keep the windows clean, and to mow the grass. By the time he was ten his father allowed him to take the horse and wagon into town for supplies and over to the farm across town to pick up milk and eggs. He groomed the horse and took care of their two dogs. He walked three miles to school every day, and at his mother's command, devoted two hours to his studies every night: "Nae son o' mine will grow up to be an ignoramus." And he never got sick. Other than childhood diseases during school years, he was never sick a day in his life. Why should he be? To McIver Watson life was absolutely wonderful.

Probably the one extravagance that Gordon indulged in was the shiny new black Model T Ford he purchased for six hundred dollars in 1918, the summer after McIver turned eleven. It was the very latest model, with every novel feature money could buy. He built a sturdy garage connecting the shed where they kept the wagon and stabled the horses, and put it safely away there except on the occasions when the family would drive proudly into town or over to Lakeland, and, of course, every Sunday to church. Every Saturday it was McIver's chore to wash and polish the car.

By 1923, three years into Florida's real-estate boom, Lakeland boasted a population of twenty-two thousand, but the fifteen-hundred-kilowatt turbine would give way in just another decade or so to one producing ten thousand kilowatts of power, proof that a galloping population was swelling this rich and rolling highland section of Florida. Asphalt roads, nine feet wide, had replaced the town's narrow double-rut dirt paths of transportation, making way for the horseless carriages that by now had taken Florida, and the rest of the nation, by storm. And as Lakeland and Grove Dale grew, the Watson Groves grew. Before McIver left for his freshman year at the University of Florida in Gainesville in 1925, their holdings had increased to two full sections of land, twelve hundred and forty acres. By now another room had been added onto the house, a sewing room for Mary Alison, plus that genuine luxury, an indoor bathroom.

In 1926, McIver's second year at the university, the Watson family suffered through the great Florida crash, the end of the state's real-estate boom that literally crumbled under its own drunken spree. The bust plunged Florida into economic collapse three full years ahead of Wall Street's Black Monday in October of 1929. Money became tight, and times were hard, but the wise land acquisitions Gordon had continued over the years and the increasing productivity of the acres of healthy fruit trees provided the family with the security they needed to survive. Still, all of them were faced with difficult times ahead.

McIver announced he was quitting college to help out, but his parents would have none of it. His education was the very thing they had been working for, and he was halfway into reaching his goal, too close to throw it away. Before he left to enter his junior year, he sat and had a long talk with his father. "I'll go back and I'll earn that degree," he said earnestly. "I make you that promise, Father. But the Grove will be my whole world in two years, and this black depression has cast a new light on things. We've got to take the bull by the horns. Now is when we must buy more land, not simply try to hang on, don't you see? We've got to take the gamble."

"But our savings—you don't mean we should rob oursel's o' our savings! Surely not, son!"

"If that's the only way, yes. We can pick up land for the price of taxes alone, Father, land that will be worth a fortune when the economy turns back around. When else will we ever be in such a position?"

Reluctantly the senior Watson agreed. Quietly he began to buy. Every single weekend McIver drove home from Gainesville, and together father and son attended auctions and were present at foreclosures. They made no real show of it, but they bought and bought again. Land that sold for one thousand dollars an acre before the crash could be gotten for a hundred now. Within two years the Watson holdings exploded from fifteen hundred acres to three thousand. The entire time the family continued with its business of grafting and raising new sapling trees and planting every newly acquired acre of their land—Valencias, Pineapples, Hamlins, Parson Browns, and Temples—plus acres and acres of grapefruit and tangerine trees as well. When other businesses in Florida were on their knees, Watson Properties, Inc., as their company was now called, continued to show a profit and give jobs to men whose families might otherwise have starved.

In June of 1929, just weeks after McIver's graduation from the university, he brought his eighteen-year-old bride Alliene Carrington Todd home to the Grove to the cottage his father had just built by the main gate leading to the highway. It was small but perfect for the young couple, and equipped with every modern convenience. The rooms were few but big, a living room with a fireplace, a bedroom, kitchen, and bath. Like the family home just up the path, the ceilings were coved and supported with huge oak beams, and there were paddle fans in both living room and bedroom. Quite naturally the cottage became known as the Little House, and from the day McIver brought his bride there to live everyone referred to the family home as the Big House.

Throughout the early thirties, the lean, hungry years in which the entire nation endured total depression, Watson Properties continued with productivity and quiet expansion. Life at the Grove had settled into a pleasant normalcy for the two families, enriched in February of 1935 on the day Alliene delivered her first healthy son. They named the baby Gordon William for his grandfather. It was then that Mary Alison decided the two families should swap homes, insisting it had been her plan for years to live out her life in the Little House by the gate.

Not long after Gordie's birth the Watsons were wooed to enter the juice-processing business as a natural high-profit sideline to their groves, but McIver said no. His interests lay only in young-tree sales and the production and shipping of top quality citrus. Besides, juice processing presented nothing but problems. Storage in the thirties was difficult, and spoilage was rampant. And pasteurization by high temperature or the steam process was useless because it destroyed the taste of the juice.

But in 1937 something happened to pique McIver's interest. It was in October that he first heard about it. Ironically (because he absolutely believed all along that someone would one day find the answer to safe and delicious juice processing) the discovery took him utterly by surprise. Further, never in his wildest dreams did he conceive of himself as one of the industry's pioneers. God knows he felt no need for a career shift of any kind. At thirty he felt himself coming into his absolute prime, with energy yet unleashed. Alliene seemed in excellent health and grew lovelier in his eyes with each passing year.

Their fine young son would soon be three years old, and his parents, though still quite fit, had at last slowed down a bit and begun to enjoy life. They had even returned to the old country this past summer on a holiday. The Big House just last summer had undergone its third remodeling since 1916 and now included an enlarged, fully electric kitchen, an enormous dining room with a bay window overlooking the lake, and a total of four bedrooms and two-and-a-half baths. The new freestanding garage housed Gordon's 1936 Ford and a shiny new black Packard that McIver had surprised Alliene with on their eighth anniversary in June. Yes, things were going along very smoothly; McIver had no wish to change a thing.

But quite by accident he overheard a conversation one lazy October afternoon at the local barbershop that changed the entire thrust of the Watson family's business. It seemed there was a young engineer down in Grove Dale who'd been nosing around asking questions over at Pearson Brothers' Machine Shop on Lemon Street. The story had it that this engineer had come up with a discovery in the lab where he worked up north, an invention that would be the answer to keeping the flavor in orange juice when it was processed. He'd figured a way to boil the juice in some new way, drawing off all the water into a vacuum, which left behind a kind of slurry. Then, when the slurry, or particles of fruit and left over pulp, was remixed with water, it became whole juice again, just like fresh-squeezed. The engineer was calling the product concentrate.

And now gossip around town had it that this engineer, who had been in the area for weeks looking for a partner to build the machinery he'd need to experiment with the process, had finally found himself one, a guy in Dunedin who owned a packing plant. Together the two of them had every key ingredient but one. They needed financial backing.

McIver realized this was it. This was the first time he'd felt like embracing any part of the citrus business other than the agricultural end of fruit growing. And, if it were really true—if this engineer had conquered the problem of maintaining taste in the pasteurization process of canning citrus juice—it promised to be the biggest boon to the industry since its start.

The next day he set the wheels in motion. He met with the partners and agreed to supply the money to tool up for the commercial production and marketing of concentrate in exchange for ten percent of the corporation and first right of purchase of the remaining ninety, should the partners ever decide to sell. The three men shook hands, and the new company was formed.

The first four years in the venture were slow. Coolly McIver and his father stood by and watched as tooling up, production, and test marketing of orange juice concentrate took place. And in the meantime life for the Watson family continued to go on very much as before. Slowly, steadily, the Watson Properties' acreage continued to expand, and as each new parcel of land was acquired, it seemed magically, overnight, to be planted in rows and rows of healthy sapling citrus trees. For many years now Ben Hewett had been foremen for the properties, and each year the list of steady, full-time employees increased. And always McIver was there, never missing a trick or a spoken word, yet quietly running the business from the background. At home all of his attention in 1938 was devoted to his wife and the delicacy of her state of health during her second pregnancy, and on September twenty-seventh of that year she delivered her second son, another wee black-haired boy who looked exactly like Gordie.

They named the baby Arthur Todd, for Alliene's father.

McIver continued to keep a weather eye on the fledging concentrate business, deliberately keeping his distance to give the eager young inventor and his partner plenty of breathing space. To him patience was the key, but the partners were subject to increasing fits of depression with each promotional setback. McIver wasn't worried because he knew the process was a good one, and the minute they proved it to the proper party, he was convinced there would be a stampede within the juice-processing industry. All he wanted was to be among the first.

Then it happened. On December 7, 1941, when the Japanese attacked Pearl Harbor and the nation was plunged into World War II, British importation of citrus from Spain came to a halt and our allies across the Atlantic became an obvious source of need for citrus. Six days after Pearl Harbor the Department of Agriculture placed an order to the young company for one million dollars in concentrate, and within weeks the Reconstruction Finance put up a one-and-a-half-million-dollar loan to construct a bigger plant.

At war's end the partners decided to take their money and run, keeping their promise to sell their ninety percent share to Watson Properties. McIver met with Dwight Anderson, the company attorney, and added another corporate name to the property holdings, Watson Sundrenched, Inc., then settled into competition with the new kids on the block: Snow Crop, Minute Maid, Tropicana, and a score of lesser-known Florida processers. Within a decade concentrate bearing the yellow-and-orange Watson Sundrenched logo was being shipped and marketed all over the world, and the cornerstone for the family's incredible wealth was laid long before Alison ever decided to make her surprise entrance into the heart of the Watson dynasty.

The week before Christmas of 1949 Mary Alison Watson died, plummeting the family into shock and a deep, black period of mourning. For McIver life on the Grove would never seem quite the same. But by late summer of 1950 he announced it was about time they all had a good cheering up. What he meant was that the Big House was about to undergo another remodeling. The improvements were so vast, the projections to date of completion were for at least eight months, and, blueprinted, the floor plan had absolutely no rhyme or reason; like the leguminous cover crop that crawled along the ground in the aisles between the rows of fruit trees in the groves, it simply sprawled everywhere.

If all went as the contractor promised, the place was to be ready by late spring, and now with the news of the new baby, plans were set in motion to redecorate the former master bedroom in organdy and pink. There was no budging her; Alliene stubbornly continued to insist that the baby was going to be a girl. The new master bedroom, with its adjoining sun room and bath, would be just steps across the hall from the baby's room and would bring the number of bedrooms in the house to six, the number of baths to five and a half. Other additions would be the mammoth family room, plus a game room on the west wing that was big enough to house not only a Ping-Pong table but a pool table, too. One corner of it was designed for McIver's poker table and chairs, and along the north wall was a sixteen-foot-long bar. The plans included two new fireplaces, bringing the total now to five, and best of all, the new plumbing would be put in throughout the house. The frosting on the cake was the wonderful new luxury one could buy these days: central air conditioning and heating. With over seven thousand square feet of enclosed space, it promised to be a jewel indeed in the heart of the sprawling groves that now encompassed twelve sections, or just under eight thousand acres, altogether a very nice place for a new baby to make her home when summer came.

Minerva stood at the kitchen window on that stifling late July day, silently watching. With one son on either side of her, Alliene waved a weak good-bye to her father-in-law as she walked slowly down the porch steps, stopping twice before she reached the car, each time to bend forward in pain. She was enormously big in front; this fetus seemed abnormally large compared to her own slim frame.

The black girl shook her head in anxiety, wiping her hands on her apron, wiping them again and again as though there were moisture on them. The baby was coming early. There were supposed to be two more weeks before the baby came. She fixed her eyes on the family, wishing to be out there helping. But there was no need. This was family time. Both boys carefully assisted their mother into the passenger side of their father's car, a 1950 black Buick sedan, then piled in the backseat as McIver impatiently started the great engine and sped off, spinning pebbles from the circular driveway skyward as he raced away. In agony Minerva watched Alliene's face contort in pain through the car window and saw her golden red hair fall against the glass as she rolled her head in labor. Silently she watched as the car took the circle around the Little House, then disappeared among the rows of orange trees that bordered the main drive to the gate. Then, quietly, she joined McIver's father in the living room where he stood at the picture window, also to watch the disappearing car. "Can I get you some breakfast now, Mr. Gordon, suh?" she asked softly.

He turned, startled. "Oh, no, thank you, Minerva. I've had m' two cups o' tea. I'm no' really hungry this morning."

"Don't you worry 'bout Miss Alliene, suh. She's gonna make it jus' fine. She's a strong lady, even though she don't look it."

Gordon Watson walked over and smiled into the black girl's eyes. "Aye, you're right, girl. Alliene is a verra strong lass. She'll hae a wee bit o' struggle, but she'll make it. She struggled wi' Gordie and Todd, too, you know."

"Yes, suh. Mr. McIver told me 'bout that."

The old man turned and gazed back through the window. "Yes, a verra strong lass. She'll make it just fine."

As silently as she had entered, Minerva retreated from the big room to her kitchen, which had become her haven. Already she had grown to love the lady of the house a great deal, and the lady didn't look any too strong to her, no matter what she and Mr. Gordon had just been telling each other.

2

From her earliest memory there was not a day in which Alison Carrington Watson had not been the absolute hub in her isolated little universe. She never expected it; neither was she surprised by it. It was simply so. She never experienced a feeling of rejection, because there was none. She never yearned for something she didn't have, because she had everything she wanted. If she wished for something new, it was instantly there. If she wanted someone to talk to, someone was always around. It didn't occur to the tiny redhead to question anything whatsoever about life there on the Grove. She was, contrary to the extent of her pampering, the most unspoiled of children.

Not having a mother in the home didn't upset her. How could she miss something she could never recall having? She really couldn't remember her mother at all. From the time she was able to listen and understand she'd been told nothing but loving, wonderful things about her beautiful mother, the lovely Alliene, whose mirror image she was, or so everyone said. There were pictures of her mother everywhere, but to Alison they seemed unreal; rather, only imaginary pictures of some distant person she didn't know.

But McIver was real. He was big and ruddy and had shiny black hair and great, huge hands that scooped her from the swing and lifted her high over his head each night when he came home. He had nice brown eyes and white, even teeth. She always noticed his teeth when he smiled, and around her he always seemed to be smiling. He wore rough overalls a lot of the time because he spent most of his days in the jeep traveling around the groves, but in the evenings before supper he would bathe and change into a soft shirt and pants, and when he pulled Alison into his lap, she loved to lay her cheek against his shoulder and feel the cleanness. It was her favorite time of day. Everyone always rushed back out after Minnie's big noon meal, which was the family's main meal of the day. But evenings . . . well, evenings seemed to belong to her. Sometimes McIver would come in through the kitchen with the great screen door slamming behind him, all smelly and wet from a rough day, exhausted, even distant and detached. But the instant he laid his eyes on her, he would pull her into his arms and call her his little red-haired fairy princess.

And Gordie and Todd were real. Her brothers were different from each other, yet so alike. From the time Alison could first perceive character traits in people she knew that, although her brothers looked very much alike—both looked remarkably like their father—they were entirely opposite in personality. Gordie was proper and straight and reliable in every way. Gordie had impressed her from the start. She loved him immensely. But Todd was different. "Todd's like the Todds," McIver always said. Todd was more of a dreamer, a musician, someone who teased her mercilessly and horsed around with her, often tumbling for an hour or more together on the floor. Every word out of his mouth was a tease. But it didn't matter. Todd was super. He tickled her fancy, and she adored him.

Grandfather was special, different from the rest.

He was a wonderful old man who talked in a funny way, with a guttural brogue and rolling Rs. His hair was gray but had been black like McIver's when he was young, and, like his son, he was a ruddy, brown-eyed Scot. He was much shorter in stature but slender and unbowed. He was always immaculately dressed. Alison liked that. He smelled good. Grandfather shared Alison's favorite time of day, her daily late-afternoon visit to the Little House. She loved to watch him make a pot of tea, then dilute and sweeten a portion before pouring her share into her little china teapot. Together they would sip their tea, nibble on shortbread, and pass the time of day.

And she loved Minerva, her Minnie, the special person who silently placed each plate before her and who gently tucked her into bed at night before she caught the bus that would take her to her little home in the black section of Grove Dale. Wonderful Minerva, big and tall, with black skin that shone with cleanliness, and wearing starched white aprons that magically never seemed to stain.

But this lady everyone spoke of, this Alliene Carrington Todd Watson, was only a fantasy, a fairy-tale princess with golden red hair and fair skin, a delicate person who was slim and elegant and not really very strong.

Yet, oddly, it was not Alliene's delicate health that was the cause of her death. In fact, in spite of all the warnings she had been given during her pregnancy with Alison, she had sprung right back to her normal state of health within weeks after the delivery. But on September 27, 1953, Alliene Watson died in an automobile accident, a horrible, senseless accident that took place on a hot, late-summer afternoon less than two months after Alison's second birthday. Alliene was hurrying to prepare for the big barbecue party they were having that night to celebrate Todd's fifteenth birthday. She'd driven over to Lakeland to have her hair done and had stopped at the market to get some last-minute things. She never saw the car that hit her; it crashed through the intersection and onto the highway without stopping. The doctors at Lakeland Memorial assured McIver she never knew what hit her, nor could she have lived long enough to suffer.

The suffering came for those who were left behind. McIver was thrown into utter, black despair. He was absolutely inconsolable, and for his sake, his father and sons bore their own grief as best they could, keeping to themselves.

Throughout the long period of mourning the only spark of joy in their lives was the little girl who was totally unaware that she had become the only female left in the Watson family. McIver vowed to become both mother and father to her now, to bring no other wife into their home. What's more, Alison's brothers became father and mother to her, too, caring for her with the same sort of fierce desire to make her happy that McIver expressed. As for her grandfather, Alison was the main source of happiness that remained for him.

McIver asked Minerva to stay on. Quietly she continued to run the two households, to manage the other servants, and to take full command as Alison's nursemaid and companion. As such, she became the only real female figure in this tapestry of men that wove the web of security tightly, strongly around Alison's little world. Through it the incredible little redhead unconsciously began to wrap all four men ever so tightly around her tiny pinky finger.

As it is generally true in any person's life in which there is no memory of special pain or discomfort, Alison would recall only fuzzy patches of events that were a part of her earliest years. Her memories, instead, were all good. She felt secure, loved. Her daily activities fell into a disciplined routine, guarded over and directed by Minerva, the kindly black lady who was her special friend. She could never remember a time in which there weren't other servants about the sprawling house and grounds, but the child didn't spend any time alone with any of them; Minerva never allowed it. To Minerva Alison was her personal and private charge. Mr. McIver had declared it so, and jealously the woman guarded this honor, and focused her undivided attention on the child; in fact, watched her like a hawk. The situation was amusing to the family and their friends, but Minerva's zeal didn't bother the child herself. Alison felt no real need for privacy from the servant, at least not until a few years later. Like everything else around the Grove it was a condition that simply was so.

And so the days rambled lazily on, turning into a jumble of hazy memories in the little girl's preschool period of life. But something happened a couple of months after Alison's fifth birthday of such immense interest to her that it stood out from all the rest up to that point in time. It occurred on a lazy hot September evening in 1956, during her nightly prowl. She had waited, as she always did, until Minnie had been gone awhile and the men in the house believed her to be asleep. Of course, the idea that she would be asleep by eight-thirty was ridiculous. It wasn't even quite dark by then. And, besides, she was never tired at all by that hour. How could she be when Minnie forced her to take long naps right after dinner every afternoon? "You rest now, you heah me, Miss Alison? A good nap'll he'p you to grow up to be strong an' healthy like your big brothers. Besides, you know you cain't go outdoors in the hot sun of an afternoon, anyhow. You'll turn into one big brown blotch of freckles."

It was true. When Alison played out in the strong Florida sun, her entire little body became sprinkled

with light brown freckles, a generous smattering of
them on her cheeks and across the bridge of her nose.
Try as Minerva might, none of the lotions she slath-
ered on the child's skin seemed to help. So one day
the black woman just decided to keep her child away
from the rays of the sun—period.

Alison always protested her nap, but each day,
soon after she was forced into her big bed, she fell under the mesmerizing motion of the ceiling fan. She
always woke in time to run down to Grandfather's
house for afternoon tea, then enjoyed her play period
when the sun's rays had diminished sufficiently in
Minerva's judgment to allow her outside.

Alison's play area was enormous and entirely safe.
A sturdy six-foot-high chain-link fence surrounded
the three acres of land where the two family dwellings were situated, rich ground sodded with thick St.
Augustine grass and groomed to perfection by Willie
Fursan, the full-time gardener. A wide pebble path
connected the Little House to the back porch door behind Minerva's kitchen, and a sizable vegetable garden nearby provided fresh vegetables to the family
year round. The flower garden, which was Grandfather's pride, was just yards away from the open front
porch of the Little House. Nearly every afternoon,
when he and his granddaughter had finished with
their tea and visit, he would walk with her to the
garden and clip a fresh rose for her bedroom.

Alison owned two sets of swings with adjacent
sandbox and jungle gyms, one near the kitchen window of the Big House where Minerva could watch
her at play, and one beside Grandfather's garden.
There were climbing trees everywhere inside the
fenced area, and of course there were dozens of the
smaller straggly fruit trees—orange, tangerine,
grapefruit, lime, and kumquat. One of the fine
young orange trees was Alison's own, planted as a
sapling by her chubby two-year-old hands the spring

after her mother died. "Here's a good place, pet," Mc-
Iver had said to the toddler. "Here under the dining
room window where we can watch it grow right
along with you." They had all gathered to watch the
planting ceremony: McIver, her brothers, Grandfather, Minerva, and Ben. "And when the first fruit
ripens, darlin'," her father added, "it will be as
orange as your wee head."

Two gates led from the child's fenced-in world to
the great universe out there. One was about twenty
yards from the steps at the end of the open porch that
spanned the lakeside of the Big House. The other,
just beyond Grandfather's rose garden, was the gate
nearest the main driveway into the Watson groves,
on an angle, a short turn off the highway.

The latches on both gates were high. Even an
adult had to reach up to open them. And they were
strong and difficult to operate. Furthermore, McIver
drilled it into the boys that no guest was to leave
either gate until the latch was fixed firmly in place.
For added security there were dogs, two magnificent
black German shepherds, Great Bear and Diablo.
They had been trained from puppyhood to protect Alison. They slept in her room during naptime and at
night, and wherever she set out on foot, she was
quietly flanked by both animals. Together with her
yellow-striped cat Honey, the inseparable band of
four were an amusing sight.

Always the last servant to leave at night, Minerva
generally caught the seven-thirty bus for home. This
was Alison's friskiest time of day, but she was too
clever to let the black lady who listened to her pray-
ers know it. Instead, she piled into bed on command
and lay wide-eyed to watch her friend stop at the
doorway, as she knew she would, to blow her a kiss
and say, "God keep you safe till mornin', Miss Alison."

Tonight there was an aura of excitement around

the house. At five years old there was little that the intelligent youngster didn't observe. All week Minerva had been in a frenzy, overseeing Lonnie's laundry room activities and getting big trunks packed and shoes polished and clothing mended. Both boys were leaving the next day for the university, Gordie to begin his senior year, and Todd, who would be eighteen the next week, to enroll for the first time. Alison watched from her favorite stool as Minerva lifted sheet after sheet of cookies from the double ovens, then packed them, still warm, into tins. "It don't seem right for two hungry boys to be agoin' off where they cain't get no home cookin' till Thanksgivin'."

Even dinner tonight had seemed festive. Both boys had been allowed to invite their girl friends, and Minerva had saved the main meal of the day for evening, outdoing herself with a southern-style feast. Afterward Gordie and Margaret took off for a movie in Lakeland, and McIver decided to stroll back to the Little House with his father for a game of chess. Alison listened attentively, but Todd never said what he and Sharon were going to do. It looked like they were going to stay home. Good. Maybe they'd listen to records and dance. It was easy to sneak down the hall to the family room unseen and watch from behind the big sofa. She loved to watch when her brothers brought their girls home to dance.

With Minerva gone, Alison waited patiently until the house was quiet. There was no music coming from the family room yet, so Todd and Sharon must have gone for a walk. She climbed down from her bed and pulled on her seersucker robe, then sat on the floor to yank on her little slippers. The shepherds roused and shook. Standing, the child methodically kissed each dog on the face, just as she did every morning when she got up, and called them by name. "I love you, D'ablo," she said. "Love you, Bear."

Then she gathered the reluctant cat from his comfortable place on her pillow and carried him like a rag doll through the dark hall to the kitchen. She left the house through the back door, but not before she grabbed up a couple of tangerines, one for each pocket of her robe. The two dogs bounded on protectively in front of her, then fell in at each side as she began her routine, nightly trek down the hundred yards to the Little House. Alison never concerned herself that McIver would be beside himself with fear if he knew she were wandering around the property with only slippers covering her feet, down paths where they occasionally killed rattlers or coral snakes. But the child was careful. She always watched where she was going, and she had a healthy fear of snakes, drummed into her by Minerva. Besides, Diablo and Bear were forever at her side.

A few yards before reaching the Little House, Alison whispered her command for the dogs to stay. Obediently they sat, watching as she climbed the porch steps and peeked through the open window. Both men were silent, intent on their chess game. Then she climbed back down and set her cat on the ground before circling to the bedroom side of the cottage, again followed by the little band of animals. She stopped at her favorite tree, a mulberry tree with a trunk that split into a wide *V*, perfect for climbing, and took off her robe and laid it on the grass. Then her slippers, neatly, side by side as Minnie always instructed her to do. She squatted down and pulled one of the tangerines from the pocket of the robe and placed the fruit in a low crook in the tree, then turned to the cat and whispered, "Come on, Honey." The dogs positioned themselves at the trunk of the tree and watched.

The cat scampered up ahead of her and handily beat her to the nice flat branch that was Alison's favorite perching place, about halfway up the tree. Her climb was slower because she had to stop and find a nook for the tangerine all along the way. But she could see quite clearly from the light through the bedroom window, and from the moon that was still three-quarters full. Once settled, she sat, swinging her little legs happily, and peered down through the open bedroom window, which lent a perfect view of the two men at the chessboard in the next room. As she silently peeled the fruit and ate it she listened to the conversation between her two men on the hot, still night. They seldom talked much during a chess game, and what they did say really was of little interest to her, anyhow, unless she heard her name mentioned. It was the joy of sneaking out and watching them unnoticed that intrigued her.

Finished with the tangerine, a little bored now, she climbed back down, careful not to snag or stain her pajamas because Minnie would soon be on to her game if she did. She pulled her robe and slippers on again and headed back up the path to the Big House. Tonight she decided to circle the far side, the bedroom wing of the house, and sneak down to the south end of the long, open porch where she knew Todd and his girl friend were bound to be, since there was still no music coming from inside. Unless they were still out walking, where else would they be than in the swing?

She was right. The couple was seated close together, and it looked like Todd had his arm around Sharon, hugging her really tight. But they weren't saying a word. That was odd. As Alison drew closer she discovered why. Todd was kissing Sharon, kissing her on the mouth. And she was squirming and making little moaning sounds and running her fingers through his hair, and between kisses, saying, "Oh, Todd. Todd, sugar!"

"Sharon, baby, you're wonderful. I want you." Alison heard her brother say breathlessly.

Utterly fascinated, the child found a good place in the grass just behind the big azalea bush at the end of the porch and settled in to watch. She sat down cross-legged and made herself comfortable as both dogs silently found a place beside her. Diablo turned his head up to his mistress and uttered a low whine of communication. "Shhh," she whispered, bending to kiss his head.

"What was that?" Sharon cried out. She jerked back in fear.

"What was what?" Todd answered, pulling the girl back in his arms.

"I thought I heard something."

"You heard my heart. You've got it hammering right out of my chest." Again he kissed her warmly, hungrily. "Holy Christ, Sharon, you drive me nuts!"

Alison's view was perfect. Even though Todd and Sharon had their backs to her, she could see everything clearly through the slats in the porch swing, their bodies silhouetted against the light from the living room picture windows.

Then Todd did something that was very, very interesting to the child. He unbuttoned Sharon's blouse and reached his hand inside it and felt all around in there, and Sharon cried out even louder and said, "Oh, Todd, Todd, *sugar!*" Then they were kissing again, and Todd left his hand inside her blouse.

Spellbound, Alison automatically reached in her pocket for the other tangerine as Honey pounced into her lap and made himself comfortable for a nap. As she carefully peeled the fruit and started to eat it, more interesting things began to happen in the swing. Todd undid all the buttons on Sharon's blouse and pulled it away to each side. Then, after first looking all around, he put both hands inside her blouse and reached around her back and undid the garment she was wearing under it. Alison had never seen a bra before. Slowly she chewed up each plug of the tart fruit and watched, without ungluing her eyes from the lovers.

Her brother lifted up the little white garment, a funny, filmy thing that you could see clear through, and bent down and began to kiss Sharon's body. Alison noticed that Sharon had pink round places in the same spot where hers were on her own body, only Sharon's were much bigger and plumper, and they were out on the tips of two round white mounds of flesh, fat places that stuck out in front like Minnie's did under her apron. But her brothers' and father's little pink circles were on flat skin over their ribs, just as her own were. She reached up under her pajama top and felt her nipples and breasts, wondering if they had changed to be like Sharon's since the last time she noticed. No, they were the same.

Then Alison watched as her brother took one of the pink circles into his mouth and began to lick it and suck on it the way she would suck a lollipop. He kissed and licked and sucked some more, then began to suck the tip of the other one where it stuck straight out in perfect silhouette against the reflected light. Sharon rolled her head back and moaned and squealed aloud, but Alison noticed that she didn't try to stop Todd from sucking on her. In fact, it seemed to her that she liked what he was doing a lot.

Then Todd did a really interesting thing. He took one of his hands away from the place that he was kissing and reached down and put it up under Sharon's skirt. "No, Todd. I can't let you do that. Not here. No! No, you mustn't!" Sharon said. But then she started kissing Todd again, really hard, and Alison saw her squirming and pushing her body against Todd's hand.

"Come down with me by the lake," Todd said to

the girl. "Come on, Sharon. We can go to the boat house."

"No. That's too wide open," the girl exclaimed. "The moon's still out, Todd. You can see straight into that place. What if your father were to come back that way?"

"Okay, okay, the potting shed then. No one will see us in there."

"Todd, I'm scared."

"I want you, baby. Tonight's my last night. We won't see each other until Thanksgiving. Don't be scared. I've got a rubber. We've never been caught before. Come on, baby, I want you before I leave."

Alison could hear Sharon's voice trail away as they ran down the yard toward the gate. "Sugar, am I crazy or did you smell fresh tangerines just now?"

Todd's laughter echoed back. "We live on a citrus grove, baby, remember?"

Alison sat very still until she heard the click of the gate latch behind them, then circled the house and reentered through the back porch. She was still lying awake when she heard McIver come home, but she pretended to be sleeping when he looked in on her. "She's beautiful, isn't she, Honey?" she heard him whisper to her cat. "So like her mother." The child lay still as she heard her father give each dog a pat. "Keep her safe," he said to them as the dogs returned to their places, Diablo at the side of her bed, Bear near the foot.

She lay awake long after her father's footsteps were gone, thinking back over all she had seen tonight. What was Todd touching up under Sharon's skirt? And what was it that her brother wanted before he left for college, something they had to go to the potting shed to find? And why would Sharon be scared if Todd didn't have a rubber? A rubber what?

Alison made up her mind then and there that the minute she was allowed beyond the fence, she was going to have a look around the potting shed and see for herself.

3

"Damn it, Alison, you told me you liked it this way."

"I do, Calvin. It's just that I don't see what harm there is in trying something different once in a while."

The boy eased off of her and swung his feet to the floor, balancing not to slip off the edge of Ben's narrow bed. He looked disgustedly around for his jeans. Spotting them, he walked over to the chair where they were slung.

"Where are you going?" Alison asked. She pulled up and leaned for a thoughtful moment on her elbow, eyeing Calvin's naked ass with approval.

Calvin took his time, keeping his back to her as he dressed, then turned and tucked his shirt into his pants. He pulled the zipper up in a snap of exasperation. "It's a long walk back. For me. I don't have a horse to get me back like you do. I told you before we ever met all the way over on this side of the grove, Alison, that my ass is gonna be in a sling if I'm late for dinner again tonight. And my old man told me last night he meant business. Said he'll ground me for a week if I'm not there by six o'clock."

"Oh," she said. She flopped back down on the pillow and folded her slender arms across her ribs. Calvin noticed that the very way she placed them under her firm little breasts seemed to make them rise higher. Incredibly, her luscious nipples even appeared to stick out farther than they had at the height of their passion a few minutes ago. He glanced around nervously, then said, "I really do have to beat it. You okay?"

"I'm always okay."

"Listen, Alison, don't be that way. You're the one who wanted to stop just when everything was going so good."

"I didn't want to *stop*, Calvin. I wanted you to try it the way I explained it to you."

"That's another thing," the boy said in frustration. He hitched on his belt, then stuck his hands in the pockets of his jeans, fixing his stare on her eyes. "How is it you know so many positions, anyhow? You're only sixteen years old and—"

"I'll be seventeen next month."

"Okay, seventeen—next month. But I can't figure out how . . ."

"I told you. I read a very explicit book. And it had very explicit pictures."

Calvin brushed away a lock of hair from his eyes and glanced at his watch. He was a fine-looking young man, only seventeen years old himself, and like Alison, a red-haired third-generation Scot. Calvin was the son of the Douglasses, who owned the grove bordering the Watson groves to the north. The Douglass family was one of the dozens of grove-owner families who'd moved to central Florida, coming from their native Scotland to settle here in clans as Scots are inclined to do. This gentle, rolling area of Florida had become known as the Highlands for more reasons than one.

Calvin was ruggedly handsome, six feet tall and stocky without being fat, just the right size for the back line of Grove Dale High's football team. He continued to gaze at Alison as she sat up on the edge of the bed and slipped into her blouse, braless. Alison didn't need a bra; her breasts were firm and nestled against her rib cage in a way that seemed just right to him. Her enormous nipples drove him nearly mad. As a matter of fact, Alison drove him nearly mad. He feasted his eyes on the beauty he'd admired from the first grade on, the girl he thought was untouchable, one who would never in a billion light-years give him the time of day. Holy Christ, but she was gorgeous.

Calvin wasn't the only one to perceive that this was a beautiful girl, beautiful in an elusive way, one that lent an aura of mystery to her, a certain mystique that strangers found fascinating. Even the way she scampered into class at Grove Dale High spelled out the message that she was independent like a cat, cool and self-contained. It shocked Calvin that day two months ago when he found out firsthand that she was, instead, every bit as torrid as she'd always seemed cold to him.

At nearly seventeen Alison had grown to her full height, a little over five feet eight inches, and was slender and straight. And now that the girl was out from under Minerva's constant watchful eye, she spent a great deal of time in the sun, so was sprinkled generously with freckles on every square inch of the body, which her tiny bikini swimsuits didn't manage to conceal. Alison detested her freckles and was vain enough to spare her face from being too heavily coated by them, usually wearing a hat when sunning or taking to the trail on horseback.

Today Alison was wearing faded jeans and her favorite cotton blouse, a short-sleeved floral print splashed with orange and rust that was tied up in a little knot just under her bust, leaving her sunbronzed midriff bare. The jeans rode low on her hipbones, and now, as she stood to zip them, Calvin noticed the tantalizing plane of her flat belly rising just above the waistband and the barest hint of her dimpled navel peeping over the center snap. He allowed his eyes to linger there for a moment only, aware that the blood would soon be surging again to his crotch if he didn't keep his mind on hauling ass out of here.

"Meet me again tomorrow?" he asked brightly, trying to mask the urgent hope in his voice.

She looked up from her zipper and eyed him quizzically. "Promise not to get fussy if I make a slight suggestion or two? I only want it to be really good for *both* of us, Calvin."

" 'Course I won't get fussy." He grabbed up her hand and kissed the tips of her fingers. "Make any little ol' suggestion you like. Same time, same place?"

"Same time, but we can't come here tomorrow. Ben will be back from market. We'll have to use the potting shed by the lake."

"You sure that place is safe? It's too damn close to the Big House if you ask me. Why not the Little House? At least we could lock the doors there."

"No. The Little House is out. It's inside the fence. And besides, McIver stops by there now and then when he's headed home. Don't worry about the potting shed. No one ever uses it that time of day."

" 'Kay," he said, kissing her fingers again. "I love ya."

He turned and sprinted from the door of the tiny cottage. The place still belonged to Ben Hewett after all these years. An old man now, Ben had remained a bachelor and liked the place exactly as it was. Other than the addition of an indoor bathroom in the late twenties and a coat of paint from time to time, the house was virtually unchanged. It had been a hideaway of Alison's for years, ever since she'd finally become old enough, at ten, to let herself through the gate.

Today Alison had arrived at Ben's on horseback,

riding one of the regular stable horses she helped exercise daily. Her own mare, Goldie, had died that spring from distemper. Like Honey and the dogs, Goldie had been her special pet, her pride. When her horse died, a little of the child died along with her. At sixteen it seemed a turning point, a time to grow up.

Bear was gone now, too, replaced by Cinder, another black shepherd puppy. And Diablo was very old but still alert and constantly true to his mistress. Honey seemed indestructible, and the teenager still dragged him around in her arms, taking him with her almost everywhere she went at the Grove. But she never brought the cat along when she was meeting Calvin.

Ben and she were great friends, and Alison knew she was free to go inside his house anytime. She spent hours there, generally as a hideaway from Minerva's watchful eye. It was a great place to read the off-limits books she snitched from Todd's bedroom. Only Lonnie was on to her, threatening more than once to tell Minerva if she didn't stop sneaking them out of the house. "Hush, Lonnie," the teenager defied. "You'll do no such thing, and you know it. Why would you want to upset Minnie by telling her a story like that? She'd never believe you, anyhow. So mind your own business, okay?"

Alison had learned a lot about sex from books, but she gained her firsthand knowledge about the sexual act and its different and interesting positions from watching the very thing over the years, not once but many times. From the moment her curiosity was piqued when she saw Todd reach under Sharon's skirt that night in the swing, Alison had developed a keen interest in anything sexual that happened between her brothers and their lovers. And between McIver and *his* women, too.

Though fixed in his determination never to marry

again, McIver was a virile man, and his sexual assignations generally took place in the bedroom of the Little House after his father had died. The cottage was a perfect stopping place when he was returning a lady home after she had shared dinner with Alison and him at the Big House. Perfect, except that he didn't know his daughter had continued her pattern of making a beeline to the Little House and climbing up the mulberry tree outside the bedroom window. Of course, he assumed her to be in her room, reading as she always did after dinner. "I've never seen a child in my life who could spend so much time with her nose in a book!" he exclaimed over the years. And certainly it never occurred to him to close any blinds at the cottage.

Alison was only seven years old when she first stumbled onto what was to become the typical after-dinner routine between her father and his current lady. Grandfather had been dead less than a year then, and recently McIver had begun to bring a particular woman to the Big House for dinner. Her name was Elaine. Alison liked her all right but remained distant from her, as she did with everyone except her family and Minnie and Ben. Still, the child rather looked forward to her visits because she liked seeing McIver laugh. Strangely she was never a whit jealous of Elaine, nor of any that were to follow; she knew instinctively that none of them would alter McIver's devotion to her or change his mind about remarriage.

The first two or three visits, McIver and Elaine sat after dinner and played cards or watched television with Alison snuggled comfortably on her father's lap until she could no longer hold open her eyes. But on the fourth evening something happened to get the little girl's feelers up. Soon after Minerva left McIver told Alison he and Elaine were going to go out for a while but that she would be safe in her room with the dogs there. He promised to be back soon. "We won't be far away, pet," he assured her. "We're just going to take a little walk down by the lake."

The Little House. They were going to walk down to the Little House. Alison knew it instantly. So, of course she gave them a head start, then followed. When she tiptoed up the steps to the front porch, she got her first surprise. She'd assumed they would be seated at the chessboard, just as McIver and Grandfather had always done. Instead, she saw her father guide Elaine through the door to the bedroom, each of them holding a glass of brandy. Wide-eyed, the little girl watched as her father stopped Elaine at the bedroom doorway and kissed her on the lips. Her father was doing the same thing Todd had done with Sharon in the swing.

Swiftly the child retreated from the porch and motioned to the dogs to follow her. The animals sat patiently and waited for her to settle herself in the tree. Now the lovers were inside the bedroom. There were no lights on there, but Alison could see from the light that beamed in on them through the living room door. Extremely interested now, she watched as her father took the brandy glass from Elaine's hand and placed it beside his on the dresser. Then he pulled her into his arms and kissed her passionately again and again, reaching down as he did to grasp both sides of her bottom with his hands. Elaine seemed to like it a lot and clung tightly to him, then ran her hands along his back, then up into his hair. Then McIver did exactly what Todd had done with Sharon. He unbuttoned the top of Elaine's dress and reached in and began to feel around inside it.

Before the astonished girl could take it all in, suddenly Elaine's dress was lying on the floor at McIver's feet, and then her slip, and there she stood,

clad only in her panties and the same sort of filmy
garment Sharon had worn on her top. McIver
seemed to be very excited about it all, and Elaine
moaned aloud and rolled her head backward as Mc-
Iver leaned in and began to kiss the flesh over the
sheer white garment. Then, quick as a wink, he undid the hooks from Elaine's back and lifted the garment away. Well! The flesh that spilled from it was a
lot different from Sharon's; the two white mounds
were enormous, and the pink places stuck out like
Alison's pinky fingers. She had never seen anything
like it.

Then, sure enough, just as Todd had with Sharon,
McIver leaned in and began to suck on Elaine's pink
places. Alison stared, completely absorbed, as her father led Elaine over to the bed. Gently McIver
slipped Elaine's panties away and tossed them on
the floor, leaving her completely naked. Then he
pulled off all of his own clothes before lying with her
in the bed. They hugged and kissed for what seemed
a very long time to the child. Every so often McIver
took his lips away from Elaine's mouth to lean down
and suck her pink places again. And then Alison
caught a glimpse of a fascinating part of the male
anatomy, one she hadn't seen before: an erect penis.
She'd had fleeting looks at the flaccid penis and
thought little of it, on such times as one of her brothers dashed from the bathroom and the towel fell
away, or before her father turned his back to her if
she entered his room when he was dressing. But this
was something new, something terribly exciting. It
was so big! And it stood away from her father's body
on a hard angle. It showed in perfect silhouette
against the light before it penetrated the shadow between Elaine's legs. Right after that Elaine cried out
McIver's name, wiggled hard for a while, then fell
back and sighed.

Alison knew she had stumbled onto something

really special this time. When her father and Elaine were dressed and back in the kitchen, she scampered back down the tree and hurried up the path to her bedroom. She lay in the darkness for a long time that night thinking. So *that* was what Todd and Sharon went to the potting shed that night two years ago to do! It wasn't to *get* something, it was to do this thing. And doing it was good because McIver liked doing it, too.

After the first experience Alison watched McIver with several different ladies. In fact, there was a steady procession of them over Alison's early teen years, and she spied on every one of them the first time they disappeared with her father down the path to the Little House. But she only watched each new lover once. She just wanted to see if there would be anything different about the new one. Each lady was interesting in her own way, and Alison knew one thing for sure: Going to the Little House seemed to be McIver's favorite part of the evening when he brought a lady home to dinner.

Alison also watched her brothers escapades from her perching place in the mulberry tree. And, amazing as it seemed to the child, none of the three seemed to know that the others were using the place for the same reason.

The girl noticed that Todd was careful never to go near the place unless McIver was off the family compound, but her canny brother didn't miss a chance when he thought nobody was around. Unknowingly Todd gave Alison an expanded knowledge of the various sexual positions. When she saw Todd engaging in oral sex for the first time, the crazy upside-down position he got into with his girl friend intrigued the child completely. Plus, Todd did many interesting things with girls in the armless chair near the desk, and standing up, too, right smack against the wall. Alison watched Todd and his partner in untold positions right up to now with Jennifer, the girl he was going to marry this coming fall.

But she only saw Gordie in the sex act once. He was plainly in love with Margaret long before his grandfather died, and so was hardly inclined to bring a succession of women to the Little House as his father and brother regularly did. But one very cold early December afternoon when McIver was away at market and Todd hadn't arrived home yet from school, Gordie and Margaret slipped away from the Big House as Minerva was preparing dinner. Instinctively Alison knew where they would be and, when she approached the Little House and saw smoke curling from the chimney, knew they were inside. Climbing up the tree to watch, Alison discovered that her brother and Margaret weren't in the bedroom. She waited against the approaching darkness, aware that the couple were no doubt enjoying the fire and that perhaps they would make love in there, out of her sight. Shivering, she decided to wait a few minutes longer. At last a light appeared from the kitchen that reflected into the bedroom. She watched as Gordie led Margaret to the bed and gently removed her clothes, kissing her all the while. After the long and tender lovemaking, Alison knew inside herself that she would want something just like that to happen to her someday.

The canter back from Ben's house to the stables took only moments, and Alison was relieved to find that one of the stable hands hadn't left yet for supper and would rub down and feed her horse for her. She couldn't wait to get into the shower. Ben's cottage had been hotter than the hinges. Even though McIver had tried to persuade him otherwise, the man had stubbornly refused to have his place air-conditioned. Then, on the ride back, there hadn't been a breath of air on the trail. Summer at the

Grove had set in. It felt like a hundred and ten out there. She hurried up the path from the stables, anxious to jump into fresh jeans and a halter before time to get dressed up for dinner. She had promised Minnie she would help out in the kitchen before everybody began to arrive. Dinner would be very late tonight. Tonight was going to be special.

It was not yet seven o'clock when Alison watched Minerva put the finishing swirls of icing on the layer cake she had baked that afternoon. The girl sat with her chin on her fists at the big round oak table that stood near the corner fireplace in Minerva's great kitchen. She observed, impressed as always, as her friend rounded the bend in her day's work, doing the thing she did best, which was to organize a marvelous meal and serve it within minutes of when McIver finished his nightly routine. Alison smiled to think about it. Always her father's pattern was the same. He would rush into the kitchen through the back door, disappear to shower and change, then sit in his recliner in the family room to enjoy exactly two Scotch and sodas while he read the evening *Grove Dale Courier*. And each night, even though his time of arrival often varied as much as an hour or more, magically one of Minerva's meals was placed before him the moment he folded his paper and strolled back through the kitchen.

Alison sat angled in the chair and pulled her bare foot up under her leg to watch Minnie's extravagant decorating finale to the cake. It was going to be a work of art in yellow and pale green, big yellow sugar roses atop, with delicate swirls of green stems and tiny green leaves. This was the teenager's favorite hour of the day. Unconsciously the girl was replaying an old tape, a hark back to the happy late afternoons she had spent in her grandfather's company over tea and shortbread.

And tonight promised to be extra special. Tonight

they were having dinner, not a cold supper of left-overs from the noontime meal, and the cake Minerva was decorating was certainly no ordinary cake. This was the dessert that was to follow a feast of celebration. Minnie had spent today preparing one of her extravaganzas, and the dining room table was already set with Alliene's best bone china and sterling silver and centered with a cut-glass bowl filled with roses from Grandfather's garden. Only this week Todd had shared the news of his engagement to Jennifer Brandt from Jacksonville, and tonight the family was gathering to celebrate. It was the tenth of June, 1968, just a week after school was out. Alison had just completed her junior year at Grove Dale High School and was off for the summer, feeling deliciously carefree and completely happy with her world.

"Where's my straight-*A* student?" McIver shouted. As the big man entered the room Alison looked up from the cake and grinned, then rushed across the kitchen into her father's arms. "McIver, hello!"

"Miss Alison, you know it ain't respectful to call your father by his given name," Minerva chided.

"McIver loves it," Alison answered. She hugged her father again and ran her hand across his cheek. "Don't you, McIver?"

"Love it or not, you'll do as you please," he answered, smiling.

"You know you love it." Turning, she added, "Look at Minnie's cake, McIver. It's Todd's engagement cake. Have you ever heard of an engagement cake?"

The big man stood for an appreciative moment to eye his daughter as she left him and hurried back across the huge room to watch Minnie at work. She was dressed in worn-out-looking jeans and a halter top, with her golden red hair caught up in a ponytail by a narrow yellow ribbon, yet somehow she looked as elegant to him as if she were wearing a gown and going to a ball. He noticed her poised with her hands on her hips as Minerva added the final yellow rose, and his heart swelled with love. So lovely, so incredibly lovely. He fixed his eyes on his daughter's freckled shoulders and chest and smiled. He could see that in spite of Minerva's protective grumblings, Alison had been spending many hours in the early summer sun. Her face shone with good health, and her tawny eyes flashed the occasion's excitement. She was his heart, the apple of his eye, his joy.

"I have a present for you, Alison," he said tenderly. "A reward for bringing home such a splendid report card."

The girl spun around, not masking her excitement. "Really, Daddy?" Minerva's head shot up, and she eyed the teenager with a satisfied smile. Catching it, Alison said, "Really, McIver? Where is it?" She darted over to him and peeked behind him where he held his hands clenched, then pried them open to find nothing there. She squinted into his shirt pocket and frisked his other pockets for some bulge, some sign of the gift, jumping up and down and giggling in delight.

Finally he said, "It's outside."

Alison sprinted through the screen door with her father close behind. When Minerva heard a screech of excitement, she hurried to the porch to watch. Standing with its reins looped through the back porch railing, was a magnificent golden palomino mare.

"Oh, Daddy, oh, Daddy darling, oh, McIver, I love her so," said Alison, running over and throwing her arms around the animal's neck.

"She's all yours, Princess."

"Oh, Daddy, I love her! What's her name?"

"You must name her, Alison. She's yours."

The young woman stepped back and eyed the horse in appraisal. She cocked her head and stuck her fingers in the back pockets of her jeans, turning her hands palms-out in a gesture that always amused McIver, one he knew his daughter assumed when she was ready to solve a problem. Leaving them there, she pranced all the way around the animal. "Well," she said seriously, "I can't call her Goldie II. I wouldn't feel right about that." She cast a sidelong glance at her father, silently asking him for help. He grinned and shrugged his shoulders. "Nugget," she announced finally. "I'll call her Nugget." She walked over to kiss the horse on her long face. "Hello, Nugget. My name is Alison. I'm going to be your new mother." Then, turning, the teenager ran to McIver and threw herself into his arms.

Minerva stifled tears and retreated to the kitchen. It was family time.

Margaret was the first to notice Alison on her new horse as their car entered the drive. She nudged Jennifer's arm and pointed. The two women were seated in the rear of Gordie's car, with Gordie at the wheel and Todd in the front seat beside him. When Todd caught sight of his sister, too, he said, "Hey, Gordie, wait. Look. They've delivered the new horse."

Gordie chuckled and set the brake, then swung around to watch through the rear window. When Margaret shifted to get out, he said, "Let's sit here a minute, hon. Give Pop this time alone with her."

Margaret cast a knowing glance at Jennifer, then turned to watch, curious, like the rest. By now Alison had mounted the mare and was riding her bareback in a small circle, guiding her only with the loose rope McIver had fixed in the horse's bit. Alison laughed and gestured in delight, and her father laughed, too, then waved to her as she dug her sneakers into the horse's sides and set off at a trot around the house.

"Okay, come on now," Gordie said, jumping out and quickly assisting the girls from the backseat. The two young men fell into stride and walked in the direction of their father. Jennifer took a step to follow but hesitated when she felt Margaret's hand on her arm.

"Wait," Margaret said softly. "Let them go on." Jennifer turned in question to the woman who was to become her sister-in-law in October. When the brothers were out of earshot Margaret said, "Don't try to enter their world just now. You'll be left out. I'd hate to see you hurt."

Up ahead Gordie turned and hollered back, "Hurry up, you two."

"We'll catch up with you," Margaret called out.

"What do you mean, *their* world?" Jennifer asked haughtily.

"Listen, darling. It's not a bad thing but something you must accept. You're going to be a Watson, so you must. Alison is special. She owns them."

"Owns them! You can't *own* anybody. That sounds horrible."

"It's not. It's beautiful in a way. But they don't let anyone inside." Margaret gazed wisely at the family of four, now clustered around the new mare, all talking animatedly among themselves. "I think it has a lot to do with the child's not having had a mother. But trust me when I tell you that you must never try to step inside at moments like these."

Margaret could see Jennifer's anger rising, the challenge to compete. "But she's only a child, she's—"

"She's their heart. Accept it, and Todd will love you more."

The two women looked a moment longer at Alison and her men before climbing the porch steps. Jennifer studied Margaret, watching the graceful way she moved, admiring her for her ladylike poise. Thirty years old now, Margaret had settled into a lovelier stage of womanhood than the young girl who had married Gordie in this very room over eight years ago. She was of medium height and trim, with the sort of figure that looked best in tailored clothes. Her dark brown hair was cropped short and shone with good health. She had clear blue eyes, a slim nose just a bit on the long side, and extraordinarily pretty lips that generally were smiling, but her real beauty came from within. Jennifer liked her from the start and realized that she was about to become best friends with this young woman, the person she would be living close to for the rest of her life. After almost ten years away from home, first in college, then time spent in service in Vietnam, then back to the university's graduate school, Todd finally had decided to join Gordie and his father in operating the family corporations. The construction crew had already broken ground just across the lake for the home he and Jennifer would share when they returned from their honeymoon in November. The Watson compound would then grow to five family dwellings inside the now cultivated six acres in the heart of the eastern section of groves. The young woman glanced briefly at the sprawling structure that was already rising across the lake, then back into Margaret's cool blue eyes. She and Margaret were destined to become close in many ways.

The two women who had won the most eligible and sought after young men in central Florida were an interesting physical contrast. Jennifer was a tall, sun-streaked blond of German extraction who had a certain flair about her. Alison considered her to be not only extravagantly beautiful, but also by far the best of all the lovers Todd had brought to the Little House. At twenty-eight Jennifer had just entered her seventh year in her career as a model, and in Jacksonville and on certain location bookings to Atlanta and Miami, commanded top union fees. Her figure was a knockout, with large, firm breasts and a trim, athletic waistline and fanny. Her smile was open and appealing, and, magically, she managed to hold a tan year-round.

Margaret smiled into Jennifer's crystal-clear eyes. "I guess this is a round-about way of warning you that Todd will probably save a part of himself for Alison. It's just their way. Don't be upset by it or by the fact that Alison probably won't open up to you right away; it's her way. It took me a long time, but it finally happened." She laughed. " 'Course it helped that I presented her with her two nephews. That put me right up there with Ben and her animals and just a cut behind Minerva."

"What's she really like, Margaret? She's such a quiet thing."

"Bookish. When she's not in school or down at the stables, her face is forever in a book."

"What about boys? She's nearly seventeen and simply stunning to look at."

"Alison doesn't seem to care about them. Oh, there's Calvin Douglass from the grove next door, but even when he comes over she doesn't pay much attention to him." Margaret pondered a moment, then added, "I'm sure they're just buddies."

Jennifer shook her head. "I just don't get it. I've never heard of a sixteen-year-old who wasn't interested in boys. Maybe she has you guys fooled. Maybe she's still water that runs deep." Giggling,

"Maybe she has a mad sex life going on some-where."

"I really don't think so. She just hangs around here and studies, honest. The bulk of her time is spent with her books or horses, or chewing the fat with Minerva. Minerva's her only buddy. Alison ignores the other servants. Minerva guards her against them like an ogress at the castle gate."

"That must go over big."

"It's almost funny. I'm not kidding, Minerva is fiercely protective of her. I've known Alison since she was four, and in all these years I have never once seen Minerva allow any of the others to baby-sit her for an hour."

"Not even Lonnie? How odd. Isn't she full-time, too?"

Giggling, "Oh, my, yes, but they're very competi-tive, Minerva and Lonnie. Minerva is kingpin, and in her quiet way lets ol' Lonnie know it, especially where Alison in concerned."

"I'm surprised the others don't resent the girl."

Margaret looked pensive for a moment. "You might be right. I think Lonnie resents her terribly. She tat-tles to Gordie about Alison all the time. Gordie's her favorite. She helped raise him."

"You mean Lonnie's been around that long? No wonder she resents Minerva! But tell me, what sort of juice does she tattle to Gordie?"

"Oh, she claims Alison makes a beeline for the hot books Todd brings home—reads his *Playboys*—*you* know."

"How hysterical! If that's the worst thing she does it still sounds too good to be true."

"Well, Lonnie thinks she spends too much time with Calvin. She keeps trying to get Gordie to watch them more closely when they disappear together. But that's ridiculous. Nobody has time to be the girl's warden."

"Ah, ha! Maybe I was right."

"Oh, no, it's just Lonnie being a busybody, I'm sure of it."

"No, Calvin, the book said like *this*," Alison insisted as she pulled away from the boy's embrace and struggled to get over on top of his eager body. "There," she said, welcoming his young, willing penis as it penetrated deep inside her. "Oh, yes, now that's really good."

"Jesus God, baby, you're killing me! No kidding, you'd better stop!"

"Wait, Calvin," she commanded. "Shhh. Stop now. Just relax and think about how extra good it can be this way if you just don't rush it."

"Oh my achin' ass, Alison, you're killing me, don't you know that?"

"Okay, let's stop," the girl said. She lifted herself off him and lay down at his side, trying to find a comfortable place on the floor of the potting shed. It really was much better in Ben's narrow bed. Here there was nothing between their bodies and the cement floor but an old picnic blanket, plus it was insufferably hot in the tiny room with the only window open just a small crack. The late-afternoon sun beamed relentlessly through the high window over their heads, and the call of a mockingbird echoed back from across the lake. She laid her head against Calvin's chest and felt his heavy breathing begin to subside. "Did you like it with me on top?" she asked.

"Cheesch."

She smiled. "Want to try it again?"

"If you're ready for me to get off I do. I can't take you up there on top of me, Alison. When I look at your nipples bouncing, I'm gone."

"You can hold off, Calvin," she coaxed. "Close your eyes if it bothers you to look at me." She

reached down and caressed his cock. It quivered at
full erection. She lifted her head and checked to
see that the rubber condom was still fixed securely
in place. "I really want you to love me that way,
okay?"

"Okay." They boy squeezed his eyes tight and took
a deep breath.

She kissed him on the cheek and silently mounted
him again to begin her rhythmic motion back and
forth, leaning back against the air, arching her back
and smiling. Oh, how she loved this feeling! She
loved every wonderful sensation, every tingly moment as she began her climb to the height of her climax. Then she began to feel it, the maddening
prickle of a thousand needles as she rose higher and
higher, cresting the summit at a wonderful, perfect
pace.

With his eyes still shut tight, Calvin rolled his
head backward and took another deep breath. He
had to hold on! Suddenly Alison cried out, "Calvin,
oh, my God, Calvin! Oh, Calvin, oh, yes, now, now—
now!"

The boy let loose and began to drown in the delicious heat of his passion. As he groaned aloud Alison was motionless with him for a heavenly
timeless beat, feeling his bare shoulders with her
fingers, then the deep heaving of his chest under
her open palms. Eyes still closed, she ran both
hands down his torso then fell across his body with
her face on his damp chest. Together their breathing became less labored, their heart stilled to a
normal pace.

"Looky there, Mr. McIver, see fo' your*self!*" Lonnie's voice broke the silence like a knife.

The girl shot up on top of Calvin and jerked around
to see her father's face, set in stony agony, through a
crack in the doorway. As he opened the door wider,
the late-afternoon sun silhouetted his enormous

frame. Then, slowly, the brilliant light edged around Lonnie's ample figure before spilling across Alison's body, then Calvin's, in a warm impersonal path of light.

4

Alison insisted on the marriage although it was doomed before the teenagers ever stepped before the altar in the tiny chapel of Grove Dale Presbyterian Church. To her it was the only way. Being reared in a loving home so steeped in old country traditions by a father who was the soul of propriety, a man who had valiantly tried to do better than his best to compensate for her losing her mother, had bred an obligation of morality deep within her heart. Sure, she had been playing with fire. Of course she'd been up to things nice girls aren't supposed to do. But it had all been a game with her, an experiment, a romp. In no way was it intended to change the plans she had for her future. Her growing-up years had been fixed on one dream, to fall in love and share a lifetime with only one man. She wanted the joy her father had known with Alliene, the life-style her brothers had chosen for themselves when they were ready to settle down. How could a little sexual fling harm anyone as long as she never got caught?

But she *had* been caught, and now the only action left was to swear she was in love with Calvin and that it had been their intention to run away and get married this summer, anyway. She simply could not face up to the admission that the only thing she loved about Calvin Douglass was making love with him. To wound McIver so deeply was the last thing she wanted.

The wedding ceremony was hastily arranged and performed by the minister who had served the Watson family for three decades, with only Alison's and Calvin's families present. The marriage lasted less than three months, and before Labor Day had rolled around the seventeen-year-old divorcee was accepted for enrollment in a Georgia boarding school. She withstood the dreaded decision as proper penance for the terrible thing she had done. For a girl whose life had seemed enchanted, one careless moment had catapulted her world into an abyss of total misery.

It had been a summer of black despair. The young couple set up housekeeping in the Little House, ironically the one shelter they had avoided inside the Watson property when they had eagerly met to engage in sex over the previous couple of months. To Alison it was not a love nest but a trap. She felt trapped for life with a young man she not only didn't love but clearly overshadowed in every way. Even their sex life quickly soured for her. It became a duty, and to lie all night beside Calvin repelled her.

Until time for school in September, Calvin went to work in the groves, taking his assignments from Gordie. At first Alison stayed home in the Little House. She couldn't bring herself to hang around Minnie's kitchen anymore. Next to McIver, she knew that her black friend had suffered the most hurt over what she had done.

Each morning after Calvin left she lay in Grandfather's big bed and sobbed herself into exhaustion. Her afternoons were spent in mesmerized devotion to the soap operas on television, but they really didn't interest her. Nothing interested her. She refused to go anywhere and couldn't force herself to eat. In spite of the elaborate dinners Minnie brought to them on trays, she simply could not face food.

She covered her misery as best she could whenever McIver stopped by to see her. He didn't do so often, respecting the youngsters' privacy, but occasionally he popped in on his way home for supper. From the beginning McIver was deeply worried about his daughter. He noticed that the sparkle had gone from her eyes, no matter how cheerful she pretended to be, and before long it was evident that she was losing weight.

Without overstepping the boundary between fatherly concern and what he felt to be interference, McIver did all he could to please the young couple. He encouraged Alison to redecorate the Little House, to do it completely over to suit her taste, but she refused. Frustrated, he did the next best thing he knew. Until now he hadn't bothered to have the Little House air-conditioned. The two paddle fans and shade trees were all the cooling his father had ever wanted. But now, with the midsummer heat dragging down on all of them, and with his daughter's increasing listlessness, McIver sent over to Lakeland and ordered the job done.

The day the workmen arrived, Alison walked down to the stables for the first time since the wedding. She spent the morning grooming Nugget and visiting with Ben. Ben, of course, said nothing to her about her marriage; instead he visited with her like old times. He disappeared at lunchtime and in a half an hour came back carrying a brown paper sack and a Thermos of sweetened iced tea. Together the old man and the girl sat under the shade of a sprawling water oak and ate the clumsily wrapped lunch that Ben had fixed at his house. Nothing had tasted so good to Alison since the feast Minnie prepared for Todd's engagement party six weeks ago. She ate her peanut butter sandwich slowly, then carefully peeled the tangerine Ben had placed in the grass in front of her. "You're a good cook, Ben."

"It's nice to be eatin' with you again, honey. I've missed you." After an awkward pause, "You goin' to be exercisin' Nugget from now on?"

"Yes. Thank you for seeing about her for me."

"She's a fine animal, Alison." He gathered the lunch wrappers and stood to leave. "I'll be agettin' back to work now, honey. You okay?"

"I'm fine, Ben. Honest."

The old man dug his toe in the grass and asked, "You happy, child?"

Alison burst into tears and Ben stooped beside her and gently stroked her shoulder. "Go ahead and cry," he said. "Cry it out, child."

Finally she sat up and accepted his wrinkled handkerchief. "I'm all right now." She smiled weakly into his eyes. "Really."

"You've got to tell your father, child. Tell McIver. He will he'p you to get out of this thing."

"I can't! I told him I love Calvin. I can't break his heart."

"His heart's already abreakin'. Don't you see how worried he is about you? He's agoin' crazy with worry. Tell him. He'll understand."

"No! And you musn't either, Ben."

Alison's seventeenth birthday came and went. She submitted to a dinner party at the Big House, dragging the reluctant Calvin along, pretending to be cheerful, but no one in the family was fooled. As August wore on, everything began to settle into a regular routine, a dull, deadly routine. She was bored beyond belief, and each day was more miserably unhappy than the day before. She and Calvin had nothing to say to each other, nothing. Her mornings with Nugget and her quiet lunches with Ben were the only pleasant hours in her day, but at least she had begun to eat a little again, and she regained some color with her daily rides in the sunshine. She was amused when Ben began to slip extras into the lunch sacks, goodies unmistakably from Minnie's oven. But she ate them without questioning him.

On the last Friday in August, when she was rubbing Nugget down after their morning ride, she looked up in surprise to find not Ben but McIver standing at the stable door with a picnic basket in his big hands. "I'm wondering if I can have lunch with you today, Alison," he said gently.

She walked over to hug him. "I'd love that, Mc-Iver. Did Ben tell you he and I have been eating together every day?"

"No. Ben doesn't talk to me about you. Minerva figured it out. You know Ben's not a sweets eater, and he's been plaguin' Minerva lately for her cookies and cakes. She knew he must be taking them to you."

"Minnie's smart. She always was."

Alison opened a wrapper and nodded. A chicken salad sandwich on home-baked bread, Minnie's specialty. She handed it to her father and lifted another from the basket for herself. There were four of them altogether, a large plastic container filled with fresh diced fruit, and two huge wedges of Minnie's pound cake. "I smell a conspiracy," Alison said with a small smile. "There's enough food here for an army."

"You're too thin, pet. You must force yourself to eat more."

"I'm all right, Daddy. Really I am. I've just had a little adjusting to do."

McIver cleared his throat and looked earnestly into his daughter's eyes. "There's something I must say, pet, that won't wait any longer. You can be honest with me, Alison. If you're not happy with Calvin I won't be hurt by a divorce."

"Have you been talking to Ben?"

"No. I've discussed this with your brothers only. Something's terribly wrong, Alison. We all know it. We love you, darlin'. Calvin's a fine young man, but it's *you* we love. You are ours. If Calvin is wrong for you, you must get out of this marriage now. We'll stand behind you all the way."

Alison gazed gratefully for a long moment into her father's brown eyes, eyes so big and gentle and filled with love and concern for her, then put her face in her hands and silently began to weep.

Clumsily McIver pushed aside the picnic basket and reached over to pull his daughter into his arms.

The divorce was finalized, and Alison already had six weeks of classes at Brenau Academy in Georgia before Todd and Jennifer's wedding day rolled around on October seventeenth. A bridesmaid at the wedding, she walked down the porch steps and over to the flower-decked altar on that lovely autumn afternoon, quite as though nothing had ever happened. The wedding was beautiful, and the party lasted long into the night, with all of Grove County and prominent citrus people from the entire state there to dance to the music that filled the air. Even the Douglasses came. Alison held her chin up and greeted them warmly in the receiving line, laughing with Calvin and accepting his kiss on her cheek as lightly as if their nightmare marriage had never taken place.

Actually, once Alison was convinced that her family wouldn't be disgraced by the divorce, she didn't feel a bit bad about it. Calvin was plainly relieved. Even though he insisted that he loved her, the boy wasn't ready to settle down. When McIver threw him back into the wonderful world of teenage singlehood, he threw him straight into the brier patch.

Alison settled into life at Brenau. She never glanced at a boy, although Riverside Military Academy was only three miles away, and potential young suitors were crawling out of the woodwork. She'd made up her mind there would be no time for that. She had one goal only over the next nine months, and that was to rebuild her father's confidence and trust. Somehow she must convince McIver that she should go to the University of Florida next September, not be sentenced to four more years at some far-away cloistered school for girls.

Alison worked hard her full senior year and on May 28, 1969, stepped forward to accept her high school diploma from the Dean of the Academy, handily walking away with valedictorian honors. The family drove up in force for the ceremony. Gordie and Margaret even brought little McIver and Robert. And, of course, Minnie was there. Of all the people Alison loved in the world only Ben was missing. When she finished her commencement address and caught sight of her father grinning up at her from the front row, Alison knew that she had made everything all right again. So it was done; the slate was clean. The nightmare mistake she had made was a page from the past that was forever turned, never to be reopened.

At her father's insistence Alison applied to every major school in the east for entrance in the fall. She was accepted by them all, but when the time came for a decision, she stubbornly insisted she wanted to go to the University of Florida. "But, pet," her father protested weakly, "look how you've honored yourself. Don't you think one of those fine schools up north . . . ?"

"I don't want to go away, darling. I've *been* away. I want to be back where the sun shines again and I'm

not cold all the time. I want to go to college where
you went. You didn't make Gordie and Todd go
away." She patted her father's cheek and smiled into
his eyes. "Besides, Gainesville's close enough for me
to drive home lots of weekends. Don't you want to see
me?"

Of course, McIver melted. After all, he rational-
ized, the girl had studied hard and deserved to get
her education in the place where she'd be happiest.
Why, he was hardly able to persuade her to take a
moment to herself anymore. Her sailboat and her
horse were the only recreation she indulged in anymore. The rest of the time, only books and more
books.

In late September when Alison drove up to the university in the baby-blue Camaro McIver had given
her for graduation, it was with a happy heart. She
had found her academic home. She sailed through
university life with a goal-oriented ferocity that almost alarmed her father. Because her intention was
to graduate in three years, she attended classes nonstop, winter and summer. "You must slow down a
bit, pet," McIver protested. "You'll make yourself
sick."

"Nonsense, darling. I've never felt better in my
life."

It was true. Alison had never been happier. The
only thing that happened in her freshman year to
mar her joy was that her precious Honey finally died.
But the week they buried him, a yellow-striped female kitten was waiting when she pulled into the
drive. She named the new cat Amber. And there
were other attractions to pull her like a magnet to
the Grove: Bruce, Gordie and Margaret's third son,
was almost two now, and come spring, Jennifer was
due to have her first baby. Truly, all was right in her
world again.

At the university, Alison lived in a little world all

her own, carved out right smack in the heart of the bustling throng of students at the enormous institution. She drove to class, to the library, and to her apartment, period. She loved her apartment, the indulgence her father had allowed when she begged never to suffer through dormitory life again. "Honestly, Daddy, in dormitories all they ever do is talk about boys and send out for pizza. I'm going to college to *study!*"

Around every third weekend Alison drove home. Even there, except for a lazy hour or two out on her sailboat, she took her nose out of a book only long enough to eat or sleep. "She'll ruin her eyes!" McIver would roar. And back at school she seldom socialized. She didn't need to. The companions of her choosing came to her.

University men were magnetically attracted to Alison, and each of them, every one she allowed close to her, was madly infatuated with the elusive, intellectual redhead from Grove Dale. From Grove Dale? Could she possibly be real? The guys from other areas of the state knew vaguely where Grove Dale was and considered it a real hick town, and those attending the University of Florida from out of state had never even heard of it. But there was nothing country about this Alison Watson who'd lived in the sticks all her life. On the contrary, she exuded class from every pore. Even the guys who knew nothing of her wealthy background (very few did, and Alison liked to keep it that way) spotted the coed as a gem in the heart of the bustling school. Her clothes were exquisitely coordinated and terribly expensive—and it showed. Quite amazingly Alison seemed to grow prettier with each passing year, with a sort of elegant bearing, a loveliness that was made more appealing by her quiet and seclusive ways. Alison wore her hair down and loosely combed from a center part. Under Jennifer's guidance she learned to apply

makeup expertly. Her sprinkling of facial freckles
concealed, she never looked artificial, but rather was
fresh and young and lovely.

To many young men she met in class Alison Watson became an instant challenge: how to land a date
with her and ultimately, of course, their minds raced
ahead to the biggest how-to of all, how to maneuver
her into bed, because each of them saw it, the kitten-
ish sexiness that lurked beneath those serene and ladylike catgreen eyes. Quite a number of them met
the challenges, too, and a few even accomplished a
sexual interlude with her. Like her father, Alison
settled for one lover at a time and never played the
field. The trouble was that as soon as she went to bed
with a man, each one of them demanded instant own-
ership.

Possessiveness was the one trait she just couldn't
reconcile right now. It wasn't so much a question of
fidelity; she had no quarrel with that. When she was
involved with one person, she had no wish to be with
another. It was more the little things they began to
do that grated on her, things like questioning where
she was every minute, or why they couldn't go along
on weekends when she traveled to the Grove. But to
take a man home to meet her family was out of the
question.

All in the world McIver really wanted for her was
to marry and settle down at the Grove. He had already picked out a site for the home he would build
for her and had openly declared that if she continued
to insist on a career as *well* as marriage, well, there
were plenty of opportunities right there at Watson
Properties.

The situation truly bothered her. Someday when
she was ready to settle, maybe. But not now. Lately
she had been thinking ahead to a career in communications, a career of her own making, and definitely
not with Watson Properties.

In the spring of her senior year Alison thought she had finally found a lover who wouldn't strangle her independence. He was her poetry professor for an elective class she picked on at last-minute impulse. His name was Bryan Mainente, a sensitive man of Italian descent, with graying black hair and wonderful brown eyes that seemed to look straight into her soul. Sensitive to the stigma of an involvement with one of his students, Bryan didn't ask Alison out. But one late afternoon on a crisp spring day when she lingered after class for his critique on one of her poems, he asked her to have coffee with him. The next day he called.

Soon they were meeting at Alison's apartment where they could be quiet together, read aloud to one another, and make wonderful, sensitive love again and again.

Bryan was a gentle man. She adored the relationship, looked forward to being with him, fantasized about him when they were apart. Could she have fallen in love at last? He was so much older—thirty-nine—three years older even than Gordie. But he was young-looking and wonderfully virile and so very dear. She could even picture herself in his world, living the life of a college professor's wife in this small Florida town, abandoning her thoughts of a career in a city with a bustling newspaper or a thriving television station. She even felt she could live with the problem of an ex-wife in town and his twelve-year-old daughter, who spent weekends with him. She thought everything through except for one very important reality: Bryan never mentioned a future with her. Foolishly that didn't worry Alison. After all, he told her he loved her and adored her. Loving a person meant fidelity, of course. What was so special was that he loved her without trying to possess her as all of the others had.

When Alison went home for spring week, unlike the rest, Bryan made no show of jealousy. Instead he seemed happy for her. It made her love him more. "Have fun with your family, darling. Patricia will keep me company on the weekend. Just call me the instant you get back." Eagerly she hurried back to him after the holiday.

The day before the family was due to drive up for graduation, her security was shattered. For the first time in her life Alison Watson experienced rejection. She and Bryan were sharing dinner together, knowing that tomorrow she'd be swamped with family and would have no time alone for him. He had cooked the meal, and they'd gotten deliciously drunk on a special bottle of French wine, then spent the lazy, warm evening inside her cool bedroom making love. As he was leaving he faced her with some devastating news. "Alison, darling," Bryan said, holding both of her hands inside his as he stood at the door to leave, "this must be good-bye." She stared into his eyes, incredulous. "Pamela and I have reconciled," he added softly. "We're to be remarried next week."

The blow stunned her so much that she never closed her eyes all night, instead spent it in tears and torment. Graduation the next day was a blur. She only knew she had to get through it somehow, to hold her chin up in front of everyone, then to get home, back to the Grove, back to her big bedroom where she could be alone.

What a fool! What a vain fool she had been to suppose Bryan wanted only her. Now, at last, it was clear why he had been the one man who never tried to possess her. He never really wanted her. She felt chagrined, used, ill.

So was that it? Was there no in-between? Could there possibly be a man out there who would want only her and yet allow her to be herself?

Men! So all right. She would be all right, just *fine* without any of them. She could live without sex; she proved that to herself the year she was at Brenau. She could get along very well on her *own*.

5

It was accomplished almost before Alison herself realized she had done exactly what she had set out to
do. Before June of 1972 had wound down, after only
three years, she had earned her Bachelor of Arts degree in communications, walking away with Phi
Beta Kappa honors and had traveled down to
Sarasota, Florida, that very week, interviewed for,
and nailed her first job. And it was a terrific job, the
exact thing she'd dreamed about the last two semes-
ters at school. It was exciting! Suddenly, happily, she
was behind her own desk and in front of a television
camera five days a week, with a good toehold on a
promising career. The best part was that she'd done
it on her own, without a single boost from her family,
without anyone's even knowing she was a Watson of
Watson Sundrenched fame. It was wonderful, a
heady feeling like none she'd ever known. There had
been little time for reflection in these last few
months, yet when she did look back, she had difficulty believing that any of it was true.

And now it was April, ten months later; nearly a
year had streaked by like a flash of lightning, and
she was leaving today to fly to New York City. New
York, the most exciting spot on the face of the earth!
She'd never been to a city bigger than Atlanta, and
now Sam was sending her to New York.

Nervously she checked the zipper pocket of her

bag to be sure her plane ticket was safe, then went
through the papers in her briefcase for the dozenth
time in the last hour. Sam would be here any minute, late as always. She smiled. Sam Abrahmson was
more than just her boss; he had become her mentor.
He had been wonderful to her from the start. He was
manager here at Channel 32, with all of the pres-
sures such a job entails; still, he found time every
day to talk to her, to listen to her ideas, to take her
quite seriously in a way that made her feel important. And now he was sending her to New York
alone, trusting her to represent Channel 32 at a seminar on television programming right in the heart of
the country's broadcast capital.

She sat back and tried to relax; she still had a few
minutes to wait. It was all so exciting. She wondered
what she might be doing today if she had never
driven down to Sarasota that day for the interview.
Who knows? She knew one thing for sure: already
she loved this city. It was a fast-growing Gulf coast
community, huge compared to Grove Dale, yet still
with the feel and look of a sleepy Florida coastal
town. It was a growing young people's town, with
lots of energetic college graduates and newly mar-
rieds choosing it for their home, even though it
boasted a swelling population of Florida retirees as
well. It was no wonder. The climate was great. To
her it seemed exactly like home, just a bit south of
Grove County in latitude, with long summer months
and balmy winters. Yet enough cold snaps came
along to enjoy wool suits and sweaters now and then,
usually in January and February. But as is true of
all of Florida, the cold times never lasted more than
a few days, and usually by the weekend the beaches
would be filled again by sun worshipers and water-
sports enthusiasts. Alison was lured by the Gulf and
spent time on the beach every chance she got, when
the weather permitted. It was all so new to her.

She'd grown up in lake country, and aside from occasional vacations over on the Atlantic coast of Florida, lakes were the only waterfront living she knew. But now she was in love with the Gulf of Mexico. The waters around Sarasota and its string of keys to the west were an exquisite, almost shocking shade of blue-green. She loved everything about it—to swim in it, to sit on the sand and look out at it, to go boating on its emerald surface.

She'd gotten settled right away in a little efficiency apartment in a neat complex on the mainland, very close to Channel 32, a property that rented exclusively to young singles. The more plush apartments faced right on Sarasota Bay, but her own tiny place was a long block off the water, down a winding drive around some of the units. She didn't care. On her day off she often walked lazily down and spent the morning in the sun; other times she sat by the pool and visited with some of the other people who rented there. It was terrific. She had never felt so good about herself, or about what she was doing.

She loved her job, but more than that she realized she liked being independent. The distance between Sarasota and the Grove was about ninety miles, close enough to get home when she wanted to but not too close. She felt comfortable with the separation between herself and her family. She needed this latitude if she were really going to make it on her own.

The phone at her elbow startled her from her reverie. "Hello, this is Alison Watson. May I help you?"

"Don't give up on me, kid. I'm on my way."

"Sam!" Quickly she checked her watch. "It's okay. We've tons of time. But if something's come up, I'll grab a taxi."

"Nah. Stay cool. I'm at a gas station at the corner. See ya in five."

"Don't park. I'll watch for you from the lobby."

Sam. A fourteen-carat sweetheart. She smiled.

The affection she felt for him was similar to the love she felt for her father. What a sight she must have been when she stormed his office last June looking for a job. She had driven down to Sarasota the day after graduation and walked in on him cold.

Things had happened fast—the deadening rejection by Bryan, the flurry of the family's arrival for her graduation ceremonies. Every one of them came up to watch her this time, even Gordie and Margaret's three boys and Todd and Jennifer's wee McIver, too, the boy they'd nicknamed Trey because he was the third McIver in the family. This time even Ben was there. Wonderful Ben, who was getting ready to turn seventy-six on his next birthday and had probably never owned a full suit of clothes in his life. It warmed her to think of his driving over to Lakeland to buy the suit to do the proper thing.

Then came the excitement of the graduation ceremony itself. She'd worked to earn that Phi Beta Kappa key and was proud of the honor, and it was evident, from his show of emotion, that it meant the world to McIver.

The next morning her father loaded up the Watson Properties pickup with her trunk and luggage, her collection of paintings, and plants and other possessions she'd acquired in her three years at the university. Always the practical Scot, McIver hadn't been too proud to drive up in the truck. Ben kept him company on the trip, and it didn't bother McIver Watson in the slightest if people didn't know he had a finer car, though he had at last made the step from a new Buick sedan every two years to a fine Lincoln Continental just this past fall. Even that he found to be ridiculous, frivolous, and unnecessary. "Why not, Pop?" Gordie had persuaded. "Look at all the traveling you'll be doing now that you've decided to run. Now, just how would it look for the state senator from the Thirteenth District to be driving around in a two-year-old Buick? You know you want the car. Do it!"

It was true. McIver had finally succumbed to the coaxing of his throng of friends in central Florida to run for political office. It had been several years since he had needed to devote himself full-time to the running of Watson Properties, fulfilling a carefully planned semiretirement by his early sixties. He'd spent the previous decade easing Gordie into full control of the reins of Watson Sundrenched, Inc., and now that Todd had taken over responsibility for new land acquisition and management of the agricultural aspects of their business, he actually could retire completely if he chose to. But full retirement was out of the question for the active man. Perhaps if Alliene had lived, they would have done some traveling. But without her McIver could find no joy in travel; rather, on the one European tour he had taken in 1970, he'd found it a lonely and exhausting experience.

The first time one of his cronies mentioned the idea of political office to him, McIver scoffed. The very idea was absurd. He had no law degree, nor any of the credentials he'd always considered necessary for those who sought a public position. The Grove, his land, and its massive production of citrus fruit had been the entire thrust of his business career until he landed nose-first in the concentrate processing industry in the thirties. Once into it he found he had a tiger by the tail; it was years before he was able to slow down. Still, this venture alone had given him a canny grasp on big-business and finance. Plus, he had experience in funding in another field: education. As an offshoot to the tremendous dollars that steadily rolled in came McIver's wish to share some of the wealth with those less fortunate. In the early fifties he had begun to fund the education of promising students in colleges around the state, setting up

a major scholarship program that bore Alliene
Watson's name at the university in Gainesville.
Honorary degrees followed, and seats on various ed-
ucational boards around the state of Florida, as well
as directorships in banks and other lending institu-
tions, suddenly were conferred upon him. Quite logi-
cally, when the vacancy of the seat for state senator
from the six-county Thirteenth District loomed on
the horizon, the name of McIver Watson was tossed
around.

Jim Laskell, who was Editor of Sarasota's
Suncoast Star, and McIver's good friend, was the
most persuasive of all. "You're a natural, McIver.
Whoever said a degree in law was a prerequisite to
holding political office? You're a citrus man and a
damn good one. You know the industry inside out,
and, my God, man, what better knowledge could a
senator have for a state whose backbone is the citrus
belt? Plus you're a business man, a merchant. It may
never have been your idea to get into the concentrate
game, but once you did, once you started stocking
grocers' shelves with those little cans of pure gold,
you *became* a merchant. Don't forget, my friend,
Harry Truman got his start in the haberdashery
business!"

Well, that did it. McIver's admiration for Truman
was unabashed, and he agreed to run. He was
getting one helluva late start, but he'd do it. After
all, it was only a race, and all logic had it that the
electorate would go for a much younger man. But the
political masterminds who were backing him had decided to chance it, and so had he. It was official:
McIver's hat was in the ring for the race of seventy-
two. And now that Alison had completed her education, she could use up some of her energy in helping
him to map out his campaign. Maybe he would even
name her assistant to his campaign manager—after
a nice rest, of course, a few weeks out to enjoy her-

self. It was still five months away to election day, but there was a great deal of work to be done.

Alison had other ideas. Still smarting from Bryan's blow to her ego, she decided she didn't want to sit at home. It was time to go on with her life, to go after the career she'd spent three years planning for. She had made up her mind on the job she wanted and knew she was going to go after it before some other coed in Dr. Sewell's class beat her to it. Her favorite senior professor, Dr. Nathaniel Sewell, had planted the idea last semester. Looking back, she realized now that it was the sly old professor's act of premeditated reverse psychology, boldly directed at her. She smiled every time she thought about their talk that day last November.

"It's not what you're going to want, Alison," he'd said. "It will be a far cry from the big time. If I know you you'll be better off job-hunting in Jacksonville or Miami or Tampa. Channel 32 will be brand-new and small, a fledgling. It will only be the second television station in Sarasota County, and green as grass. They won't even have their license to get on the air until next April."

Then, when her final semester was winding down and Alison sat in Dr. Sewell's office for a conference on career placement, he had mentioned Channel 32 to her again, just as a possibility. "I still don't believe it will be right for you," he had said earnestly. "I see you in a much bigger operation, maybe in Atlanta."

"Maybe I'll drive down and look around, anyhow," she'd said casually. "I don't have any immediate plans for summer."

"Well, if you do decide to, you could mention to Sam Abrahmson that Nat Sewell thinks you have a hell of a lot on the ball . . ." Grinning now, he added, ". . . for a feisty little redhead from a hick county in central Florida."

She wondered, if she'd had the maturity to think it through first, would she have dared barge in on Mr. Abrahmson the way she did? She was terrified. She'd presented herself at the switchboard and heard Sam's friendly "Come on in!" before it flooded over her that for the first time in her life she was actually doing something on her own, walking into a situation where the Watson name and influence hadn't preceded her. What if he didn't like her? What if he spotted how utterly green she was, how she was bluffing to cover her fright?

Into it now, and too late to retreat, the girl strode across the small office and shook hands firmly with the man who stood to greet her. "How do you do, Mr. Abrahmson? I'm Alison Watson. I asked to see you because I'd like to come to work for you at Channel 32."

A smile played at the corners of his eyes. "Would you, indeed!"

Alison liked him right away. He was of medium height, a little on the stocky side, and balding just a bit, but his hair hadn't a sign of gray. She guessed him to be somewhere about Dr. Sewell's age, maybe in his early fifties. His clear hazel eyes looked wonderfully kind, and when he smiled, laughter spread all over his face. He had a deep tan, like he spent his weekends out fishing or on a golf course. His clothes were rumpled in the way she pictured an absent-minded professor's or a busy city news room editor's would be. He wore a dress shirt and tie, but the knot was pulled down, and his sleeves were rolled up. On the edge of the desk was a photograph of a pretty lady taken at the beach with a collie dog beside her. She looked nice. Alison glanced at his hands. He was wearing a wedding ring.

"Dr. Nat Sewell from the university suggested I come."

"I see."

"He said to tell you that for a feisty little redhead from a hick county in central Florida I have a lot on the ball."

"Are you feisty?"

"No. I think Dr. Sewell just likes to kid with me because I have some spunk." Embarrassed now, her voice faltered. "I think that's why."

"Well, you also must have a lot on the ball. If Nat Sewell says so, anyhow. Good school, the University of Florida. How close are you to your degree, Miss Watson?"

"I graduated yesterday."

"Yesterday. My."

Alison ducked her head and grinned. "I guess it was pretty obvious, my rushing down here like this."

"I'm flattered. Not too many folks know about us yet."

"Well, Dr. Sewell certainly does, and he's the most brilliant man in the University Communications Department. Everyone says so."

"Is your degree in Broadcast?"

"Yes, with a minor in Marketing."

"Do you fancy yourself a newsie?"

"Yes."

"Anything else appeal to you?"

"I think there a couple of other places I'd fit here. I've taken two excellent courses in commercial production."

"We plan on being competitive in commercial production for this area of Florida eventually, but it's a long-range projection. We haven't acquired the equipment we'll need to offer our clients a professional job."

"Oh."

"And right now we're fully staffed in the newsroom."

"Oh," she said again, plainly disappointed. She hesitated for a long moment and glanced around the room. The office was small and had the smell of newly laid carpet. The only furniture, other than Sam Abrahmson's huge desk and the two chairs facing it, was a console television set, plus an ancient coatrack. Rows of paper-filled boxes lined one wall, and on another a couple of framed prints were stacked against each other near three bedraggled-looking potted plants.

Alison didn't see Sam's delight in watching as she collected her thoughts before plunging into her next plan of attack. He rocked back in his swivel chair and gazed at her over the tops of his half glasses. The girl was everything in the world Nat Sewell had led him to believe, and more. She looked like ten million bucks in a perfect beige linen suit, with the smart brown leather envelope bag on her lap. He studied her in silent amusement. Boy, oh, boy. He silently chuckled at how she had twisted her incredible red hair up in such a tight businesslike bun on the crown of her head, and that her enormous eyes pierced his from behind ridiculously huge hornrimmed glasses. She didn't need them—he'd bet fifty bucks on it! The little minx had probably decided they would make her look more serious and help her land the job.

Alison drew a short breath, looked Sam Abrahmson square in the eyes, then said firmly, "Well, okay. Then I also think I would fit in somewhere on a talk show, a show such as the noon programs I've watched on the Tampa channels. You know, news, weather, and sports—and features. Features would be where I'd come in. Are you airing anything like that?"

"Not yet—but such a program is in my plan for the near future."

Brightening, "Really?"

"Yeah. Our daytime hours are being filled temporarily with old movies. We'll be moving away from that format just as soon as we can. Tell me, just where is it you think you'd fit into such a show?"

Alison sat forward eagerly. "I have a million ideas. We could have a cooking segment maybe three times a week, and regular information on fashion and makeup. We could even stage short fashion shows every couple of weeks or so, or at least once a month. And there's entertainment, local entertainment playing the night spots in the Tampa Bay Area. I'm sure they'd love the exposure. And how about a regular feature on diet and exercise?" Without pausing for breath she said, "And there could be a five-minute block for public service announcements, plus perhaps a weekly update on what's new in medicine, and—"

"Whoa!" Placing his fingertips together, Sam rocked for a moment in his swivel chair and gazed at her across his glasses.

Alison's heart jumped into her throat. He wasn't smiling. He was just sitting there studying her. Had she just made a fool of herself? No smile at all! Still, she could swear there was the tiniest hint of a twinkle in his eyes.

Finally he spoke. "I like your enthusiasm, Miss Watson. If we can come to some sort of agreement on salary, you may have yourself a challenge—and a job." Sam watched Alison's back relax and a nice smile fill her face. "When could you start?"

"Tomorrow."

He broke into laughter. "You're not going to ask what the job will pay?"

"I just want the chance. If I'm good I know you'll pay me what I'm worth."

"Tomorrow's too soon. I'll have to set up an office for you." Motioning to the stacks of boxes, he continued, "I'm not even unpacked in my own office yet. Why don't you plan to be on board at nine o'clock next Monday?" He glanced at his calendar. "That will be June nineteenth—perhaps an historic day for Channel 32 if you turn out to be the fireball Nat Sewell tells me you are."

Astonished, Alison felt her face flush and asked, "Dr. Sewell's already spoken to you about me?" Sam grinned. "Why, that old sweetheart. He never told me." She stood and extended her hand again. "Thank you very much, Mr. Abrahmson. You won't be sorry, I promise. I'll be here at nine sharp on Monday."

"Right, Alison." He smiled. "May I call you Alison?"

She grinned in response. "Of course."

Alison smiled again, thinking back on it. Sam had liked her right away and had shown her nothing but support from the start, including sending her to this seminar for delegates from independent television stations all around the country. The agenda looked impressive. They were to be given a tour of all the major network stations, workshops headed by top industry people, and a final day for exchange of ideas. She was eager to get started, and as the sole representative of the tiny local station, she was determined to pick up lots of information and make her organization shine.

"Better get a move on, Alison," Sam said. She jumped, snapping from her reverie, and saw him standing at her office door, leaning with his shoulder against the jamb. He wore a broad grin on his face. He had his jacket on, and even the knot of his tie was pushed into place.

"Oh, my gosh," she said apologetically. "I was sitting here daydreaming." She jumped to her feet, her face flushing crimson in embarrassment. "I'm sorry you had to park and come in, Sam. I feel like a fool."

"Nervous?"

"A bit."

"Come on. You'll be fine. You mustn't miss your flight."

She grabbed up her briefcase and slung her bag over her shoulder. At the door she turned and hurried back to her desk. "Almost forgot my tape recorder," she said, looking up at him sheepishly. She pulled open her top desk drawer and lifted out the small black case.

Sam took her elbow and together they hurried out the side door. On the drive to the airport Alison fished through her briefcase one more time to be sure she hadn't forgotten anything.

"Got your ticket?"

"Uh huh."

"Cassettes for the tape recorder? Camera and film?"

"Yep."

"The videotapes of clips from your best shows?"

"Yes." She grinned over at him and began to relax.

"How about a fresh change of underwear?"

Laughing, she reached over to touch his arm. "Really, I want to tell you again how much I appreciate your sending me to this thing."

"Just promise me you'll come back."

"Very funny. What on earth could possibly keep me from coming back?"

"Oh, I don't know. You could fall in love with the big city. Or with someone who lives there."

"Little chance of that," Alison said calmly. "I'm already in love." Sam turned sharply in question. She smiled over at him. "With Channel 32. *And* with my job. That's the only love affair I can handle at the moment."

He returned her smile. "For a minute I thought you were holding out on me," he said. "Thought one of the Longboat Key lotharios that hang out around the bar at the Buccaneer on Saturday nights might have gotten to you."

"I don't hang out at the Buccaneer bar, or any of the others." She slipped her sunglasses on and watched Sam pull a parking ticket from the machine, then glanced around the small airfield to see if her plane was in yet. "Might give me circles. Gotta keep looking my best. You know, for my audience," she joked.

At the gate Sam gave her the ticket folder along with an affectionate pat. "The baggage claim checks are stapled to the back, and here's your boarding pass on top. Got you no smoking section, right?"

"That's right." Eyeing Sam's glowing cigarette, she said, "If you and I ever fly together we'll have to sit in separate sections."

"I'm going to break this habit one of these days."

She smiled tenderly at him. She really had grown fond of him in the few months she'd been working for him. "I wish you would. So you could be around forever, like McIver's going to be."

"I'm flattered. I like the company that puts me in." He patted her again and said, "Take care of yourself, Alison. The city's full of lecherous old men. I'll worry if you leave your hotel at night without an escort."

"Sam, you *are* just like McIver. I went through all this last night on the phone with him. Honestly! I'm a big girl. Of course I'll take care. And when I get back Saturday, I'll grab a cab to my apartment. Please don't come out on the weekend to meet me."

"Nonsense. I'll be here. I'll be anxious to know how it went."

The loudspeaker sounded, "Delta flight three-four-three now boarding at gate ten."

"Oh, that's me!" she said excitedly. On an impulse she threw her arms around Sam's neck in a warm hug. At the door she blew him a kiss.

Once airborne she tried to read some trade publications, but it was useless. With each mile they trav-

eled her anticipation grew. When she caught her
first glimpse of the New York City skyline, she
gasped at the impressive sight.

"You get used to it," a voice said.

Alison jumped and noticed that the man in the
seat next to her was finally awake. "Oh, not me,"
she said. "I'd never get used to that. I've never seen
anything so beautiful in my life!"

"And we'll ask you to be quiet as soon as you see
the red light go on," whispered the guide. It was the
afternoon of the third day, and they had been broken
into groups of twenty. Alison's group was there to
watch the final hour of today's shoot of one of the network soaps, *In Seasons of Change*. Alison knew it
well. It was one of the daytime dramas that had hyp-
notized her in that dreadful summer she'd isolated
herself at the Little House when she was married to
Calvin. And she'd seen it since then. It was a favorite
in the dorm at Brenau, and Minnie's small television
set in the kitchen was always tuned to *Seasons* week-
days between three and four P.M. Alison had to admit
that it was one of the good ones. It was skillfully
written and acted, and now she found it exciting to
watch it performed. The three actors involved were
taping the same segment for the fourth time.

"That's Hunter Ames," whispered a woman from
Channel 42 in South Dakota. "He's my favorite. He
plays Barrington Dodd."

"Hunter who?" Alison whispered. She winced
when the guide waved her forefinger at them and
motioned silence.

The actor's voice carried out over the studio, dramatic, powerful, in command of the scene. "Have it
your way, Melissa, I won't take it to your father this
time. But if you ever behave that way again—"

"You can't threaten me, Barrington!" the actress
playing Melissa shouted.

Alison was caught in the scene when the South Dakota lady's voice said in her ear, "Hunter Ames. He's the head writer for *In Seasons of Change,* too."

Alison smiled at the woman and edged closer to the two actors and positioned her tape recorder. Wait till she played these tapes for Sam!

The seminar had been outstanding. To see what went on from behind the scenes in newscasting and regular entertainment programming such as they were watching now was a learning adventure it would take years of experience to match. Already she was putting together dozens of new ideas she wanted to use on *Sarasota Midday,* if Sam agreed.

Actually Alison could have written her own ticket with Sam Abrahmson at this point. He was flabbergasted by the girl from her first day on the job. When he received Nat Sewell's call last June, he knew to expect an exceptionally bright young lady, but Nat couldn't have predicted—no one could have—how fine her performance would turn out to be these last ten months. She was a dynamo. She assembled good material for the show and wrote every word of her copy. And then on camera she was a natural. She built an audience almost immediately. Mail started pouring in from the Sarasota County retirees who tuned to *Sarasota Midday* when they came in off the golf course or from tending their yards to sit down for lunch. They seemed to regard the serious young redhead the way they would their granddaughter back home in Michigan. And there was younger response, too. Alison's peers identified with her as well. The girl was with it, on top, uptown.

Perhaps Alison's best asset to Sam was that, from her first show on, she was a professional. He knew how terrified she was on opening day, but she went on like a pro. She looked like she'd been in front of a camera all of her life. And she was industrious almost to a fault. In fact, he had to admonish her to slow down from time to time. Then the icing on the cake was that she turned out to be very well read, a real asset during interviews. A book review evolved as a natural weekly feature, often with author interviews. The girl managed to hold her own with the best of them. "What did you do, spend your life with your head buried in a book?" Sam asked her one day.

She laughed. "According to McIver, yes."

If Sam was standing by in awe Alison was unaware of it. It was taking every ounce of her energy just to keep on top. The amount of work that went into five half-hour shows a week was incredible. Her job consumed her, was her world now. She was jaundiced after her last disastrous experience and allowed absolutely no time for anyone. She meant what she'd said to Sam on the way to the airport. She was in love with her job at Channel 32. For a local independent the little station was steaming. When they'd marked their first anniversary on the air last week, the local ratings were on the rise. Commercial sales were up, and three more people had been added to the sales staff. Sam had confided to her that when the new rating book became due in June, *Sarasota Midday* was likely to inch a couple of points away from the strong Tampa noontime shows. When she got back from this seminar, she'd work even harder and boost their ratings.

Alison jumped when she heard the director's voice boom into the studio, "That's a wrap." She glanced back at the three actors as the guide began to herd her group in the direction of the big barn door. The actors were talking animatedly among themselves. The main actor, Hunter What's-His-Name, was shouting and gesturing with his hands. He was angry about something. Oh, great, a fight. Alison quickly checked her tape recorder. There was still plenty of tape. She stepped a little closer.

"Come along, please," the guide called back to her. "This way."

Noticing her for the first time, Hunter Ames said, "What have we here? A beautiful lady trespasser!" He walked over and traced his finger along the edge of Alison's tape recorder. "A trespasser with a recording device, perhaps an espionage agent from another network."

Embarrassed, Alison flipped the button off and tried to stuff the machine into her shoulder bag. "I'm sorry," she said coolly, trying not to glance anxiously after her disappearing group. Thank God the guide was out of sight. She looked back into the actor's eyes. They were as blue-gray as two chips of slate, and fiery, with highlights of anger—or amusement, perhaps—dancing there. But he wasn't smiling. "I'm sorry," she repeated. "They assured us it would be okay to bring recorders on the set."

Still, he didn't smile but continued to stare into her eyes. "They?"

Alison felt weak. In all her life she had never seen so handsome a man. She'd seen him on the screen, but this was different. On television he seemed suavely handsome, of course. But the man who faced her was spellbinding. And she had made him angry! Her heart pounded inside the walls of her chest. "Our tour guide," she mumbled, her calm evaporating. "I-I'm with a group of independent network delegates touring . . ."

Suddenly he broke into a broad grin. The muscles in his face relaxed. His gray eyes began to twinkle, and his smile exposed flawless, incredibly gorgeous white teeth.

Alison took a deep breath and returned his smile. "Then it's all right?"

"This time, my little interloper," Hunter said to her. Turning to the other two actors, who by now were in quiet discussion between themselves, he said, "We'll go over it tomorrow, you two. Be here thirty minutes early."

Alison looked around the studio, wondering if her group had left the building. She felt a moment of panic when she realized she'd no doubt lost her ride back to the hotel. Oh, well. It wasn't that far to walk. "Thank you," she said to Hunter Ames, then turned to leave.

"Wait. I said it was all right *this* time," Hunter said, catching her by the arm. "But there's a condition." Alison gazed at him in question. "You must have dinner with me tonight."

"Oh, no, I can't possibly. I—"

"I won't take no for an answer. I could report you as a spy. You wouldn't want that to happen, would you?"

"But I'm supposed to . . . Tonight's the banquet, and I've really *got* to—"

"Nonsense. Plans are made to be broken," he said smoothly. "Where are you staying? I'll pick you up at seven o'clock. Have you tried the Four Seasons yet? Well, no matter; we'll decide after I pick you up. Where did you say you're staying?"

"But really, I . . . ." Suddenly she smiled. He was handsome, and maybe she could pick up some material to use on a feature. "The Hilton on Sixth Avenue and Fifty-Third."

"Wonderful. I'll see you at seven." He took her arm to lead her to the door. "Do you know your way out of here?"

"I'll find my way."

"Oh, one more thing. Tell me your room number. I'll need that when I call for you." Grinning his incredible grin again, "And your name."

"I'm in 832. My name is Alison. Alison Watson."

He bowed extravagantly, then lifted her hand to his lips. "Lovely. Alison." Looking deep into her eyes, he said softly, "I'm Hunter Ames. Tonight, Alison, we shall begin to get to know one another."

"Hello?"

"Were you asleep yet?"

"Mmmm, unh uh. But almost."

"I don't want you to fall asleep yet, Alison. I want you to concentrate on something before you drift off."

She began to smile. "What?"

"Me."

She laughed aloud. "Hunter, hang up and go to sleep."

"I can't sleep. That's why I called. It is absolutely unfair to think of your sinking into the deep sweet slumber of youth while I am unable to close my eyes."

"You're silly."

"I am enchanted, Alison. Perhaps I am the most enchanted I have ever been in my life. I want to lie here and think back over every moment of this evening with you. Beautiful Alison, seated across my dinner table. Alison with the yellow eyes. Alison in my arms on the dance floor. Alison's silken lips brushing mine when we kissed good night. Lovely Alison of the lovely kiss." After a long silence, "Alison?"

"Mmmm?"

"You wouldn't dare go to sleep on me, would you?"

"Of course not. As a matter of fact, I've been thinking about this evening, too. It was a wonderful evening, Hunter."

"Do you miss me?"

Alison laughed aloud again. "You've only been gone from here a half an hour."

"I miss you. I wish you were here with me. You should see the view I have of the skyline, sweet girl. From my balcony we could touch the stars."

"Oh, my. But Hunter, you must let me get some sleep. Our wrap-up session begins at nine sharp downstairs, and I've got to be wide-awake. It's bad enough that I missed the banquet tonight. My boss will think me ungrate—"

"Alison?"

She snuggled down closer in the pillow and listened to his beautiful, resonant voice. There was soft music coming from somewhere near his phone. "Yes?" she whispered.

He spoke softly, breathlessly. "I am mad about you."

"Hunter, don't be absurd. We haven't known each other twelve hours."

"Ah, but we have. It is after four in the morning, my sweet child. It has been twelve hours now and"—pausing—"twelve minutes."

"Good night, Hunter."

"Because I love her I will let my beautiful red-haired princess sleep. Sleep, sleep, my angel. And dream of me."

"I think you've been on the stage too long. Now turn off your light and get some sleep. Don't you have to be at the studio in the morning?"

"Yes. Early, too. Have to finish chewing out those two imbeciles who call themselves actors. Throw away *my* lines, will they!"

Alison stifled a yawn. "Hunter . . ."

"Yes, yes, my darling. Sleep. I'll pick you up at seven tomorrow evening. In the meantime I'll think only of—"

"But . . . we didn't make any plans for tomorrow."

"We're making them now. See you then, my angel. Remember that I am mad about you."

Alison listened to the click of the receiver and smiled into the darkness. She fumbled for the telephone and cradled the receiver in its place. Crazy. This was the craziest night of her life. The man

was like no other. Mad about her, indeed! Hunter
Ames probably didn't understand anything but extremes. Still, it had been wildly exciting. That incredible dinner—the wine, the music. How many
places did they go after the Four Seasons—four,
five? Oh, God, what a dancer. She felt as if she had
been molded into his arms. She wanted the music
to last forever. Hunter Ames. So handsome. So
witty. And really so very smart. His mind was like
a steel trap.

She rolled over and punched her pillow. She had to
get some sleep! She pulled up and peeped at the digital clock. Already four twenty-five. She groaned. She
couldn't get the man out of her mind. Hunter Ames.
He had no flaws. His features were chiseled, almost
not real, yet masculine. All male and handsome. She
liked his thick shock of silver hair.

She turned on her back and pulled the pillow over
her face. Too old. The man was entirely too old for
her. He had a daughter almost her age, a twenty-
year-old off somewhere in college. And the girl had a
mother out there someplace. Alison thought fleet-
ingly of Bryan and shivered. Then she smiled, remembering Hunter's words, "Oh, yes, Ann has a
mother. I just never remember Louise as my wife.
Really, Alison, the first one doesn't count, does it?"

Alison winced. Mustn't forget Calvin. No, the first
one doesn't count.

She got up and stood for a moment at her window
looking out. The city lights excited her. She went in
the bathroom and brushed her teeth for the third
time since she got home. Too much wine, too many
drinks. How many? Too many. She wasn't used to
drinking. "A little cognac after a nice meal isn't
drinking, my sweet, it's dessert, to complete the
meal." She wondered if he always drank that much.
Surely not. She'd hate to be judged on how much she

drank tonight. It was just a special, extravagant, fun-filled evening.

She jumped back in bed and rolled over on her stomach. Too old. He was older than Gordie, older even than Bryan. At least he hadn't backed off from telling his age—he'd be forty-two on Christmas Eve. That was too old.

What was the matter with her? She sat straight up and plumped her pillow. Go to sleep, Alison! What difference does it make how old he is or anything else about him? Don't be a little fool. The man is a celebrity. An evening that had been so exciting to her was probably commonplace for him. He was just playing games, having fun with the green kid from Florida. By tomorrow he'll have forgotten her name.

Still, did he mean it that he'd be here for her at seven? Could there be two evenings in a row like the one tonight? He was so proper. Except for on the dance floor, he never tried once to hold her. Just both of her hands in his when they stood at her door to say good night, then his lips glancing hers, so soft, so gentle, like butterflies' wings.

She wrapped the pillow tight around her head. She had to get Hunter Ames out of her mind. In another day it would all wind up, and she'd be winging back to Sarasota, back to tell Sam how wonderful the seminar had been. There would be no way she could see Hunter Ames at seven. She'd promised some of her new friends to dine with them on their last night in the city. Already they must be wondering what in the world happened to her tonight. She'd have to think of something to tell them before the wrap-up.

Go to sleep, Alison. Hunter Ames. Nice name. Wonder if it's his real name. Felt so good when they danced. Such a nice body, nice shoulders. Sexy. Hunter. Those incredible eyes, blue like slate, icy blue, murky blue. Tall and lean. Oh, how they fit when they danced, how her head spun when he pulled her tight against his body.

What in the world would she wear if he did come? She'd worn her very best dress tonight, the one she'd have worn to the banquet. Oh, dear, the banquet! No way she could see Hunter again. He was probably only kidding, anyhow. He probably teases every stranger he meets at the studio. Probably wines and dines them all—once.

Sleep, Alison. You'll probably never hear from him again.

She drifted into a deep, wonderful sleep with Hunter Ames's name on her lips, his face in her mind as she fell, spinning, spinning down, spinning as she had on the dance floor in the dizzying, heady whirlwind that was Hunter Ames.

Alison did see Hunter again that night. Incredibly it was the same as the night before had been—a fairy tale, a magic evening filled with romance and music and wine and dance. And she did see the city skyline from his balcony, that magnificent sight she had seen only in movies, had always supposed existed just for others in a world so far from her own. Again Hunter was proper. All evening he was proper. For the first time in her life here was a man, a total man, virile, appealing, strong, who didn't spend their time together in an obvious, one-tracked sexual maneuver. Instead he entertained her, shared the excitement of another evening in the city with her, seemed only to care for her and her reaction to all that was so new. All evening long, except for when he held her in his arms on the dance floor and for one magic moment when he caught her hand across the dinner table, he held himself back from her, caressing her only with his eyes.

It was late, very late, when at last they kissed.

This time she felt more than butterflies' wings. The butterflies were in her stomach. Together they stood looking out over city lights as the first hint of approaching dawn began to cast silver into the sky. They stood side by side leaning against the railing, with one of her hands held firmly in both of his. She was dizzy, dizzy from the height, from the brandy, from the headiness of being in the presence of this magnetic man. They stood for many minutes without exchanging a word, silently watching the slow stream of lights that twinkled between the railings of the Queensborough Bridge. The view of the East River was breathtaking to her, with Manhattan's skyline looming to the south.

Finally Hunter turned toward her. "I am, you know."

She returned his gaze, not daring to speak.

"Mad about you," he whispered. He released her hand and placed his open palms on her shoulders, turning her to face him. Then gently he stroked her cheek, and with his lips only inches from hers, said, "More than just mad, Alison. I am falling in love with you. It's happening. It's really happening." He bent to her and took her lips in his, slowly, gently, then fiercely, hungrily. She felt his tongue warm inside her mouth, the fire of his lips burning hers, his hands on her back, around her waist, circling lower, then swiftly up to her shoulders, stroking, feeling, then a tangle of fingers in her hair. With a strength she had never felt before he pulled her body against his, laying one hand on the small of her back to press her pelvis hot against his own. She felt heat from his groin, heat from his hands, and whimpered in ecstasy beneath the crushing strength of his embrace.

Then suddenly she felt his face buried against her hair, his breath hot on her neck as he breathed the words, "Oh, Alison, I want you so."

Then they kissed again, a maddening, devouring kiss that made her head spin, an escalating vertigo, a breathless, consuming feeling like none she had ever known. It was more, much more, than a feeling of desire. Oh, God, what was happening to her? What did it mean?

Breaking away, he looked into her eyes. Alison had never seen an expression quite like it before. He seemed to be searching inside her soul, seemed to be offering something to her that she had never been given—a rare gift, a wonderful, precious gift. Surely she must be mistaken. It couldn't be. It couldn't be happening this fast, this feeling she'd yearned to know someday, the feeling she'd wished for all of her life.

A little sigh caught in her throat as again Hunter leaned in to kiss her, this time softly, gently, and only once. "But I can't ask you, can I, darling? How can I?"

"Hunter, I . . ."

"I know." He sighed dramatically. "I know I must get you back to your hotel. I'll take you home, my darling. You must get some sleep before your flight." He drew back and gazed deeply into her eyes once more. He sighed again and shook his head. "It's wrong with an angel such as you, with someone so young and innocent, to feel such desire so soon." Whispering now he closed his eyes briefly and said, "I know I must wait. It would be wrong." He took her hands and bent to kiss her fingertips.

Gently she pried one hand from his and placed her forefinger under his chin to lift his head. With her eyes fixed on his she laid that same finger across his lips and, smiling, slowly nodded her head no. "No, it's not wrong," she said softly. "It seems right. I want you to love me, Hunter. It's all part of the magic. Tomorrow it will all be gone. Tonight wrap me in your magic."

She watched him close his eyes and draw a deep
sigh, then felt herself folded again inside his arms.
For the longest moment he merely held her, wrapped
her in a gentle, caring embrace. Then the sparkling,
twinkling lights on the distant bridge spun around
as she felt herself lifted and carried across soft carpeting through a dimly lighted room and through a
door into near darkness where soft music seemed to
surround her, where distant lights reflected through
walls of glass, twinkling city lights that faded into
the hazy silver dawn.

Then she felt the soft bed rise up against her back,
felt his fingers on her collar as he began to undress
her, following each movement with his lips, gentle,
burning lips that sought her own in passion. She felt
transported as suddenly he was lying beside her,
their naked bodies warmly touching, seeking, find-
ing one another. She clung willingly to him and rose
higher with each kiss, with each impassioned mention of her name.

"Alison," she heard him say again and again.
"Oh, Alison, you are magnificent, so beautiful. . . .
Alison, beautiful."

She rose to her passion's height and, as she
crested, could hear him still softly calling out her
name. Then she felt him burst inside her, his body
arched above her for a breathless time, before he fell
in against her, breathing heavily, whispering more
words of love. He rolled onto his side, pulling her
with him, and together, for a moment only, they
seemed to sleep.

At her hotel they rode the elevator in silence. A
light kiss at her door, just another glance of a kiss,
and then Hunter said, "I'll pick you up at ten-thirty.
You'll be in plenty of time to check your baggage."

"You're taking me to the airport? I can't let you do
that. It's such a hassle."

"Nonsense, sweet child." Touching her cheek, he

smiled into her eyes. "I'll call you at nine. I'll be your wake-up call. Sleep now."

Alison fell into bed and into a deep dreamless sleep.

It was like McIver or her brothers or Sam. Hunter took care of everything. He was her wake-up call. He patiently waited while she finished packing. At the airport he checked her luggage and handed her the boarding pass. He even bought her a magazine. Then he said, "Come, darling, we must talk." He picked a corner table in the busy coffee shop and ordered for her. Nervous now, she toyed with her coffee. "Alison," he said earnestly, penetrating her with his steel-blue, hypnotizing eyes. He's telling me good-bye, she thought. "Darling, I refuse to let you go," she heard him say. He reached across the table and took one of her hands in a strong grip. "Listen to me, Alison, I cannot let you go."

"Hunter, my plane is due. I'm—"

"I'll let you fly away today, sweet child. But I cannot allow you out of my life."

"Hunter, it's insane. We hardly know each other. We—"

"Shhh. We have only a few minutes, so listen to me. I want you, Alison. I want you desperately. Possibly I have never wanted anything so much in my entire life as I want you now. I am alive again, young and alive because you walked into my world."

"You don't know what you're saying. Two days ago you didn't know I was alive. I—"

"Today is what's real. I have you today." He lifted her hand to his lips, then turned it over and gently kissed her palm. Sighing deeply, "Alison. Alison."

She heard her flight called. "That's mine," she said.

He tossed a bill on the table and took her arm.

"Think about me, darling. You're mine. I'll be coming for you soon."

At the gate he again kissed her hand, then held it for a long moment as he looked deep into her eyes. They parted without another word.

6

Sam was standing just where she had left him last Monday afternoon. "Hi, kid," he said brightly. "How'd it go?"

"Oh, Sam, just super. I can't tell you how great this trip was!"

In his car he studied her for a long moment before he started the engine. "You look different, Alison."

She smiled self-consciously and cast her eyes away. "I guess I am in a way. So much has happened."

He studied her for a few seconds more, than began the twenty-minute drive to her apartment, listening attentively as she bubbled on about the seminar. Was he nuts, or was something terribly different about his Alison? It seemed to him she was overexplaining every detail of the trip.

The calls came every evening and every day. She'd only been home for minutes when the first one came. "Alison, darling, are you safely home?"

"Hunter, you're insane," she said, laughing.

"I miss you. I miss your gorgeous face."

Within an hour the first bouquet of roses arrived, magnificent long-stemmed white roses. "No beauty can rival your loveliness, my sweet," the card read, "but let these roses try. Yours, Hunter."

Before sundown he called again. "Alison, I tried to reach you. It rang and rang."

"When, just now? I drove to the vet's to pick up Amber." Alison sat stroking her cat as they spoke.

"No need to explain. I only called to say I love you."

There were calls to say good night, wake-up messages of love every morning. Somehow Alison didn't feel threatened by them or closed in, just wanted and adored! Was it really happening to her? She began to look forward to the calls, to wonder if anything were wrong when an expected one didn't come.

Jealously she tried to guard the secret of what was happening to her. At first it was easy to hide from her family. After all, they were ninety miles away. But Sam knew by Monday, and before the week was out, everyone at Channel 32 knew she had a suitor. Her office was filled with flowers. Her phone rang off the hook. But most of all, Alison had the unmistakable glow of a young woman in love.

Before long Hunter's calls said more than "I love you." "I can't wait to hold you," he whispered with his good-night call. The next day: "It won't be long now, darling. I'm getting the story in order."

"How can you possibly be coming down so soon? I've only been gone a week."

"It seems an eternity. But don't forget I have power over Barrington Dodd. We've written him out of the script for a while. We're in rehearsals now. We'll tape his last show by the end of next week."

Alison giggled. "Where's he going, to the hospital?"

"Oh, no, my sweet. The fans *love* to visit the characters in the hospital. That's their favorite place for them to be. No, I had to get him out of the country. He's off to Switzerland for three glorious weeks in the Alps."

Alison began to think about what it would be like

to have Hunter visit her in Sarasota. For the first time the tiny apartment she had leased last June seemed embarrassingly inadequate to entertain a man whose life-style was so extravagant. It had appalled McIver from the start. "Alison, pet, you can't live like this," he'd said on his first visit. "Why, this place isn't big enough to swing a cat around by the tail."

His daughter sat stroking Amber and smiled. "I like it."

"Where's the bedroom?"

"You're in it."

"Where's the bed?"

"You're sitting on it. The sofa opens out."

His great shoulders sagged. "You'll ruin your back."

"I've explained to you, McIver, it's all I can afford for now."

"This Abrahmson fellow has you working for peanuts. It's a disgrace for a girl of your talent and education. Sweetheart, if you're determined to live in this town, let me get Jim Laskell to give you a decent job at *The Suncoast Star.* I've talked to him about it and—"

"McIver, no! Everything I get from now on I want to be on my own. You've already invested a fortune in me. Tell Uncle Jim I said thanks, anyway. He'll understand."

"At least let me put you in a proper place to live. You can pay me back later if you're so determined to be independent of me."

"No, Daddy. I love my apartment. When I have something better, it will be because *I* can afford the rent. And I will one of these days, you'll see."

And she would, too, but she couldn't swing it right now, no matter that Hunter was liable to show up in less then two weeks. It took all of her energy to keep ahead of her shows. After Sam's show of confidence she couldn't let the quality slip now. In fact, she and Sam were already at work to incorporate some of the new ideas she'd picked up in New York.

So Hunter would have to take her as she was. No pretenses. She liked it that he hadn't a notion she was a Watson of Watson Sundrenched. He'd find out someday if they stayed in each other's lives that long. It was far too soon to project past his visit.

The day of his arrival took her by surprise. She expected him the next day, on Saturday. Instead, he walked into the studio just minutes before time for her to go on. When she caught sight of him, she almost fell apart. It was the first time she'd ever lost it. She had less than a minute to greet him before taking her seat on the set. Instantly she was given her five-minute cue. It was horrible. For a second she thought she might actually faint. Hunter couldn't be here already, he just couldn't. She wasn't *ready* for him yet.

"Two minutes, Alison."

She glanced meekly into the camera, its red light glowing relentlessly at her, mercilessly exposing that her confidence was lost, and displaying her destroyed composure before thousands of noontime viewers. Her cheeks flushed scarlet, and her heart beat wildly under the folds of her dress. She cast her eyes down for a moment at the tiny note pad she held in her palm, saying a little prayer under her breath that she might last until time for the first commerical break. Although she felt anything but, Alison looked stunning today. In an impetuous mood this morning she had chosen a vibrant dress to wear, a vivid Kelly green silk. It seemed to have been designed just for her, wrapping a soft surplice bodice across her firm breasts, then falling in feminine gathers around her lap and hips. Her eyes flashed in matching green reflection, and her tawny red hair seemed, in contrast, to punctuate the gorgeous shade, while framing her cheeks, both flushing deeper now in the warmth of Hunter's approving gaze.

"Stand by, Alison," the voice boomed into Studio B. She nodded toward the booth where the invisible director was watching her from behind black glass. Her knees were jelly. She cast a sidelong glance at Hunter. He was in a shadow beside one of the cameramen, with his arms folded across his chest. He was smiling. She felt sick.

"You're on, Alison," Rick said.

Her back stiffened. Somehow she forced a bright smile, but instantly she blew her first cue. From there it went rapidly downhill. She stumbled over her lines and repeated herself self-consciously. She did the first bad interview of her career. It was a nightmare.

Somehow, mercifully, the commercial break came. The instant the red light went out she rushed to the water cooler. With her back to Hunter she took repeated long, deep breaths, steadying herself with the flat of her hand on the wall. She had to pull it together. Oh, dear God, don't let me disgrace myself in front of him, please!

Moments before Alison went on, Sam happened to walk through the studio. Quietly he had watched the handsome stranger throw Alison into turmoil. Now inside the booth, he observed without comment as Alison gave herself a talking-to. "Who's the dude?" he heard the director ask.

"He must be the one who's been sending the flowers," the audio man answered. "I never saw Alison lose it before. She's messed up four times already, and we're only twelve minutes in."

"I know," said Rick. Then into his mike, "Okay, guys. Tell Alison one minute."

Sam was silent. So this was the man. He was too

old for her! My God, he had to be forty. Had she lost
her mind? The girl was only twenty-one. Sam felt
rage, an unexplained rage. When Hunter turned
to smile at a crew member who asked him to move,
Sam got a good look at him. God knows he was
handsome, but the girl had sense. Looks would
never be enough for her. Reluctantly Sam had to
admit there might be more to him than that. But
in his gut he didn't like him worth a crap.

His eyes narrowed, Sam watched as Alison took
her place in front of the camera. She didn't say a
word to the stranger and kept her eyes downcast.

"Stand by, Alison," Rick said over the intercom.

She lifted her eyes to the camera and smiled. Sam
stood with his hands thrust deep into his pockets. He
winced when she flubbed her opening cue again. Oh,
damn. The kid had gone and fallen in love with a
slick-looking dude from the big city.

Alison sat facing him across a table by the window. The sun lay low in the clouds, ready to embrace
the green Gulf of Mexico. Already the orange mist
surrounding it was beginning to pattern the pale
blue and silver horizon with patches of color. She recognized it as the sort of sunset that would be even
lovelier after the sun had disappeared. Her hands
trembled with excitement when she lifted her wine-
glass to her lips.

Hunter looked wonderful to her, carefree and
rested, seeming somehow already tan, as though
he'd been out on the beach for days, not just hours.
His off-white shirt was open at the collar, exposing a
tiny edge of chest hair that was as white as the sand
beyond the window, as white as the row of teeth behind his smiling lips. His jacket was almost white,
too, a nubby linen, shot with beige streaks of silk.
White shirt, white jacket, white teeth, silver-gray
hair. Even his eyes looked lighter somehow. They

were almost a crystal blue in the setting sunlight, instead of the shade of slate that they had seemed to her in city lights. Her heart began to trip, and she felt a surge of sensuality throughout her body. "How ever did you know to pick this place?" she managed to ask.

"I asked for a map of the city when I rented my car at the airport. Longboat Key seemed logical. It was on the Gulf and far enough away from Channel 32 that you wouldn't feel cramped."

She began to relax. "What time did you check in?"

"Oh, around breakfast time. I caught the night flight."

Astonished, "But I talked to you last night at eight o'clock! You didn't say a word."

He grinned and sipped his martini. "I wanted to surprise you."

"Well, you did just that." She ducked her head, then shook it slowly. "I was just awful today. Awful."

"I thought you were wonderful."

She lifted her eyes, pleading with them. "Don't tease me, Hunter."

"I'm not teasing. You were a delight."

"It's the only bad show I've done in almost a year. I can't believe it yet. And Sam had to be in the booth. Normally he's at lunch when I go on. *You* were there, and *Sam* was there." She groaned. "I was mortified. Thank God our signal doesn't reach over to the Grove."

He reached across the table and lifted her hand to his lips. Tenderly he kissed each of her fingertips. "Don't be so hard on yourself, Alison. I upset you by coming in unannounced. It was my fault. But don't you see, darling, you're so good that those tiny flubs you made were nothing? We do worse on network every day, much worse, and that's after hours of rehearsal before we ever begin to tape. I shudder to think what those birdbrains I'm forced to work with would do before a live camera."

She eyed him gratefully. "Anyhow, it's done. I can't get today's show back. I can only do another that's better on Monday." Settling in now, "But let's talk about you. You're here. You're in Florida! You're here for three weeks, right?"

"I wish. No, old Barrington has to make an appearance in about ten days. We're building a set to look like a room inside a Swiss chalet. He'll be on the trans-Atlantic phone from his room in Switzerland screaming obscenities at someone or other in the States." He laughed.

"Do you like playing a bastard?"

"Barrington's my alter ego. I like getting my bastard side out and over with." Suddenly serious, he lifted her hand again to his lips. "So that I can be my real self when I'm with you, Alison." He waited until she took another sip of wine. "You do know why I'm here, don't you, darling?"

"For sun and sea and relaxation. At least that's what you said."

"Yes, for all of those things. But I flew to Florida to ask if you will marry me."

Alison sat back and drew a deep breath.

"How lovely you are," he said. He reached across the table and ran his forefinger down the outer strands of her hair where the light from the setting sun reflected a perfect golden rim along the fiery mass. "So incredibly lovely," he repeated.

"Hunter, I don't know what to say. I keep feeling like I'm in a dream every time I'm around you. It can't be happening this fast."

"It has happened. It's too late to change a thing." He leaned forward on both forearms and gazed hypnotically into her eyes. "Tell me that you'll become my wife, Alison Watson. Alison Watson Ames.

Alison Ames. See? Doesn't that have a lovely sound?"

"Hunter," she said, carefully measuring her words. "I'm really not ready for this. I . . . I don't know what to say to you. You've turned my life upside down. I was just beginning to feel right inside myself, someone real and, well, kind of important." She cast her eyes down modestly. "At least important inside my own little world."

He leaned forward and smiled reassuringly. "But, darling, I've no desire to uproot you from your world. I'll give you all the time you need to make the transition."

"To New York City?"

"It's where I make my home."

She shook her head slowly. "I can't, Hunter. I can't move up there."

"But you don't understand, sweet child. I'm in *love* with you. I want to marry you. I want to spend the rest of my life telling you good morning and kissing your sweet lips good night."

She turned away and stared out at the Gulf. The sun was gone; the sky was a brilliant watercolor of bright red and orange and yellow and blue, all running together behind streaks of white clouds, clouds edged in silver gray. "I haven't had time yet. You haven't given me time to know if I'm in love with you." Facing him again, "I think I am." She watched him smile and close his eyes for a moment. "I know I *could* be. You're everything wonderful, Hunter. You charm me completely, but more important than that, you show me that you care about me. And you do it in a strong and protective way that I love—like my father and my brothers. Like Sam." She watched him smile again. "And something else: you're on my mind constantly. But—how shall I say this—I don't want to hurt your feelings or lose what we've begun. But, Hunter, I'm not ready to follow you anywhere.

Don't you see, I am a person, too? I have to be good for me if I'm ever going to be good for anyone else. What I've been building here is special to me. I can't ditch it now."

"Your career?"

"Yes."

"Do you like New York?"

"Oh, yes, but—"

"But?"

"It's like the old saying, I guess. I wouldn't want to live there. Don't you see, I'd be *lost* in New York. I'd be nobody up there. Down here I'm somebody. And I'm two hours from the Grove. My family means the world to me, I've told you that. The people there are my heart. I can't move away and leave everything I love and understand." Shaking her head, "Maybe someday I'll be ready for that. But right now I can't."

"Listen to me, angel. I don't want to *own* you. I want to marry you! Your independence is one of the traits that attracted me. You will need to call on every ounce of self-reliance you can muster if you embark on a life with me. At times it will be very rough, Alison. I want to warn you about that. When we're plotting each thirteen-week segment of *Seasons,* our writing team holes up for two or three weeks at a time. We don't even come up for air. I *want* you to work if it pleases you. I *want* you to have babies if it pleases you. Do both! That would be even better." He leaned forward eagerly and took both of her hands in his. "I only ask you to let me come to you at the end of every day to share, then hold you inside my arms all night."

Alison sat back, overwhelmed. She sighed deeply and closed her eyes.

She heard his voice ask softly, "Is the only issue moving to New York?"

"I . . ."

He released her hands and drained his glass. Signaling the waiter, "Another, please." Turning to Alison, "How's your wine, darling?" She indicated no, touching the rim of her goblet. "Just the martini, thank you." He grinned broadly and said to her, "Well, then, it's settled."

"What are you saying?"

"I'll move down here." Looking around, "I like it here. I really like it quite well. It will probably give the show an entire new shot in the arm. Certainly the writing will be no problem. Perhaps we might even shoot some segments in Florida."

Astounded, she said, "Are you serious? Will they let you do such a thing?"

"They? My producers? Oh I don't think that will be a problem. I'm head writer for *Seasons,* Alison. The drama is my baby, my creation. But an enormous amount of my time is spent in playing the part of Barrington. I have a staff of writers who execute the actual scripting of the dialogue. My function is to draft the plots, then approve the scripts. I'll fly to New York for that. Other times I can bring my writers to me. I'll have to fly up when Barrington's on, of course, but I've been thinking of easing him out a bit, anyhow." He patted her hand. "It will work out. Leave everything to me."

"Then you mean . . . ?"

"If Mohammed won't come to the mountain, my darling . . ."

The wine filled her head. His room was dark, but the sound of the surf pounding outside the wall of glass beat a muted rhythmic assurance that everything was going to be all right. They had lingered over dinner, then Irish coffee, taking nearly three hours to go over all their plans. Yes, she was going to be his wife. It was decided. The date was set. Now they wanted to be alone.

Inside his room he folded her into his arms. "Alison, my darling, you've made me the happiest man on earth." He kissed her tenderly, then pulled her inside a savage embrace, devouring her, burning her lips with his.

His hands were hot on her back but he still had not touched her breasts, had not yet reached down to feel her ass. Suddenly he pulled her into an embrace so strong that it took her breath away, then groaned and buried his face in her hair. "Oh, darling, I want you so desperately."

"And I want you, Hunter. Hunter, love me. Love me now."

He leaned to kiss the back of her neck while he undid the tiny hook and slowly slipped the zipper down, following his fingers with his lips. When the folds of green silk fell away from her shoulders and her dress slipped to the floor, she heard him catch his breath, then murmur sweet words that she couldn't fully hear.

Then, gently, he undid the tiny hook that held her bra, slipping the garment from her breasts in the same motion that he bent his head to take her nipple in his lips. She cried out in pleasure as he took both of her breasts in his hands and kissed each of them, whispering his love. Then she felt herself lifted in the darkness and carried across to the bed. In a sweep he pulled down the bed cover, then placed her head in the center of a pillow before falling in against her neck, speaking soft words, whispered promises of love.

"Hunter," she called out softly.

"Yes, my darling?" he answered before he muted her cry with his lips, devouring her in a kiss more powerful than before.

It became like the spinning dream in which they danced into the night. It was slow and beautiful, like the dances they had danced. He kissed every inch of her body, drowned her in the ecstasy of two bodies moving together, rising, falling.

He kissed her, caressed her, tormented her to the moment when she cried out for him to be inside her, longed to have him there. Then she felt him, hot and strong and better than anything she had ever known in this world. Everything felt completely right. "Hunter," she called out, "Hunter, I . . ."

"Do it, darling. Come to me."

"Hunter! Yes, yes, now!" She felt him wait until she had passed her crest, then clung tightly to him as he sighed deeply in his own passion.

Drained and weeping softly now, she lay cradled in his arms until she began to drift into sleep. Sleep came with his strong body against her back, his hand caressing the rim of her waistline and the curve of her hip. She felt the warmth of his kisses on the nape of her neck and heard him whisper over and over again, "Alison Ames. Mine. Mine forever. Sweet, sweet Alison. Mine."

The wedding was set for May twenty-seventh at four in the afternoon in the garden near the porch of the Big House, the exact spot where Todd and Jennifer had exchanged their vows almost five years before. "Please be happy, Daddy. I am so in love. I'm happy, darling. I didn't know it was possible to be so happy."

Too stunned by the announcement to protest, at first McIver only sat and listened to the plans. All of the plans had been made, it seemed. Everything was set. Alison was to be married in just a bit over a month's time. Married to this stranger from New York City, to this man almost twice her age. Surely not. Surely the child would come to her senses in time.

"I don't think so, Pop," said Gordie sadly. "You're

going to have to convince her she has your blessing,
then pray for the best."

"Gordie's right, Pop," Todd said. "But don't look
so worried. I think she's going to be happy with the
man. He has a lot of good things about him. I think
he covers up what a special person he is with all that
show-biz flamboyance. But that's the business he's
in. He's an actor." Todd watched his father continue
to shake his head gravely.

"The point is, Pop," interrupted Gordie, "that
Alison is going to be twenty-two years old in three
more months. We can't tell her what to do anymore."

McIver looked from his oldest son over to Todd. "Is
that what you think, too, Todd?" His younger son
nodded. "And did you know, either of you, that the
man has had *two* bad marriages; not one but *two?*"

"Pop," Gordie soothed, "it's like Alison explains.
The first one really doesn't count. It's like her mistake with Calvin."

Ignoring him, "And he has a daughter from the
first one who is almost Alison's own age!"

The three men sat facing each other on the narrow
benches that circled the walls of the boat house, the
place they had gone for privacy. The Big House
seemed to ring with merriment. Alison was home
with Hunter to make her marriage announcement,
and Minerva had prepared one of her famous feasts.
His grandsons were running around wildly, the dogs
were barking their heads off, and music boomed
from the open windows. What was worse, Margaret
and Jennifer seemed to be utterly charmed by this
intruder, this polished stranger who had stolen his
daughter's heart away. They seemed to know exactly who he was, even followed his ridiculous drivel
that filled the airwaves every afternoon, his own
daughters-in-law! Until now McIver had considered
them among the most intelligent women he had ever
known. They watched it, they actually *watched* this

program Hunter Ames was associated with. They seemed highly honored to have this *actor* at the Grove.

He shook his great, dark head again. When he and the boys left the Big House to come down for their talk, Margaret and Jennifer were gaily setting Mary Alison's big dining room table for the celebration. He groaned inwardly. A celebration. Already they had gotten out most of Alliene's best china and crystal. Alliene. His beautiful Alliene. What would Alliene think? "What would Alliene think?" he asked aloud. Not waiting, "She'd think I'd failed."

"Don't, Pop," Gordie commanded. "You've done everything in the world for Alison. But she's a woman now, grown and responsible, just as Mother was when she made the decision to marry you. Don't underestimate her. She has flat-out refused to move to New York with him. She has a handle on what will make her happy. It can be a good marriage."

McIver heaved a great racking sigh and fell forward with his face in his hands. In agony his sons watched him sob for minutes, then slowly recover himself. He fumbled in his pocket and finally found his handkerchief. He sat for a long beat with his forearms on his knees, then, shaking his head sadly, said, "First a boy, now a man twice her age. I'd so hoped her second time would be the right one."

After many moments more he straightened and looked from one son to the other. "But I know you're right. To forbid it would only make her move to New York with him. We must bless it and at least keep her close by. At least close by, maybe we can pick up the pieces."

Only a month to prepare. The sheer excitement that Alison felt was on a high pitch. She was so very much in love. From the moment of their engagement

announcement that April afternoon at the Grove she
and Hunter had been together incessantly. Hunter's
trips to New York were frequent but brief; always he
was back in Sarasota within a couple of days. They
were driven, both of them, to be together. The motel
room on Longboat Key where they had gone to make
love the night they decided they would marry was
Hunter's now, booked for him until their wedding
day when they had plans to fly to the Bahamas for
their honeymoon. Each night that he was in town
Alison rushed from her office to be with him. And
when he was gone, she took quick trips to Atlanta for
her trousseau and worked on wedding arrangements
with Jennifer and Margaret. It was a rushed, but
happy, time.

With each day that passed Alison felt more sure
that Hunter was her wish come true. If the age gap
that separated them had bothered her in the beginning, soon all of the anxiety was forgotten, and
within no time at all it became unimportant. This
was the youngest, most virile man she had ever
known. They had everything in common, could
talk for hours or be quiet together for hours—no
matter. Whatever they chose to share seemed
right.

To her their sexual encounters were beautiful beyond belief. Each time they were alone in Hunter's
room they rushed into one another's arms as though
it were the first, and always she felt transported,
wrapped in an aura of sensuality, on a physical pin-
nacle that became intertwined with spellbinding,
breathtaking love.

Alison's mistake of the past was forgotten; Hunter
had only laughed when she told him about Calvin.
And, strangely, she didn't seem to care at all when
he talked about some of the personal, private happenings during his marriage to Christina. Today
they had decided to escape from the pre-wedding

frenzy and spend the last quiet Saturday before the
wedding week on their own. They were lying together in Hunter's bed, listening to the sounds of the
distant surf, muted by the massive glass wall that
overlooked the green Gulf of Mexico. Alison loved
these private moments. She felt so much a part of
Hunter, even when he spoke of unpleasant things.
Today he wanted to talk about Christina, as if wanting it said, then forgotten.

Christina had been Hunter's second wife. "I was
in love with Christina," Hunter said, "or so I
thought. I never loved Louise, and she knew it. I only
married her because a baby was on the way. We split
soon after Ann was born. But ten years ago
Christina and I thought we had something permanent."

"What went wrong then?" Alison asked.

His voice became brittle, hard as he cradled his
head in his arms, staring at the ceiling. "What
went wrong? Everything. Christina was head-
strong, but that came as no surprise. I admired her
spunk. But as soon as she got that ring on her finger she seemed to change. She is the most utterly
demanding, perhaps the most selfish, woman I
have ever known. She claimed to love me but
thought first of herself—always." He rolled over,
pulled himself up on his elbow, and stroked
Alison's cheek, then bent to kiss the place he had
touched. Then his lips brushed her breasts, lingering to kiss one nipple, then the other. "Christina
was," he said against her breast, "your diametric
opposite, Miss Watson." He lifted his head and
leaned in to kiss the top of her nose. "Lovely Miss
Watson, the soon to be Mrs. Ames."

She smiled and snuggled her shoulder closer to his
chest. "Go on. Tell me more. Tell me about
Christina. I don't want to make the same mistakes
she did."

He rolled onto his back again. "That could never happen—never. But, Alison, in fairness, so much of it was me. I wish I could blame it all on Christina, but I can't. We lasted almost seven years, you know." Sighing, "It was a rocky seven years, but in her own way I think she tried."

"Did you . . . did you ever think of having children? Maybe that would have—"

"No," he said emphatically. "Neither of us wanted them. Christina's career came first with her, and I was wise enough to know she would have resented even a few months away from her public." He snorted. "Christina is an incompetent actress, but she *is* an actress and must always be on call."

"Do you ever hear from her now?"

"Regularly. On the occasions I am two hours late with her alimony check."

"I guess I don't fully understand what finally brought the split."

He gazed deeply into her eyes for a long moment. As always, when he did, she felt weak, felt that surge of warmth in her groin, the increase in her heartbeat. It was late in the afternoon, and they had been lazy together all day long, first on blankets in the sun, then floating in the gently rolling surf, then together in the shower, and now naked in bed. For hours now they had lain together, making love and sleeping, then making love again. It was a timeless, rapturous escape for her, a sort of never-never land in which there were no clocks or schedules to keep, no responsibilities to meet. She only knew that she was in love and wanted to wile away the endless hours with this man whose lips now smiled just over hers, whose breath was warm and sweet upon her lips. On an impulse she lifted her head from the pillow and glanced his lips with a kiss.

He grinned, then quickly leaned in and returned it, kissing her warmly, passionately. "Be careful, you vixen. You're going to start things up again. Don't forget, it's you who've been fussing that you're fed up with room service." He squinted at the clock on the night table. "We have a reservation at Café L'Europe at . . ."

Alison lifted herself to him, circling his neck with her arm, pulling her breasts up against his strong chest. "We could cancel."

He flopped backward on his pillow and hooted with laughter. "You *are* a vixen! An insatiable vixen, insatiable. My God, woman, I have never known another like you. Don't you ever tire? Other women tire. Other women have headaches."

"Maybe you've never come up against anyone normal before. Maybe you've only encountered cold, uninteresting women until now."

First sighing deeply, he then chuckled aloud. "Perhaps, perhaps."

Radiant, exquisite, wearing ivory Swiss organdy and carrying orange blossoms, Alison clung to McIver's arm as they walked down the five porch steps to the flower-decked arbor where Hunter and the minister stood waiting. Along the way she glanced around the crowd but was in too much of a daze to recognize many of them. All of Grove Dale was there, and half of central Florida it seemed. After all, Senator McIver Watson was their boy! His campaign lieutenants were still basking in the landside sweep he had pulled off last November. State Senator McIver Watson from the Thirteenth District! What's more, the groom was a celebrity.

Alison trembled all over with excitement. Up ahead, Margaret and Jennifer, wearing long yellow organdy gowns and carrying yellow roses and daisies, took their places on the left. Her eyes traveled quickly over the setting. Gordie and Todd were up there, too, beside Hunter, with Gordie as best man. From the corner of her eye she could see her nephews giggling with excitement, adorable in their little white suits. All of them were there surrounding Minnie, who was trying to keep them in tow; all but little Keith, Jennifer and Todd's newest, who was too tiny to attend.

She couldn't find the others who were so dear to her, Ben and Sam and Uncle Jim, but she knew they were all there somewhere. She caught a glimpse of Hunter's daughter Ann, standing on the sidelines, looking nervous and out of place.

Before she left her father's supporting arm, Alison turned to him and smiled. The big man's eyes were full, but no tears fell. As best he could he returned her smile. Lifting her lips to his ruddy cheek, she kissed him tenderly. Then she turned to her groom. Their eyes met and clung in a perfect, precious moment in time. "You are my life," Hunter whispered for her ears alone. Together they turned and faced the minister.

Alison felt as though her heart were going to burst. Never, ever had anything felt so right.

7

It was five years before Alison began to accept that never had anything been so wrong. Actually, had she not chosen to ignore them, there were telltale signs before the first year was out. But her world was a flurry of activity then; everything good seemed to be happening at once.

Soon after they returned from their exotic two-week honeymoon in the islands, Hunter plunged into a new dimension of his career, and within months hers took a challenging new direction as well. Both of them were happy with the changes; they were stimulating, fun to talk over with each other. Things were happening exactly the way she had pictured in her dreams. Both she and Hunter were busily fulfilled by day, yet hurried to be together at night.

Hunter's time at first was spent in structuring the new system his writers must work around with the distance between them and him. Further, Hunter's character, Barrington, was deeply involved in an important plot segment, one necessary if the writers were to edge him out of total dominance in the drama. This meant he had to travel to New York often over the summer. But new things were beginning to happen for Alison, too. In late June the couple moved into a house on the mainland, an old Spanish-style two-story stucco home, one that had been built in the early twenties during Florida's real-estate boom. Alison fell in love with the place the moment she saw it. Excitedly she went with Hunter when he met with the real-estate agent to close the sale.

Between the move and renovation and keeping up with her job, Alison literally fell into bed each night, too exhausted to feel lonely for Hunter. But she never slept until his good-night call came through. "I telephoned to say I love you, my sweet."

"And I love you. When are you coming home?"

"This weekend, but I have to fly back up Sunday night. Only a couple more months of this, though, sweet thing. Everything is falling into place. Old Barrington hasn't realized it yet, but he's becoming a supporting actor."

"Are you sure you really want it that way, Hunt? You're not doing it just for me, are you, darling?"

"If it would make you love me more I would say I'm doing it so I can spend all of my time with you."

"I couldn't love you more. And, guess what? The land deal closed today at Sunfish Key. Daddy says as soon as we okay the blueprints they'll start construction of the A-frame."

"Fabulous. I'm still a little staggered by your father's wedding gift, I must admit."

She laughed. "McIver can be staggering at times. But he has it in his head we need a beach hideaway. He thinks we both work too hard."

"Whatever the motive, I accept. It will be a wonderful writing retreat."

"You'll have your typewriter under the big window facing the Gulf inside six months. Oh, Hunt, I'm so excited!"

It was true. The gift was extravagant, but McIver wanted to do it. He'd been feeling twinges of guilt for the negative thoughts he'd entertained about Hunter before the wedding. There could be no denying it, his daughter was blissfully happy; no way she could be pretending. He knew the girl far too well. She had never been lovelier. Maybe things were going to be all right. God knows he prayed so.

McIver had little time to spend in worry the summer after Alison's wedding, anyhow. With only a few months under his belt since he had taken the oath of office, the enormity of the seat he had won had descended upon him. For a post he'd been more or less talked into seeking, he had discovered a new excitement in the world of the legislature that caught him by surprise.

Furthermore, he was enjoying a gay spark of romance in his life. There was a new woman he met at one of the rallies last summer, a lady who had just inherited a rich grove of Temples over near Auburndale. She was young for him, only forty-seven, and a divorcee, but what matter? He'd no intention of marrying her, anyhow. Yet she was a total delight, a stimulation like no other he'd known in many years. Her name was Clair Hill.

The moment he met Clair he began to feel that old familiar spark, and the woman was plainly intrigued by him from the beginning. He still found it a bit hard to grasp that she was; after all, he was sixty-five years old when they met. But it didn't seem to matter to Clair Hill, and she knew full well he'd turned sixty-six this past March. She simply laughed and said, "Senator, you're the youngest man I know." Yes, Clair Hill was quite a woman. McIver felt the youngest, the most vital he had in years.

Alison liked Clair. She approved of the relationship completely. It was one of the things that happened that year to make her world fall into place. She really didn't see it as a situation in which McIver would marry at last, but she loved all she'd begun to observe in the past several months. She per-

ceived a decided spring in McIver's footstep and the
sort of sparks she'd seen flying back in the days
when he'd hustled all those ladies down for a romp at
the Little House. The old rascal! Well, it didn't surprise her a bit.

Alison's fledgling career had been so all-consuming to her in the heat of the campaign last summer that she hadn't been able to take part in it. It
bothered her that she couldn't, but she didn't have
the energy a weekend commute would have required. But now it was different. She felt more sure
of herself in her job, and Hunter seemed to be in New
York so much of the time that there was little to
keep her in Sarasota when her weekends were free.
In a way there was even more going on at the Big
House now that her father had won the election than
during the frenzy of getting him the seat. There was
an endless round of parties, something happening
every Saturday night at one house or the other on
the family compound. The people who attended were
interesting, stimulating. She loved being around it,
was immensely proud of being McIver's daughter.

"Oh, Hunt, I wish you could have seen Daddy last
night in the midst of his cronies. There were two
other senators there, and a member of the House.
And a lobbyist from the Citrus Commission. The conversation that went on at the dinner table boggled
my brain."

"You're being ridiculously modest. You probably
had the best brain in the room."

"I wish. I felt like a kindergartener. I was smart
enough to keep my mouth sealed. I didn't want to
open it and humiliate McIver."

Hunter chuckled. "You were out of your realm,
that's all. I'd like to see what one of those geniuses
would have had to offer if the conversation had been
about the inner workings of a television station."

"You're prejudiced. But, honestly, darling, I wish you could have seen Daddy."

"I'm glad you have fun when you go, sweet. You didn't mind that I couldn't join you?"

" 'Course not. I know you need to get a few days' rest before you fly back to New York. Just as long as you didn't mind my leaving you."

"You're back now, that's what counts," he said, gently stroking her cheek.

"I do love you so, Hunter. You seem to understand me completely. And you never smother me. Instead you make me know you care."

"I will always care. You are my life."

"Oh, do love me, Hunter, love me always."

"My sweet, darling child, how could I ever not love you?"

As he pulled her passionately into his arms she felt it all over again, the same breathless feeling that each time wrapped itself around her. Together they rose to rapturous heights, each giving everything, each responding in total love. Later, when they lay in each other's arms in the midsummer's twilight, they were quiet together, quiet and cozy and belonging to the moment. Always together—whispering, joking, playing, just being—with each day falling more and more deeply in love.

It really hadn't begun to bother Alison yet that Hunter rarely went to the Grove with her for any reason. After all, he was working very hard, and it thrilled her that he seemed to be enjoying their house. Besides, it seemed healthy to her that they were not lost without each other. Hunter liked to read and have a little glass of wine there in the quiet coolness of their bedroom. She was never gone longer than a night or two.

He didn't make it home to Florida for her birthday, but that didn't upset her. She had a marvelous day at home with her family. Minnie fixed her favorites, and her brothers were there with their families in force, five active little nephews to liven the day. She eyed her father tenderly when he proposed the toast to her twenty-second birthday. Clair was at his side, looking up at him with a definite twinkle in her eye. Suddenly it hit Alison that the two of them had been making love all afternoon somewhere. Her father had been gone for hours, not at all like him when he knew she was there at the Big House. The old sweetheart, a matinee at his age! He looked wonderfully rested and relaxed, younger than she'd seen him look in years. His ruddy skin was barely lined, just the nice, deep character lines she always remembered. And his shiny black hair was hardly laced with gray. "To my beautiful daughter, Alison. May she always be as radiant, as happy, as she is tonight." The family applauded and smiled at her. Fixing his nice brown eyes tenderly on hers, McIver said to his daughter, "Happy birthday, pet. We love you very much."

Alison was especially radiant that night. By the end of August she was told the best news of all, a secret she had been suspecting for a month now. She was pregnant. "Hunter, come home! Darling, when are you coming home?"

"What's wrong, Alison?"

"Nothing. Everything is right. I just want you home with me."

She could hear him chuckling softly. "We're winding down now. In about ten days I'll be home for a long while. I'm going to see to it I'll have only two more short trips before New Year's."

"Ten days!" Her disappointment showed in her tone.

"Alison, tell me what it is."

"I wanted to see your face, but I can't wait. Hunt,

it's true. The doctor told me this afternoon. It's true!"

He sighed deeply. "Oh, my angel, what wonderful news."

"I've never felt so good."

Alison drove to the Grove that weekend to tell her father the news. Why had he been so quick to worry? His daughter had settled down, just as he'd prayed she would. He couldn't say he knew Hunter well, but he did seem to be a hardworking man, devoted to his girl.

By late fall Alison was three and a half months along in her pregnancy and feeling terrific. She'd had a few flashes of morning sickness, but she didn't miss a single episode of *Sarasota Midday*. Best of all, Hunter was home now, and except for one more brief flight to New York when Barrington had to be on the show, he'd be home until after the first of the year.

By early December she knew she must prod Sam into a decision. "Look at me," she said, pointing to herself. "Better not drag your feet in hiring the new person."

"Haven't made up my mind yet. None of 'em are any good. You've spoiled me."

"Nonsense. That little brunette, Betty Sue What's-Her-Name from Tampa, seemed good to me. I was just back in the tape room viewing her audition."

"She'll do, I guess."

"I'm not kidding, Sam. I'm popping out of my regular clothes. No way I can hold off on maternity clothes much longer. Pretty soon we'll be getting mail if you don't get me off the air." She giggled. "If Rick gets his camera shots any closer around my face, everybody'll figure it out, anyhow."

"Are you planning to start your leave before Christmas?"

"No, I only mean that you've got to get me off the

air soon. I'll keep working till spring if there's anything else you can let me do around here."

"Whoever replaces you on *Sarasota Midday* will need your help in putting the new show together for a while. But, yeah, there is something else I have in mind. Our new Sony cameras are due for delivery sometime in January. And we've got a switcher ordered for the booth that'll knock your eyeballs out. Are you still game to get into commercial production?"

"Oh, yes! I'm dying to try it."

"Let's play it by ear and see how you're feeling. You never know. By January you may want to get off your feet."

"Come on, Sam, you know better. I've never felt this good."

Having Hunter home full-time seemed an almost idyllic time to Alison. While she was at the studio he spent a lot of his week out at the construction site of their new beach house on Sunfish Key. At home he seemed to read constantly or, when the urge moved him, sat down at his typewriter for hours. It was an almost musical sound to her. She'd never have considered interrupting him; she knew he would always come to her. They made love often, beautiful, passionate love. And often they lay awake afterward for hours, talking, sharing, exchanging their deepest secrets of love. Was it right, was it be possible to be this happy?

They celebrated Hunter's birthday on Christmas Eve. His daughter flew in the day before, and the three of them enjoyed a late supper by the Christmas tree. Alison liked Ann. She was a lovely girl, with some of Hunter's physical features but few of his ways. As Alison watched the father and daughter together she noticed there was a certain affection between them but no real warmth. But then how could there be? By Hunter's own admission he had seen

little of Ann from the time he'd split from her
mother. The situation was hard for Alison to grasp.
How could he have gone all these years from the
girl's infancy until Ann sought him out recently,
without seeing her? "Not all families are close like
the Watsons," had been his only comment when they
discussed it.

Christmas morning they rose early. Anxious to be
on her way back to New York to spend the holiday
with her mother, Ann caught an early flight, and
Alison and Hunter headed on to Grove Dale when it
was not yet noon. All day Hunter was a total delight,
charming the women in the family, and was even at
the beginning edge of winning McIver over. In fact,
he gave special attention to McIver and Clair,
escaping with them Christmas afternoon to the family room. They opened an exotic bottle of brandy
someone had sent McIver for Christmas, and by dinner the three of them were pretty tipsy. Alison
watched it all from the corner of her eye and was
amused.

The whole family gathered before dark for Christmas dinner. Hunter was a little loud and a trifle long
in the dramatic toast he offered after the meal, but
no one seemed to notice or mind. It worried Alison a
little. She never had seen him quite so unsteady. But
then so were McIver and Clair. Oh, well, it was holiday time, and everyone was entitled to relax.

That night, after the house was quiet and she and
Hunter lay cuddling in her bed in the room that was
home to her, she nestled back against his chest. He
was breathing heavily, and his breath smelled
strongly of the pungent brandy that followed Minnie's rich dessert assortment, but it didn't matter.
Nothing mattered except the exceptional feeling of
warmth and family time that filled her heart tonight. More than ever Hunter had made himself part
of the Watson circle and, what's more, had seemed

truly happy with them there today. She had been so
proud to be his wife, watching him from the corner of
her eye as he enchanted her sisters-in-law, and later,
wisely on to him when he played hooky with her father and Clair. He even seemed interested when he
asked all the right questions of Gordie and Todd. He
must have been doing a good bit of homework, too,
because the probing questions he'd asked Gordie
about the intricacies of the juice-processing business
had been downright intelligent and informed. She
was overwhelmed with pride. Yet never did he hint
that he was interested in a mercenary way regard-
ing the various Watson Properties' enterprises. On
the contrary, Alison's vast personal wealth seemed a
matter entirely unimportant to him, other than that
she be happy and have all the things she was accus-
tomed to. If they were more than he could provide
and her trust fund needed to be dipped into, well,
that would be up to her and the family's financial ad-
viser. From the beginning he had assured her that
his own income was more than enough to support
them both handsomely, and that for Alison to continue on with her career was a matter solely up to
her.

She lay beside him, listening to the gentle whine
of the wind in the trees outside her huge bedroom
window. It had turned cold yesterday, and there always seemed to be a special sound to the wind in the
groves during a cold spell. It was the sort of mysteri-
ous whispering of leaves and creaking of branches
that had given her the urge to snuggle deeper under
the huge comforter Minnie had tucked over her as a
child, and tonight it only made her push closer
against Hunter's warm, naked body. It was in the
low thirties outside, but a fire of crackling pine logs
flamed in the hearth across the room, and so both of
them slept, as they always did, bare. She lay with
her back to him, his left arm tucked under the crook

of her neck and his right hand gently circling her breasts, circling over and over again. Every now and then she thrilled to the touch of his lips on the nape of her neck.

"Hunter, I love you so much."

"I adore you, Alison. You are everything to me."

"I was proud of you when you spent so much time with my brothers today. You knew all the right questions to ask."

"I enjoyed being with them. They are highly intelligent men."

"Still, I know it's hard on you, darling. Your worlds are so far apart. I want you to know it means everything to me for you to seek out the things that they know to talk about. I know you're not interested in sports, and—"

"Don't be silly, sweet. They are just as considerate of me. When Todd took me out in the Jeep to tour the south grove this afternoon, he had dozens of questions about New York and the theatrical world. I found it delightful—amusing and delightful. I realized how hard both of us were trying to become friends."

"I'm glad. Hunt?"

"Hmmm?"

"I think you really won over McIver today."

He chuckled wickedly. "By getting him bombed, you mean?"

"Well, I'd say you got each other embalmed."

"Nonsense. I was in total control. But it was entertaining to ply him and Clair with that thirty-year-old brandy."

"Just as long as everyone had fun."

"Oh, indeed. We did that."

Again Alison thrilled to the touch of Hunter's lips on her neck. She felt his fingers slip from her breasts and down to her abdomen where its flat athletic plane was now replaced with the curve of the fetus

inside her. "You are so lovely, darling," she heard
him whisper, "lovelier than ever in motherhood, did
you know that?"

"Am I?"

"Oh, my, yes."

As she turned to face him he leaned over her to
gaze tenderly into her eyes, eyes now flashing their
tawny reflection of the flickering firelight. Slowly,
he kissed her lips. She rose to meet his embrace,
warmly welcoming his tongue, rising passionately
as his body moved agilely above her own.

Much later, as the fire flickered and died, she still
lay awake. It had been many minutes since Hunter
had fallen into a deep, dead slumber, breathing
heavily—an odd, heavy sleep, it seemed to her. She
couldn't sleep. In spite of the excitement and packed
activity of the day, she simply could not get her mind
to be still. Something new had happened—a first.
Their lovemaking had been long and tender, and as
was most often true, she had reached a full and satisfying climax. But this time his did not follow hers in
the same pattern as before. This time he had simply
fallen away and drifted into sleep. It was as though
he hadn't been able—just couldn't . . . Could it have
been all that brandy? Reluctlantly she forced herself
to think it through. She had begun to notice that
Hunter seemed to be drinking more and longer these
days. Could it be her imagination? she wondered.
When he first got home from the north, he seemed
content with a couple of martinis before dinner, then
a little wine with the meal. But gradually he wanted
to put off eating, and he seemed to be drinking more
and more. But, so what? After all, this really was the
time of year to unwind. He'd worked hard pulling
Seasons together, so that he could be down here more
often with her. To scold him now about how late he
wanted to dine seemed an awful thing to bring into
their marriage. And today, well, for goodness' sake,

today was Christmas, their very first Christmas together. As for their sex tonight, it was still wonderful. He was gentle and caring and sought only to please her. And the truth was that they just about *had* worn each other out in these last eight months. "A marathon!" Hunter constantly shouted. "We're on a sexual marathon, and I have become the sacrificial lamb. There will be nothing left of me for my adoring public." So it was time to grow up. A man should be entitled to fall asleep once a year, especially on a holiday, with a little too much brandy under his belt. Besides, she had so much else. The baby was kicking strongly inside her, their new home was decorated, she had broadened career horizons, and her father was the state senator from the Thirteenth Senate District of Florida.

Of course she could go to sleep. The very hint of any anxiety was absurd. Still, she saw light breaking across the distant rows of orange trees and heard a cock crowing from someplace far away before she was able to drift off.

By January Alison got her first taste of what it was like to be around Hunter when he worked closely with his writers. Five of them were down as their houseguests in town, because the Sunfish Key A-frame was too long a drive out. Besides, Hunter refused to leave Alison alone in these last months of her pregnancy.

What Alison hadn't bargained for was the tension. And she was shocked when she stumbled onto the first loud argument among the men. Perhaps she should have remembered that scene she'd witnessed at the network studio in New York when Hunter scolded those actors on the set. She was stunned by the side of his personality that suddenly reemerged.

She walked in on the incident one night after work. She was excited, full of her day. She couldn't wait to tell Hunter the news. She had just produced her first commercial, one commissioned by a chain of west coast Florida grocery stores. Alison laughed to herself, knowing Hunter would kid her about that. Okay, so her first spot featured hams, Idaho potatoes, and a sale on butter—not glamorous at all. But she had written the copy and designed the camera moves, and it turned out to be a nice, clean thirty-second commercial. Best of all the client was pleased, and it appeared Channel 32 would land the annual account. Sam was ecstatic. "Ya done good, kid," he said enthusiastically. "This will be a nice soup-bone account if they sign, Alison."

"I'll keep my fingers crossed."

"Did you enjoy making it?"

"Oh, Sam, I loved it!"

He glanced down at her figure and smiled. "I may not let you go back to *Sarasota Midday* after Junior arrives, not if you turn into a commodity around here."

Alison drove the fifteen minutes to their house feeling good about this job shift. April was just around the corner, and with the baby here, she knew she'd want a little less frenzied pace than the daily show required.

She could hear shouting when she pulled in the drive. At first she thought the men were laughing over cocktails as was often the case when she drove up. But tonight these were shouts of anger, and Hunter's voice echoed across the patio over the rest.

As she hurried from her car she pulled her coat tighter around her. It was entirely too chilly for them still to be out on the patio. "I'm home," she called out. No one answered. The voices rose higher as the argument raged on. She hurried upstairs, cringing at what she overheard. Hunter was being a wretch, an absolute bastard! Suddenly she remembered his words, "Barrington's my alter ego. I like getting my bastard side out so that I can be my real self when I'm with you, Alison."

She paused at the landing and glanced down on the scene. She was stunned to see her husband moving angrily around the patio from man to man, waving his arms wildly and continuing to shout.

She flipped her radio on high before stepping in the shower, anxious to get the angry sounds from her ears. She felt terribly upset. It was true that Hunter had never once been a bastard with her, but ever since the writers came—almost two weeks now—he seemed to have changed. It had spilled over into their lives. Now nothing pleased him. At night he seemed drained, exhausted, and irritable. It was new to her to be unable to reach him.

By the middle of the third week she waited until very late one night before speaking up. Hunter was alone out on their balcony having a few brandies before bed. The house was dark, and she could see no light coming from the guest quarters over the garage. It was certainly no wonder. At dinner the men had drunk heavily. The air in the restaurant was electric. She didn't ask, didn't even want to know what had happened this time but knew it had to be some terrible new disagreement late this afternoon. Now she felt depressed, lonely. For one thing it was cold out, and Hunter had been outside for more than an hour with that damn bottle of brandy at his side. She walked to the French doors and opened one a crack. "Hunt, aren't you cold?"

"No. It's like spring in the city."

"Well, I'm cold."

He turned and eyed her in surprise. She was wearing a warm robe over her gown, and fuzzy slippers. He threw back his head in laughter. "Impossible. You're bundled up like an Eskimo. Besides, the fire is still going, and we have marvelous heat in the house."

Even in her anxiety it was wonderful to see him laugh. She spoke very seriously. "I stay cold inside when I can't get close to you. You've blocked me out for going on three weeks now. Is it always like this when you're working on *Seasons?*"

Slowly he put down his glass and stood, steadying himself on the arm of the chair. Slowly he walked over to the door, weaving just a little, as she opened it wider for him to come in. Inside he took her tenderly into his arms. "Oh, Alison, my love, my only true love of my life. How foolish of me." He buried his face in her hair and sighed deeply, sadly. "Can you forgive me?"

She felt him begin to sway, steadied him, then guided him over to the bed. "Of course I forgive you." She sat on the side of the bed while he pulled off of his clothes and crawled under the covers. "But won't you let me share? I thought that's what marriage was supposed to be about, Hunt. If all this gets you down, let me help just a little. *Tell* me if you're frustrated, if you're angry. Perhaps telling me will vent some of it, and you won't have to get so emotional with your crew."

He snorted. "My *crew,*" he said, closing his eyes dramatically, "is made up of imbecilic shits!"

Watching him closely, she hurried around to her side and crawled in beside him. She snuggled against him, enjoying his naked body against her warm gown. "Hunter?"

"Hmmm?" He didn't open his eyes.

"Can you feel the baby kicking?"

"Yes. It's wonderful."

They lay for moments in the darkness with only the low flicker of the fire to light the room, Alison's cheek against his shoulder. "Hunter, I think it's all become too much for you because they're staying here in the house. Don't get me wrong, darling, it's no bother to me. The new help is working out won-

derfully well. It's just that I believe it is too much for
you. Why don't you just take everyone out to the
beach house and hole up until you wind up this segment?"

Hunter was slow to speak. He spoke from almost
far away; his words were slurred. "Because I will not
leave you alone with the baby practically here. I
'splained that to you."

"Darling, this is only February. I'll be perfectly
safe. If you're worried I'll get Minnie to come over
and stay with me."

He lay for minutes without speaking. Alison wondered if he had gone to sleep. Then he said, "You're
right about the togetherness. It's getting to me. The
nex' time they come down, they'll simply have to
stay in a motel. We were too generous."

"I think Sunfish Key is the answer. After all, we
have that fabulous place to do with as we please.
That's what McIver meant it for."

Opening his eyes, he rolled on his side and gently kissed the tip of her nose. "You are so lovely,"
he whispered. "An' so smart. All right, my angel,
here's what I'll agree to: We'll move out to the
beach, those imbeciles and I, but I'll drive home to
you at night. Will you be nervous if it gets to be
midnight?"

"Of course not. I'm working on decorating the
nursery. I'm having a wonderful time, Hunt. Can
you believe I have only two more weeks to work,
then I'm on leave till July?"

He turned her on her back and leaned over to
kiss her lips warmly, hungrily. Her heart began to
beat faster. He lifted his lips from hers and gazed
into her eyes. "Alison Ames, I am desp'rately in
love with you." Alison watched his face in the
flickering reflection of the firelight. Suddenly the
tension was gone. The beautiful planes of his fore-

head and cheeks relaxed. He looked young and so terribly handsome.

Then he fell back against his pillow. Instantly he was in a dead, heavy sleep that gave her a little shiver of anxiety. It seemed the sleep of a man who'd been drugged.

On April 16, 1974, right on schedule, Alison gave birth to a seven-pound eleven-ounce child, a beautiful strawberry-haired daughter. It was an easy delivery, after only six hours of labor, and the joy of the moment when she first held her in her arms was one she would treasure the rest of her life. "Oh Hunt, isn't she absolutely exquisite?"

"Exquisite. Like my exquisite Alison."

"Are you happy?"

He lifted Alison's hand and kissed her fingertips. "It's everything now, complete. My life is complete. I thought you had given me all there ever could be." She smiled up into his eyes. "But now you've given me more."

When McIver looked down on the baby for the first time, he thought that his heart would burst. Together he and Alison stood in the hospital corridor and watched through the nursery window as his precious granddaughter balled up her little fists and screamed lustily. He turned to Alison anxiously. "Why doesn't someone pick her up?"

Alison laughed. "They will. It's healthy for her to cry. Oh, darling, isn't she beautiful?"

"Beautiful. Oh, my, yes."

"And a girl! The little granddaughter you've been badgering me to have."

"She's exactly as I pictured her."

"We're naming her for mother, Daddy. Alliene Carrington Ames."

She watched her father's eyes fill with tears. "We're going to call her Carrie."

* * *

It was less than eleven months later that the two of them stood looking through the same window at little McIver Watson Ames. In the dawn hours on March 6, 1975, another baby had been born to Alison and Hunter. Only Hunter wasn't in town at the time. Little Wattie had arrived a few days early. McIver and Minerva held watch in the St. Vincent's Hospital maternity waiting room.

The next day, as father and daughter stood together to look down at the newest child named for McIver, he said, "He's fine, darlin'. A fine boy."

"Isn't he, Daddy? I'm so happy. But this is it. Don't expect any more grandchildren from me. Hunter and I have our family now. Oh, darling, I feel so fortunate. Everything is going just right."

Things were anything but right, but the last person in the world she wanted to suspect it was her father. Alison's second pregnancy hadn't come as a surprise to her, but the news stunned Hunter. "My God, Alison, not so *soon!*"

"I'm a little in shock myself, Hunter." She tried to mask her astonishment that he wasn't prepared for the possibility. "But there it is. The doctor says around March tenth."

Hunter stood and walked over to his bar. He poured three fingers of Scotch and dropped a couple of ice cubes into the glass. "March! Carrie won't even have had her first birthday. Christ."

"That's right, but let's look on the positive side. We'd talked about having two children. Now we'll have our babies close together and that will be it."

"I certainly hope so. I'm too old to keep going *this* route much longer." He drained the glass and walked over to pour another. "I'm going ahead with the vasectomy now—this week."

Tears stung at Alison's eyes. What about her? How did he suppose she felt about going through the whole thing all over again? Carrie wasn't even four months old yet! She watched him walk over to the French doors and stare out across their balcony. "Aren't you the least bit pleased about it, Hunt? I'm not crazy about the timing, either, but I'm grateful I'm healthy."

He turned and eyed her apologetically. "Forgive me, sweet thing. Of course I'm happy. I was just shocked, that's all. I hadn't thought of another baby so soon."

Alison kept her hurt inside herself but was indignant that Hunter had behaved so selfishly. After all, she hadn't exactly managed her condition on her own. It, of course, had to be that rainy Sunday afternoon when Hunter's car came screeching in the driveway. He had been out at the beach place. She knew instantly that he hadn't been at Sunfish Key to write; he'd been out there drinking. But he was happily drunk at least, not somber and moody like he'd been since Carrie was born. In the entryway he pulled her into his arms and kissed her passionately. "I came home to ravage you," he whispered in her ear.

"Hunter, Minnie's in the kitchen. She'll hear you."

"Then we must escape upstairs." Laughing, he caught her hand and led her up to their room. Almost before she could close the door he'd begun to undress her, and within seconds they were flung naked across the big bed, and she felt him penetrate her, hot and deep, pounding without stopping.

"Hunter," she said. "You'd better stop! I haven't had time to—"

Suddenly he cried out exquisitely, and she knew it was too late. He groaned and lunged inside her again and again, then sighed a wonderful, ecstatic sigh. She could feel his heart pounding through the walls of his chest. Finally it began to slow. He lay on top of her for minutes, as heavy now as lead.

From the bassinet near the window the baby whimpered. "Hunter," Alison said, "let me up. Carrie's crying." Then the infant let out a wail.

Hunter groaned, then rousing, mumbled, "Oh, yes, the baby." He rolled over on his back and dropped off into a dead sleep.

Quickly Alison wrapped a robe around herself and lifted the baby to change her. She heard Minnie outside their bedroom door. "Miss Alison, do I hear Carrie?"

"Yes, Minnie. Just a minute." To the baby she crooned, "Shhh, darling. It's all right. You're going to eat now. Shhh." She opened the door only wide enough to step into the hall.

"I have the formula warmin'. You want me to feed her?"

"Would you, Minnie? Hunter's taking a little nap."

She hurried to the bidet. She had to get washed out. Please, God, don't let it be too late. What in the world had gotten into Hunter? He had never been so brutal, so uncaring. He had hurt her when he first entered her. She stepped into the shower, downright angry now. It was only the second time they'd had sex since Carrie was born. She could have understood his passion if it had been the first after so long a wait, but just the night before last they had enjoyed a wonderful, satisfying evening of lovemaking, their first in almost three months. So Hunter couldn't have been hungry. What *was* the matter with that man?

He was half-drunk, that's what.

But once the news of the baby was confirmed, she decided to make the best of it. She had to, even though she thought often about Hunter's original carelessness and his selfish attitude when he'd

been given the news. Was it possible he didn't remember taking her upstairs to bed that day at all?

As with Carrie, Alison worked until the end of her
seventh month. She had made the permanent switch
to commercial production now and had no wish to be
back on *Sarasota Midday*. She enjoyed the pace of a
comfortable nine-to-five, five-day week and was
getting good at her craft. The household was running smoothly because Minnie was with them full-
time now. McIver had made the offer to give up the
woman's services at the Big House when Carrie was
an infant. Minnie had agreed to make the move although she had originally expressed her doubts
about Hunter's enthusiasm in having her in his
house.

Minerva had begun to age but ever so subtly. She
still stood tall and proud, projecting a strength of
body and character that were impossible to disguise.
At forty-two she had not yet the first line on her face,
nor gray in her carefully combed black hair. But
there was something, an almost imperceptible something, that Alison could see in her that whispered
that she, too—even Minnie—was growing older. Alison hadn't wanted to face it, but she also saw decided signs of aging in McIver, and even Gordie had
gray in his hair. She didn't want Minnie to grow old.
She didn't want any of them to grow old. Instantly
she put the thought out of her mind as Minerva
voiced her doubts.

"What about Mr. Hunter?"

"What do you mean?"

"How would Mr. Hunter like havin' a full-time
black woman in his house?"

"Why, he'd love it. We've already decorated the
garage apartment for a guest house, but it will be
yours instead if you'll only say you'll come." Alison
began to slow the rocker where she sat with her

baby, feeling a certain uneasiness. "Of if you want to stay with us here in the house, that will be fine, too."

"That ain't what I mean. Mr. Hunter, he's . . ." Minerva suddenly turned and began to do busy work again at the sink.

"Go on, Minnie. I want to know what you're thinking."

She spun back around and exclaimed, "He's *different* from all us Watsons, Miss Alison. He's a fine man I know, and he loves you, but—"

Abruptly Alison got to her feet, holding her baby against her. "Don't worry about the differences, Minnie, please don't. Hunter will be pleased, very pleased, to have you with us. I know him better than anyone, and I'm sure of that." She walked slowly to the bay window and gazed out at her flower garden. So she knew. So Minnie already knew that things were no longer blissful. Covering, she turned back around and smiled brightly. "Well?" she asked.

Minerva smiled then, too, a broad, wonderful smile that showed her row of snow-white, perfect teeth. "I'll stay. Since you're sure Mr. Hunter will be pleased, I'll stay."

Minerva did stay on. Alison never bothered to talk it over with Hunter. She had learned long before Carrie was born not to concern him with any of the details of household management. It hurt her that he remained distant in decisions such as these. She had grown up in an atmosphere that was the opposite. Her brothers were in on everything that involved their households and seemed to thrive on it. But not so with Hunter Ames. "That's much better than hiring a stranger," had been his only comment when Alison told him Minerva was staying on.

Reluctantly Alison admitted to herself that Hunter was even less interested in the news of her world after Wattie was born. He still listened politely when she talked about her day, but she could tell his thoughts were miles away. He seemed tuned in only to the trivial happenings he'd begun to occupy himself with since Barrington had become a sub-lead in *Seasons,* a decision Alison wondered more than once if he regretted. He was restless now, and terribly moody. She learned to steel herself against the yo-yo of his emotional extremes. His New York trips came up every few weeks or so, and always he complained about having to go. Yet, oddly, he seemed happy just before the trips. Once there, in a complete flip, he called her every night, swearing he was lost without her and couldn't wait to come home. What would it take for him? Was there no place he could be happy, no situation that would please him? She had to face it, the man was a malcontent.

The nightmare ordeal of the writing team's descent upon them came like clockwork four times a year. The first experience had been a keen lesson for Alison. "Darling, just take over the beach place as long as it takes. I won't bring the children out, I promise." As always, Hunter was a bear while the writers were down. Alison kept as far away from them as she could. Unlike the first time Hunter rarely made the long drive in late at night during the weeks he now referred to as their brain blitzes. Well, that was fine. After all, moving south must have been an enormous adjustment for him to make. Born and raised in New York City and having had an entire career in the theater, with all its exhilarations and depressions, was a high that must have been hard to come down from. It must be the new environment. She simply had to be patient. It couldn't be solely the man's personality. Could it? Her life was very full now. She could be content with her husband's absences and even put up with his bad moods when he was around.

The summer after Wattie was born Hunter began to dabble in the local Little Theater. Alison was relieved. It could be the perfect answer to his restlessness between trips. But his severe mood swings continued to puzzle her. He was fiercely proud of the children but gave almost nothing of himself to them. In crowds he was quiet and withdrawn unless someone pulled him to the center, then at those times he was flamboyantly entertaining. On the infrequent times he went with her to the Grove he was a constant delight to her sisters-in-law and Clair, but in his everyday dealings with people he was icy cold, cutting even strangers dead. When alone, their sex, while infrequent now, was still good. He was an entirely separate person then, gentle and sweet, steadfastly declaring his love. Altogether life with Hunter Ames was an enigma.

Over and over again Hunter's words rang in her ears, that one statement he had made on the lazy Saturday afternoon before the wedding when he wanted to talk about Christina. They were words she had fluffed aside at the time, choosing to believe they could not be true. But now they came back to haunt her. "In fairness, Alison, so much of it was me. I wish I could blame it all on Christina, but I can't." Still, she decided to make the best of it. This was the man she had married, and there was no margin for error—not this time. She was going to *see* to it that this one worked.

From all outward appearances the marriage was working beautifully. Alison and Hunter Ames seemed the ideal couple in town. They fit right in with Sarasota's most vital social set, an outstandingly attractive pair who led creative and fulfilling lives. They had two beautiful children and apparently a great deal of money, judging from the two homes they maintained, the cars they drove, the clothes they wore, and their general life-style. They became part of the community and, within a few years of their marriage, had a host of friends, among them prominent young professional people in the Sarasota area, the movers and the shakers. They attracted others magnetically; theirs were by far the most glamorous careers of all their crowd. It was fun to be invited to their parties, and people scrambled to reciprocate. Alison and Hunter entertained frequently at their home on the mainland, and on weekends the family retreated to Sunfish Key. They never seemed to be apart. They were the envy of all who knew them.

Alison was determined to carry the image off. No one was going to know that much of her time was spent in worry and dread, endless hours fraught with anxiety. Life with Hunter had become a nightmare monument to his vacillating moods and lengthy bouts of heavy drinking. The thing that saved her was that on occasion he would dry out completely for a month or so at a time. But the sober periods didn't last. His drinking always began again, usually precipitated by some holiday or crisis. And when Hunter began to drink again, his highs and lows were worse than ever. He was an actor, it seemed, destined for a role of personal tragedy.

There was a bit of the actress in Alison, too, and she called on it constantly to present the carefree happy front she intended for others. For years her family didn't suspect she was unhappy, and she was even able to hide it from Sam. She was positive she protected the children from the brunt of Hunter's moods, but the one person she was never able to fool was Minerva.

Alison wrapped herself in two things, her children and her career. She doted on Carrie and Wattie, hurrying to be with them at night. She laughed with them, read to them, took them on picnics and to the playground. They went often to the Grove, but always without Hunter. And at Channel 32 big things had begun to happen. Within two years of the first grocery-store spot, their commercial business caught fire and mushroomed. Sam named her Creative Director and gave her a plush office in the brand-new wing, just down the hall from his. Before long she needed a secretary, then an assistant, then another. By 1979, when Carrie was five years old and Wattie four, Alison had a five-person staff working under her, and the Channel 32 production facilities were booked sometimes weeks in advance. She had become the very thing Sam predicted, a commodity, and she loved it. At work she was able to push back all that was pressing in on her at home, able to quell the tide of emotion that flooded her these days—the anger, the bitter disillusionment she felt in Hunter. Their relationship had become so sad to her, a broken dream.

Something happened that same year, something she ached over, something that took the carefree girl out of her forever. For the first time in her adult life she lost someone dear that she loved. Her friend Ben Hewett died. The night of the funeral she wanted to turn to Hunter for consolation, but when she rushed home to the house on the mainland, she found a note from him that he'd decided to spend the night at the beach.

Three days after Thanksgiving of 1979, Hunter hit her with some stunning news: He had written Barrington Dodd out of *Seasons*. He didn't mention it to her until it was over and the segment had been recorded on videotape. Alison knew his New York trip was a little longer than usual this time; he hadn't gotten home for Thanksgiving. But she was shocked, totally speechless, when he told her why.

They were sitting together on the sofa in their

bedroom, enjoying an open fire. It was chilly outside, a cloudless, gorgeous Sunday afternoon. Things were anything but right between them, but Alison felt fairly content that day. She was addressing Christmas cards, and Hunter was deeply engrossed in a book. Since early morning he'd had a lighthearted air about him, one of his festive holiday moods. She could take him when he was this way. He'd had some wine at lunch but, at least for the moment, didn't have a drink in his hand. He glanced over from his book and smiled at her. As always she felt a little tug, a thrill. She doubted that his smile would ever cease to enchant her. "Did you make my apologies Thursday at the Grove?" he asked.

She put the cards aside and turned to face him, pulling her knees up under her to settle in closer. Moments like these reminded her of old times, of the wonderful afternoons they'd shared at the beginning when they would talk for hours. She was glad he wanted to talk. " 'Course. Everyone missed you, but they understood."

"Everyone feeling good in the Watson clan?"

"Really good. The Laskells were there for the weekend. Uncle Jim was asking for you."

"And how is Sarasota's claim to fame in the world of visual media?"

"Don't be mean, Hunt. Just because you don't agree with Uncle Jim's editorials, you mustn't lose sight of the fact that he's my father's closest friend."

"Has it gone to his head that he's become publisher of *The Suncoast Star* now, too?"

"Not in the slightest. He's been editor for years. Publisher and editor only makes sense. Uncle Jim's a sweetheart. He's like family to me. He and Daddy were fraternity brothers back in the thirties. Did I ever tell you he was the one who introduced McIver to Mother?"

"No."

"I do wish you could have been with us Thursday. You've never been around the Laskells except at stuffy old cocktail parties here in town. At the Grove they're so at home, so relaxed. You'll be crazy about Aunt Millie when you get to know her. She's one of Barrington's most rabid fans."

"Next time they're scheduled over there I'll make a sincere effort." He reached over and stoked her cheek. "Truly I will, sweet." He smiled his devastating smile again.

"I do hope you can come home with me more often, Hunter. Everyone just loves it when you're there. You should see Carrie and Wattie with their cousins lately. They eat up the attention the boys give them."

Hunter turned abruptly and glanced in the direction of his liquor cabinet. "I'm sure," he said detachedly.

Alison struggled to keep the conversation alive, aware he was beginning to be bored. "Uncle Jim says McIver's landslide election in seventy-six clinched his political future, that he can be state senator from the Thirteenth District the rest of his life if he wants it," she said, laughing. "He's a born vote-getter. Uncle Jim says—"

Hunter jumped to his feet and stood over her in irritation. "I just told you I'll make an effort to hear out good old Uncle Jim, Alison." He walked over to the tiny bar and began to mix a pitcher of martinis. "I'll be with you to listen to the entire *bunch* more often now," he added dramatically.

Stinging from the chop, she stared at him in silence.

"Don't you want to know why?"

"I guess so," she said quietly, struggling to keep her own temper under control.

"It's because I'll be doing very little traveling to New York from now on."

"Really?" Alison winced as her husband poured a goblet to the brim and popped in a skewered pair of olives. It was only twelve-thirty in the afternoon.

"Yes, really. Join me in a toast, my dear? It's a special occasion."

"Oh?"

"A martini or some wine?"

"I think I'll have a martini today. Sounds important."

He grinned broadly. "What a delightful surprise!"

"What is it, Hunt? You've got my curiosity up."

He made himself comfortable and clinked his glass to hers. "We're drinking to Barrington's sad demise. Old Barrington Dodd is now an ash." He threw back his head in laughter. "Yes, you might say that Barrington has made a final ash of himself."

"Stop joking, Hunt." She sipped the strong drink and made a face.

"The funeral extends for four days. That's why I was longer in getting back this time. All four episodes were loaded with flashbacks."

Suddenly she sat forward and stared at him. "Are you serious?"

"Completely." He continued to chuckle and drink.

"Barrington's *dead*, written out of the script for good?"

"For good and all."

"Hunter! I can't believe my own ears. Barrington's dead? You let Barrington die?" He continued to chuckle. "But why? Why on earth would you do a thing like that?"

"Barrington was the type who wanted to die while he still looked good."

"Okay, Hunter, game's over. Now you can stop this nonsense. Honestly, sometimes you can be such a tease." She bent down to pick up Amber and plopped the cat in her lap, then eyed her husband suspiciously. "You *were* teasing, right?"

"Tune in two weeks from Monday, my dear, and see for yourself."

"It can't be. Barrington's the main character in *Seasons*. I don't care if you *have* reduced him to a sub-lead. Barrington Dodd *is Seasons*. Hunter, your fans will be devastated." She shook her head in astonishment. "I simply don't understand it at all." After a long silence, "Why, Hunter?"

"Look at me, Alison. Look carefully. What do you see?"

"I see my husband, possibly the handsomest man I've ever known."

"You see an aging actor."

"Don't be absurd, darling. You can't be serious. Why, I think you look wonderful—better and better all the time."

He stood and walked dramatically back over to the liquor cabinet. "For God's sake, Alison, open your eyes. Listen to me, my little child bride, I am going to be forty-eight years old on December twenty-fourth. Forty-*eight!*"

"So?"

He rolled his eyes. He walked back over and stood in front of her, then began to slap himself under the chin with the backs of his fingers. "Don't you see the loose skin here—the lines around my mouth, under my eyes?"

"Oh, Hunt, for goodness sake. You're being ridiculous. I don't believe this. You look maybe forty at the most, a wonderful forty, a marvelous forty! I just hope I look half as good when I'm forty."

"That's right. Rub in the gap between us."

Recoiling, "Hunter, how can you say such a thing? I've never, not once, even noticed the age difference between us, let alone rubbed it in. Please take back what you just said."

"No, because I meant it." He marched back to
the bar and poured himself a double. Alison
watched him in bewilderment, stunned, hurt by
the words that still hung brittle in the air. "And
I'll tell you why!" he exploded. "Because I think
you've been thinking it all along. I think there is
never a day in which you aren't aware you are
young enough to be my daughter." He sneered.
"My perfect sweet little daughter, Alison. Alison,
the perfect homemaker. Alison, the perfect career
woman. Alison, always the perfect little mother,
forever running off and frolicking on picnics with
the children." He flopped back down on the sofa
and sighed deeply. "Forever with them, never
with me."

Fighting tears, "You've never wanted to go with
us."

"Oh, why don't we forget it, shall we?" He laid his
head back and closed his eyes. "Shall I tell you how
Barrington checked out?" Alison was silent. He
opened his eyes and smiled over at her. "He did it in
a very dramatic way."

"He did it? What are you talking about?"

"Suicide, what else?"

"Hunter!"

"Think about it, darling. What better way for a
man of such utterly low moral character to die? His
death was in total keeping with his life." He let out a
low, sadistic chuckle. "Of course, he chose the painless way. No guns or razor blades for Barrington.
Just a nice quiet overdose, a delightful handful of
pills."

"Oh, my God. I don't believe this."

"Don't you think that would be the painless way to
go, my dear? A nice quiet handful of Seconals? Why,
it would be rather like passing out, I would think."
He laughed again. "Only you'd never wake up to a
hangover."

"I think it's absolutely macabre. I'm amazed your producers allowed it."

"Alison, when are you ever going to understand that *I* am *In Seasons of Change? I* write the drama. *I* decide the direction the characters lives—*and* deaths—will take. When I decided Barrington's time had come, it was done." He laid his head back and closed his eyes again. "I think I chose a brilliant way. Suicide; nice quiet, painless suicide. Delicious." Chuckling again, "I could have had him murdered or die in a bloody automobile accident. I *could* have had him get cancer. Oh, my, that could have been drawn out and sad."

"Hunter!" Without opening his eyes Hunter drained his glass and continued to lie back and laugh. Alison watched for a moment only. Totally disgusted, she stood and quietly left the room. That night she slept on the sofa bed in the den. As far as she knew Hunter drank till he passed out.

The next morning Hunter rose while she was still dressing, something he hadn't done in years. He stood behind her at her dressing table and gently took her shoulders in his hands. "Can you forgive me, darling?" Their eyes met in the mirror. Alison struggled not to cry. "I was a monster yesterday," he said. Bending to kiss the top of her head, "I wouldn't blame you if you don't forgive me, but I am asking you, humbly *begging* you to. Oh, Alison, my lovely Alison, my life! Why would I ever be cruel to you? You've never been anything but wonderful to me, supportive and kind. Darling, I didn't mean the things I said." Meeting her eyes in the reflection, he said, "Can't you see, I am flailing out against myself, not at you?"

"I can see that, yes. But it doesn't make it hurt less."

He circled around and crouched beside her.

"Please forgive me, Alison, please." He laid his head
for a moment on her lap and began to cry. "Alison, I
want so to hold you." He waited, pleading with his
eyes.

Finally she nodded yes. He got to his feet and
pulled her gratefully into his arms. She felt his
kisses on her neck, then more tears. It was sad. It
was pitiful. Breaking away, she said, "I have to go.
I'm late."

"Alison, let's be alone tonight. I'll take a room
at Longboat Key, *our* room. Let's be alone again
in our room, darling. Let me show you my love
tonight."

"More than anything I want things to be right
between us, Hunter, but I'm terrified that you're
destroying us." She gazed seriously into his face.
"Isn't it time you faced up to your drinking problem?"

"Yes." Sighing deeply, "I'll make things right
again. You'll see. These aren't just words. You'll see
because this time I am going to show you."

For a time things became good again between
them. For something over two years Alison was
happy a great proportion of the time. Things were
better. Hunter seemed to have changed. Finally he
was ready to embrace life and all of the fine things it
had to offer. At least he gave a very convincing performance that this was true. Beginning with that
night they shared on Longboat Key until Christmas
Eve 1981—Hunter's fiftieth birthday—he did not
take a sip of alcohol. But on the morning of that day
he began the combined celebration and commisera-
tion that marked his half century milestone, and
before the hour came to tuck the children into bed
and put the packages under the tree, Alison knew
the misery had begun again.

The misery, the slow, destructive defeat that

Hunter had chosen, with all of its mighty and wretched force, picked up at the precise place where it had left off, quite as though there had never been that peaceful period of time in between.

8

"Which one's the shrimp dip?"

"It's in that big green bowl with the tinfoil on top."

Alison smiled. Tinfoil. Minnie would never give up any of her childhood words. "Can you think of anything I've forgotten?"

"Cain't think of a thing. It's too early to put out the food." Minerva eyed her girl appraisingly. "You ain't dressed, chile, and it's seven-thirty."

"I'm ready all except for my dress. No one ever gets to these things on time, you know that. It's fashionable to be late." She reached across Minerva's worktable and scooped up a finger full of chicken salad and popped it in her mouth. "Mmmmm. The best yet."

"Won't be enough if you go eatin' it now." She slapped Alison's hand with her spatula. "I know you and chicken salad."

Alison giggled. "I could eat a bucket of it." She watched the black woman add another to the great pile of tiny sandwiches on Alliene's best silver tray. Quick as a wink she grabbed one and ran from the kitchen.

"You're bad as the chillun," Minerva called after her.

It was the night of December 23, 1983, the night of their fifth annual Christmas party. It had become a tradition to have the party on the twenty-third, a combined celebration of Christmas and Hunter's birthday on the twenty-fourth. It was going to be a huge affair tonight. Each year it seemed to get a little bigger. Everyone in their social crowd looked forward to it, and it paid back business obligations as well.

Tonight there promised to be an odd mixture of people. Suddenly, in only the last few months, Hunter had begun socializing with a strange group of actors in local theatrical circles, something he'd never done in the past. He'd invited a group of them tonight, plus his actor buddy Josh Meriweather from New York. His daughter Ann had flown in on her annual trip to see him, and there were dozens of new people coming, friends Alison had made in the past year. She didn't care how big the damn thing had gotten, just as long as it didn't rain and force the crowd indoors.

She hurried up the stairs and paused at the landing to glance out. Darkness had already fallen, but the lighted patio winked warmly in its dressing of multicolored lights. It was a gorgeous night, brisk but not too cold. No sign of rain. Good. On the way to her dressing room she noticed Hunter on the balcony. He was leaning on the railing with a drink in his hand. Alison thought wistfully about how nice those first three holiday parties had been when he'd drunk only plain tonic and lime. Unhappily, the sober period was now over, but the subject was never discussed. It was forbidden. She had argued with him only once, just days after his fiftieth birthday on the day following the third in their string Christmas parties. "Is it all going to start again, Hunt?"

In a rage he shouted, "I *told* you I could stop drinking, and I *showed* you I could stop. Don't ever speak to me about it again."

Well, she never had, and she never intended to.

From then on it had become only a question of time
until she screwed up the courage to divorce him or at
least legally separate. She dreaded taking the action, detested the idea of being a twice-divorced
woman, and managed to keep putting it off. But
she'd pretty well decided 1984 was to be the year.
One of the reasons she so wanted tonight's party to
be a happy one was that she felt it would be their
last. She'd see it through the holidays, then in January meet with Dwight Anderson and get on with it.
Dwight had been the Watson attorney for thirty
years, and it might take his wizardry to untangle the
financial complication of the mutual holdings she
and Hunter now shared. It was going to be a horrible
mess.

Alison's heartbreak was complete. The last two
years had been bearable only because she rarely saw
Hunter anymore. They were practically separated,
anyhow. Except for very occasional trips to the mainland, he lived at Sunfish Key, surrounding himself
with his strange bunch of friends: actors, musicians,
and artists who were constantly at the beach house
whenever Alison took the children out for a swim.
She disliked most of them intensely. They dressed in
a bizarre fashion, wore punk haircuts, and were
vague and hazy in their speech; evidence, no doubt,
that they were into drugs. She didn't think enough of
any of them to care. Eventually she quit going to the
beach altogether.

Besides, her life apart from Hunter was full. Her
career was at its peak, and she and the children
spent most weekends at the Grove. An active child,
Carrie was almost ten years old, and Wattie was a
quiet youngster who enjoyed the political action that
surrounded his grandfather.

Alison liked it, too. It was fun, exhilarating to be
with her father's friends. Someone important was always around. There were intimate dinner parties at

the Big House, and frequent cocktail parties at Gordie's and Todd's. Alison didn't miss one. If people wondered why she was there without her famous husband they never said so. McIver was the last person to question her. On the contrary, without her ever asking him to, he covered for Hunter. More than once she heard him say, "Oh, Hunter couldn't make it tonight. He's working on a novel, you know. He needs time alone for that. Aren't we fortunate that he urges Alison and the children to come without him."

A novel, ha! She'd bet that he hadn't accomplished ten pages, total, in three years. The reason Hunter spent all that time out there alone was to feed his habit without her anywhere around. Well, fine. That was just fine. Pretty soon he'd be having plenty of time without her *any*where around. She squared her shoulders and faced herself in the mirror. And he'd better not ruin things for her tonight. Tonight, as she never had before, she intended to play out the charade of the happily married woman to the hilt.

It promised to be her Academy Award. Her Christmas party was the social high point of her year. She loved to entertain, and weeks of planning went into the party. Of the more than three hundred guests, only Patsy and Jim Peterson, their next-door neighbors, were aware that Alison was anything other than the happiest, luckiest lady in town. She slipped her dress off the hanger and stepped into it. She was wearing silk tonight, in a shade of light sherry, an Yves St. Laurent original she'd paid an extravagant price for. She adored it. It was fashioned with a deep, square neckline that plunged to a deeper square in back, all nipped to a tiny waistline with folds of silk falling softly to the floor. Her only jewelry was the magnificent topaz pendant McIver had given her on her last birthday, with tiny, exquisite, perfectly matched stones for her ears.

She thought about her birthday as she fastened
the slim gold posts behind her ears. July twenty-
ninth, her thirty-second. She'd chalked up a couple
of birthdays herself. After all, she'd turned thirty
the same year as Hunter's fiftieth, only she didn't
freak out over it. It had pinched a little, too. Hunter
didn't have a corner on the vanity market.

She struggled with her zipper and thought of
going out on the balcony to ask Hunter for help. No.
Why bother? She did everything else without him
these days. She could manage her zipper. There.

She stood for a moment in front of her full-length
mirror, eyeing herself critically, turning to peer over
her shoulder at her back as she tugged at the folds of
silk. Actually she was lovely, perhaps lovelier than
she'd ever been, now in the full bloom of womanhood.
She wore her hair down and loosely turned under,
falling from a center part. It formed a shiny halo
around her face, which was carefully made up in
tawny shades of blush and eye shadow, understated
and elegant.

She heard Hunter call down to someone at the
party below. Maybe some of the guests were on time
after all. She braced herself and hurried across the
bedroom carpet. Please, Hunter, not tonight, okay?
Don't screw things up tonight. She wanted tonight to
be so special. All her family had come over from the
Grove. The boys were quite grown-up now. A couple
of them drove over in their own cars. Her father, of
course, brought Clair. Very properly, Alison had
given them the two separate upstairs guest rooms.
She thought it was funny. Adorable and funny. They
really had lasted a long time, over ten years now.
Gosh, was Daddy really going to be seventy-seven in
March? She couldn't believe it. To her he would always seem young. But he looked tired to her lately.
She was going to have a talk with him about seeing a

doctor just as soon as the excitement of the party died down.

Alison smiled to see him standing at the foot of the stairway when she walked down. He was looking up at her eagerly, wearing his best little boy expression, the look he had given her so many times over the years. "My, but you're beautiful tonight, pet."

"Thank you, darling. You're mightly handsome yourself." Alison stopped on the last step and looked down into his wonderful face. She patted his cheek, then bent to kiss the place. "I'm wearing my topaz. I bought this dress just to show it off."

"Beautiful. Just beautiful."

Together they joined Clair by the fire. "How lovely you look tonight, Clair," Alison said.

"I was just thinkin' that about you, darlin'. My goodness, Alison, you always manage to make us poor mortals look pale by comparison. Why, you are absolutely gorgeous tonight!"

In truth Clair was gorgeous herself in bright, Christmas-red peau de soie. The diamond jewelry McIver had given her reflected flashing colors from the firelight. Clair was a handsome woman, full-bodied and sensual. Her short hair, frosted only lightly with gray, framed lovely hazel eyes and incredibly young-looking skin. Alison gazed at the two of them fondly. They seemed totally content with one another. She'd given up wondering why they never married. Everyone had. It really didn't matter.

Alison heard Hunter's loud laughter from the patio. When did he come downstairs? He must have used the backstairs through the kitchen. So he didn't care to do the proper thing and be host. She shrugged. That was quite all right with her.

When she heard another raucous burst of laughter, she turned to look through the French doors. Hunter was bent over, broken up in glee. Ann stood beside him, laughing, too. Then she saw Josh. So—he was already here. When did he slip in? True to his pattern, he was early. Josh always came early and stayed late. Why did that annoy her so? She detested the egomaniac, that's why. She studied the young actor for a long moment. He was in the animated act of telling her husband another joke. He'd been in Sarasota for weeks this time, lingering long after the writers had left. He was the only actor in *Seasons* who came to Florida when the writers did, and he never seemed to understand when the time came to leave. Alison didn't understand it. What was the deal with this kid, other than the fact that he was Hunter's obvious successor to Barrington Dodd, the new man in the drama the fans were swooning over? Josh Meriweather, the fair-haired boy from the big city who was daytime's answer to J. R. It annoyed her to admit it, but Josh played the character brilliantly. She wondered how he could get by with being in Florida so often. Oh, that's right, Hunter masterminded his part.

Hunter suddenly whooped with laughter again and reached over to lift a glass of champagne from Delilah's tray. Alison felt a little shiver of dread. It was shaping up to be a tension-filled night. From outside she heard the car doors slamming, then chatter and laughter. She paused only for a split moment to gaze back out at her husband again, then, taking a deep breath, linked her arms through McIver's and Clair's, walking between them toward the dining room. "Come on, you two. Wait till you see the food. Daddy, I know you'll never believe this, but I made the shrimp dip all by myself. I want you to taste it before I start playing hostess."

The house was still, a lovely contrast to the music and laughter that filled the air until after three in the morning. Alison always liked the afterglow. It was her quiet time, her time to putter. It seemed es-

pecially right to her to be done with the festivity by
Christmas Eve, to settle into the serenity of Christmas and all it meant to her. She enjoyed taking her
time cleaning up after the party and thinking back
over the fun of it. And, too, Christmas Eve was such
a special day for the children. Their pitch of excitement grew stronger by the hour.

The house was quiet now. Ann had risen early and
caught the limo to the airport. And after a big breakfast McIver and Clair left for the Grove, the last of
the family to leave. It had been a super party, one of
the best. That is, up to the very end. Patsy and Jim
Peterson had been the last to leave at three-thirty,
except for Josh, of course. Patsy lingered in the
kitchen with Alison and Minerva, helping to put
away the food. "Don't bother with anything else,
Patsy," Alison said. "Minnie and I will finish."

"Just let me get the mayonnaise out of this silver
dish. It'll turn. Don't worry, Jim's not on call again
till the twenty-sixth."

"Terrific. How'd he swing that?"

Patsy laughed. "Maybe by being chief of staff at
St. Vincent's. God knows, it seems like he's on call
every other holiday of the year."

Jim ducked his head through the kitchen door.
"Come on, Patsy. I'm fading fast."

Alison turned to hug her friend. "Thanks, Patsy.
You're always wonderful at these things."

If Alison had a special friend in town it was Patsy
Peterson. Still something of a loner, as in her college
days, she found it hard to give herself freely to any
girl friend. But Patsy was dear. She and Jim were
marvelous next-door neighbors, undemanding and
always there. Alison knew they'd observed more
about Hunter's problem than they let on, but, of
course, nothing was ever said. Jim had been their
family doctor for ten years now. Even so, it was impossible to get Hunter in for a checkup. "Nonsense,"

he always shouted at the suggestion. "I'm the picture of health. *You* go, Alison."

When Alison watched her friends leave the party, walking hand in hand through the opening in the hedge, she wondered if Hunter even bothered to say good night. He and Josh were still drinking together on the patio. Hunter was sprawled out on a lounge by the pool, arguing heatedly about something or other. She dried her hands and turned to Minnie. "Get some sleep, darling. You've outdone yourself today."

"You all right, Miss Alison?"

" 'Course. It was great. Thanks for all you did."

Minerva cast a worried glance through the window at Hunter. The argument was getting louder. She hesitated, then said, "See you in the mornin'. God keep you safe, Miss Alison." Then she disappeared to her apartment.

Alison toyed with the idea of going to the patio to say good night before going upstairs. It suddenly struck her that she and Hunter had not exchanged a single word all night, not a syllable. They had just mingled, greeted, laughed, the perfect host and hostess. But she hesitated and turned away at the French doors when she saw how hot the argument had become.

She tiptoed up to her room. There were no lights evident from the guest rooms. Her father's rhythmic snoring sounded throughout the house. Alison smiled. It was familiar, comfortable. When she looked in on the children, they were sleeping soundly. She was ready to fall into bed when she heard loud, angry shouts from the patio below. My God. She stepped onto the balcony and called out, "Hunter! It's almost four o'clock!"

He was standing over Josh's lounge with his fists doubled up. The actor was laughing at him. Hunter turned angrily and shouted up to her, "Keep out of this, Alison. It doesn't concern you."

"It concerns me that you might disturb our guests—and our neighbors." Alison pulled her robe closer around her. It was chilly, and a heavy fog was beginning to settle in. Josh continued to laugh, rolling his head from side to side on the cushion. "Hunter, why don't you call it a night?"

"Keep *out*, I said!"

Alison retreated and pulled the doors firmly behind her. It would only enrage him further for her to say more. She cringed when she heard louder shouting. Josh wasn't laughing now. In a few minutes she heard a car door slam and the screech of tires in the pebble drive.

In bed she tossed angrily, unable to sleep. It had been such a nice party until the end. Why did he always take everything to the point of destruction? She hoped Clair hadn't heard the argument. No worry about McIver. McIver could sleep through a hurricane.

Finally the bedroom door opened, and Hunter fell across his side of the huge bed, fully dressed. He didn't even bother to pull down the covers. Alison inched as far away away from him as she could, over to the farthest edge of the bed. The stench of liquor filled the bedroom. She hated Hunter, *hated* him this minute. It had finally come to that. Well, this was it, *out.*

When she left the bedroom at nine the next morning he was still in bed, flat on his back, dressed in the clothes he'd worn to the party. Now, standing at the kitchen sink and nibbling one of last night's leftover sandwiches, the anger came flooding back. It was after two in the afternoon, a new record of sleeping in, even for Hunter. Minnie was humming to herself as she wrapped the sterling silver before storing it. "Where's my babies?" she asked Alison.

"They're over at Patsy's. It's okay. I called. Patsy says Jim's been up since noon. Jimmy needs the company. The three of them are going to string popcorn for the tree Patsy's letting them decorate in the yard."

"It was some party," Minnie commented. "Long time awindin' up."

Alison shot her a sidelong glance. Of course Minnie would have heard every word of the fierce fight between Hunter and Josh with her apartment so near the patio. "Yes. Josh always overstays his welcome."

"Ain't it sorta strange for Mr. Hunter to be sleepin' this late?" She gestured her head upstairs. "I mean, it seems mighty quiet up there to me."

Suddenly Alison felt the blood drain from her face. It *was* too quiet! The house was as quiet as a tomb. She turned and sprinted from the kitchen and raced up the stairway. She burst into their bedroom with his name on her lips. "Hunter!"

The bed was empty. Thank God. Why had she panicked? She knew why. It was the old, nagging dread that she would one day find him passed out from the drunk he'd never wake up from. But it was all right now. He must be in the bathroom. She turned to leave, then stopped dead. Something was wrong. She could feel it. The bathroom door was open a crack; a narrow path of light spilled in an ominous slice across the ice-blue bedroom carpet.

She tiptoed across the bedroom and pushed the door open wider. "Hunter?" She saw him then and screamed, her voice rising in hysteria. "Minnie! Minnie, come quick!" He was lying on the floor, crumpled against the vanity.

"Miss Alison?" Minerva's voice was breathless.

Alison crouched beside him, feeling his forehead. "Call Jim Peterson. Tell him Hunter's had an attack. Tell him not to tell the children." She unbuttoned Hunter's shirt and reached inside to feel his chest for a heartbeat. Oh, God. Why wasn't it

beating? She ran her hand across his chest. It was
warm. It had to be beating! Where was it? Why
wasn't it beating? Oh, Jesus God, don't let him die!
Oh, God! Oh, God, no!

Suddenly she noticed something. A bottle was lying on its side on the bathroom carpet. The lid was a
few inches away. Shaking all over, she picked the
bottle up. It was empty. Her vision blurred for a moment, then she forced her eyes to focus on the label.
Seconal. Chilled now, her heart sank. The prescription was made out to Hunter Ames. She squinted,
trying to see how many milligrams were in the tab-
lets. What *was* Seconal, anyhow, some sort of sleeping pill? She knew she'd heard the name someplace.

All at once she felt the blood drain away. She felt
faint. Seconal! She'd heard Hunter mention Seconal!
It was the drug Barrington Dodd used to kill himself
on *Seasons.*

Everything was over and all right before anyone
knew it happened. No one except Patsy and Jim and
Minnie. No one must know. No one must ever know
what he'd tried to do.

Somehow the three of them, she and Minnie and
Jim, had gotten Hunter into Jim's Cadillac and
raced the clock to the clinic. Thank God Jim had his
own private clinic. And thank God it was Christmas
eve. The nurses were all home for the holiday.

Alison watched in horror as Jim forced Hunter
through the grizzly process of pumping his stomach.
She turned her head away but listened as her husband retched and caught his breath and retched
again and again. "Can't let him sleep," were the
only words Jim said. Together they paced the floor,
he and Minerva, with Hunter dragging between
them.

When Alison tried to take her turn, Minerva

wouldn't let her. "I'm stronger than you, chile. I ain't tired. Just set down."

By the time they pulled back into the driveway, it had already turned dark. All of the houses on the block twinkled gaily with Christmas lights. Christmas! She had forgotten about Christmas. For the first time in hours Alison thought about the children. Patsy was at her front door. "They're in the kitchen eating supper. Jimmy's over here eating with them. Take it easy, hon. They're fine."

Once Hunter was in bed Jim turned to Alison. "He'll sleep normally now. Don't expect him to wake until tomorrow. He's going to have one helluva hangover this time, the granddaddy of them all. He'll wish it were simply the kind you get from booze."

Outside in the hall Alison asked, "Where would he have gotten those pills, Jim? I didn't know he had a prescription for Seconal."

"Not from me. He's apparently found himself a doctor up in Bradenton. The label on the bottle is from a pharmacy up there. Better face it, Alison. I think Hunter is into more than alcohol these days. I've been thinking it for a while lately."

Stunned, and feeling suddenly weak, she leaned against the wall. A chilling numbness crept around her like a shroud. Jim's voice seemed distant, as from the end of a tunnel far, far away. Her voice trembled when she spoke. "Do . . . do you mean you think Hunter's taking drugs?"

"Yes. And he's taking the real danger route this time. You just can't mix downers with alcohol, not if you want to see what Santa Claus dropped down the chimney." He crossed the few steps that separated them and hugged Alison tenderly. "But it's okay this time, hon. Hunter beat the odds. He's going to be all right. He's a lucky man that you checked on him when you did."

* * *

Zombielike, Alison managed to get through the balance of the holidays. The only thing that mattered to her was to guard the secret that Hunter's illness was a suicide attempt. The minute McIver heard that Hunter was ill, he rushed back to be with her, but she stuck to her story that he had suffered a heart attack. Yes, an angina attack, she insisted, and she and Minnie had rushed him to Jim's clinic in time, and he'd been put on the respirator, and with rest he was going to be just fine. Her father sat with her in her kitchen listening to the story. Minerva stood straight and tall at the kitchen sink with her back to them.

"What does the doctor say, pet?"

"Bed rest. Just lots of rest, and no more smoking or drinking, of course. You know, the rules they have for all cardiac patients."

"But shouldn't he be in the hospital—on one of those monitors?"

"No. Jim says it's fine to keep him here at home. We can take care of him, can't we, Minnie?"

"Yes, Miss Alison," she answered softly. "We'll take good care of him."

Yes, they were going to take care of him. It was a close call, but things were going to be all right now. In her heart Alison felt that there was hope for their happiness at last because surely Hunter would follow the doctor's orders and never abuse alcohol or drugs again. He would need her help, and it was her intention to stand by him. There would be no divorce. Not now.

She could help him, she knew she could. She would be his strength. This time he had really touched bottom. The only way now was up.

Part III

1

"Look at you, kid!" Sam let out a low whistle and rocked back in his chair. "You look like a *Vogue* cover. Where are you off to?"

"Believe it or not, they've asked me to speak for the Sales and Marketing Executives today. A luncheon at the Hyatt House. Do I really look okay?"

Sam hesitated for a long moment. Too long. It made Alison shift nervously. He was studying her in a strange way. "You *look* like ten million bucks, Alison. All except . . ."

She squared her shoulders and asked, "Except?"

"Alison, I'm worried about you. You have a troubled look, a—well, a lost look these days. Say, I know it's none of my business, but if you ever need a listener . . ."

Alison flushed and cast her eyes away. "I . . . I don't know what you mean, Sam." Then, returning his gaze, she smiled shyly and said, "Honest."

He eyed her seriously a second longer, then began to nod his head. Slowly his famous smile lit up his face. She relaxed. Everything was all right. He was smiling now. "Must have been my imagination. Go to it, kid. What's the speech about?"

"Low-budget commercial production, what else?" She sighed. "My specialty these days, remember? Everybody wants the no-frills model."

"It's coming up on eleven years since the day I

hired you. 'Bout time you started specializing in something."

She stopped at the door and made a face at him. "Just for that, don't expect me back till three o'clock."

Stuart Stratton noticed her the minute she walked through the doors. He was stunned. He'd never in his life seen such an attractive woman. He was standing among a small group of businessmen sipping a cocktail. Who was she? She'd never been to any of the meetings before, and he'd been a member of SME for over two years now. Must be new. He pretended to listen to the man next to him, but his gaze followed her when she melted into a cluster of people near the bar. She smiled her thanks to the waitress who brought her drink: A Bloody Mary. Stuart made a note of that.

"Don't you think so, Stu?"

"Huh? Oh yeah, sure. You bet."

"It's the way to go, right?"

"Hmmm?"

"It's like I just told Hank here, you're beginning to invest in property over near Sea World in a big way. It's the way to go."

"Can't lose." Stuart forced himself to listen, but he was straining to get a better look at her, whoever she was. A small crowd had gathered around her now. He could only see the top of her head. When the man who was blocking the way stepped back over to the bar, Stuart caught a full front view of Alison for the first time. Then she saw him. Across the room their eyes met. She gazed at him for a moment only, but it was one long moment. It was a special look, right square in the eyes. It was crazy as hell, but in that single instant he actually felt his heart beat faster. There was something private in the look. Instantly it was gone. Could he have imagined it? She was still facing his way, but now she wore a cool little smile, and her eyes had become distant.

Before Stuart could edge through the crowd he saw Harry Matheson lean in and say something to her, then take her elbow and guide her to the head table. Ah, so, she was the speaker. No wonder he'd never seen her before.

Stuart kept an eye on her during lunch and afterward pulled his coffee cup around to settle in and listen, turning his chair to get a better view. He couldn't hear everything the program chairman was saying over the din, but he caught her name. ". . . honored to have with us the creative director of WSBV, Channel 32, here in Sarasota. Alison Ames."

Alison Ames. He liked it. And now he knew where he could see her again. Channel 32 wasn't ten blocks from his office.

Alison answered the buzzer. "Yes, Diana."

"Your ten-thirty is here. Stuart Stratton, Stratton Real Estate."

Alison extended her hand across the desk as he entered. "Hi. I'm Alison Ames. I understand you're interested in television advertising, Mr. Stratton. Please have a seat. Let's talk about it."

"I wish you'd call me Stuart."

This was the man, the man across the room at the Hyatt the other day. "If you'll call me Alison . . ." she heard herself say. He was the one who stared so long at her, the one who seemed so familiar.

"I heard you speak at SME last week. I was impressed with what you do here at Channel 32. It seemed a relatively inexpensive way to get a project of mine in front of the central Florida viewers."

Alison listened and vaguely heard every word he said, but she struggled to concentrate. She was suddenly wrapped in the oddest, the strangest wave of emotion. She felt it all over again, that fleeting instant of communication she had experienced last week at the Hyatt. It seemed she had met him somewhere. College, maybe. But who? Why couldn't she place him?

He was explaining his project, and she pulled her attention to his words. "There's a development I'd like to advertise. It's a whole community, single-family homes, clusters, some condos. Two nice golf courses, tennis courts, a lake, a riding stable less than a mile . . ."

Her thoughts drifted away. He really was good-looking. He had an appeal, a strong look that drew her to him instantly. He was splendidly dressed. Awfully young to have that shock of gray hair; hardly out of his twenties, it seemed to her.

". . . actually it's situated near a hammock, you know, one of those central Florida thickets that . . ."

Alison felt her heart begin to trip oddly. This was a stranger, yet she felt as if she'd known him for years. He had that dark-haired look, gray now like Gordie's and Todd's, but she'd bet that his hair had been coal-black like her brothers' used to be when they were younger, like McIver's once was, too. Maybe that was it, a sort of Scottish look. But his eyes were clear blue. None of the Watsons had blue eyes except Keith, and he took after his mother's family. What was it, then, that made this man seem so familiar? She was positive now she hadn't known him in college. She'd have remembered. This reaction to him was insane.

Stuart was leaning forward now with his forearms on her desk, speaking earnestly. Suddenly he wasn't saying a word, just staring at her in question. "Excuse me?" she asked, embarrassed.

His eyes twinkled, but his tone was serious. "I just asked if I could air my commercial on any station I choose."

She watched him settle back to wait for her answer. It almost irritated her how comfortable he seemed to be when she was so ill at ease. He fixed his eyes on hers, seeming to appraise her, smiling a charming, utterly disarming smile.

Alison was dressed, as she generally was at the office, in a business outfit, a nubby linen suit with a loose jacket that hung long, and a skirt that fell below it into box pleats. It was a pale shade of yellow, like rich cream just before it turns to butter, and the collarless blouse peeping from the open jacket was silk, in the exact same shade. Her golden-red hair was caught up in a bun on the crown of her head, and her jewelry was elegant and simple, all of it gold except for a stunning topaz ring on the index finger of her left hand, two fingers away from her wide gold wedding band.

Alison tried to concentrate on the answer to Stuart's question. "Any station you choose?" she asked, too brightly. "Oh, you mean do you have to air *only* on Channel 32. Heavens, no. I mean, heavens, yes, you can air anywhere you choose. We simply produce it for you. It will be yours to do with as you please." He was staring at the rings on her fingers, staring at her wedding band. She flushed deeply and quickly moved her left hand to her top desk drawer, fumbling for the rate sheet. Where was it? What had she done with the damn thing? It was right here the day before. She caught a glimpse of him from the corner of her eye. He was grinning broadly now. "Of course we'd love it if you decide to place some air time here on Channel 32," she stammered. She was making an utter fool of herself. What was the matter with her?

"Does it cost a lot more to go out on location when we make the spot?"

"About double, but let me explain what you get when we take the crew out. It's a lot less expensive than it used to be when we had to take the truck. We have hand-held cameras now—they're the best—and it will depend if you want the type shots that will require one camera or two. I can show you some sample commercials and you'll see what I mean. But first let me show you the rate sheet. I—I have it right here somewhere. It's . . ."

"I want my first one to be right," Stuart said firmly. "I don't care what it costs. I prefer to go out on location. You really have to see Woods Acres with your own eyes to appreciate how terrific it is."

"Well, the cameras should certainly capture . . ." Gratefully she spotted her appointment book lying near her typewriter. That would do! She grabbed it up and began to leaf through it. "Fine. Let's find an opening for you. Woods Acres. I don't believe I'm familiar—"

"It's over near Sea World. A multiowner development in its fifth year. They just signed me on an exclusive."

"Really? My."

He grinned. "Yeah. They're taking a chance on me. For a year, anyhow."

"And from so far away."

"I have a small branch office in Kissimmee. It's tiny, just two salesmen. But my main office is here in town. I prefer to live over here. I love the Gulf."

Alison smiled. "Oh, so do I." She wouldn't remember the details later, but somehow they worked them out. When she found herself walking Stuart to the outer office, she had managed to place a rate sheet in his hand and her business card with his appointment scribbled on the back.

He lingered near the outer door. "Incidentally, do you go along on the location shoots, Alison?"

"Sometimes. I don't have to, or I can. It's up to the client."

"I'd like for you to." He smiled boyishly. "I'm wondering, is it allowed—is it all right for the client to go along and watch? I promise to keep out of the way."

"Of course. We'll have your script for approval by the end of next week. Let's see, that will be the sixteenth. Diana will go over it with you if I'm not here. Then I'll meet you bright and early the morning of Thursday March twenty-second. We'll need to get a seven-thirty start."

Alison stood at her open door until he disappeared, noticing his lanky frame and the energetic way he moved when he headed for the lobby. He had a vitality that was contagious. How nice to be around a man who seemed to be in a hurry to accomplish things for a change, not like those burned-out vegetables Hunter hung out with on the Key. It was nice, really nice.

She turned and slowly closed her office door, oblivious to the look exchanged between Diana and Jackie, and the expressions of astonishment on their faces.

March twentieth fell on a Tuesday. Alison cleared it with Sam to take the day off. She wanted to be with McIver on his birthday. "I'll make up for it before the week's out. I'm taking the crew clear over to Sea World Thursday," she said to him. "It will be a very long day."

"You doing a spot inside the amusement area?"

"No. This is a real-estate development not far from there." She didn't tell him how much she was looking forward to this appointment—or why.

After the birthday dinner Alison and her father lingered longer than the others over coffee. "Will you take a wee walk with me down to the lake, pet?" he asked her.

"Of course, darling."

They sat in the boat house enjoying the sunset on the water. Alison studied her father's face carefully.

He looked tired to her, drawn. "You feeling okay, McIver? What did the doctor say last week?"

"I'm fine. The doctor says I'm fine. But I'm hurting, sweetheart. That's why I want to talk to you. I'm hurting inside my heart."

"Darling! Why?" She leaned forward and took one of his big hands inside both of hers.

He gazed at her tenderly, searching for the words. Finally he spoke. "I'm hurting because you're hurting, Alison."

She cast her eyes away. "How long have you known?" she said.

"For many months. It wasn't a heart attack Christmas, was it?" He watched her sadly shake her head. "An accident then? An accident from drinking?"

"Yes," she whispered. Tears brimmed over and rolled down her cheeks.

"Don't be ashamed of it, Alison. Divorce the man! He's not deserving of you. No man has the right to make you weep."

"Oh, darling, please try to understand." Wiping away the tears with her fingertips, she went on, "Hunter's sick, Daddy. He's not a bad person, he's a sick person. I guess I've hung on this long because—well, I just kept thinking that if I stuck it out a little longer, maybe he would seek help. Jim Peterson says they have to hit bottom before they reach out." She drew a deep sigh. "I thought he had at Christmas, but apparently it's still to come. But don't you see, I'm letting him alone right now? He's out at the beach all alone." She stood and walked slowly over to gaze out at the lake. "Maybe out there he'll take a good look at himself and realize the things he really wants he already has—me, Carrie, Wattie." Softly she began to cry again. "The house, everything."

McIver shook his head sadly. "Oh, Alison, pet."

She spun around, gaining control now. "I don't want you to worry about us, Daddy. I realize the odds and won't be foolish about it. Hunter swears he loves me, and in his way I think he does. But I suspect the rest is a lie. He says he's out on the Key to work on his novel, but I'm pretty sure he's hiding because he's begun to drink again. I haven't caught him yet, but when I do . . ."

McIver rose and stood beside his daughter. "More than my life, Alison, I want your happiness. I'll stand behind you, darlin'."

"I know you will. I just have to wait and see. I can't be his warden. I refuse to drop in on him to spy. He's either going to pull it together or be a dead man. Jim Peterson spelled out those options to him with me as a witness." She squared her shoulders and faced her father. "You've lost respect for me, haven't you?" Without waiting, "For staying?"

McIver cleared his throat and said gently, "On the contrary, Alison, I admire your loyalty. Just please don't hang on because you're worrying about what *we* think, darlin'. Promise me you won't. We love you, Alison. You'll never be a failure in our eyes, no matter what you do with your life." He bent to kiss the top of her head. "Don't give the man much longer, darlin'. Set a date, then stick to it. Make him realize he can't play with your heartstrings forever. Set him a date, child, and if he hasn't taken hold of himself by then, come home. We'll take it to Dwight Anderson."

Thursday was the craziest, most carefree day Alison had spent in years. Stuart Stratton was plugged in nonstop. It wasn't that he interrupted her work but rather that he got such a kick out of seeing the video shots on the little monitor they'd brought along. He was like a little kid on a picnic. He seemed to approve of everything she did.

What flabbergasted her was that he put out so much energy. He seemed so happy, so lighthearted. She'd almost forgotten there were people who still knew how to laugh, a refreshing change from that damn Russian tragedy she'd been playing out for over ten years now.

Stuart had asked if she'd drive over with him. Diana wanted to ride in the station wagon with the crew, and it did seem silly for Stuart and her both to take cars when they could ride in one. He was walking around the Channel 32 parking lot when she pulled in at seven-thirty on the dot. He took her elbow and guided her over to his car, a shiny-new black Porsche.

"Neat car."

He nodded enthusiastically. "I've always wanted one. One of my goals."

"Do you have lots more?" she asked. "Goals?"

"You bet. I'm just getting started."

She slipped on her sunglasses and sat back, unaware of how closely Stuart was observing her; he was managing to catch tiny glances without really taking his eyes off the road. He relaxed as best he could but was about to go crazy with excitement. His last thought in the world ten days ago was to produce a television commercial to advertise Woods Acres. He chuckled inwardly. Who knows? Maybe the damn thing would actually pay off. All he knew was that the minute he saw her he wanted to get to know her, and by the time she finished with her spiel at SME he'd figured out exactly how he was going to do it. This was business, and everything was as proper as hell.

He took his time studying her, taking longer now because she was gazing out of the window to her right. She was wearing pants, and they gave her a long-legged look. They were a khaki color with a matching jacket. When she started to peel off her jacket, he reached over to help her and glanced for an instant at the full curve of her breasts under the soft cotton shirt. He couldn't help noticing the beautiful contour of her nipples. "Is it too hot in here?" he asked, quickly reaching to adjust the air.

"No, it's just right. I just wanted to get comfortable. It's a long ride over."

When she settled down for the three-hour drive, Alison felt a sense of closeness to Stuart in the tiny car that made her almost edgy. It was a sexual feeling that wrapped her in a mood of sensuality like none she had experienced in years. For all of the grief she had endured with Hunter, it had never crossed her mind to be unfaithful. It had been over two years now, from the day of their bitter clash following his fiftieth birthday, since they had made love. She thought about it sardonically. How sad. A relationship that had crested the heights, a love affair written in the stars. Their sexual relationship alone had been incredible; a marathon, as Hunter used to call it, that burned early, then began to die out. With each new disillusionment, with every new allegiance to his mistress, alcohol, Hunter had driven them further and further apart, until finally she cringed at the thought of being with him at all. Well, no matter, he rarely approached her anymore, anyhow. And on the few times he had approached her since the wretched day of his suicide attempt, she had always found some reasonable excuse to say no. He really didn't seem to care—not at all. In a way that had hurt her most of all.

No, sex was not a part of her world now. Just as surely as she had put it from her mind that miserable year she had spent at boarding school, she had erased it from her thoughts these past many months. Sex and misery didn't seem to go together. At least not for her they didn't. What on earth had gotten into her now? This was a total stranger she was seated beside, and they were traveling together on a very proper business trip. She didn't know a thing about the man. Probably had a wife and ten kids somewhere. She stole a glance when he wasn't looking. No. No, he didn't have a wife. He was single, she'd bet on it, and he attracted her completely. Again the feeling of familiarity came over her. He was someone comfortable to be around. And there was more. Whether she wanted to face it or not, she had a strong sexual pull to the man. It was his personality. She liked his looks, but it was really his personality that attracted her. He was so wide-open and positive in his ways, so funny and fun-loving. Around him she felt a release from the pent-up side of her she hadn't let loose in years. All those years of being so damn serious. What if . . .

Stop it, Alison. Stop it right this minute. There was absolutely no room in her life for a complication of any kind.

A strange and wonderful thing began to happen to Alison that spring, an entirely new experience to her. She found herself falling into the most delightful of friendships. For the first time in her life she discovered she could be friends with someone of the opposite sex. Except for the kind of support she had always enjoyed from her brothers, and with people like Sam, she'd never known the feeling before. Now, suddenly, she was face-to-face with a man, a young stranger her own age, who was offering to be her friend, no strings.

It was amazing how nicely she was able to block out Hunter and his destructive ways these days. How nice to laugh again, how nice not to make decisions, *not* to be responsible. How lovely to be with someone who enjoyed her company and made no demands at all.

In the spring of 1984 Alison and Stuart Stratton became fast friends, and it took her by surprise. That first day they traveled across the state was a busy one, and the following Monday when they sat in the dark booth at the studio to postproduce the footage they had shot at Woods Acres, she felt it again, the closeness, the warm feeling that came over her when she sat next to him. This time she didn't feel guilty. She had received no suggestion from the man that he intended to make any advance. She felt, instead, quite relaxed around him. He constantly made her laugh.

When the commercial was complete, Stuart turned to her and grinned. "I don't believe it. It's great! You're terrific."

Alison stood to shake his hand. "I'm glad you're pleased. Hope the sales at Woods Acres double. You were wonderful to work with, Stuart."

"Now I want to make another couple of spots."

"But you haven't even gotten this one on the air yet. Surely—"

"I don't need to. It's going to work for me, I'm sure of it. Now, let me tell you what I want you to book time for next. I want a commercial just to let them know who we are, a plain old Stratton Real Estate spot. I think I'll go for the low-budget model." He grinned. "See? I was paying attention. You said you can make one cheaper if you shoot it here on the set, right? Any problem?"

"Well, yes. I mean, no. I mean, no problem." Laughing, "And yes, we can make one in the studio. I just thought you might like to wait and see if this first one works. Don't you?"

"It'll work." Taking her arm, "Come on. Let's get some coffee."

"Why doesn't that Stratton guy take up an office in the space next to yours, Alison?" Sam asked. "I could move Diana out and start charging him big rent."

"Sam, you're funny."

"I'm not kidding, kid. You'd better watch yourself. I think the man's got a case going on you."

"Sam!"

"I'm serious. I've seen how he looks at you. Can't say I blame him."

"Sam, stop it. You're being absurd."

"What's he doing with all these commercials, Alison, eating them?"

Indignant now, "As a matter of fact he's *airing* them. You, my friend, if you'd bother to check with your sales department, are enjoying a very nice profit these days from Stratton Real Estate. Not just in production dollars either but in sales. He's airing like crazy on Channel 32. Don't you ever watch television?"

"Not if I can avoid it."

"Well, you should. You might just happen on a very nice spot I've done lately. Or two."

"Like maybe Stratton Real Estate spots?"

"Yes."

"And Stuart Stratton is doing it all to increase his business."

"What else would it be for? Sam, it's happening already. Stuart says he felt an immediate response the first week he went on the air. He's already hired a new salesman, and he's getting ready to enlarge his building. He says—"

"Well, you tell Stuart Stratton for me that I'm delighted he's found it pays to advertise."

"Sam, you're behaving like a jealous child. I should think you'd be pleased by all this."

Sam put out his cigarette and stood to leave. He lingered a moment, studying her seriously. "As a

matter of fact, I like the guy. I like him a lot. And I'm
pleased about one thing. I'm serious about this, Alison. I'm pleased, for whatever the reason, that you
don't seem to be so troubled lately."

"You sound just like McIver."

At the door he said, "Oh, almost forgot what I
came in for. Got a bit of news for you, kid."

"What is that?"

"I'm retiring the middle of July."

"Sam! No! I won't let you."

He chuckled softly. "It's done. I've turned in my
resignation. The ink's dry on the paper. The new
man will be on board June fifteenth. His name is
Fred Ingalls. He's coming from Channel 9 in
southern Utah, a real hotshot I understand, here to
look us over, kid. He's with our parent company."

She sat back, saddened, feeling suddenly lost. "So
you decided on early retirement after all."

"Had my sixty-second birthday last week."

The change Sam had spotted in Alison was true.
She was a lot happier lately. She had quit brooding
about the situation between herself and Hunter, had
put off thinking about it for a while. It was something she knew she must grapple with, but she
wasn't ready to face it, not now, not when she was
having so much fun. Still, her father's words stayed
with her, "Set him a date, child, and if he hasn't gotten hold of himself by then, come home."

She continued to drive to the Grove on weekends,
and occasionally she and her father talked. "Have
you come to a decision yet, sweetheart? April is almost gone."

"Not quite yet, Daddy. I know I have to, that I've
been an ostrich. But, oh, I don't know. I've been so
busy at the office. We're going crazy with new business in my department, and I've got to have things in
shape when Mr. Ingalls gets here the middle of June.

Honestly, I've hardly had time to think. I haven't seen Hunter in weeks."

"You don't talk on the telephone, either?"

"Oh, he calls every few days. Says he's working till all hours on the book. Says it's coming along," she added skeptically.

"You're looking better, pet. A bit more relaxed these days."

"I am, darling. It helped me to be open with you about things." Patting his arm, "Don't worry about me, McIver. I'm working things out."

When the time came, the decision was easy. It happened on a Saturday, the twenty-eighth of April, on one of the rare days she took the children to Sunfish Key. Alison decided to go at the last minute. "I hope you don't mind if I put you on the bus for Grove Dale this weekend," she said to Minerva. "I have an awful lot I need to catch up on here around the house. I think I'll take the children out for a swim Saturday. They haven't seen their father in weeks. And Hunter and I have some things we need to discuss."

Alison had fun on the drive out. With every passing year she'd begun to enjoy her children more. Alison thought wistfully of how nice it would have been to have their father's strength to lean on as well, but that was never to be. Apparently Hunter didn't have it within him to give of himself.

"I hate this car," Wattie said from the rear seat. "I like the 'vette."

"I'd no intention of going through the hassle of who held who on whose lap if we'd brought the 'vette."

"It was his turn for the bottom," Carrie said. "He ought to be happy you brought the wagon."

"Yeah, fat as you're getting, you're right."

"Watson Ames, I am no such thing!" Indignant,

the child turned to her mother. "Mother, make him take that back."

Alison laughed. "He's only trying to aggravate you, honey. Of course you're not fat. And you never will be if you pay attention to me instead of Minnie. If I'd eaten all Minnie put in front of me all my life, I'd be as fat as a butterball."

"That's what Granddaddy always says, 'fat as a butterball,' " Wattie chimed. "I think he means Carrie."

His sister turned in the front seat and swatted at him. "You're the one who's liable to be fat, Wattie."

"Hush, both of you," Alison said. "Nobody's going to be fat. Now pay attention and help me. We're getting into traffic."

Actually both of the children were very attractive. Carrie had turned ten nearly two weeks before and was almost the identical height and build that her mother had been at that age. She looked remarkably like Alison, although her hair was a deeper, more fiery shade of red. Her little nose and the shape of her mouth were Alison all over again, and her eyes were shaped like her mother's, but they were darkest blue. Carrie had something that was all her own, a combination of Alison's features and Hunter's way of looking out of his eyes, sometimes murky, sometimes crystal-clear—a haunting, lovely look.

Wattie was the family maverick. Sometimes his mother stared at him for minutes at a time trying to figure out who it was he took after. Her Todd grandparents had died before she was born, but she had seen many photographs of them and decided that if Wattie looked like anyone it had to be his great-grandfather Todd. McIver often said that he did. And there was something, a hint of something, that reminded her of Hunter's daughter Ann. Whoever he looked like, she loved it. He was an adorable nine-year-old, husky and cute. He had soft, light brown hair and big hazel eyes. His skin was unfreckled and tanned. Sometimes Alison thought he looked like Hunter; he had a way of setting his mouth in exasperation that was identical to his father's. And his smile was very much like Hunter's, too. But mostly Wattie was just Wattie. He was a happy child with a mind of his own, and he simply approached life head-on, undaunted by much of anything that came his way.

"It's my turn to throw the money in the basket," said Carrie as they approached the final toll.

"You're on the wrong side. I get to do it. I told you you should sit in the back. You never plan ahead, Carrie."

Alison sighed and handed the quarter over her shoulder to her son, glancing apologetically at her daughter. "He's right, honey. The one on the side of the basket gets to toss it, remember?"

"I get the backseat coming back." The child gazed out at the Gulf and asked wistfully, "Do you think Daddy will go swimming with us today?"

"It will depend if he has a stopping place. I tried calling him but kept getting a busy signal. Probably out of order from that storm yesterday."

When she approached the circle, Alison wondered if one of the neighbors was having a party. But when she spotted five cars crammed into their driveway, she had an uneasy sense of what was happening. She told the children to wait in the car and hurried up the walk. Loud music was blasting from the far deck, an ugly sound. She stepped into the cool entry and recoiled. The house was littered. People's clothes—jeans and bras and wet swimsuits and sneakers—were scattered everywhere. An empty beer can lay on its side on her beautiful antique credenza. She heard loud conversation from the deck and whoops of laughter from the loft upstairs. Her bedroom! There were people up there, more than two.

She recoiled from the sweet, pungent odor that filled the air, then marched angrily into the living room. Papers were strewn on the floor. Every ashtray was full. A man in a swimsuit was asleep on the floor near the picture window.

She looked around the room. He was there, sprawled out on her white sofa, dressed in jeans and a denim shirt. He was barefoot. He was lying on his back with a drink resting on his chest, balanced loosely in one hand. He was in a state of semi-sleep. "Hunter!" she shouted.

He opened his eyes and smiled. "Alison, my angel. What a delightful surprise." With a little effort he pulled himself up to a sitting position and patted the sofa beside him. "Come, my dear. Come sit with me. What can I fix you to drink?"

"Who are all these people?"

Looking around, "Who? You mean my guests? These are our guests, dear. Friends of ours. You met them at the Christmas party, remember? I invited them over for a little swim. Seemed such a lovely day."

"I want them out of my house."

"Alison, they are our friends."

Almost snarling now, "They are animals!" She stepped closer to him. He had an eerie look about him, a strange expression in his eyes. He was blinking a little in the bright sunlight that bathed the room. His blue-gray eyes looked weird, strangely blank. Then she realized why. They were dilated almost by half.

Suddenly she was aware of someone standing very close behind her. When she heard a soft chuckle, she whirled around to face Josh. He was laughing, laughing at them! He was enjoying the whole thing. Quickly she turned back to Hunter. "I'll be at home tomorrow, Hunter. We're not going to the Grove this weekend. I'll expect you to drive in in the morning. There are things we need to straighten out." When he opened his mouth to answer, she said, "I have nothing to say right now. You're not coherent enough to listen and retain. I'm leaving. Don't follow me in tonight. You're in no condition to drive. And don't phone. I don't intend to answer the telephone. Just get yourself down from this high you're on—whether it's booze or pills or pot or cocaine or all of them mixed together—and be at the house no later than noon tomorrow."

"Golly gee, Hunter," Josh said sarcastically, "sounds like the little lady means business."

Alison whipped around and slapped him full across the face with her open palm. Then she turned angrily back to her husband and said, "No excuses this time, Hunter. No promises. No apologies. No big fat declarations of love. You've worn them out. Just be there tomorrow if you ever expect to see me again." In a rage she tore from the house.

The phone began to ring shortly after dark. Alison let it ring. The children were asleep for the night. She was sitting on the balcony in the dark, trying to think things through, trying to come down from the destructive rage that was tearing at her insides. This then was it. She would tell Hunter to go back to New York, away from the children, away from all of them. And if he had any ideas about taking along any of the Watson money with him, well . . .

Part of her anger was at herself. What an utter, total fool to think she could have helped him pull it together. What a joke. If he wouldn't do it for himself, how vain to have supposed he would do it for her!

Well, there would be no changing her mind this

time. Tomorrow she would give him the news, and he
damn well better get here sobered up. She'd no intention of going through the speech more than once.

The phone began to ring again. Let it ring. He
only wants to tell me how much he loves me. He
wants to tell me I am his life. Disgusted and an-
grier still, she marched into the bedroom and
placed the telephone on her bed, muffling it with a
pillow, worried that it would soon wake the children. Before she reached the balcony, it rang
again. It ran incessantly. Why doesn't it stop ringing? Alison counted the rings. Eighteen. He was
really determined. Well, he wouldn't get his way
tonight. Then she thought she heard her name
called out. It was a female voice, high, childlike.
Startled, she jumped to her feet. Carrie? No, Carrie would never call her by her name.

"Alison!"

It was from the patio. It was Patsy. "Oh, my God,
Patsy! You scared me half to death."

"We knew you had to be home. Your car's in the
drive." Alison noticed her friend in a new way; she
looked odd to her. "Alison," Patsy asked, "why
wouldn't you answer your phone?"

"It's Hunter. I don't want to talk to him tonight."

Suddenly she knew. Something terrible had happened. The children! No, the children were safe in
bed. Then a feeling of total horror washed over her,
like a wave, a wave that came up suddenly, unex-
pectedly, from the Gulf. "My God, Patsy, tell me!
What is it?" Oh, God. Oh, God. It was terrible. She
knew from her friend's face. "Oh, Jesus God," she
said, "tell me."

"Alison, it's your father. He's in Lakeland Memorial. He's in Cardiac Intensive. You must hurry, Alison. Jim will drive you over. He's bringing the car
around. Don't wake the children. I'll bring Jimmy
and we'll sleep here. Gordie says for you to hurry."

2

The saddest part of the funeral was the graveside
service. She held up fairly well until then. She had
cried intermittently for three days and the three tormented sleepless nights since McIver had gone. Still,
somehow she held up. But at the grave it all became
too much.

Alison sat in the center of the first row that faced
the casket. Her brothers were on each side of her,
each of them holding one of her hands inside both of
his, holding them tightly. She could feel her brothers
near her, their strong bodies there to protect her,
their arms and shoulders pressing close, supporting
her, seeming a shelter, the strength it would take to
hold her up. She didn't release their hands to wipe
away the tears. She simply let them flow down her
face while the minister spoke. He was new. She
didn't know this one. He wasn't the same one who
had married her and Hunter. He stood facing them
on the far side of the casket. McIver's body was
closed inside that casket.

". . . And now hear the comfortable words of Our
Lord Jesus Christ . . ."

A terrible racking pain shuddered through her
body. He couldn't be gone. Not McIver. I love you so
much, McIver. Oh, Daddy, I love you so. Daddy, if I
am anything good in this world it is because you
made me that way. You gave me so much. You gave

me your love. "More than my life, Alison, I want your happiness, I'll stand behind you, darlin' . . ."

". . . In My Father's house are many mansions. I have come to prepare a place for you. . . ."

What will I be now, McIver? Who can I come to the Grove to visit? It was always you that I came to see, did you know that? Oh, I loved you all, but it was you, darling. Who will walk with me to the lake? Who'll sit with me in the swing?

Such pain. She felt such terrible pain. A hollow ache filled every fiber of her body, an ache you don't get over. The ache you die from. Her throat felt dry, closed over, sore. Her ribs heaved in agony.

"Our Father, Who art in Heaven . . ."

I love you, Daddy. I will miss you every day until the day I die.

She felt her brothers stand and pull her up between them. The minister was facing her now, leaning in very close, saying something. Please move. You're standing in the way. I can't see the casket unless you move. Why wouldn't he get out of the way? McIver was in that casket. Soon she wouldn't be able to see the casket. They're going to bury it. They're going to put it down there in the ground.

She felt Gordie turn her to lead her away. "Wait," she said. She stepped forward. She wanted to be close to him this one last time. Gordie and Todd went with her, supporting her. She smelled the roses. McIver loved roses. Grandfather grew such lovely roses. McIver always had fresh roses in the house, Grandfather's roses. Yellow roses. McIver loved yellow best. She knew why. It was because she told him once that she loved yellow best. His casket was covered with yellow roses.

She stood for a long moment with her head bowed and both hands on the casket. Then she took a single yellow rose from the roses that covered McIver. A rose to keep. Sadly she turned to leave.

Her brothers led her away, back to the black limousine. She heard Minerva behind them, weeping softly. She had been there in the first row with them, seated between the children with an arm around each of them, supporting them. But she knew Minnie's own heart was breaking, too. She caught a glimpse of the three of them when she turned to leave. Carrie was crying openly. Wattie just looked sad. Behind them were the boys, McIver's other grandsons. The three big boys were holding up, but Todd's boys were wiping tears away.

Then she passed the others. Hunter stood on the side between Jennifer and Margaret. Hunter was there, looking proper. He even looked sad. He'd been right there behind her, seated with the rest. Then she saw Clair. Jennifer had her arm around Clair. Clair was weeping into her handkerchief.

They were all leaving the cemetery now. Hundreds of people were leaving. Soon they would put McIver into the ground. Up ahead, her eyes focused on the black limousine. She stumbled and looked down. She had stumbled on the edge of a granite marker. BEN HEWETT, Born 1896—Died 1979.

If Ben's grave was here, then her mother's must be nearby. She looked around but couldn't find it, her final control slipping away, and she sobbed openly. It had to be here some place! Where was it? Oh, yes, it would be back there under the canopy, in the grave next to the one where they were going to put McIver. The next time she came here McIver would be down there, down in the ground beside her mother, back with his Alliene at last.

It was over now. At the limousine she started to look back. "Don't, Alison," said Gordie. "That's not McIver back there. McIver's at home, back at the Grove. Come on home now, sis. Come home with us to the Grove."

* * *

The only thing that made it bearable was that she'd gotten to the hospital in time to see her father alive. She was alone with him when he died, standing beside his bed, holding one of his big hands inside both of her own. He had hung on. He had held onto life so that he could see her one last time.

If he had already been gone there would be no way Alison could have endured ever looking at Hunter Ames again. As it was, she bore a consuming resentment toward him, a near hatred for what he had done that day, for being party to the debauchery she had stumbled onto at Sunfish Key. Hunter was why she wouldn't answer the phone. She'd have had other precious moments to be with McIver at the hospital if it hadn't been for Hunter. She shivered with rage each time she thought how close she came to missing those last few minutes of his life.

Her brothers assured her she couldn't have been with him any longer, anyhow. The visits were limited in Cardiac Intensive, with one family member allowed in at a time, and spaced very far apart. When she ran up the corridor, Gordie met her and put his arm around her. "He's been asking to see you, Alison. You can't stay in there long. The doctor says not to let him do much talking."

She stood at his bedside, holding his hand. He looked suddenly very old to her, lying there inside the oxygen tent. For the first time ever, McIver looked like an old man. His color was ashen, and the gray streaks in his black hair looked more pronounced with his hair against the pillow. But he was awake and he smiled warmly when he saw her. "Are you in pain, darling?" she whispered.

"Not now, sweetheart."

"You're going to get well, Daddy. You must do everything they tell you to and try very hard and get completely well. I'm going to come home to the Grove to take care of you myself. Minnie and I are going to come back home. We'll live with you now, the children and I. I'm going to quit my job and come back home."

He smiled weakly. "Are you now? Well, I'd like that, Alison." She watched him anxiously. She could tell it was difficult for him to speak. He closed his eyes for several moments, then looked tenderly into her eyes. "Alison, pet, there's something I need to say."

"Don't try to talk, darling. They'll only let me stay for a few minutes. The doctor wants you to rest. I'll be here, though, right outside your door. I won't leave, I promise, not for an instant. I'll come back in as soon as they'll let me."

McIver gripped her hand tightly. "I must say this now, sweetheart. Don't leave until you hear me. You must promise me something, Alison."

Tears began to roll down her cheeks. "Anything," she said.

"Promise me you'll leave the man soon." She nodded, unable to speak. "Promise me, sweetheart. He's not going to change. Don't waste another minute of your life with someone who won't be happy for you. You've a wonderful life ahead of you still, and there will be someone to share it with. You'll find him, pet, just as I found your mother. I promise you that. Like a wind that whistles in from the grove, when you least expect it, something wonderful will happen. Your mother fell into my world in just that way, and I have loved her deeply all of my life."

"I know, I know," she said. Tears fell openly now, down her cheeks and into their clenched hands.

McIver spoke with great difficulty now. "The right man for you will be there, darlin'. You'll see." He closed his eyes and grew very still.

Alison's heart raced wildly. "McIver? McIver?"

Slowly he opened his eyes, so slowly. He looked so very tired, but he smiled again, a tender, sweet smile intended for her alone. "You'll find him, Alison. You'll see, pet. The third time is bound to be the charm."

"I love you with all my heart, Daddy," she said, "with all my heart."

He nodded and smiled, then closed his eyes again. She felt his hand relax inside hers. When he died, there was still a tiny smile on his lips.

The rest of the month passed very slowly. Alison stayed on at the Grove, needing to be near the people she loved. "Stay as long as you need to," Sam said. "The girls are managing very well."

Patsy offered to keep the children until school was out, to spare their being uprooted. Weakly Alison said yes to anything and everything others offered that would help her. She was exhausted, drained, utterly void of any good feelings now. She knew that with time it would begin to pass, aware that time was the great healer but, for now, could only submit. For the first time in her life she had lost her fight. Everything was wrong, everything. She had lost her beloved father, the man who had given her life, the person who was her strength. In a few weeks' time she'd be losing Sam. Her marriage was shot, and with it her hopes and dreams and beliefs that there could be such a thing as happiness with a man. She seemed jinxed, doomed, and she didn't understand why. Her whole world, her feeling of security, was hanging by a thread. Little Alison Watson Ames, the rich and beautiful Alison Ames was lost. Rich and beautiful, the envy of everyone. What a joke. A sick, sad joke. None of it meant a thing, not now. A sob caught deep in her throat. Her feeling for life was wrapped darkly, gloomily, in a helpless, hopeless shroud of defeat.

Then another thing happened, a minor thing by comparison, but the same week they buried McIver they buried Amber as well. To lose her cat at that particular time triggered a new torrent of tears. She cried until her ribs ached from heaving, until her throat was raw. She lay for hours in her room in tormented agony over all of the things that had turned her world to black.

"Here, sis, open your eyes. I have a present for you." Todd dumped a beautiful yellow-striped cat on the pillow beside Alison's face. "He's a teenager. Couldn't find a yellow kitten, and you needed a cat today."

"Todd, he's beautiful!" She sat up and gathered the animal in her arms. "I love him! What's his name?"

"Nobody knows. I got him at the animal shelter. He was destined for the old gas chamber tomorrow."

"No!"

Todd grinned. "Yep, I got there in the nick of time. He's yours, Alison." He reached down and tried to grab him from her. "Unless you want me to take him back."

Alison swatted her brother's hand and cradled the cat. "Let's see," she crooned to the animal. "What shall we name you? I want a good Scottish name." She lifted him and studied his face as he hung limp in her hands. "I know." She grinned up at Todd. "MacGregor. Todd, meet MacGregor Watson Ames."

Alison grinned up at her brother, her eyes flashing her appreciation, and watched as he rested his shoulder on the doorjamb. Although she refused to think of any of her family as getting any older, Todd was beginning to show a little age, though a far cry from his forty-six years. He had stayed remarkably young and handsome. Always Gordie's look-alike until the last few years, lately there had been a decided separation in their appearances. The difference was about twenty pounds. "I keep tellin' you, man, it's those high exec killer lunches you're into," Todd loved to jab at his brother, "the high-on-the-hog meals and desk job routine that's getting to you. You can keep your office, I'll take my Jeep any day."

Gordie had settled into a dramatic resemblance to McIver, and McIver had taken on a little paunch at just about that same age. Todd was still lean, partly because his job entailed a more energetic outdoor day than his brother's did. Inside the Watson Properties network of corporations, the brothers were competitive in a fiercely loyal, friendly way. Over the years the empire had continued to grow, and the legacy that McIver had left behind was so huge and complex that it would take many months and teams of lawyers to organize and sort it out. Try as both sons might, they never had been able to get their father to keep Dwight Anderson, nor even them, fully informed of certain new pieces of property he decided to buy. The attorney was doing some grumbling this week over a couple of deeds the boys had uncovered in a small bank in Auburndale, from a safe-deposit box McIver had never bothered to mention owning. McIver had been a trustee there, and he had no doubt opened an account and taken a safe-deposit box as a gesture of confidence to the president of the young business.

But the details would clear themselves in time. The concentrate processing business was in excellent shape, just a cut behind the giants of the industry, and profits were high. Gordie prided himself on the kind of management that kept Watson Sundrenched quality at a premium. There were managers on many levels under the wing of both Watson men, but land acquisition continued to be Todd's particular baby. The total Watson holdings now exceeded fourteen thousand acres of rolling citrus-producing land, and they were buying more all the time. Gordon Watson's old original business of tree

grafting was still operative, giving work to dozens of
full-time employees and their families.

The company owned three citrus-packing plants
now, one in Grove Dale and two out in the county,
plus a huge chemical plant over in Auburndale, the
sole purpose of which was to discover productive uses
for citrus byproducts and waste. Company funding
was always behind the Citrus Agricultural Experiment Station over in Lake Alfred, and Gordie had a
team of Watson's own young engineers working on
creation of the one device no one had yet come up
with, a citrus harvester.

Both men sat on various boards in the surrounding communities, many of the spots having been va-
cated by their father as he slowed down the last few
years of his life. Yet it was Gordie who put the company's official foot forward; Todd saw to it that he
did. "Aw, come on, Gordie, you know you don't want
me to embarrass you today over at the Tower Club in
Tampa. They're downright ugly to folks who try to
get inside in jeans. Get some wear out of those three-
piece vested suits Margaret keeps havin' to let out
for you. Be my guest. Represent us both!"

"You're a regular asshole, you know that, don't
you, Todd?"

"Me? Aw, man, I'm doin' you a favor! I hear the
food in that joint is great."

Actually Gordie was more at home in jeans, too,
and generally wore them most days.

Life on the Grove was good. The two young women
who had married the Watson boys were into their
middle years now, too, and handling it with ease and
grace. Each ran a sprawling home, entertained frequently, and managed activities of teenage sons and
a staff of servants. Unlike her husband, Margaret
had not allowed an inch of extra weight to creep onto
her body; if anything, she was more slender than she
had been as a bride. Her hair was graying, and nice

comfortable lines had begun to settle in around her mouth and eyes. She was the energetic mother of three sons and was a regular volunteer at the learning disability institution over in Lakeland, with a specialty in helping autistic children.

Unlike her sister-in-law, Jennifer had to fight to keep her athletic body trim, but she did it with disciplined diet and exercise. She'd begun modeling again when Keith entered grammar school, and now she was in demand in central Florida, spending a great deal of her time commuting over to Orlando or Tampa on assignments. She was a perfect mother for boys because she was so sports-minded, and she could beat both of her sons at tennis.

The family was close-knit and strong, and life for them was exceptionally fine. The business was intricate and complicated, but every facet of it seemed to be thriving. Indeed there wasn't a person who knew the Watson bunch who didn't consider them among the most fortunate clan of Scots ever to grace the highland section of central Florida. But right now Alison didn't see anything good about anything. Her world was ebony-black, with no light visible ahead. It meant nothing to her that she was now one-third owner of all that had been McIver's. She didn't want his money, she wanted him back. From the moment Patsy told her to hurry to his side until this very instant she looked down at her new pet, nothing had interested her, nothing had made her smile. It was a tiny one, but this little spark of pleasure became the turning point in her recovery.

Typical of his contrary behavior, Hunter emerged during the week of the funeral as a prince. It took days before Alison could bear to look him in the face. Her heart was still so filled with rage for that insulting encounter at the Key that she could only tolerate being in his presence for minutes at a time. Everyone thought her grief caused her withdrawn behav-

ior. Only Hunter knew how angry she was with him.
But Hunter knew.

He had arrived at the Grove by noon the day following the death. To look at him no one would have
guessed that only yesterday he was lying in a stupor
of alcohol and drugs, wearing filthy jeans and shirt.
When he arrived, he was clear-eyed and clean-
shaven and dressed immaculately. He immediately
assumed a strong family role and was quietly supportive, helping the men make the funeral arrangements. He even took long walks with the children so
that Alison could be alone. He received the droves of
friends who called, and from appearances he was
everything in the world that Alison could want him
to be, the admiration of all.

From the shadows of the butler's pantry Alison
watched a scene that repelled her totally. Hunter
was seeing two elderly neighbor ladies to the door.
He spoke softly, attentively to each of them, and
shook hands warmly with them when they left. Alison heard one say to the other, "My goodness, what a
prize Alison got for herself in that man. Why, he
seems perfect in every way." What an actor the bastard really was. Alison had to admire him for that.
Until now she had never properly appreciated how
terrific he was at his craft.

The day after the funeral Hunter walked into Alison's room with a small bouquet of daisies. "Here are
some flowers sent especially with your name on
them."

"Who are they from?"

"I don't know. Do you want me to open the card?"

She lay with her back to him, wishing he would go
away. "Yes, read it."

"Alison, you are in my constant thoughts. Stuart
Stratton."

She rolled over on her back to look at the flowers.
"Oh."

"They're really quite lovely. Someone must know you well to know how you love daisies. Stuart Stratton. Anyone I know, dear?"

"He's a client. I made a few commercials for him this spring."

Hunter placed the flowers on her bedside table and left without comment. Alison reached over and read the card again, then quietly began to cry.

At night, when Hunter lay with her in her big bed, he didn't touch her. He knew how angry she was and was sensitive enough to keep away. They never talked, never exchanged a word, except for the times that she wept. Then he would ask, "Do you want me to hold you, Alison?"

"No."

"Is there anything I can do to help?"

"No."

"Then I'll leave you alone with it, darling. But I want you to know how very sad I am. I wish I could take away some of your pain."

But for everyone else's eyes the two of them were sharing a loving, comforting marriage, with Hunter as Alison's caring support. He carried off his role like a prince, never tasting a drop of alcohol the entire week he stayed at the Grove.

On the day he left he asked to see her alone. They went into Alliene's sun room and sat facing each other. Alison liked to sit in McIver's favorite wicker rocker now. It was the place she spent a great deal of her day.

"Alison, I want to ask you to let me work things out between us."

"I am very angry, Hunter, and very hurt." For a moment only, she turned her face away and drew a weary sigh. Then, fixing her eyes on his, she said firmly, "Just as soon as I gather the energy I'm divorcing you."

"Alison, no. I'm going to show you this time, darling. I'm through with words. Now I'll show you."

"You've said that before."

"I know, I know. But this is now. Things have changed for me. Everything has changed." He rose dramatically and began to prowl around the room. "My eyes are open at last. I *must* make you understand that!"

She continued to sit, expressionless, with her head back on the cushion.

In a rush of emotion he crouched beside her chair and implored her, "Please, hear me out. There's more. I have a new appreciation for life. Your father's death has done something urgent that my own brush with death didn't stir in me." He watched as tears flooded over and ran down her cheeks.

"Don't," she whispered. "Don't say those things if—"

"I want to live, my darling. And I want you with me. I want a proper home for the children, the sort of atmosphere McIver gave you to grow up in."

"McIver knew you were ruining my life."

Hunter winced, then stood tall, looking down at her. "I was. But that will never be again."

"We talked about your problem. He believed your only hope was with professional help."

"I don't need professional help, Alison. I can do it myself. It's just a question of willpower."

"You've batted zero in your efforts to do it yourself."

"I won't this time."

Cruelly she stared into his slate-blue eyes. "My father's deathbed wish was for me to leave you."

Hunter hung his head. Alison could hear his breath catch. "Please, Alison," he begged, "just one more chance. Please."

She closed her eyes in pain. "I'm so tired. I can't

think about it now. I'm going to stay here another couple of weeks. I'll call you when I get back."

A spark of hope kindled in his eyes. "You'll see. I'll show you."

"Show yourself, Hunt. I'll know when you show yourself."

"Will you promise to come back to me if you see the change?"

"I promise to think about it, that's all. I'll call you when I get back to Sarasota. I want you to stay at the beach house until I decide what to do."

"My first project is to get the place back in shape. It will be exactly as you like it, I promise. I'll confine the mess to the living room when the gang arrives Monday."

Alison looked puzzled. Then she remembered. "Oh, I'd forgotten. The brain-blitz boys are due, aren't they? What about those—those other people?" She made a face of distaste.

"None of them will be invited back. You have my word."

"Not even Josh?"

"Especially not Josh. I know you don't like him. I sent him back to New York before I came over here. I've already told him never to come down again."

"I almost believe you mean all this, this time," she said, eyeing him sadly.

He lingered by her chair. "You'll see, my darling. Without you, Alison, I would not wish to have life." He lifted her hand and, with his lips, brushed each fingertip, then opened out her palm and kissed it tenderly.

For a fleeting moment she felt a tinge of the old warmth there used to be between them, the gentle love that once had been so sweet. She saw a side to the man, a tender, boyish side that pulled her to him, especially now, when he seemed so vulnerable, so openly undeserving. Silently she watched tears form in his eyes and fall on her fingers. Then he was gone.

During the balance of her stay she heard from Hunter regularly. He sounded productive, happy, sober. He wasn't drinking, she was sure of it. But she didn't trust it, not for a minute.

Before she left Grove Dale, Alison met with the family lawyer. "Did McIver share anything with you about the problems I've been having at home?"

"Yes, he did. Please don't be angry with him for that, Alison. He was terribly worried about you and knew he'd have my confidentiality."

"I'm not angry. I'm glad. Perhaps you've gone ahead with some of the details."

"You're going through with the divorce then?"

"I'm not sure, Dwight. Hunter's being good right now. He's terrified of losing me, so he's promised to reform. But I don't trust it to last."

"Has he ever dried out before?"

"Oh, God, yes. Many times. It usually lasts three or four weeks. There was one time that he made it a bit over two years. But, you see, he always finds some reason that he needs to start again, either some trauma or something to celebrate."

"Why don't you just get it over with, honey?"

"I guess I'm a stubborn Scot who hates another failure. I just hate it, Dwight, hate it!"

"Hell, child, no one in the world even remembers about Calvin. Surely you're not still whipping yourself over that."

She smiled. "You sound like McIver. But there's more to it. The children, a unified home—you know. I guess I'm just too numb right now to be decisive. I'll give him a few weeks, I guess. If Hunter does all he's promised . . ."

"The old carrot."

"Hmmm?"

"The old carrot-and-stick routine."

Wearily she admitted, "I know. Look, Dwight, I'm sadder and a lot wiser these days. I really don't trust him at all. I want you to go ahead and draw everything up. The first time he falls off, and I mean this, the first time, then I'll give you a call and you're to get it through the courts as fast as you can. For one thing he's refusing professional help, and I really don't think he can pull it off alone. He means to, and I actually think he wants to this time, but I'm wondering if he can." She gazed away for seconds, then said wistfully, "Still, I believe in miracles. It would be so wonderful for the children. . . ."

Dwight studied her and shook his head. "I'll get things in order."

"You think I'm a fool, don't you?"

"It's your life, Alison. You'll turn loose when you're ready. No one can make that decision for you. But I will tell you this: You are a very wealthy woman now, and it's my job to see that you and the children are protected. Divorces can be very messy. And the scorned partner usually gets mean. It was McIver's strongest wish that if the man abuses you again, mentally or any other way, that we get him out of your life, hopefully back to New York, away from your homes and bank accounts by the fastest jet."

Alison drove back to Sarasota the last Saturday in May. She was so happy to be with her children that her grief, at least for the moment, was assuaged. Work would be good for her, too. She looked forward to Tuesday when the long Memorial Day weekend would end, and her life would take back up its regular pace.

She'd been giving some thought to driving to the beach to see Hunter, to see for herself how he was getting along. His calls had been tender lately, more lighthearted than in years, almost like the first Hunter she knew. There was no denying it, he had turned back into the charmer who swept her off her feet eleven years ago. Eleven years! Tomorrow would be their eleventh wedding anniversary. Maybe she might just drive out and surprise him tomorrow. She knew the writers were flying back to New York this afternoon; he would be out there alone. She decided to do it. She would know when she saw him if there was a spark of the old feeling left.

As she crossed the small bridge to Sunfish Key she enjoyed a certain feeling of contentment. It felt good to know Hunter had banned all those horrible people from the house. She'd never have to brace again for the hoards of strange types who used to wander in and out unannounced. He was certainly firm in that promise. When she entered their circle, she saw his light blue Mercedes backing out of the the driveway with the great electric door swinging shut behind it. Maybe he was running up to the store for something. Then she noticed it: There were two people in the car. When she got closer, she saw who it was. Josh. Josh was at the wheel, and Hunter was in the passenger side, looking at him and laughing. He didn't notice her until she pulled alongside and stopped.

Josh rolled to a stop and lowered the window. "Alison, darling. How stunning you look! But then, you always do, don't you, doll?"

"Hello, Josh. Have you been down long?"

"Just popped in on old Hunter last night. He wouldn't let me come last week. He tells me I get in the way when the brain-blitzers are at work."

Hunter leaned across Josh and said, "Alison, Josh came in unannounced. His arrival was a total shock. He's leaving now. I've made it plain that—"

"Where are you two off to?"

"Didn't Hunt tell you, doll? We're on our way to the big city." Josh checked his watch. "As a matter of fact, if we don't tear out to the airport this minute, we'll miss our flight."

"No, Hunter didn't tell me."

Anxiously Hunter explained. "Alison, this is an emergency trip. I called the Grove. They said you'd gone home yesterday. Then I tried the house. I've called steadily for the last hour. Honestly, darling, we just got the call this morning. The girl who plays Susan fell and broke her arm. She was written into every day of next week. We'll be working on rewrites all weekend."

"Gotta go, Hunter, babe," Josh interrupted. "They won't wait for us."

"Yes, go, Hunter, babe," Alison said sarcastically.

As Josh sped away Hunter called back, "It's only for three days. I'll call you, darling."

Alison sat for a moment, stinging from the encounter, feeling more than just anger. Adding to the shock, she felt rejected and betrayed again. He promised to keep Josh away. And he obviously had forgotten that today was their wedding anniversary.

Slowly she circled the cul-de-sac, not bothering to go inside the house. She drove aimlessly for minutes, smarting in pain. Suddenly she thought of Stuart. Around him she never felt sad. She would call Stuart, that's what she would do. Stuart would make her laugh today. To hell with Hunter Ames and his endless string of broken promises. Today she needed to laugh.

On the mainland she stopped at a pay phone, fumbling with the clumsy book for the number. It rang six times. Please, God, make him be home. Seven, eight . . . She wilted in disappointment. She was ready to hang up when she heard a breathless "Hello?"

"Stuart?"

"Yes?"

"This is Alison. Alison Ames."

"Alison! Fantastic! What a surprise. I was outside by the pool. I wasn't sure it was my phone. Hey, it's terrific to hear your voice. On a Sunday, too. What's up?"

"Stuart, I have a free afternoon. I was wondering, could we have lunch?"

Stuart watched her closely over lunch. She was different today, and he couldn't exactly figure out how. She seemed more—well, relaxed and eager. She drank a lot of the wine he ordered, and he could tell it went to her head right away. They lingered over the meal for two hours; still, he dreaded for it to end. She didn't mention her husband, but then, she never did.

Then she surprised him by suggesting they take a drive out to the beaches. They drove and drove, going first up to the tip of Anna Maria, then a lazy turn south to Longboat Key, then Lido, then Siesta Key. He enjoyed every minute of it. His brain raced ahead, wondering where to suggest that they go next.

She saved him the decision. "You know how to swim?"

"Sure."

"Want to go for a swim at my place?" When he looked surprised, she said, "I have a house out here. On the next key south, Sunfish Key. If you like, we could take a swim before sunset. I think I can find you some swim trunks." She eyed his skinny frame. "You'll probably have to put a string around them to hold them up, but I'll scare up a pair somewhere."

When they walked inside, Stuart whistled his admiration. "I didn't know you had this gem tucked away out here."

She was delighted. "I absolutely love it. I'm glad you like it, too. McIver—my dad—gave it to us for a wedding present."

When they passed through the center hall, Stuart noticed that the sprawling living room over to the left was a regular mess. It was littered with books and papers and file folders, ashtrays were full, and there were glasses everywhere with stale-looking drinks in them. It was odd because the rest of the house was immaculate. But then Alison explained why. Hunter was in the middle of a writing project for that soap opera of his, and the room was hands-off to everyone until he was through.

In the kitchen Alison pulled out a bottle of wine from the pantry. They sat on the full deck over-looking the Gulf drinking wine out of heavy, lead-crystal goblets, talking and laughing their heads off before the sun came down. And again and again he kept noticing it: She was different today, so different, not reserved and cool like at work.

Pretty soon she disappeared and came back dangling a pair of men's swim trunks from their drawstring. "There's a bathroom down off the center hall, between the bedrooms," she said, pointing the way. "I'll go up to the loft and change. Last one in's a rotten egg."

When he hurried back out to the deck, he saw her already on the deserted beach, running like a young filly down to the water. She was wearing an orange bikini, as orange as the sunset, as flaming as her hair. He had to hold the trunks up to keep them from falling off but managed to overtake her at the water's edge. She looked down at the swim trunks and laughed hysterically, then raced him to the Gulf.

The surf was up. A high wind was rolling big waves into the shore. She dove through one of them and came up laughing. Then another one, a big one, came crashing in, and they went into it together. They swam and laughed in the sunset. They frolicked like little kids. He'd never seen Alison like this before, so happy, so warm. He hadn't known what to expect when she came back from the funeral. He only knew she left Sarasota in a hurry and that her father died minutes after she reached him. And he knew this: She loved that man. He was practically the only person he'd ever heard her talk about besides her kids. She never mentioned her husband, and he didn't ask. In fact, the few words she said today about where he did his writing was the most Stuart had ever heard her say about Hunter Ames since he'd known her.

They sat on the sand and watched the beautiful afterglow when the big orange sun went down behind the Gulf. Suddenly she got a devilish look on her face and said, "I'll go get our wine. I want some more."

He caught her arm. "No, I'll go. I'll be right back." He found a couple of paper cups and brought the bottle down to the beach. As he approached he held the cups high and grinned at her, shouting "Voilà!" over the breeze that had sprung up.

"Terrific!" she called back.

She sat cross-legged at the water's edge, laughing lightly as his jog slowed to an easy gait. She felt warm, tingly all over. The air that bathed her was warm but not hot; the tiny waves that slapped at her were as deliciously warm as a tepid bath. He knelt down on the sand facing her, with the paper cups and bottle resting precariously between them. Alison watched as he poured her wine, then sipped before tracing little overlapping circles in the sand with the bottom of her cup. He drank, too, without saying a word, his eyes fixed on hers. She loved watching him there in the dusk, felt the overpowering presence of his sexuality. It was unreal, almost surreal. They were not touching. Their knees were inches apart, but she felt his electricity, his magnetism. "Stuart," she said very slowly, "I have a confession to make. I am getting very . . . very drunk."

"I got drunk the first time I laid eyes on you."

"Do you remember looking at me that day, you know, that day at the Hyatt? You stared at me from across the room. It was a—private look."

"Yes. I didn't think you would remember."

"Oh, I remember. You seemed to see inside my soul that day."

"You opened yourself up to me for a tiny moment. Then you took it away."

It was nearly dark now, but when she leaned over to gaze straight into his eyes, she could see quite clearly. "Why did I do that, I wonder; to you, a total stranger?"

"I felt honored. It made me want to protect you." He drew closer to her face. "I felt you calling out to me. Alison, I . . ."

She felt his breath on her face, melted under the passion she saw flashing in his eyes. Then they kissed. He kissed her lightly at first, leaning across the sand without touching her body. Suddenly he pulled her close against him as he plunged his tongue deep into her mouth. She cried out in ecstasy as he fell back on the sand and eased her down with him, rolling her over on top of his body. Shivers of excitement rippled through her as he ran his hands across her back and down to her ass, feeling his long fingers inside her tiny bikini bottoms. She moved on top of him, returning his kisses passionately, giving him her tongue, then taking his back. They both were sticky and covered with sand, but she didn't care. She didn't care about anything, not anything but now and how wonderful it was to feel his body hard against hers.

Gently he rolled her over on her back and leaned over her, kissing her again and again. His kisses were deep and hard. She responded wildly, passionately. She loved his kisses, loved his hands on her body. She wanted more. She lifted herself to him, and as he ran his hand across her breasts, he lifted the scanty swimsuit bra aside and bent to kiss her nipples. They stood full and erect, welcoming his kisses, wanting his kisses, there in the darkness. "Jesus God," she could hear him say. "So beautiful." Again his lips were on her nipples, her neck, her ear. "Alison," he whispered, "I want you."

"I want you, too. I want you now."

He pulled back on his haunches and lifted her to a sitting position against him, kissing her again and again. At her back he untied the skinny string that held her swimsuit top closed, then let it fall to the sand. "Jesus God," he said again, "how lovely you are."

Then, very gently, he slipped the swimsuit bottom down across her ankles, kneeling still, bending as he did to kiss her navel, her triangle of auburn hair, her clitoris. Then she felt his tongue plunge deep inside her and sighed in ecstasy as he devoured her with his lips.

In a blinding flash of passion he was naked, too, and breathlessly she cried out to feel him plunge deep, then deeper still inside her, deep and hot and filling her with a force that tore her apart, catapulted her into delicious vertigo, left her tingling and weak. She was hot, burning hot, wet and willing. Oh, God, yes, willing! She wanted him, wanted this feeling never to stop. She felt no passage of time; there was only now as together they climbed to the peak of exquisite pleasure, of heavenly rapture, with every fiber of her body responding to his strength. She felt him wanting her, savagely, desperately wanting her, straining in the heat of his own passion, wanting her now in a plea that was somehow more fierce, more commanding than she had ever known before. She loved it, adored it, wanted him to want her in just this way, to take her, caring only to surrender to the mood, the moment, the heavenly thrill. It was electrifying and complete.

In only minutes she cried out, "Stuart! It's happening already. Oh, God, you're going to make me come."

"Come! Come, Alison. Alison, Alison, come."

She clung to his shoulders and pulled higher. He lifted her ass from the sand and pressed her body tighter to him. She felt him wait, pulling her tighter still until she cried out exquisitely, then felt him burst inside her, sighing in his passion. With her ass still lifted off the sand he lunged forward again and again. "Alison," he said. "Oh, Jesus God."

They lay close together for a few breathless moments as tiny waves lapped at their feet, bubbling phosphorus around their toes. Then, catching hands, they ran naked back across the sand in the cool evening air, trailing their swimsuits in the breeze. The beach was very dark now. It was a starless night. "Come," she whispered, "let's get the salt and sand off." She led the way down a narrow cypress deck to the bathhouse. Inside, she flicked on a night-light, and he took a minute to let his eyes adjust. There was exercise equipment, a whole room of it, and on the far side a huge redwood Jacuzzi. Alison turned a switch, and the water began to swirl. "It will take a while to heat up," she said. "But it's wonderful even now." They stepped into the swirling water and sank down to their shoulders. She faced him, smiling. Circling his neck with her arms, she whispered, "I love being with you."

"I love it, too."

"You've been on my mind, Stuart. I was touched by the flowers you sent me at the Grove. Could you have known? Daisies are my favorite."

"I heard you mention once that they were. Alison, I felt terrible when I heard about your father. I know you loved him very much."

In the semidarkness he could see tears spill over and roll down her cheeks. "I loved him too much. I am very lost right now, Stuart."

"Thank you, then."

"For what?"

"For letting me share today with you."

"Stuart?"

"Yes?"

"I want to lie down with you. I want to lie with you in a cool, clean bed. I want you to hold me before we have to leave. Will you?"

"I wish I could hold you all night."

"No, we can't do that. Patsy's bringing the children home around eleven o'clock. I need to be there." She checked the hands on the big clock across the room. "But that will give us almost an hour. We can lie together for an hour and still be home by eleven."

Inside the house again, she caught his hand. From a dim light coming from somewhere he could see her lithe, naked body as he followed her swiftly up the stairs to the loft. It was like a dream to him to feel her cool and bare against him, to lie in each other's arms on crisp linens, with the strains of music coming from muted speakers across the room. The only light came through the high, pointed window that stretched from the floor of the loft to the top of the A-frame. A patio light cast up an eerie, magical illumination that bathed her body and made her seem yet more exquisite to his eyes. Neither of them spoke a word. They lay in silence but for the constant pounding of waves outside.

There was no clock in the room, but quite as if she knew exactly how much time they had left and without saying a word, Alison put her lips up to his. He felt her wanting him again. And this time there was no sand, just cool, sleek skin and cool sheets and kisses burning hot on his lips.

Alison's car was where they'd left it in the restaurant parking lot, the only one there now. "Well," she exclaimed, "talk about a sore thumb."

"Don't worry about it. They were open till ten. Besides, this really is an inconspicuous place. It's why I chose it." He leaned in to kiss her.

"No, Stuart. Not here. I can't take a chance in public."

"Will I see you again?"

"She laughed. "Tomorrow in Studio B."

"You know I mean alone." He lifted her hand and held it tightly.

"I want it, too. We can't go back to Sunfish Key, though. Tonight was pretty unusual. Hunter rarely travels anymore."

"You can come to my place. Will you come, Alison? It's a big complex. Nobody pays any attention to who comes and goes."

"Yes, I'll come there. I'll come in the evenings on my way home." She laughed again. "Sneak me a map tomorrow."

Quietly she slipped from the car and hurried to hers. Stuart sat watching until the golden Corvette was out of sight.

"Hello?"

"Alison, sweet. I've been calling for hours. Where in the world have you been?"

"I was out."

"But no one answered. I was worried sick. Where are Minerva and the children?"

"The children are in bed. They've been at Disney World. I told you Patsy was going to take them over today. And Minnie's always in Grove Dale on Sundays, remember?" Her voice was sharp.

"Alison, can you forgive me for letting our anniversary slip past me? This emergency in our story line threw me totally off. I remembered the date the instant we boarded the plane." She was silent. "Alison, I'm doing so well. I'm doing everything I promised I would the day I left the Grove."

"You've broken at least one of your promises."

"I swear to you, Josh barged in uninvited. I would take an oath to that on our children's heads. I was hurrying him out, darling. Please believe me." Wading through her silence again, his voice sounded too eager. "Did you notice the place today, Alison? Didn't I get it back in shape? And now that those birdbrains I work with are gone, I'll tackle the living room next." He listened a moment, then asked, "Alison, are you still there?"

"I'm here."

"I haven't had a drink. Not one since April twenty-eighth."

"I'm tired, Hunter. Please let me get some sleep."

"I'll be back Tuesday night. Let's celebrate our anniversary then. Let me come directly there and—"

"No. Our anniversary was today."

"I want to come home to you."

"No. Go on back to the beach. Good night, Hunt. I'm going to hang up now."

She lay for a long while in the dark thinking back over the day. She had begun to believe such excitement could never happen to her again. It was wonderful, terrifying, something she should have guilty feelings about. But, strangely, she didn't feel guilty at all. Hunter was the one who had betrayed *her*. In a very real sense he had been betraying her for nearly eleven years while he soothed his own selfish wishes and needs, deserting her, turning his back on her.

She rolled over and thought again of Stuart. Her friend, her special friend. Only now he was her lover, too. She liked what she had just found and had no intention of giving it up.

She fell asleep with a picture of his face in her mind, Stuart's nice, smiling, happy face.

3

June sped by and then suddenly July was half-gone, too. Alison stayed caught up in a whirlwind of activity. The children were packed off to summer camp in a frenzy of excitement. Sam wound things up at the station, and then there was the last day of sad farewell. Alison gave a party for him in her home. Most of the guests were Channel 32 employees, but she included a few special clients, too. Sam noticed Stuart standing at the buffet. "I see your shadow's here, kid."

Alison made a face at him. "So are a dozen others from my best accounts."

"Yeah, so there are." Looking around, "Why isn't Hunter here tonight?"

"He couldn't make it," she lied. "He's in New York." Squirming under Sam's scrutiny, she changed the subject. "I'm going to miss you, Sam. You've been wonderful to me. I don't know if I could have made it working anyplace else."

"You'd have made it if they had TV stations on the moon, Alison. You helped make this old man look good. It felt great today when I turned over my figures to Ingalls. All that nice black ink on the bottom line was a gorgeous sight to behold. You helped put it there, kid."

"I'm glad." Alison caught sight of Fred Ingalls and his wife out on the patio. They were talking to

Mary Abrahmson. "What do you think of Mr. Ingalls, Sam?"

"Can't really tell. He's a hard one to figure. I have a hunch he's a tough cookie. No time for fun and games."

"You're making me shiver."

He patted her lovingly. "Like I said, kid, whatever you've been doing, just do more of the same. He'll probably end up a little in love with you, too." Alison eyed him inquisitively. "You didn't know?" he asked tenderly.

"Sam, I . . ."

"Well, now you do."

"I wish you could stay all night."

"So do I, but you know that's out of the question."

He sighed and lifted her hand to kiss it. "Yes. I know."

The room was almost dark, with only the last rays of daylight visible through the cracks in the mini blinds. Stuart lay crossways on his huge bed, leaning on his elbows to gaze down at her. Every time they were alone like this it seemed to him that he found some wondrous new thing to worship about her. Today they had giggled together when he announced he had decided to kiss each freckle on her shoulders, all of them individually, if it took a light-year. "Ninety-seven," bending to peck her shoulder, "ninety-eight, ninety . . ."

She cackled with laughter and rolled away from him. "You are a total nut!"

Swiftly he rolled her back into the same position, pinned her arms tightly to the mattress, and continued seriously with his task. "Ninety-nine. See? You can't possibly go yet. I'm only on the first shoulder, and I haven't even flipped you over yet." Reaching his long fingers across the top of her back, he said, "There's a whole bunch of them back there and—"

She sat up straight and teasingly slapped his hand away. "Next time," she promised.

He flopped onto his back and grinned up at her. "Nice. I like the sound of that."

"So do I."

"Tomorrow?"

"Yes."

"Promise?"

She laughed softly. "I promise. But now I really have to go."

"I was hoping that maybe now, with the children in camp, you could spend the night—"

Interrupting, "No. Minnie's still there. She hasn't left for Georgia yet. Minnie'll scold me if I'm late."

"You sound like a little girl who's stayed too long at the playground and is going to get her bottom spanked." Stuart watched her as she walked agilely to the chair where he had slung her bra and panties when, in his passion an hour ago, he had hurriedly undressed her. It was the same every time; each afternoon they rushed into each other's arms, desperately, hungrily, as though they had never made love before. It was as if neither of them could wait, neither wanting to wait, both of them plunging headlong into the torrent of desire, of hot, burning skin and delicious, warm lips, lips that were warm and willing and hungry for more. Today was no exception. Today was wild. He had unlocked the key of Alison's fierce sexuality and had learned how to make her reach climax after climax, always stopping at last only because time ran out for them again.

She looked up from buttoning her blouse and appraised him seriously for a long beat before breaking into a smile. She stepped into her skirt and walked back over to the bed as she pulled the zipper over her left hip. "Around Minnie I will always be a little girl. She's the only mother I ever knew."

He reached up and caught her hand, pulling her

down beside him, then sat up to take her into his
arms. Sweetly, softly, he kissed her lips. "She did
one helluva good job raising you, lady," he said at
last. "She must be quite a person."

Tears filled Alison's eyes. "She means everything
to me."

"I love you for that." He pushed her back to her
feet, then swatted at her fanny as she turned. "Yes,
hurry home to Minnie. But hurry back to me. I've got
as many new ways to fuck as you have freckles on
those gorgeous shoulders, and I don't *think* we've
gotten to ninety-nine of 'em yet, but I may have lost
count about three weeks ago."

She laughed gaily as she scooped up her bag and
hurried from his bedroom door. "Oh, I do hope so. If
you've lost count that means we have to go back to
square one and start over, doesn't it?" Glancing imp-
ishly back over her shoulder, she lingered for only a
moment at the open door. "Don't bother to dress, Mr.
Stratton. I'll see myself out." Blowing him a kiss,
she disappeared.

Alison had kept her promise to Stuart. It was a ritual. She went to his place directly from her office
every night of the week, and as soon as the children
left for camp, she was able to see him on weekends,
too. The affair had been going on the entire summer
now, and she found it wickedly exciting. He always
made her laugh. At the studio they were businesslike, as before. But in the cool darkness of his bedroom they whispered lovely, private things, tiny
words of endearment mixed together with kisses.
Yet neither of them spoke aloud the word *love*.

Hunter called constantly, but still she refused to
see him. The new direction her life had taken on
filled all of her time and thoughts these days. Everything at work was different. It was frightening in a
way. Alison didn't feel exactly insecure in her position, but working for Ingalls was in no way as com-

fortable as working for Sam. He called daily meetings that were tiresome and repetitive. Sam never stood over her shoulder, instead trusted her to do a good job. Ingalls watched her like a hawk and demanded daily, sometimes hourly, reports.

"Sam, I miss you," she wailed over long distance. "Come back. I'm coming up to the mountains to get you."

"You'll have to buy a ticket to Hong Kong, kid. Mary and I are leaving Saturday for eight weeks."

Alison stayed busy, working in a frenzy to get her office in shape for Diana to take over the month of August. Her vacation had been set for months, and she planned on taking it. Dwight had called only yesterday; there were a bunch of papers he needed her to sign. She had no idea how complex McIver's holdings had been.

She couldn't wait to get home and unwind. The terrible sadness she felt in the loss of her father was softening some now. She was able to think of him without so much pain. She wanted to take time to go through his papers and sort out his personal things, to feel him near her at the Big House. She needed this vacation badly, needed to feel the closeness of her family around her.

Minerva was scheduled to spend the last week in July in Macon with her sister. Then they'd all converge on the Grove on July twenty-ninth—Alison's thirty-third birthday. This time there would be a family birthday dinner without McIver there to propose the first toast to her. It would be a difficult moment but one she needed to embrace.

The only thing she dreaded leaving behind were her nightly visits in Stuart's apartment. She certainly was able to leave Hunter behind without a backward glance. Yet she knew she had to face meeting with him before she left to have it out. She had to make the decision now, before she went away. There would be no putting it off any longer. She was either going to take him back and give their marriage one more try or tell him she'd given Dwight the go-ahead to file the papers.

The last Thursday in July she drove out unannounced to Sunfish Key. She decided the best time to face the beach traffic was midafternoon. "Stuart, you'll have to forgive me tonight. I have an errand late today that I can't put off. Things are starting to crash in on me. I have so much to do to get away Saturday."

Obviously he was disappointed. "Oh. Well, then is there a chance I'll see you tomorrow night?"

She laughed. "You know I'll try, but it will only be for a moment. I haven't even begun to pack."

"And your birthday. You promised me some time to celebrate."

"I'll have lunch with you Saturday on my way to the Grove. That's a promise."

When she crossed the bridge to Sunfish Key, she wondered what she might find waiting this time. She frankly wanted to surprise Hunter. His stories about how good he'd been were getting almost saccharine. She glanced at her watch. Almost four-thirty. If he were up to his old tricks he'd have an alcoholic glow going by this time of day.

As she entered the cul-de-sac, it suddenly struck her that she hadn't seen Hunter since the day she watched him speed away with Josh, the day she had first made love with Stuart. May twenty-seventh, their anniversary, two months ago tomorrow. Well, this was it. Her decision was overdue. So now to see for herself if any of the promises were being kept.

His car was in the driveway, but she didn't see any sign of him in the house. "Hunter?" she called out. The place was immaculate. That, at least, hadn't been a lie. Even the living room was relatively clean. Not a sign left from the brain blitz in May, just Hunter's usual personal clutter when he was writing. His desk was a mess, and there were pencils scattered on tables around the room. But, no, it wasn't a mess, really. Not at all. She walked over to Hunter's typewriter. A page half-filled with copy was there. She read a few lines. It was the typical soupy dialogue the fans who doted on *Seasons* would drool over. She shook her head and whispered, "So he *is* out here writing."

She wandered through the dining room and called his name again. "Hunter, where are you?" In the kitchen she opened the refrigerator. No beer. No wine. Just normal-looking food—healthy looking food, in fact—lots of fresh fruit and cheeses. She checked the pantry. The wine rack was exactly as she'd seen it last, the day she and Stuart were here. She opened the liquor cabinet. It was stocked, looking undisturbed. Could it be that Hunter really was behaving himself?

She heard music from the stereo in the loft. Ah, he must be taking a late-afternoon nap. She tiptoed upstairs. The bed looked slept in, but he wasn't in it. Well, then, there were only two places left, the Jacuzzi or the beach.

Suddenly she began to feel very uneasy. It was all too good to be true. She'd really driven out expecting to have it out with Hunter. What if he actually were going to keep his promises this time and do as he said he would? What now were *her* wishes? Was *she* ready to try again?

She left by the side door and walked the narrow deck down to the bathhouse, its door ajar. She braced herself, not really knowing where their conversation would lead. Well, whatever, she was ready. Stepping closer, she smelled that odor again, the pungent, burning smell she had recognized the day she stumbled on the wild party. So no wonder he wasn't drinking. She shook her head angrily. Pot, and probably cocaine, too. How could she have been so stupid? Furious now, she reached for the doorknob, then stopped dead. She heard laughter, a man's laughter. Only it wasn't Hunter's.

She stood transfixed at the opening in the door, recoiling at what she saw. Hunter was in the Jacuzzi smiling up at him. Josh was lying naked at the edge of the pool with his back to her. The two men were passing a joint back and forth and deep in intimate conversation she couldn't quite hear. A chill washed over her. It was like nothing she'd ever seen two men do before. Suddenly her flesh began to crawl. She felt sick. Dear God. She watched in morbid horror as her husband reached up and stroked Josh's cheek, then bent down from her sight.

"Hunter," Josh cried out. *"Do* it to me Hunter, baby, do it!" When he threw back his head, he noticed Alison, then bent forward instinctively and rolled into the water.

Hunter whipped around and stared wildly at her. "Alison, I . . ."

She stayed only long enough to cast him a look of the vilest, the purest contempt.

On the mainland she stopped at the first pay phone she could find and blindly dialed the number. "Dwight? Alison. Process the papers, Dwight. I want you to expedite everything now—right away." She glanced at her watch, a blur through her tears. "I guess it's too late for today, but can you do it first thing tomorrow?"

"Of course."

"Dwight, I'm going to need your help on something else. I want to have Hunter evicted from my beachhouse. Can you get the property put solely in my name so I can have him thrown out?" Without waiting, "I want him out no later than this weekend. And he's never to be allowed near my house on the mainland, either. What will it take to get all the papers in my name alone?" She rushed on crazily, almost hysterically. "McIver paid for the place on Sunfish Key, and the down payment on the house in town was written on a check against my personal account. I—"

"Easy, honey."

There were tears of anger in her voice. "Dwight, Hunter Ames is never to set foot on any property belonging to me again, do you understand me? I'll go to the Sarasota police department for a restraining order. I'll—"

"Is it that bad, Alison?"

Almost snarling, "Oh, yes, Dwight, it's that bad. Whatever you consider to be bad, it's much, much worse." He could hear her utter a pitiful sob, then say softly, almost breathlessly. "I want my name legally changed back to Watson. And the children's names, too. Hunter must never be allowed to come near my children again." Suddenly strong again, "They're *my* children now, and they will never carry the name Ames as long as I draw breath."

"In the name of God, what has happened?"

"I have grounds, Dwight. I can't talk about it now. I'll tell you when I see you. I'm coming to the Grove Saturday. We'll talk then. I'll be home for a month."

Alison checked her watch. Nearly six-thirty already. Just a couple more notations for Diana and she'd finally get out of here. She couldn't wait to leave everything behind. She congratulated herself on getting through this final day. Already she visualized herself relaxing at the Big House, feeling the pull to her own bed and the circle of the overhead fan that had rocked her to sleep during her childhood. She longed for the cloistered simplicity of life at home. The world outside had taken on a sordid look to her, one she couldn't wait to escape.

She snapped her briefcase shut and eyed the telephone with a smile, thinking of the words she'd just exchanged with Stuart. What a love. Of course he had understood that she was too rushed to come by his place tonight. After all, they still had their date tomorrow. She smiled. He was going to fix her a birthday lunch himself, he'd said. The phone jangled again, startling her. Then she relaxed. Of course it would be Stuart again with some crazy, trumped-up excuse to talk to her once more before she went home. Seductively she said, "Hello."

"Alison, my child, how alluring you sound."

Recoiling, her voice was charged with disdain, "Hunter, I've told you never to call me. I have nothing to say to you. Dwight Anderson will communicate—"

"But this is urgent, sweet thing. I'd never have called otherwise. Alison, you must hurry straight home tonight. Don't make any stops. And freshen your makeup so you'll look your best in front of the gang."

"What on earth are you talking about?"

"The guests—*our* guests, Alison, are due at seven o'clock. Almost everyone I called was able to come. They were delighted I'd called. *You* know how everybody loves a surprise party."

Alison felt the heat of anger flush up her neck. "Hunter, you're drunk. I'm going to hang up now."

"No! I'm sober as a judge. Ask anyone. Lis'n to me, darling." Alison cringed to hear him slur his words. "I've created a birthday party for you here at the house—now—tonight. You mus' hurry, sweet child. It's all arranged." He laughed dramatically. "Jus' be sure to act astonished when you walk in and everyone shouts 'surprise.' These mad fools all love s'prise parties."

"I refuse to believe that you're inside my house. It's impossible. I've had the locks changed."

She could hear him chuckling softly. "Ah, Alison, Alison, but I am. I am calling from our bedroom."

"I don't believe you."

"Oh, my sweet lovely child bride, you mus' think me such a fool. I know your ways, dear heart. I know your eccentric little ways so very well. Of course you'd have a spare key at the Petersons. It was like taking candy from a baby to charm it away from the maid." Hunter was speaking slowly now, very oddly. "Sweet, trusting Lulu."

Alison's heart began to pound wildly. Could he? Had he actually had the nerve? Oh, Jesus God, where was Patsy? Suddenly she remembered that Patsy took Jimmy down to visit her parents in Venice today. Jim was in San Francisco at a medical meeting. All at once she felt fierce rage, then panic. Patsy should have warned Lulu. But how could she have guessed Hunter would dare go to Lulu? Oh, yes, he'd have been able to charm the spare key away from Lulu with ease.

She took a moment to collect herself. Slowly she spoke, slowly and with determination. "I'll have no part of your latest trick, Hunter. I advise you to get on the phone and *un*-invite everybody. You can tell them the guest of honor has other plans." Then she heard her own voice, stern, slow—brittle. She was hearing a new person, someone she'd never met. "I'll give you exactly thirty minutes. If you're not out of my house by then, the police will physically—"

Hunter's loud, raucous laugh interrupted her. "Oh, no. You'd *never* humiliate yourself in that way. You're too proper, too perfect. My perfect, proper little Alison would never cause a scene in front of her guests. Why, some of them must already be on their way to this side of town. Really, darling, it's entirely too late for you to do a single thing except wind up those important little papers of yours you're forever fussing over and come home."

"I detest you, Hunter Ames."

He sighed dramatically. "Ah, yes. I suppose it has come to that. Then why don't you think of tonight as our divorce party?"

Alison took her time before answering. "I may just do that." Fiercely, deliberately, she added, "I *will* do just that. I will be home tonight, Hunter, but I'll not only announce our divorce. I'll tell them all what a miserable slime you have become."

"How deliciously dramatic. Do it. Do it, darling! It will be such fun. Listen to me, Alison. Just let's have fun with each other this one las' time. Let's check out of this marriage with class. I'll be out of your life after tonight, out of it forever—you'll see. Trus' me."

Then he paused and chuckled. Alison could hear the sound of ice clinking and the unmistakable gurgle of liquor from a bottle.

Then his words seemed to fade away. "Get ready to start a new page. By your birthday, I promise. On your birthday you'll have a whole new start. This party's a big celebration. Three's my lucky number. Now you'll be my little double-three. My child bride is growing up at last."

Hunter was silent for a very long time. Alison listened closely and could hear only his deep, deliberate breaths. He laughed dramatically again, then spoke slowly, so very slowly, in a way that seemed weird to her. " 'Xcuse me, my soon to be *ex*-child bride. But jus' laugh with me one more time, that's all I ask. Don't be nervous about it, darling. Relax. I'll never sleep under your roof again, that's a promise. But get ready for a birthday party you'll never forget!"

There was a long hush. For a moment Alison thought he had passed out. Then she heard a distant, audible sigh. "Good-bye, my sweet," he said. "You were my life."

In a blinding flash of realization she knew what he

had done. Terrified, she reacted instinctively. She
grabbed up her purse and sprinted for the lobby,
grappling inside it for her keys in her race to her car,
knowing in absolute certainty that she would not get
there in time.

For some odd reason she noticed how elegant the
shadows were. The sun was still low in the east, and
because of it they were long and black, each different
from the other, just as each grave marker was different. Still, they looked orderly. They looked clean to
her, neat. Her car's engine seemed clean, too, effi-
cient and unsputtering. She sat, numb, and listened
to its hum, then, bracing herself, turned off the igni-
tion and opened the door against the already stifling
early-morning heat.

She forced herself to look at Hunter's grave. She
stood for a long moment in the sweltering sun, leaning full weight against her front fender, gazing at it.
It stood out from the others because the flowers from
yesterday were still there, all the standing arrangements jabbed awkwardly into the earth on the far
side of the grave, and more, dozens and dozens of
bouquets spread flat across his grave. Today they
were no longer beautiful, but rather, forlorn-looking
in their decay.

She took a deep breath and walked slowly, deter-
minedly through them until she stood at the grave-
site. She spoke aloud into the ground. "You lowly
coward. You destroyed it all, everything good we
once had. You killed everything you touched, even
before you decided to kill yourself."

Alison longed for tears, but they wouldn't come.
They hadn't come Friday night when she'd rushed
home to find him dead, nor Saturday when she se-
lected the casket and finalized the arrangements.
They hadn't even come when she watched the children climb out of Gordie's car and took them, first

Carrie, then Wattie, in her arms. And they didn't come yesterday, not at the funeral, not at the graveside service, not ever. There was only anger, an intense anger that raged like a fire through every fiber of her body.

She squeezed her eyes tight to block away the sight, but there was no erasing it from her mind. Again and again she relived the frantic fifteen-minute drive home after his call had come. When she rushed in, she found the house extravagantly decorated. Music was blaring, and the food was already set out. Candles were burning, and there were flowers everywhere, stunning bouquets of yellow roses and daisies. Even in her blind rush to find him she noticed them. And the cake. It was huge, an elaborately decorated, monstrous thing. Inscribed on the top in yellow sugar icing were the words, "Alison. You are my life."

She spotted him near the pool. He was lying sprawled out on a lounge with an empty martini pitcher on the table beside him. Feeling dead inside, mechanically she went to him and reached for his pulse. Nothing. Then a pill bottle rolled from the lounge to the flagstones—an empty pill bottle. She picked it up and read the label, knowing already that it would be a prescription for Seconal. Swiftly she hid it in her skirt pocket.

Vaguely aware of car doors slamming and the sounds of happy chatter from the yard, she went through all the motions. But she knew before the paramedics arrived that this time Hunter had succeeded.

From a pay phone in the emergency room she called Uncle Jim. Even before she was given the final news from the ER Intern that her husband had been pronounced dead, Jim Laskell set in motion the cover-up story that might keep the media from discovering that the celebrated Hunter Ames had taken his own life. Alison knew that if anyone could do it, it would be Uncle Jim. He would do it for her and for McIver's grandchildren. He would use McIver's influence to do it for them.

Now with a victorious nod, she smiled down at the ground. "So we robbed you of your final satisfaction, didn't we, Hunt? I've got to hand it to you, though. You even planned your curtain bow for an audience, didn't you?" Her voice rose. "But you didn't get your way this time. Even from his grave McIver was too strong for you!"

"Are you all right, ma'am?"

Alison jerked around to see the old cemetery caretaker behind her. "Oh—oh, yes. I'm quite all right, thank you."

"Anything I can do, Miz Ames?"

"You know my name?"

Nodding down, "That's Mr. Hunter Ames down there."

"Yes," she mumbled. The man smiled at her compassionately. "No, no, thank you," she said as she turned toward her car. "I just wanted to be alone with him this morning."

"Yes, ma'am."

As she drove slowly out the winding road she thought briefly of what lay ahead for her today. Well, she'd make short order of it. Just a few minutes in her office, then her appointment with Ingalls and she'd be headed for the Grove. Home. Soon she would be home.

As she completed the arch that wound around the grave site she looked back one last time. "You actually *planned* it, didn't you, Hunt?" she whispered. "One final wound to everyone who loved you because you had stooped so low you detested even yourself?" Sobbing now, "Did you know all along you were going to do it?"

She braked her car and turned around in the seat.

The old man was still moving some of the flowers back into place around the grave. "I think you even figured it so that your funeral would take place on my birthday!" she shouted. "Was it your final, rotten, stinking joke?"

She gunned the engine with such force that the caretaker looked up in surprise. He stood watching as the sleek sports car tore out of the cemetery, tires screeching at every turn.

Part IV

1

The late September heat was oppressive, and the days dragged endlessly on. McIver always called them dog days. The only relief came after dark. Actually it was no hotter in late September in central Florida than it had been in July and August, but this was the month that seemed to get everyone down. When Alison exercised her horse early each morning, there wasn't a breath in the grove.

Of course it was deliciously cool indoors. The great screen door slammed behind her as she dragged wearily into the kitchen. "Help! Lemonade!"

Minerva smiled and filled a tall glass with ice. "You ought to let one of the hands take him out on a mornin' when it's hot as this, chile."

"I just may do that—like tomorrow." She gulped the icy liquid and leaned back and closed her eyes.

"Ain't nobody gonna be exercisin' your horse tomorrow if that storm keeps movin' our way."

"Did I miss another weather report?"

"Uh huh. It's a big one, they say. It's almost to the Keys."

In her bedroom Alison snapped on the television set and listened to the announcer as she began to peel out of her wet clothes.

"A hurricane alert remains in effect for the Florida Keys and southern peninsula as far north as Ft. Myers. This fifth hurricane of the season has been named Eloise. Eloise is headed in a northerly direction, crashing now across central Cuba and expected to sweep across the Keys onto the Florida mainland by late morning. Evacuation of the Keys began yesterday, and mainland residents are advised to prepare for one of the most wicked—" She flipped off the set on her way into the bathroom.

In the shower she turned her face appreciatively into the clean spray of water. It hardly seemed possible that a few hundred miles south, this huge storm was brewing. Not a leaf was moving when she was on the trail. Her house on Sunfish Key crossed her mind. It looked like Eloise was going to slam straight up the west coast. Well, there was nothing she could do that hadn't already been done. What she should have done was put the damn thing on the market six weeks ago. But she'd let Stuart talk her out of it. Stuart. She smiled. His calls got funnier all the time, and those constant, zany cards of his were a delight.

Alison strolled from the bathroom, blotting her body lightly with a soft towel. She threw herself across her bed and lay for several seconds to enjoy the gentle breeze the paddle fan cast down on her naked body. Rolling over, she stared up at it, watching its lazy circles, appreciating the hypnotizing comfort the turning wooden blades gave her. She thought about her father, about her childhood. She simply had to get over being so sad. McIver wouldn't want her to be this sad. She thought of Stuart again. It was hard to brood with a wonderful man like that, even out there on the perimeter of her world.

Still, the days had gone slowly, and the steady melancholy she felt bore down on her. Not sadness over Hunter. The grief was all for her father. The only emotion she had left for Hunter was relief. She could barely remember any of their good times. Just the wretchedness of his final two years seemed fresh in her mind. As for the good parts, it was as though Hunter were merely a player, a character in her life put there briefly, to act out a role. This person who had been her husband, the man who was the father of her two beautiful children, was no more. The actor, Hunter Ames, had properly acted out his part and disappeared early in the second act of her life.

So, all right, Alison, look ahead. That's what McIver wanted for you. "You've a wonderful life ahead of you still, and there will be someone to share it with." She smiled. Her father's voice was vivid in her memory. "Like a wind that whistles in from the grove, when you least expect it, something wonderful will happen. You'll see, pet. The third time is bound to be the charm."

The charm. She rolled over on her belly and lay with her face on crossed arms. There will be no charm or anything else if she didn't move herself out of this lethargy. Here it was September nineteenth and she was still lying around. She simply could not keep this up. She had been only two places since coming home, to shop for the children's school clothes and to a land auction in Lakeland with Todd just yesterday. The auction had been kind of interesting, too. She enjoyed watching her brother in action. When he won the bid, he turned to his sister and winked. "See, sis? Hope you were paying attention. Gordie and I are are sending you on the next one."

Her thoughts jumped back to Stuart. She couldn't wait to tell him she'd finally gotten herself out of the house yesterday. He'd been urging her almost daily—urging her in a nice way, a caring, friendly way—to get involved in something. She knew that sooner or later each one of his calls would get around to, "Well, what did you do with yourself yesterday after I called?"

It was good for her, really, that he'd been putting her on the spot like this. It gave her a clearer picture of herself, of just how ridiculous it was always to answer him with something inconsequential, like, "Well, I helped Minnie snap the beans while we watched a soap opera" or "I sorted through the dresser drawers in my bedroom." The man was used to a career woman, a fireball who never before had produced enough minutes in the day for all she wanted to accomplish, who had never even been patient with people who steeped their lives in monotony and boring pastimes.

She really did care very much what Stuart thought. She was aware he was doing the probing only for her, that in actuality he would only laugh if she told him she'd laid flat on her back and slept all day, for that matter. He'd never care. But *she* cared. She cared a lot. His daily telephone call had become the absolute high point of her morning, and she always felt a little lost and hollow inside when it came time for them to hang up. She missed him terribly. To figure this out had stunned her, but it was true. Once the activity of Hunter's funeral week had died down and she'd tended to the sympathy cards and gone over the business details with Dwight Anderson, she'd suddenly found herself with an amazing amount of time on her hands. Her children rarely came home until dinner time, their days filled to the brim with their cousins' lively escapades, their new school, and happily caught up in the beehive of activity that forever went on around the family compound. The one left out was Alison. Her own children didn't seem to need her.

There was Minnie, and she loved being around her. She supposed the two of them would never entirely wear out all there was to say between them. And, too, some member of the family or other constantly charged through the Big House. But there was something missing. Some*one* was missing besides her father.

She moved from the bed and strolled over to gaze from her enormous bedroom window across the lawn, into the fertile grove that lay just fifty yards or so away. She loved this window. It was a wonderful window, reaching from just inches above her feet to well over her head, with its oversize panes that were separated by immaculately painted strips of wood. It was part of this room that had been her refuge all of her life, the bedroom that Gordon Watson had built onto the first great room here at the Big House so that his Mary Alison could have some privacy at last. And it had been fixed over just for her during the months of the last remodeling, in the weeks before she was born. It was hers, and it was home.

Something caught her eye at the edge of the grove. A little breeze stirred and gusted, bending a tiny branch low on an orange tree straight across from her view. It was just a tiny breeze, an odd little tornadolike gust that left the other branches undisturbed, one that disappeared just as swiftly as it had come. She waited and watched. All of the branches were still now, as though poised, waiting for something to happen. How strange it had been. Just the tiniest breeze, a wind whistling in from the grove. She thought instantly of her father. A wind from the grove. Then she thought of Stuart. The charm. The charm.

Oh, *is* he the one, McIver? She thought. Can I dare to hope again? I'd given up believing I could be happy, as if happiness were never meant for me. But he's wonderful, McIver. He's like you. He's happy and alive and full of positive, wonderful thoughts and ideas. He's a happy person, darling. Suddenly she remembered something else her father had said to her in those final minutes at the hospital. "Don't

waste another minute of your beautiful life with
someone who won't be happy for you." But, Stuart *is*
happy, he is! Hunter would never be happy, could
never be happy, not for me, or for himself, or for anyone.

Still, it was all too soon to be thinking these
thoughts about Stuart Stratton. After all, only a
little over seven weeks had gone by since Hunter's
funeral, and she hadn't seen Stuart in all of that
time. The phone calls and the cards, that was all
she'd really had from him. And they were nothing
but nonsense, just moments taken from his day to
tease her, to say meaningless things that made her
laugh. Why couldn't she get him out of her mind?
She couldn't allow herself to depend too strongly on
these phone calls. She simply had to get her mind
going on other things.

The phone rang and she smiled. "Miss Alison,"
Minerva called out. "Telephone. It's long distance."

"Hi, Stuart."

"How did she know that? I direct-dialed."

Alison laughed. "Because she knows your voice,
and knows I get calls from my real estate broker in
Sarasota."

"Is that what I am?"

"That's what I told Minnie you are, only she
doesn't believe a syllable of it." Alison immitated
Minerva, " 'Seems mighty quare to me you keep
gettin' all those *real* estate calls when you ain't even
put a for sale sign on either one of them houses over
there yet.' "

"I could, you know. It would make it legal."

"I was thinking today that I probably should have
put the beach place on the market six weeks ago. I
just heard the latest report on Eloise. She's headed
your way."

"I know."

"Are you going to be all right?"

"Oh, sure. The complex is in a high section. I just hope I don't get any damage to my office building. But what about you?"

"Gordie and Todd are keeping an eye. They've already hired extra hands. They're picking now. If it hits us the fruit loss could be staggering. But we won't start boarding up the houses until we're sure we're in the path."

"What have you been up to since we talked?"

She laughed softly. "That's your sweet way of asking if I'm still vegetating. Well, I'm happy to say I went to a real estate auction yesterday. Todd took me."

"What did you think?"

"I really enjoyed it. Todd thinks I could handle going to one of them alone one of these days, in his place."

"I think you could, too. I think you'd be terrific at it, as a matter of fact." Alison snuggled down in her pillow and smiled. "As a matter of fact," he repeated, "I think you'd be terrific at anything you put your pretty fingers into."

"Stuart . . ."

"Hmmm?"

"I've been giving some serious thought to staying on here."

"I know."

"How? I haven't said so before."

"I just know. I've gotten to know you very well, Alison Carrington Watson Ames. At least two of those three sides I said I saw in you."

Alison fingered the triple heart necklace Stuart had given her. She hadn't taken it off since that last day they'd been together. "What do you think?" she asked.

"I think I want to explore that side you're holding back—that third elusive side—one of these days."

"I *meant*, what do you think about my resigning at

Channel 32 and staying on here? I have to make my decision before Friday of next week."

After a decided hesitation he said, "I think you must make up your mind about what's right for you. If you're happy at the Grove you should stay."

Alison struggled with a feeling of disappointment. What had she expected? Did she think he would beg her to come back to Sarasota to live? He'd never said so. Maybe he didn't care what she did with her future. "Oh," she heard herself say.

"Say, Alison, I have to sign off. Sally just flashed me a note. An important call is on hold. I think it's about that closing over at Woods Acres. Keep your fingers crossed, baby. It's a biggie."

"Oh, sure. Thanks for calling. I'll hold the right thought."

"I'll call again soon. Take care, beautiful."

Slowly she replaced the receiver and stared, crestfallen, at the telephone. What was wrong with her? He was sweet, as sweet as ever. He was just busy, that's all. Of course he had to take that other call. Why did she suddenly feel so hollow?

When she walked over to her closet, she caught a glimpse of herself in the mirror. She appeared anxious, upset. Okay, Alison, face up to this, too. You thought Stuart couldn't live without you, and he sounded casual just now.

With a deep sigh she pulled into her jeans and twisted her hair up in a ponytail. Okay, enough. You've spent enough time today being blue, Alison. Enough.

"Mother!" Carrie shouted as she tore up the porch steps. "Mrs. Solomon says we're going to have a hurricane and that I should fill all the bathtubs with water."

"Well, maybe a couple of them, darling." Alison smiled to watch her daughter drop her books and pile

into the swing beside her. She leaned in to kiss her
forehead and push back a lock of her smoldering red
hair. She ran her forefinger across the bridge of the
child's nose, tracing the fine smattering of freckles
still left over from the late summer sun. "Minnie'll
get you good," she said. "You know you're supposed
to keep indoors until late afternoon. You've been
playing out again."

Carrie unbuckled her sandals and dropped them
in exasperation. "You're not paying attention. It's a
bad storm! Mrs. Solomon says—"

"Carrie gets unnecessarily hysterical," said Wattie without emotion. He climbed the steps a few
paces behind his sister, flanked by their two dogs.
King, the black German shepherd, had been Mc-
Iver's dog and was theirs now. The other animal, a
fine three-year-old black Labrador, was the children's from puppyhood. The boy sprawled out across
a lounge and settled in for a competitive exchange
with his sister.

"I do not get hysterical, Watson Ames. And besides, there's something to be hysterical about.
Mrs. Solomon says the hurricane has turned and is
going to rip straight up central Florida now. It's
going to blow us clear off the map, you'll see!"

"Shhh," said Alison. "Now slow down. We're not
going to get blown off the map. But we do have to
batten down for the storm." She glanced anxiously
across the open porch. The winds had begun to pick
up before noon, and now they whistled menacingly
through the trees. "We still have plenty of time.
The latest weather report says the eye is several
hours away. Minnie and I have already been to
market."

"Did you get lots of candles? And sterno? Is that
how we'll cook when the lights go off?" asked Carrie.

"We have the portable grill from the camper we
can use, in the garage, and Minnie unearthed that

two-burner kerosene stove of hers. We'll be fine.
Now listen, this is serious. I'm going to need both of
you to help this afternoon. Everyone's coming here.
We've decided the Big House is the safest spot on the
Grove. We're on the highest land."

The girl squealed in pleasure. "You mean, everybody?"

"Well, all except McIver and Robert. Margaret
told them to stay put at the university. They're probably better off there."

"Maybe it will hit Gainesville, too," said Wattie
with a tinge of glee.

"Now, Wattie, hush. You're not funny."

"What about Minnie?" he asked, suddenly serious. "Isn't she worried about her house?"

"Of course she is, but she's decided to stay with us.
She'll be safer here. We've already been by her place
and brought back her special treasures. You know,
in case of high water damage."

"It's the high winds we should be scared of. The
high winds can blow us away." Carrie jumped up
and ran over to pat Blue. "I think it's exciting!"

"A minute ago you thought we should all get hysterical."

"Okay, Wattie, enough," Alison scolded. "Time
out. Come on, you two. There's lemonade in the
kitchen, then into your jeans. We have work to do."

The three families settled in to brace for the storm.
The earlier hours in the day had been spent boarding
up the other homes on the family compound. Gordie
and Margaret's home was half a mile away in the
heart of the north grove, down a shaded road from
the main gate. Todd and Jennifer lived just across
the lake, in view of the Big House. And there was the
Little House to see about, plus Ben's cottage, although nobody had lived in either place for years.
Gordie's two oldest sons were away. McIver, who had

turned twenty-one in June, was entering his first year of pre-law, and Robert, who would be nineteen the next month, was a sophomore in college. But their youngest, Bruce, was still at home. Bruce was Carrie's particular joy. The sixteen-year-old was the cousin who had taught her to ride a horse, to swim, to dance. This summer he'd been giving her tennis lessons.

Of all the grandsons, Todd's oldest son, Trey, was the one who most resembled his namesake, though all three of Gordie's boys had dark hair, too, and were ruggedly good-looking in the Watson way. But for a boy of just fourteen, Trey, was big, already over six feet tall, and his shiny black hair and brown eyes and ruddy skin were so like her father's that at times it was actually startling to Alison. Todd's baby was Keith, eleven last January, and the standout in the crowd. He was the only Watson who was a towhead, resembling Jennifer's side of the family. He was artistic like his father, and a tease. His ways reminded Alison of the teenage Todd she'd known.

Minerva put every one of the kids to work. With orders to keep out of her kitchen except when called to meals, they were dispatched to the dozens of jobs that must be done if the huge house were going to be made safe in time. The storm was bearing down now, and the outside chores must be accomplished long before dark.

Alison was standing on a chair in the dining room working with two of the boys to lay masking tape across the big windows when Minerva answered the front doorbell. The black woman returned with an odd expression on her face. "What is it, Minnie? Is anything wrong?"

"It's a visitor to see you, Miss Alison."

"A visitor? My God, doesn't he know we're practically in the middle of a hurricane?" Stuart Stratton stood on the front porch in the blowing rain. "Stuart!" Alison reached up automatically to smooth her hair. "I don't believe this. Where on earth did you come from? Come in. Hurry!"

Margaret passed through in time to hear him say, "I was over in Kissimmee closing that deal I told you about at Woods Acres. You were on my way back home. I stopped to see if you need any help. You're right in the path, and it's predicted to be a mean one." He grinned down at her, obviously enjoying her moment of shock. "Plus I have some good news on your Sunfish Key place. I think I have a buyer."

"Oh. Oh, my. Well, my goodness. Yes. How wonderful." Suddenly realizing Margaret's presence, "Oh, Margaret, I want you to meet Stuart Stratton. Stuart's my real estate broker in Sarasota. He may have a buyer for my beach house."

Margaret extended her hand. "How nice to meet you, Stuart. But look at you. You're soaked. Come back to the kitchen. Minerva has a big pot of coffee on. You're going to need a towel."

Frozen, Alison watched as the two of them picked their way through the clutter in the dining room, stopping as Stuart shook hands with Bruce and Trey. When the swinging door closed behind them, she scampered for her bedroom. Stuart was here, here at the Grove, and he'd found her looking like the wrath of God. She'd been in her grubbiest jeans since early morning, doing one filthy job after another.

She stepped from the shower and nervously dressed. Why hadn't he warned her? She'd talked to him only this morning, about the beach house, too, and he never mentioned any sale. Why? It *was* only this morning, wasn't it? So much had happened since they talked. Of course it was today. He was on his way to Woods Acres. But that was early, and now it was nearly dark. Why on earth would he come here now, of all times, right into the path of a fierce hurricane? Was he crazy?

She forced herself to slow down, taking time to style her hair with the blower, then carefully to apply her makeup. Why, she'd had a whole face full of freckles when she answered the door, a face she'd scrubbed after her ride this morning and hadn't bothered to look at since. Stuart had never seen her like this. What a mess. Why didn't he give her some warning? Her hands shook so, she could barely apply a light coat of mascara to her lashes, and she fumbled awkwardly with the buttons when she pulled on a fresh, faded denim shirt. She'd toyed with the idea of wearing a dress, but that was ridiculous. That would give her away in front of the family, and the last thing she needed right now were any wise and knowing looks passed among her nephews when she rejoined everybody in the kitchen. Yes, jeans. That's what she always wore around the house, and today would be no exception. She stepped into a clean pair and pulled the zipper up over her flat stomach, then reached for a ribbon to tie up her hair. Quickly she thought better of it. No, she'd leave her hair down tonight. Stuart had told her so many times that he liked it best when she wore her hair down. It had become a ritual on the nights she'd stopped by his apartment. Always, the first thing he did was to loosen the pins that held her hair high on the crown of her head, standing back then to smile as she shook the titian mass free. Yes, tonight she would wear it loose.

She stood for a long beat in front of her full-length mirror, which was tilted on its white wicker frame to catch the fading rays of the late afternoon's stormy sky and checked herself over one last time. Her heart was pounding wildly now; her hands were cold and damp. Inside she was an emotional wreck, but she

looked good, vital and carefree, and so very young.
Her cheeks were flushed high with excitement, and
her hazel eyes snapped in the mirror's reflection.
"Okay," she whispered to herself, "that's the best
you can do. You still look like a grub, but at least
you're a clean grub."

When she rushed past the grandfather clock, she
noticed the time: five after seven. It seemed later
with the skies nearly dark under the storm clouds'
cover. The wind out in the grove had begun to
scream shrilly now, and great spurts of rain peppered the roof. It sounded awful out there, certainly
too hazardous to be driving through. How could Stuart possibly venture back out tonight into that dangerous mess? Well, he couldn't. He'd have to stay
over at the Big House. She felt her heart begin to
pound even more savagely against the walls of her
chest.

The excitement of the evening seemed to crash
around Alison in exact proportion to the intensity
of the storm's march across the rich highlands of
Grove County. All of the Watsons were there, and
Clair Hill, too. The central hub seemed to be Minerva's kitchen. When Alison first joined them,
she found her brothers treating Stuart as though
they had known him for years. They accepted his
offer to go out in the groves with them before dark
to help with the unfinished chores. There was no
time to visit. Every man on the property worked,
back-breaking, frantic work, trying to beat the
darkness, to beat the storm. While the teenagers
hurried to the stables to feed the horses and secure
the stable doors, Carrie and Wattie carried in the
porch plants and filled large vessels with water.
There was an air of urgency throughout the house.
The women stored away the huge amounts of food
Minerva had spent her day preparing and made up

fresh beds for the crowd that would sleep at the Big House that night.

Alison watched from the dining room window as the Jeep made one more swing by the Big House to round up her nephews. She strained in the darkness to see who was at the wheel, smiling when it turned out to be Stuart. He was part of the family effort, a very comfortable-looking one of them. She was overwhelmed that he made it look so easy, when never in eleven years had Hunter managed to fit in.

The frenzy was to save as much of the fruit as they could before darkness fell. In central Florida damage from rising water was never as dreaded as in the coastal areas of the state, but wind damage—especially from the small tornadoes that preceded and followed the main thrust of the storm—could reach into hundreds of thousands of dollars of loss to crops and trees. So this was a last-minute desperate harvest to save all the fruit that could be reached before the high winds should rip it from the trees.

At eight-thirty Gordie sent the hands to the safety of their homes, and the Jeep pulled back in the pebble drive with darkness almost upon them. Alison stood at the big bay window in the dining room, relieved when she saw the yellow lights round the curve in the drive. Minerva was stirring about silently behind her. Alison noticed she'd gotten her mother's sterling flatware from its place in the buffet drawer. So Minnie planned to serve on the good china tonight. There was an extra place needed now. There would be twelve tonight, ten family, plus, of course, Clair, and now there would be Stuart, too.

"Where do you want *him* to sit?" Minerva asked her, eyeing her knowingly. "Next to you?"

"Who, Stuart? I mean, Mr. Stratton?" Alison

blushed. Minerva remained silent, studying her. "Well, yes, I guess so. Well, no, anywhere, I guess. It really doesn't matter." Alison busied herself, avoiding Minnie's eyes. So she knew. Of course she knew, because she would have recognized his voice. Well, it was proper, his being here, totally proper.

She hurried to the kitchen when she heard conversation. The men had just come in by the back door and stood inside it, dripping wet. "Alison, better lead this man to a bathroom," Todd said, laughing. "I'd say he's earned a nice hot shower."

Stuart followed Alison to the south bedroom wing. Once inside McIver's bedroom, the two of them were alone for the first time in nearly two months. "Here, let me show you where to shower," she said, hesitating before she dared look into his eyes. When she did, she felt herself go weak. His blue eyes were smiling into hers. Pausing at the bed, she said, "Here's where you'll sleep tonight. You can't possibly think of venturing back out in this thing," she added maternally. "This is—I want you to have McIver's room."

"I'm flattered."

She hurried across the carpet and opened the mirrored door. "This is the bathroom." Suddenly embarrassed, she ducked her head. "Well, obviously it's the bathroom. Anyhow, you'll find towels and all you'll need." She gazed tenderly at him. "My, look at you. You look like a drowned rat. Do you have any dry clothes in your car?"

"Just tennis shorts."

"Oh, dear."

"I'll put these back on. I don't mind."

"No. You'll catch cold. We'll find you something. Bruce is almost as tall as you." At the door Alison paused and smiled at him again. "Welcome to the Grove."

* * *

Totally exhausted, everyone went to bed early. They had done all they could. The worst of the hurricane was predicted for near midnight. Alison lay awake from the sheer excitement of the day, but she could hear Gordie's heavy breathing long before tenthirty. Stuart was sleeping just across the hall, in McIver's big bed.

She allowed her mind to go back over the moments tonight when she watched her family pull Stuart into the warm embrace that was part of being a Watson. Again she felt it, her amazement that he seemed so at home here. In just a few short hours he seemed to have made friends with both of her brothers. She wished for McIver. *I know you're here, McIver. Do you like him, darling? Is it okay that I let him have your room? I planned never to let anyone sleep in that room.*

Alison had bathed again before bed, sensing that it might be the last hot bath she'd have for a couple of days. She could only remember one severe hurricane in her lifetime, one that had hit Florida when she was a teenager. It was the monster of 1964, named Donna, which had ripped up the west central coast of the state before turning west into the Gulf of Mexico. It was a big storm, but that year they'd been lucky here at the Grove. The worst of the storm ravaged Ft. Myers to the southwest of them before lumbering up the coast to Tampa Bay, then turning out to sea, but she did remember very well that they'd been without electricity for something over twenty hours during that storm and realized now that it could be for a much longer period this time. Now they were in the direct path of Eloise, and it didn't appear that she was about to veer off her course. According to the weather maps on television, Eloise was marching slowly, relentlessly, straight toward them.

Alison lingered at her closet, wondering what she would wear to sleep in. There were the pale green baby dolls she'd never had on, or that lovely yellow, accordian-pleated gown Margaret had given her for her birthday, the Grecian one that caught up with the slim little ties under her bust. She reached for the gown and held it against her naked body to study her reflection in the free-standing mirror. Yes, this was the prettiest gown she owned, and it had a matching robe and slippers. Suddenly she felt the total fool. What on earth difference did it make? Nobody was going to see her in a nightgown tonight.

She slipped into the gown and sat at her dressing table to give her hair its nightly brushing, then smoothed moisturizing lotion across her cheeks and neck. The room in its semidarkness seemed to wrap her in an eerie mood, the strange feeling of excitement that went with darkness and stormy skies and howling winds. She switched off her bedside lamp and hit the mute button on her television's remote control but allowed the set to remain on. The weather report was continuous now, and its changing pictures cast the only shadowed light in the room. She fell across her bed and lay facedown for many minutes, with her head cradled on her arms. For a minute or two she dozed off, but a sudden torrent of splats on her windowpanes caused her to jump with a start.

She rolled over and checked the digital numbers on her bedside clock. Only ten forty-seven. She wished she could get to sleep. Why couldn't she? God knows she ought to be exhausted. The wind was screaming and moaning at the same time now, and somewhere out in the grove she could hear branches cracking from the trees. She reached over to stroke her cat. He was curled up on the pillow next to her head. "How come you can sleep through all this, MacGregor, hmmm?" She gathered the animal in her arms and silently crept over to her door, then tiptoed down the hall, noticing a crack of light under Stuart's door as she passed. Her children were in twin beds at the far end of the wing. They were both sleeping soundly. Blue was in bed with Carrie, curled up at her feet, trembling at the distant thunder. "It's okay, boy," Alison whispered. By the nightlight she spotted King's great black tail sticking out from under Wattie's bed and smiled.

Back in her room she placed her cat back in the soft place he'd made on the pillow and turned the television audio on low. The storm was right on top of them. She wondered how much longer they'd have power. The monotonous voice of the weatherman droned on: "Eloise is continuing on her wicked path of destruction in a north-northeasterly direction at a steady fifteen knots. The eye is nearing Grove County now, and it appears at this point that Orlando is going to be hard-hit if the storm continues on her northeastern curve. Residents of Daytona Beach and neighboring Atlantic coastal—"

She snapped off the set and crawled back in bed, lying outside the covers to enjoy the gentle breeze of the fan overhead, daydreaming, fantasizing a little, finally sinking into a light sleep. She woke with a start, realizing something was different. She sat straight up. What was it? The wind howled louder than before. The great old house creaked and groaned under the stress of it. But she felt no sense of fear. What was it, then? Then it hit her. The fan wasn't spinning. The power had finally gone. Fumbling for the flashlight she'd brought up to the room, she beamed it on the face of the clock. It had stopped at eleven twenty-three. She wondered what time it was now.

She made her way across the room to her dresser and picked through her jewelry case for her wristwatch. Just eleven-fifty. She had slept only minutes. She crawled back in bed and lay listening to the screeching winds and the heavy splats of rain that pelted in hard gusts against her window. She wondered if anyone else in the house was awake. Maybe she should check on the children again.

Silently she crept to her door and opened it a crack. There wasn't a sound except from outdoors. The place was dark, dark as pitch. She stood for a moment, trying to adjust her eyes. She pulled her door quietly closed behind her and, without letting herself think, tiptoed the few steps across the hall to McIver's door. She stopped, magnetically riveted to the spot. With her heart in her mouth she quietly turned the knob and opened the door a tiny crack, standing very still for a breathless moment. Then a sudden flash of lightning illuminated the sky beyond the sun room. Instinctively she began to pull the door closed but felt pressure from the other side. She could feel the air across her face as the door opened, then sensed him close to her face. "Thank you for coming, Alison." he whispered. He took her hand and led her inside the room. She could feel him reach around behind her and gently close the door. Then he pulled her into his strong embrace.

She burst into tears. He lifted her and carried her over to McIver's bed, kissing her cheek and her hair as he did. He placed her gently in the center of the bed, then eased in beside her and gathered her in his arms. "Cry, baby, go ahead and cry," he said. "Just let me hold you, that's all I ask." He kissed her cheeks, her eyes, kissing away the tears as they fell. Again and again he kissed her, caressing the soft gown that covered her lower back with his hands. "Cry, darling. I'm here now. I'm here."

Alison pulled closer to him and clung with all of her strength. He felt so wonderful, she never wanted to let go. "Stuart, I—"

"Shhh. Don't talk. Not tonight. Just let me hold you tonight."

She felt his comfort, his love. Somehow he understood all of the things she had been holding inside herself, the depth of emotion she had been hiding behind her bedroom door. The pain that was Hunter, the loss that was McIver; all of it spilled out in a torrent of quiet brokenhearted sobs. She wept uncontrollably, basking in his strokes, his kisses, trying now and then to speak, to explain. But she didn't need to. Always he interrupted her. "Don't try to talk. It's okay. I understand. Shhh, I'm here. Just cry, baby, cry it out." Wrapped up in his strength and tenderness, somehow the tears of heartache turned into tears of joy as she felt filled to bursting with love for him—strong, comfortable love. Not once did he try to hush her; instead, only held her and stroked her and gently kissed away the tears. She loved it, adored the feeling, felt totally, unselfishly loved perhaps for the first time in her life.

His body felt good against hers, strong and athletic, yet comfortably soft in just the right way, the very way she needed to be held tonight. She was aware that he lay naked against her filmy gown, could feel the hair on his chest against her breasts as he pulled her closer to him, loved the sleek strength of his shoulders and back beneath the touch of her fingers. It seemed so long since he'd held her like this, so long! But it was all right now. Now she was here with him, here in his welcoming arms, hearing his voice whisper words of consolation, expressions of tenderness for her ears alone. Oh, how she needed it. She hadn't realized how very much she needed just to be held and allowed to cry. It was only the second time since she found Hunter's dead body that she'd given in and cried. Only the day she closed up the beach house, and now—and both times in Stuart's arms.

He held her. He held her for a timeless interlude, a private period in which there were no moving clocks, nor lights to intrude, save for the occasional flash of lightning somewhere far out across the groves. She had no idea how long he held her; she only knew that it felt right. She had never experienced a feeling quite the same. For once in her life things *were* right. She belonged here, she absolutely knew it, here and now in Stuart's caring arms. Gradually, gently she dropped off into a light sleep, still cradled inside his tender embrace.

A loud crash woke her with a start. Something big had fallen on the roof. "It's a tree," Stuart said softly. "A big one. Sounds like it came from up front."

Alison sat straight up. "Oh, God. An oak. Probably one of the water oaks by the porch. Stuart, I can't let them find me here! I—"

"Shhh. It's okay. There are no lights. You have time to get back to your room. Come on now, it's okay." He guided her to the bedroom door.

Before she could bear to leave him, she flung herself into his arms and kissed him passionately. "Stuart, oh, Stuart, I . . ."

"Oh, Jesus God, Alison, tell me. Tell me!"

"Stuart, I love you so. I love you so very much."

She could hear his voice catch. "Oh, my God," he said, burying his face in her neck. "Oh, Alison, Alison." Then he quietly opened the door and guided her through into the ebony hallway. "You all right?" he asked.

She squeezed his hand then felt her way along the

hall, back to her room. She could see a distant yellow light of a lantern come on beyond the living room. Minnie was up. Minnie had no doubt heard the crash and was up preparing coffee. Alison closed her bedroom door only seconds before Gordie's flashlight shone from the far end of the hall.

The day sped quickly by. By dark it seemed barely possible to Alison that an entire day had come and gone. She could scarcely remember a time in her life when she felt so physically exhausted yet exhilarated. It had been one great adventure from start to finish. She had been in on everything, a part of it all, from the moment it was calm enough to venture out. There was no access to the highway, nor any help from the outside world. A pole had fallen across the Little House, with loose wires strung laterally across the road to the main gate. The wires were very likely live, and there was no choice but to keep away from them and wait for the power company to fix them. Stuart was stranded inside the compound.

The blocked passage was a disaster in itself, for thousands upon thousands of oranges and grapefruit now lay on the ground and would begin to rot. The Watson Properties' hired hands, the men sent home before nightfall last night, couldn't get back in to help with the collection of the fruit. The huge trucks stood silent, filled to the brim with yesterday's harvest, yet motionless until the power linemen cleared the way to their packing plants out in the county. At least for now the family was on its own.

The Big House porch was badly damaged. The first priority after breakfast was to get rid of the broken oak that lay across the porch roof. Alison watched, impressed as her nephews shinnied up the tree, first to cut away the smaller branches with handsaws, then proceed to section the tree's enormous trunk and main branches with the power chain saw. They hauled the wood to the lumber pile by the garage, load after load, until nothing remained of the tree but the stump of the once proud tree.

By late morning the weather seemed calm enough to take the horses out for exercise. Until now, Alison had kept herself apart from Stuart, afraid of being transparent in front of the people who saw them together. Even now she didn't trust herself to be alone with him; instead she asked Trey to walk down to the stables with them to help feed and water the animals.

Stuart was impressed with the horses. "Which one's yours?" he asked Alison.

She smiled and walked over to the palomino in the end stable. Rubbing her open palm up and down the animal's long nose, she leaned in to kiss the place she had touched. "This one." She whispered, "You okay, Misty? Did the storm scare you last night? I worried about you." Turning to face Stuart, "Do you ride?"

"Badly, but I'm game to try."

"Come on. Let's go check the property down by Ben's cottage. You take this one," she said, patting the horse in the next stall. "His name's Champ. He's a teddy bear. Trey will saddle him for you."

Trotting on ahead, she called back over her shoulder. "Thanks, Trey. Come join us."

"Better not. I'll stay and finish up here."

Alison trembled with the thought of being alone again with Stuart, still tingling from the nearness of him in the night. She could still feel the warmth of his embrace, felt him now just yards behind her with his eyes on her back.

Stuart's horse followed at a slow walk. The animals had to pick their way through the debris scattered along the well-worn trail. In a clearing a half-mile or so from the stables he noticed the cottage. Alison led Misty over to the open porch and dismounted, looping the reins around the wooden railing. "This was Ben's cottage until he died."

"Ben?" Stuart followed her up the steps.

"Ben was one of my best friends. He was McIver's foreman for years. He went to work for my grandparents when my dad was a little boy."

"Who lives here now?"

"No one. We let some of the hired hands have it from time to time when one of them needs a place to stay." She pushed the door open wide. The sun, temporarily out from behind its gloomy cloud, spread a sunny path across the rough wooden floor. "But no one really lives here. McIver said he couldn't feel right about anyone else's having it once Ben died." She turned and smiled at him. "Come on in. I want to show it to you. Ben let me spend hours here when I was growing up." Giggling, "It's where I came to read dirty books when I was a teenager, so Minnie wouldn't catch me."

Stuart followed, leaving the door open wide behind him. He peered around the simple room. "Is this it?"

"Yep, all of it. Well, all except the bathroom through that door."

He chuckled and paced the small room to glance in the bathroom. "Not bad. What'll you take for the place?"

"Not for sale. It's priceless. There's no way to establish dollar value on sentiment."

Stuart leaned on the doorjamb and studied her tenderly. "I think I'm jealous. He must have been quite a friend."

"Oh, I love this place for other reasons, too. This is the house my father lived in until my grandparents built the first room of the Big House. Can you imagine? The three of them lived in this little room for two entire years, and there was no bathroom then."

She pointed through the northern window. "Just a tiny outhouse over there under that tree. My father had to take all of his baths in a big old galvanized tub."

"It's incredible. And wonderful."

"Yes," she said wistfully. "They were pioneers, actually. I'm intensely proud of my Watson heritage."

"You should be." He watched her closely, with love in his eyes.

Suddenly self-conscious, she said, "They're liable to be hunting us."

He reached across and cupped her cheek in his palm. "You're incredible yourself, Alison Watson Ames. I've never seen you look so beautiful."

"Stuart, I—"

Gently he pulled her into his arms and kissed her lips, tasting her lips, hungrily devouring her lips.

A distant voice called, "Aunt Alison!"

"Oh, God," she whispered. "It's Bruce." She backed away and paused, then stretched up for one more kiss, one more quick, delicious kiss. Then she sprinted from the cottage.

Stuart lingered for a moment to collect himself. From outside he heard dialogue between Alison and her nephew. "Come on inside," she said. "We were just checking for leaks."

"Minerva sent me to find you two. She says to tell you lunch is ready and everyone's there but you."

"Oh, oh. That means she's cross." Calling back, "Stuart, hurry. We're in the doghouse. Minnie's a bear if you let one of her meals get cold."

He mounted Champ and fell into place behind the other two horses. "Seems to me all we've done since I got here is eat."

The teenager laughed. "You ain't seen nothin' yet, has he, Aunt Alison? Wait till tonight."

Before dark Alison helped Minerva prepare the

next big meal. She and the servant worked together, alone for the moment. She didn't know where everyone had gone. They all seemed to have scattered at once. "Where's Carrie?" she asked.

"She's settin' on the porch steps waiting for them to come back. I wish that chile wouldn't be so stubborn. It's fixin' to rain again, the radio says. She'll get soaked havin' to come around back when it starts." The black woman clucked under her tongue. "She knows she cain't get in the front door now, with it all boarded up."

"Don't worry about her, Minnie. So she gets wet. It won't hurt her. Just as long as the porch is safe from any cave-ins."

"Oh, it's safe. I checked on it before I let her go around."

Alison walked to the bay window in the dining room to peek at her daughter and smiled. The child sat patiently on the top step of the long porch with Blue stretched out on the grass near the walk. Alison lingered a moment, remembering all the times in her childhood when she'd had to sit and wait. She never got to go along when it was the fun or exciting thing to do but rather had to sit on the porch steps and wait for her brothers and father to return. Now here was her daughter, in a replay of the same tape.

When she crossed through the butler's pantry, she found Clair sorting out the sterling flatware for the dinner table. "Oh, Clair. I didn't see you there. Darling, you don't need to do that. Really. I want you to feel like a guest while you're here with us."

"You pamper me, child. Just like your father. Please, let me help. I want to."

Alison put her arm around the woman. On an impulse she blurted out something she'd never said before, words that had been on her tongue for years. "Clair, you look so at home here. You're part of the

Big House. Tell me, why didn't you and my father ever marry?"

The woman gazed into Alison's eyes appreciatively. "Didn't McIver ever tell you, darlin'?"

"Tell me what?"

She sighed and shook her head. A little smile touched her lips. "Oh, my."

"What is it, Clair? Is it something I was supposed to know? I've always wondered why. You were plainly in love with him, and I know McIver was in love with you."

"Yes," she said softly, "we were deeply in love. Right from the start. But Alison, darlin', he'd made that vow."

"Vow?"

"He made a vow to your mother's grave. He promised your mother he would never bring another woman to live in her house."

Alison frowned, then stared at her compassionately. Suddenly it all added up. All of those years, all of those women who tried unsuccessfully to hold her father, but he never wavered, not even with Clair. "No, I never knew. Were you terribly hurt by it? I'm sure my mother would have understood. McIver could have broken—"

"Oh, no. No, indeed, he could have done no such thing. Why, Alison child, it would have devastated your father to break that vow. And, no, I wasn't hurt. I understood. From the beginnin' I understood. Don't you see, I had him in every important way? McIver was mine. Everyone knew it." She chuckled, a low, melodic laugh. "And besides, think of the fun I've had all these years making that worm Adam Hill cough up those big fat alimony checks every month. Serves him right for cheatin' on me with that no 'count Molly Hoffman from Savannah. He was sure I'd remarry inside a year—told me so. But I fooled him. I stayed single and had my man at the same time."

Alison laughed. "Clair, you're bad." She hurried past her to help Minerva get the meal on before dark. On the porch Carrie sat with her chin propped against her fists, her elbows on her knees, wishing they would hurry and come home.

Suddenly a great streak of lightning darted down over the lake, followed by a clap of thunder so close to the house that it made her jump to her feet. Blue howled and sprinted away from her, tearing off through the open gate toward the lake. "Blue!" the child called after him.

The terrified dog continued to run, yelping as another loud clap of thunder broke overhead. "Blue!" she called again, running after her dog. The skies opened and drenched the girl to the skin. "Blue, come back!"

When the Jeep pulled into the drive, Stuart was the first to spot her. She stood at the bank of the lake, crying, watching her dog circle the north bank and disappear into the deep weeds at its edge. The north bank was off limits; it always had been. She and Wattie had been warned since toddlers never to wade in the deep weeds. There could be water moccasins over there, hard to spot until it was too late. She cried openly now, still calling out, "Blue, come back! Blue, don't go in the snakes! A snake will get you, Blue!"

Stuart stooped beside her and took her hand. "Come on up to the house with me, Carrie. You're already soaked. Blue will be all right."

The child pulled her hand away and continued to sob. "Blue! Come back, Blue!"

"Come on, honey," he coaxed. He took her elbow to guide her away from the lake. "It's dangerous out here. There's lightning across the lake. Come inside with me, okay?"

Then another flash of lightning zigzagged across the sky, followed by another thunderous, booming crack. The girl jumped and covered her ears with her hands. Stuart scooped her in his arms and ran through the sheets of rain for the back door. Inside, he sat on the porch floor and pulled her into his lap while she sobbed. "Shhh. It's okay. Don't worry about Blue. Ol' Blue knows where to go to get away from the thunder. He'll be back in no time. You'll see." Then, aware that someone was watching, he glanced up to see Alison at the kitchen door. Silently she handed him a dry towel. She watched as he patted her daughter's face and hair dry before dabbing carefully at her freckled cheeks with the corner of the towel. "My dog was terrified of thunder, too. It's in a Lab's contract."

Carrie peered into Stuart's eyes. "What contract?" she asked. Her tears began to subside.

"Their Labrador retriever contract," he said seriously.

"Do Labrador retrievers have contracts?"

"Indeed they do. How else would they know what to do?"

Alison smiled, listening.

"I didn't know you had a Labrador, too." Carrie took the towel from him and dried her bare arms, then sponged at her soaked blue jeans. But she made no move to climb out of his lap.

"Mine was a golden Lab. Her name was Annibel."

"Did she die?"

"Yes."

"How old was she?"

"Eleven and a half."

"Do you miss her?"

"Of course."

"Did she die in the thunder?"

"No, she died in her very comfortable bed, a happy old lady who'd had a fantastic life. But all eleven and a half years of it she freaked out every time it thundered, just like Blue."

"Did she ever run away when it thundered?"

"Every time. But she always came back."

"Carrie," said Alison softly. "Come along now, honey. You have to get bathed and into something dry before dinner. Wait till you see what Minnie has managed to whip up tonight on only two burners—your favorite. Come on now, darling. I've heated a pan of water so you don't have to take a cold bath."

Reluctantly the child climbed from Stuart's lap. Looking down at him, she asked her mother, "What's Stuart going to do? He's as wet as I am, and there's no hot water for him."

Stuart laughed and got to his feet. "I'll be okay. I can take it. I camped out when I was a Boy Scout. You go along, honey. I'll see you at dinner. Maybe you'll sit next to me."

Over her shoulder Alison caught his eye, just a fleeting glimpse. With it she offered him a look of admiration and love undisguised.

It was well after dark when the family crowded into the big dining room to eat. The room was jammed with furniture they had dragged in from the living room in case the porch roof should cave in and take some of the house with it. It was a tight squeeze, but no one seemed to care. They were exhausted, yet the aura of excitement still clung in the atmosphere. Two drinks before dinner and Alison felt as giddy as a schoolgirl. The very air in the room seemed heady to her. She was deliriously light-headed, with the feeling she was moving and acting in a dream.

Stuart had more than just made friends with her daughter; the child had formed a crush on him that was close to worship. She glued herself next to him at dinner and clung to every word he said. Blue, of course, was home before Carrie climbed out of her bath, and the dog now sat between their two chairs, alternately accepting tidbits from both of them. Alison was too tired to chide. She simply ate her meal and watched.

She listened, not really joining in the dinner table conversation. Yes, Todd's house was barely damaged, but no, it was impossible to get past the live wires to check on Gordie's place yet. The stables were untouched, and the horses seemed to have come through the storm just fine. Ben's cottage was okay, but the Little House had a pole down through the kitchen roof, and a live wire lay draped across the porch. They knew that the groves they had access to had been ravaged, but as for the mammoth twenty-one plus sections they couldn't survey until the highway became open to traffic, they could only guess about and assume it would be more of the same. It was impossible to estimate the extent of the damage this early. Because all telephone lines were down, any communication between themselves and their dozens of managers and foremen was an impossibility. But at least, thank God, they had gotten a large harvest of fruit into trucks from the groves east of the highway before the storm swept across them.

Alison studied all of them, listened to them, responded automatically almost in a trance of exhaustion, confusion, of starry-eyed love. She struggled to mask just how she was feeling about Stuart, but she couldn't deny it to herself. There was more than just this overpowering love she felt in her heart; he was a hero in her daughter's eyes now. He'd been wonderful with Carrie, so gentle with her when she was upset. And he fit. He fit right in with the Watsons, like one of them.

After dinner it was obvious that everyone badly

needed rest. "Come on, kids," Alison said to her two. "Tomorrow's another big day."

Stuart lingered for a moment at McIver's piano and bent over to play a couple of chords. "Do you play?" Carrie squealed. "Play for me, Stuart!" She pulled him down the the bench and climbed up beside him. "Please?"

"I'm too rusty, Carrie. I haven't played the piano since the last time I went home. The only practice I get is on my guitar."

"Just one song, please." She turned to coax her mother. "Do I have time to hear just one?"

"Just one, sweetheart." Alison leaned with her forearms on the piano and listened as Stuart played, watching his long fingers move in the amber light from the lantern across the room. She smiled to see her daughter lay her cheek against his arm, mesmerized, as his fingers moved on the keyboard. Then there were others, Clair and Jennifer and Margaret. And suddenly Keith appeared from somewhere and sat cross-legged on the floor to listen. From the corner of her eye Alison saw Wattie tiptoe back into the living room from the darkened hall. He sprawled out on his stomach on the sofa and lazily began to scratch King between the ears. The music was lovely, one of Alison's favorites.

When he finished, Jennifer was first to speak. "You've such a lovely touch. Did you ever think of playing professionally?"

"Yeah, I really did. I had illusions of my own group someday, and making it to the big time." He laughed and ran his thumbnail down the keyboard. "But I decided to make a bunch of money instead of starving to death in some dark bar."

Alison leaned in to pat her daughter's little bottom. "Okay, young lady, that's it. You'll see Stuart again tomorrow. Off to bed now. Brush your teeth." She walked over and bent to scratch Wattie's back for him. "You, too, son. Lead the way for Carrie with your flashlight, okay?"

The house was dark, dark as pitch, right away. Again Alison could hear Gordie's snoring from down the hall. She stood at her open window and listened to the wind beyond the yard, far out in the groves, light little gusts that whistled through the trees. The night was muggy but really rather cool. She could smell the pungent, wet earth and all of the damp odors cast off from the drenching rains. From a distance somewhere far away hung the sweet, delicious fragrance of orange trees in bloom.

Just minutes before, she had sat in the window seat of the children's room, waiting until they were sleeping soundly, enjoying the night air from the open window. It seemed strange. With air conditioning it had been years since the house was open wide in September. It felt good. She had to smile when she tiptoed from the room. Wattie was curled up with one fist around his oversize flashlight. Gently she pried it from his hand and laid it on the table beside his bed. She stooped to pat King's head, admiring the rim of light her candle cast against his regal head. "Keep them safe," she said to him. Then she pulled the sheet higher around her daughter's shoulders. Blue lifted his head from his place at the foot of the child's bed and wagged his tail. Alison stroked the animal and whispered to him, "You caused a lot of excitement today, you rascal you. Don't go off in snake territory again, okay?"

Back in her own room, she stripped out of her clothes and bathed by candlelight, shivering in the cool tap water. She sat naked at her dressing table to brush her hair, then slipped into a light summer shift, a pale apricot cotton seersucker gown that fell from a drawstring neckline to the floor. The glistening hardwood floors felt cool and sleek under her bare feet. She stood daydreaming now as she gazed from her big window. An icy light reflected on the glossy green leaves of the magnolia tree just outside, light cast from the moon in its last quarter, now no longer hidden behind rain clouds. Suddenly she wasn't exhausted anymore. She felt quite as though she had taken a delicious nap and awakened refreshed.

She was going to go to him. She knew she was going to go. He drew her to him with a force she couldn't defend against, one she had no power to resist. She quivered all over with excitement. Never, not ever, had she wanted anything so much as she wanted him now. She wanted to feel him take her in his arms, to hold her in his strong embrace, to kiss her, to make love with her forever.

She waited until the house was silent, all but for her brother's slow, rhythmic breathing. Then she whispered to her cat as she bent to stroke him. "You stay, MacGregor. I'll be back later." The cat lazily opened his eyes and twitched his whiskers, then closed them again. Quietly she opened her door and stood for a breathless moment to allow her eyes to adjust to the dark hall. Down at its end she could see light cast through the windows of the living room by the distant sliver of a moon overhead. She made her way across the shadowy hallway and felt in the darkness for the knob of the bedroom door. Slowly, silently she turned it. She pushed the door open wide and saw him sit quickly up, his body silhouetted by pale light from across Alliene's sun room. Alison could see that he was naked. In an instant he was by her side. "I knew you'd come to me," he said. He pulled her into his arms, closing and locking the door quietly behind her as he did. Then he kissed her, savagely, wildly, uttering tiny exclamations of passion, holding her fiercely to his chest. At last breaking away, he whispered in her ear, "Alison, oh, my Alison. Alison, you came to me." Then, magically he was kissing her again and touching her body, circling her back, her shoulders, her ass with both of his long hands. And she was kissing him, too. She responded wildly, fiercely, clinging tightly to him as she ran her fingers over his shoulders and up into his full shock of hair. Against her ear she heard him say, "Alison, I want you so."

"And I want you. I want you!"

She felt her head spin in a dizzying whirl of excitement, the vertigo of emotion, whiskey, kisses, passion, all mixed together as he lifted her and carried her swiftly over to bed. As he laid her on her back he was instantly over her, whispering to her, smothering her face with kisses, filling her ears with tiny expressions of love. He crouched beside her and gently undid the ribbon drawstring that held her gown closed, then sighed deeply as the soft fabric fell away from her breasts. "Beautiful, so beautiful," he said softly. Warmly he caressed each of them with his hands before he leaned forward to take a nipple between his lips. He pulled her firmly up until she sat facing him, then he slipped the gown up over her head. He moved silently, swiftly, and soon she was on her back again, and just as swiftly he was down with his face against her breasts. By the reflected light that embraced them, Alison gazed at his strong back, feeling her passion heighten to watch him move artfully, stealthily over her. She gripped his shoulders tightly, then felt him move, move smoothly down. She felt his lips leave her nipples and slide to her navel and down to her clitoris. She cried out in exquisite pleasure to feel his mouth hot on her, his tongue wet and warm as it explored every part of her bare body. Oh, yes, hot, and moving wickedly inside her, moving, sucking, lunging deeper and deeper with his tongue. She felt herself pulsate to his touch and responded crazily, hungrily, wanting more. "Good," she said. "Oh, Stuart, don't stop . . . oh, don't . . . Oh, darling, good . . . good . . ."

Then, in a trance, a wonderful dream, he rolled over to his back, taking her over with him, and now somehow she was on top of him with his strong cock like steel inside her. She whimpered in her ecstasy and sat back, arching her spine against the heady night air, pressing down, down against his body. "Kill me, darling," she said, then fell in to brush his lips with hers. "Kill me, Stuart. I may die. Oh, darling, stop, stop or I will die!"

"Don't wait, Alison," he said softly, smiling up at her in the darkness. "Come now, baby, come to me now. Now . . . now and always, Alison. I want you to come."

In a blinding burst of passion she could feel him lunge higher and higher inside her as he grabbed her ass, locking her body fiercely against his. "Stuart," she cried out, "Stuart I . . . I . . ."

"Do it, Alison!"

It swept over her in a wave. A wonderful, warm wave of prickly, tingling needles that rippled out from her clitoris and across her groin and down, down the insides of her legs, down to the soles of her feet. It was long, long, and so wonderful. She fell forward, her open palms against his chest, and pressed in again and again, feeling it still, wanting it all.

His hands reached up to cup her breasts, and from behind her closed eyes she could hear him say, "Oh, darling, how wonderful. How wonderful to have you come like that."

Slowly she fell in against his chest and kissed him warmly on the lips. "Yes. It was like never before, Stuart. Never. Not even with you. This was the best . . . the best. So in love. Darling, I am so in love."

Suddenly impassioned by her words, he rolled her swiftly onto her back and instantly was hovering over her with his weight on his knees. He pulled her feet up as he rose, first kissing her toes as she cried out in delight, then placing the soles of her feet on his chest. Braced against her feet, and with his hands on her breasts, he lunged and lunged again deep inside her. He was hard, he was steel, and nothing had ever felt so good to her before. He didn't stop. He stayed above her, loving her, pounding her, penetrating her in savage force until she cried out exquisitely again, "Stuart! Oh, my God, Stuart!"

"Yes, oh, yes, Alison, do it. Do it again, baby!"

Unable to stop, not wanting to stop, she burst again in a hot, delicious sensation that swept across her body and brain. It was too magnificent to describe. Somehow, from far away, from some place way above her head, she heard him cry out, too. Then he fell in against her neck and slowly began to catch his breath. "I love you, Alison."

Clinging tightly to him, she said softly, "And I love you. Oh, Stuart. I do love you so much."

After a time he rolled over to his side and gathered her close to him. They lay for many minutes without speaking, just touching, touching in an aura of total oneness as their bodies fit together, hot yet cool, cool to the fingertips, cool to the caress.

She slept. Intermittently she slept. Without words he held her, stroked her, cradled her in his arms as she slept. It was the place she wanted to be. She slept sweetly, happily, but never deeply. With each kiss she was awake again, and again and again they kissed, whispered, loved. Before dawn they made love twice again; each time passionate, fulfilling love. And again she slept. At the first gray hint of light he gently shook her. "It's time."

Startled, she sat and looked out across the sun room. "Oh, no. It's almost light."

"Shhh. No worry. They're still asleep."

"Oh, Stuart, what if they clear the wires off the road today? Gordie saw the power trucks working on the pole by the Little House just before dark. What if you go back today? When will I see you?"

"Soon," he promised.

Suddenly panicky, she said, "But we haven't really talked. There are so many things I need to say."

He grinned. "You've said the one thing that makes everything else all right." He fixed his eyes on hers, visible now in the early-morning light. "Did I dream it?"

She smiled. "You didn't dream it. I . . . I love you, Stuart. I—"

"Say it all."

"It still scares me a little to say it."

"Say it, Alison."

"I-I'm in love with you."

He drew a deep sigh. "Oh, baby. Oh, yes. Don't be afraid. I'm in love with you, too, desperately, completely in love. I have been from the start." He caught her close to him and sighed again. "You've opened up to me at last. Now it's mine, your triple heart. I've hoped all along you were saving that person deep down inside just for me."

She drew back and searched his eyes, drifting back to that day on Sunfish Key when he'd given her the necklace. "Yes, I guess I was, without even knowing it myself. I realize now I've never opened my heart completely. I thought I had once with Hunter. But a part of me held back because I was afraid." She smiled and pulled closer to him, whispering against the curve of his neck. "But I won't hold back from you, darling, not ever again. Oh, Stuart, I feel so close to you."

"It's wonderful," he said. "But now you must go." He reached down and picked her gown from the floor. With him guiding her she lifted her arms high, like a child would, for him to slip it over her head. While he spoke he clumsily tied the bow at her neck. "I'm living for the day you won't have to get dressed and hurry back away from me." He kissed her lips softly, tenderly. "It will come soon. You'll see."

At the door she turned her face up to him once more. "I may not see you alone for a while."

"I'll call you. I'll call every day." He held her for a moment, reluctant to let her go but aware that the light was coming fast. "Please tell me one more time," he said.

She smiled. "I'm in love with you, Stuart."

He gazed into her eyes and drew a deep sigh. "Oh, Alison, Alison, and I with you. So in love."

2

The agony of frustration Alison felt in the days after
Stuart left tore at her. Who possibly could have supposed it would be five full days before their telephone
service was restored? She felt marooned. Of course,
her family surrounded her, and a working telephone
was only as far away as the drugstore in Grove Dale,
but she missed her regular calls from Stuart. She felt
especially lost after all that had happened between
them. The two afternoons she drove into town to call
his office he was somewhere out of town. Then, to
add to the aggravation, one evening after supper
when she made up some harebrained excuse to go in
to the drugstore and called his apartment, he wasn't
home. She was crushed. Where would he be?

Gordie and his family were living with them now.
The third day after the storm when the power linemen finally worked their way to Gordie's property,
the bad news that lay waiting was that an apparent
tornado had ripped through the center of the sprawling ranch-style house, taking walls, roof, and valuable furnishings in its wake.

Stuart had left the day before, as soon as there was
highway access. From their last moment alone in
McIver's bedroom as dawn broke that morning, he
and Alison hadn't gotten a minute alone together.
Everyone in the family seemed to be watching them.
Alison knew Minnie had been all along, but now she

felt suddenly transparent to them all. To top things
Stuart had acquired Carrie as his shadow. From the
instant he emerged for breakfast until they walked
with him to his car, Carrie was at his side. It was
adorable, but it was aggravating, too. Alison wanted
at least a few words alone with him before he left.
She sent Carrie off on a ficticious errand, and before
she could open her mouth, Todd was there, pumping
Stuart's hand good-bye, then the whole damn batch
of them came out in a swarm. Alison wanted to
scream in frustration. She could only stand there
stupidly and shake his hand and say dumb things
like, "Call me when it's time to sign the papers."

The papers! That was another thing. She still
didn't know whether her place on Sunfish Key was
indeed sold or whether that was merely Stuart's
trumped-up excuse to come to the Grove. She expected it had been an excuse. But so much happened
so fast that somehow she forgot it entirely until the
moment he was leaving, and then it was too late to
ask. She couldn't believe it. How on earth could she
have let that get by her?

And now the damn telephone system! Well, it was
just too much. What could she do? She could wait,
that was what. Stuart promised to call. Meanwhile
she was going quietly crazy with uncertainty. She
knew he loved her, but not one syllable had been said
about a future together, not a plan had been made.
What was she to do? Time was almost up for her decision of whether to resign or go back to Channel 32.
Did Stuart want her back over there? He hadn't said
so. Did he want to marry her? If so, would he want
her to continue with her career? What if she made
the decision to resign from her job and make a new
career here? They could hardly engage in a long-
distance romance, a weekend marriage. That was no
way to start a life together.

Wait a minute! Marriage! Was she crazy even to be

thinking the word? It was too soon, too soon. Maybe it would turn out to be a wretched mistake like the others. "The third time will be the charm, Alison. . . ." The charm. Forget it, she told herself. Get that out of your mind.

Early on the morning of September twenty-fifth Alison drove into Grove Dale and called Mr. Ingalls. He was able to see her at two-thirty that afternoon. She made the drive in a little over two hours, taking a lazy pace with lots of time alone to think. She felt sure of one thing: To continue on with her job at Channel 32 just to be near Stuart would be for the wrong reason. Another day had passed with still no real communication, though this morning's mail had brought a funny card. "Get off the phone, damn it! Your public wants you. I love you. S."

The conference with Ingalls was short and painless. The man was icy cold. His personality was probably the key factor in Alison's decision to resign. It had never been the same once Sam retired and Fred Ingalls began to squelch her creativity. She felt good about her decision.

She was sadder about leaving Diana and the girls than anything else, but it was easy to leave the office behind when she glanced at the telephone and remembered that final call from Hunter. There was pain here, still too much pain. At the door she hugged Diana good-bye. "Sure you don't mind sending my things to the Grove?"

"You know I'd do anything in the world for you."

'Hold the right thought about the job," she encouraged the girl. "I honestly think Ingalls will offer the position to you. I've recommended you."

"Alison, I'm scared."

"Nonsense. You've been running this department for two months without me. You're totally qualified. I'm rooting for you."

"I'm going to miss you terribly."

Tears sprang to Alison's eyes. Squeezing Diana's hand, she whispered, "I promise to keep in touch."

When Alison pulled in the parking lot, she noticed many more cars than she'd ever seen there before. But of course, with the additional office space there would be several more employees now. She cast her eyes across the impressive-looking building that was twice the size it had been the day she'd brought the camera crew to shoot that first Stratton Real Estate commercial last spring.

She noticed that Stuart's parking place was empty. Since it was too early for him to be gone for the day, she guessed he must be out showing some property. When she entered the office, Sally looked at her in surprise. "Why, Mrs. Ames. How nice to see you. I didn't know you were back."

"Just for the day."

"Did Mr. Stratton know you were coming?"

"No. I should have called. Is he due back soon?"

"I'm so sorry. He's out of town. I'm sure he'll be upset that he missed you. He only just left. He'll be back day after tomorrow."

Alison masked her disappointment. She smiled at Sally and said, "No matter. Please tell him I stopped by."

"I'm sure he'll be calling in before six o'clock. I'll tell him."

Stunned at the depth of her reaction, Alison drove for several blocks without concentrating on where she was going. She couldn't believe how disappointed she was. Why hadn't she gone into town last night and tried to call him again? She could kick herself for feeling so confident that he'd always be around for her. She took the shaded drive that led in the direction of the old residential section of town where she and Hunter had lived for so many years. She felt empty, hollow. She had just made one of the most important decisions of her life, and she wanted to share it with him first. She hadn't told anyone yet, not even Gordie and Todd. She fought but couldn't suppress her tears.

What in the world was the matter with her? She berated herself. Grow up, Alison. You just made a decision on your own, something you'll be doing a lot of from now on. And it was a good one. No matter what might be in store with Stuart, it was time to make a career change. The page had to be turned on everything that had passed.

She found herself on her old street. As she approached the house she felt a terrible feeling of dread begin to wash over her, the dread she had encountered that awful night when she rushed home to find Hunter dead. She rolled to a stop and idled her engine, wondering whether to go inside the house she hadn't dared enter for two months. She hesitated, then inched slowly forward. Not now. She wasn't ready yet. She glanced over at the Peterson's house eager at least to visit with Patsy. It was closed up, then she remembered that they still would be at their lake house. Nothing was right today.

Without looking back she pulled away, toying with the idea of driving out to Sunfish Key. But what for? It would only be more of the same disappointment and regret. The worst memories of Hunter were out there. But she wasn't ready to go home to the Grove yet. She had told them not to expect her before evening, foolishly anticipating a few hours alone with Stuart. Tears of self-pity stung her eyelids.

She felt uncomfortable with her own thoughts today. She needed someone to talk to, someone to tell her she had done the right thing. Suddenly she thought of Sam. She wondered, could they be back home? After all, it was almost October first. Don't let them still be at their mountain retreat.

She approached the house at the outskirts of Sarasota and felt a wonderful sense of relief. Sam's gray Oldsmobile was parked in the drive. She smiled at seeing that some things were the same as ever. The car was in terrible need of a wash. She glanced inside when she stepped from her own car. Yes, Sam was home. The caddy was crammed with papers, and the ashtray was pulled out and full of stubs. She rang the front doorbell, wondering where Mary's car was. When no one answered, she felt another awful letdown.

Finally she gave up and started to leave. On a last minute hunch she walked around back. He was there on the dock, fishing. Her heart swelled with tenderness just to see him again. He was wearing sneakers and jeans and a faded shirt. His marvelous old rumpled canvas golfing hat was tilted forward to shield his eyes from the late-afternoon sun. He looked almost as if he were sleeping, relaxed on his tailbone with both legs stretched out at an angle. The fishing pole hung casually from under his armpit and rested across his knee. But he was awake. Alison watched him test the line and roll it in an inch or two. She smiled and started to approach him. When she neared the dock, Sam's collie dog woke from her place under his bench and began to wag her tail. "Sam?" Alison's voice was small, childlike.

He turned, startled, then began to reel in his line. His welcoming smile spread across his face. "As I live and breathe, Alison! I was just thinking about you. Come on over here and give these tired old eyes a treat."

Hesitating only a moment, she rushed into his open arms. "Oh, Sam, I've missed you so. I can't tell you how glad I am to see you."

He searched her eyes earnestly. "Do you have any idea how frustrated I've been not being able to get in touch with you? It's almost like the answer to a prayer, your showing up today. I was thinking of driving over to the Grove if that damn phone wasn't fixed by tomorrow. I've raised sand with the phone company since I got back in town the day before yesterday. We've been in the mountains ever since we got back from the Orient." He reached down to pat the dog. "I decided to drive on down alone to pick up Gypsy. That's when I heard the news about Hunter."

"Oh."

"Alison, we had no idea." He put his arm around her shoulders and began to walk her toward the house. "I feel terrible that you haven't heard from us. But we missed hearing about it entirely somehow. When I called Mary to tell her, she was sick."

"I knew you couldn't have known. Please don't feel bad."

They entered the house through the screened patio. Alison looked around appreciatively at the open room, filled with many personal touches. "Let's go on inside where it's cooler," he said. "Blowing Rock has me spoiled. I'd almost forgotten how hot Florida Septembers are."

Alison followed him into his den and watched him pull a couple of glasses from the bar. "Let's see. If I remember right, you're a vodka-and-tonic lady this time of day, right?"

"That sounds good. Oh, Sam, it's great to see you again. I was feeling so lonely and deserted today, I was about to head on back home."

He took his time mixing the drinks, then sat in the easy chair facing hers. "Home? That has a permanent ring."

"That's the reason I'm in town. I gave Ingalls my resignation today."

"I see. So you've hung it up at Channel 32."

"Do you think I made a mistake?"

"Hell, no. Question is, how do you feel about it?"

"It feels right. But it was really tough. If I didn't

like the work so much it would have been easier, but the other things outweighed that factor. I just can't warm up to Ingalls." She smiled. "He's no Sam Abrahmson. It's not fun performing for him the way it was for you. Everything changed when you left." She paused, waiting for him to speak, but he only rocked back silently, waiting. "Plus the memories here are pretty painful now. Maybe I'm just trying to escape something I'll have to face up to later, but things are comfortable for me at the Grove. I have a lot of healing still to do."

"Do you want to talk about it?"

"Hunter's death?"

"Yeah."

"That's not the death I'm healing from. I did my grieving for him the last few years he was alive."

"Oh."

"It's McIver's passing that I can't seem to get over." Brimming tears, she cast her eyes down, unable to catch the tears that spilled over. Then she shook her head angrily and said, "But if I feel anything at all for Hunter it's only anger and contempt."

He looked stunned. "Alison, what do you mean?"

"His death was a suicide."

He leaned forward with both forearms on his knees, studying her for many moments. Finally he said, "My God."

"We were finished," she said bluntly, gesturing with the flat of her hand. "Kaput. I'd already seen my lawyer in Grove Dale. I had a restraining order to keep him away from me and the children." She punched the arm of her chair with her fist. "So it was revenge, don't you see? His hateful, cowardly act was the only way he had left to get to me."

"Easy, Alison."

"Oh, Sam, he knew all along that he was going to do it. I know now that he had already taken the pills

when he called me and said to hurry home. I just
didn't realize it at first. I was angry and, well, I was
used to it when he slurred his words over the phone. I
just assumed he'd consumed his daily quart of martinis a little early." She made a sour face. " 'Course,
he'd done that, too. The autopsy turned up a mixture
of downers in his system." Abruptly she drained her
glass and stared down at the empty tumbler. "A le-
thal mixture," she added resolutely.

"Alison, don't."

Her face contorted in agony. "He damn near destroyed me this time, Sam." She drew a deep, sad
sigh. "He's been destroying me by inches for years,"
she added softly.

"I know." Sam gazed for a moment out at the crystal bay. "You know, it's funny. When I learned about
Hunter's death, I didn't hear the word *suicide* mentioned. I heard he had a stroke."

"Uncle Jim Laskell gets the credit for that. I don't
know how he pulled it off."

"But he did and that's what counts." Sam laid his
head back and rolled it slowly from side to side.
"You're a trouper, kid and a hell of a woman. But
now it's time to move on with your life." At his
kindly words she put her face in her hands and wept
softly. "Go ahead and cry, hon. It's all right. Don't be
ashamed." He busied himself at the bar, then disappeared to the kitchen and came back with a little
tray clumsily arranged with snacks.

Alison dried her eyes and collected herself. "My!
I'd no idea you were such a good cook."

"Yeah, me and the deli at Albertson's. Now let's
talk about the good stuff."

"Oh, yes. I want to hear about your trip. I've
talked too much."

"The monologue on the trip will go along with the
slides. We'll make you suffer through both when we
get back in November. The good stuff I'm referring

to is what's in store for you. I want to hear all about your plans."

"I don't have any that are concrete. Not yet."

"Sounds like you've decided on a permanent move back to the Grove."

"I feel content there. The children have adjusted completely at Grove Dale Elementary. I knew they would."

"Are you planning a new career, or are you going to vegetate in that moose of a house and listen to the orange trees grow while you become middle-aged and fat on Minerva's cooking?"

"I hope not." She sat forward and spoke earnestly. "Sam, today is a turning point in my life, maybe the most important one I will ever make. I've figured out a lot more than my decision to resign my job. You'll see big changes in me. I've been a mess, and I'm through with it. In a way I fed Hunter's destruction by being a party to it for eleven years."

"You're not being fair to yourself. You've made people happy with your excellence of performance at work."

"Of course I'm proud of my career, but it's not enough. I haven't been running my house, Minnie has! I've just been holding court there, getting dressed up in thousand-dollar gowns and exquisite jewelry and floating down the winding stairs to greet my party guests year after year in that never-never land I dwelled in. Do you realize I don't even know how to cook?"

Sam chuckled, then laughed so hard he strangled on his drink.

"Well, it's true! Worse than that, I've been letting someone else make my decisions for me. I'm through running away from myself. Sam, I have lain in my bed for two solid months now, almost too paralyzed with indecision to get out of bed most mornings, trying to figure out what I am, *who* I am. I have stared up at the ceiling and sunk deeper into depression. But something came of it. Maybe this decision I've just made today is the start of taking back the control on my own life which I lost to Hunter. I am through looking back." She shook her head in disgust. "I'm not terribly proud of the selfish brat I've been."

"Now wait a minute, kid."

"Don't worry, I've learned something from all this. Maybe this is the most important of all. I'm going to try to be more like the people who love me from now on. What have I proved all these years by holding everything inside and trying to seem so cool? Do you know that every person I hold dear, including you, tried to reach out to help me, but I rejected them all? I couldn't open up. I couldn't admit to anyone alive, and barely even to myself, that I had failed again. I pretended I wasn't hurting, so naturally all of you pulled back. Thank God I shared *some* of it with my father before it was too late." She brushed away a tear. "His deathbed wish was for my happiness with someone new."

"You'll find that, I'm sure of it. But you've sidestepped my question. What about a new career?"

"I want that, too. Years ago McIver tried to prod me into getting my teeth into the family business, but he saw I was determined to go do my own thing. Lately I've been giving it a great deal of thought. The Watson properties are pretty complex. I could pretty well take my choice, but Todd's pushing me into land acquisition. He's taking me to an auction Saturday to watch me bid. I'm scared. I don't know how I'll be at it."

"You'll be good at anything you decide to get into."

"You sound just like Stu—" She stopped abruptly.

A smile played around the corners of his eyes. "Is that what Stuart thinks, too?" Alison didn't respond.

"That was my next question. How are things between you and Stuart?"

For only an instant she started to protest, to pull her cool reserve up around her in one instinctive move. But then she thought, what for? This was Sam! Sam, one of the handful of true friends she had in the world. Just yesterday she'd been wishing she had McIver to talk to about Stuart. If McIver were here she wouldn't hide her feelings anymore. "Have I been that transparent?" she asked.

"Do you mean, have I noticed you're crazy about the guy?"

"I guess."

"Yes, I've been aware. But no crazier than he is about you. I'm not sure I've ever in my life seen a guy quite so smitten."

Alison grinned. "He's been over to the Grove. He came the day of the hurricane. He got stuck there for two days when the power lines fell across our road."

"You lost your electricity?"

"Yes."

"My. How romantic." He watched Alison blush deeply. "What does your family think?"

"Sam, don't be ridiculous. They only know he's my real estate broker, who stopped by on his way home from Kissimmee. He just happened to get stuck there, that's all. It was an act of God."

"Sure."

"Stop, Sam! Really, it's way too soon. Hunter's been dead only two months. It's not even proper to be thinking . . ."

He eyed her seriously. "Life is for the living, Alison. Haven't you had enough punishment for a lifetime? You're a girl who deserves the best. Don't lose it now over a foolish sense of propriety."

"Stuart hasn't said a word about a future."

"He will. Are you seeing him today?"

"No. He's out of town for a couple of days." She

cast her eyes down for a moment, then asked quietly, "Do you like him, Sam?"

He grinned openly. "He's a young man in a hurry. For the first time in your life, my friend, you may have met your match. Yes, I like him. And he has a key ingredient to happiness, a keen sense of humor. It's about time somebody made my Alison laugh."

She stared sightlessly out the window and smiled. "Oh, my, yes, he does that. He's such a friend to me, Sam. I've never had a person in my life before who could offer me so much friendship and at the same time be—"

"Your lover?" She blushed again and nodded. "Then you've found the right one this time. It'll be for keeps." He smiled as Alison spoke enthusiastically about her plans, not noticing the twinkle in Sam's eyes. To him it was like a replay of the tape the day she'd first walked into his office over twelve years ago. He only half-listened, admiring her gestures, her enthusiasm. She hadn't changed. She was more mature-looking, a little sadder but wiser maybe, but ever so much lovelier. She had a special glow today, the glow of a woman in love.

As if she were really trying to start fresh, she was dressed today in a tailored Chinese-red dress. It was silk, elegant silk from the Orient. She had her copper hair screwed up in the bun she wore when she was all business.

She was leaning forward animatedly now, explaining with her hands, when he began to chuckle aloud Alison stopped, embarrassed. "Good grief. Why didn't you stop me?"

"Like I said, kid, you'll be good at anything you decide to try. But you've left out the biggie."

"What?"

"Politics."

"Sam!"

"I'm not kidding. You'd be a natural. Our district

has state senators, too, you know. If you start on the bottom rung now you might get to be one someday."

Overwhelmed, she said slowly, "I've never even considered . . ."

"Just think about it. It could be a mechanism with which you could do good things for the largest number of deserving people." He stood and smiled down at her. "It's food for thought."

She returned his smile tenderly. "You don't know what this visit has done for me. You've given me back my confidence."

"Come on. You figured all the positive stuff on your own. You just needed a sounding board."

"I needed your approval, too. I needed to hear I'd done the right thing today. And it was important to me that you like Stuart. Don't forget, I've bombed out twice when it came to picking a man. I'm a two-time loser. Twice now, I've put my money on the wrong horse."

"Well, then, relax, kid! You've got it made. The third time is supposed to be the charm."

Slowly she began to smile. "Oh, my," she said.

"What is it, Alison?"

"McIver said those words to me once before."

Alison heard the phone ringing in the distance. It sounded good. It had been days since it had rung. She glanced at her bedside clock. After midnight. Who in the world? She heard Margaret's voice outside her door. "Alison, are you awake, hon?"

"Yes. Come in."

The door opened a crack. "Telephone. It's for you."

"I don't believe it. It's finally fixed?"

Margaret giggled. "Don't jinx it. It sounds like Stuart. Give me a minute to hang up the extension."

"Thanks." Alison listened for the click. "Hello?"

"Alison, at last. Am I actually hearing your voice?"

"Oh, yes." Finally, "How are you, Stuart?"

"Better now. Did I wake you?"

"No, I was wound up. I had a big day."

"Was that Margaret who answered?"

"Yes. They're going to be living with me for a few months. Their home was severely damaged."

"Oh, God. I'm sorry to hear that."

"It was horrible. Margaret is pretty well wiped out by it. She lost many of her beautiful treasures."

"Please tell her I'm sorry."

" 'Course I will." Pausing, "You were gone when I came to see you today."

"I know. Sally told me. I could have kicked myself around the moon for being gone, today of all days. If I'd only known. . . ."

"It was my fault. I should have called. I . . . I made a pretty big decision today. I'd hoped to talk to you about it."

"What was it?"

"I resigned at Channel 32."

"Oh?"

"Yes. After a lot of thought. It seemed the right thing to do."

"I'm very glad. You'd outgrown that place. You've better things ahead."

Alison smiled, wondering just what he meant. She could wait. It was fun to wait now that she'd had that good talk with Sam. "Are you back home?"

"No, I'm over in your neck of the woods. I have a closing tomorrow in Kissimmee and another Thursday in Orlando. I'll be here two days."

"Oh, yes. Sally said you'd be gone a couple of days."

"What did you think of my office? Spiffy, huh?"

"Oh, my, yes. I could hardly believe the changes."

"You got my ball rollin'. Say, Alison, I want to tell you it's been hell not being able to pick up the phone and talk to you lately. That's why I'm calling so late tonight. I just kept calling. I figured sooner or later somebody had to answer."

"I've hated it, too. I've missed you," she said.

She could hear him laugh softly. "And how I miss you! And I missed your first visit to Sarasota in two months."

"That's okay. I had a wonderful visit with Sam. It was therapeutic. He's such a friend to me. He took me to Marina Jack's for crab claws." She giggled. "Plied me with black coffee because he'd fed me three vodka and tonics earlier. He was afraid I wouldn't be able to drive back home. Everybody thinks I'm a baby."

"You are a baby at times. I like it. Makes me want to care for you."

Alison snuggled deeper in her pillow and smiled. "Really?"

"Oh, yes. But words over the phone aren't enough. Words aren't enough, period. I'm going to *show* you one day real soon."

She chose her words carefully. "Might . . . might you be getting back over this way anytime soon?"

"Very soon. I'm working on a deal in Lakeland. Any chance I can drop by the Grove Monday night?"

"Oh, yes, please come."

"I'll be there."

"Stuart, I still don't know if that was a myth about your having a sale of my beach house." She could hear him laugh. "So it *was* a myth. There's no buyer, right?"

"Right."

"You're bad."

"No, I'm good. Smart, too. When I heard the storm was on a straight course for you, I decided it was where I wanted to be. Worked out great. Next best thing to being marooned on a desert island with you." He drew a deep sigh. "I love you, Alison."

"Oh, darling, I do love you so much."

"Music to my ears. Okay, baby, I'm going to let you get some sleep. You've had quite a day. Anything big planned for the rest of the week?"

"Todd's taking me to another auction Saturday. We looked at the property yesterday. It's a gem. Looks like I'll get a shot at this one."

"Terrific! You're taking the plunge."

"Uh-huh. I'm scared. But he'll be there to save me from total disaster."

"There won't be a disaster. I'd like to watch you in action."

"Don't you dare! I'd freeze up tight. Call me Saturday night and I'll give you a report."

"Where is it, anyway?"

"Just east of Lake Wales, about six miles out State Road 60 among some groves. The property fronts Lake Ellen."

"Well, good luck. I'll be thinking about you. And I'll see you Monday around six o'clock, okay?"

"Can't wait."

"I'm crazy about you, Alison. Sleep warm, darling," he said. "Think of me."

3

When Alison stepped from Todd's car, she felt a gentle, cool breeze embrace her face. At last, a break from the oppressive heat of summer. There was almost the smell of autumn rising from the trampled weeds in the crowded lot where the cars were parked. She paused a moment to cast her eyes out over the beautiful lake that bordered the high, grassy bank under her feet. Beyond, on the far side of the water, a dilapidated trailer was silhouetted against a thick hedge of pines. Other than clothes hanging on a line, there was no sign of life there. On this side she was surrounded by a rich orange grove, small but well cared for. And behind her, up a gentle slope, was the hillside parcel, the land that would be auctioned after the lakefront bidding had been completed.

Positioned square in front of her was the red-white-and-blue auctioneer's tent. It was already about three-quarters full of people and filling up fast. Todd took her arm. "Let's hurry. I see a couple of empty seats down front."

Todd stopped to shake hands with a few friends, and waved to another across the tent. Alison quickly scanned the crowd, noticing only a few familiar faces. Once she sat down she was sorry to see that the speaker's platform would block the lovely breeze off the lake. It was a good thing she'd chosen jeans and a cool cotton shirt to wear. Her feet were bare inside open leather sandals, and she wore a sun visor down over her eyes. Behind it her hair was caught up in a high ponytail. To anyone who knew Alison as a fashion plate, this would have seemed another person altogether, a distant cousin perhaps, a red-haired country girl with similar features.

But this was citrus farming country, and these were simple folk. The auctioneer would have viewed her with distrust if she'd been dressed any other way. She glanced around the crowd. It was mixed but dominated by men. All the people present were obviously there on business, but for the moment the gathering also had the earmarks of a social affair. Little groups had formed, and there was laughing and chatter, like at a church bazaar. She noticed that almost everyone was older, except for Todd and herself and the couple of teenagers at the back of the tent in charge of the concession stand. She leaned in to whisper to her brother, "Think it will begin on time?"

He checked his watch. "Yeah. It's ten fifty-five. Wiggins always starts on time."

Alison noticed the people in the front of the tent with interest. The auctioneer was a decent-looking man, balding and clean cut, slim, about forty-five years old. He was bent over in whispered conversation with a drawn-looking, slender lady who was sorting out papers. Alison wondered if they were man and wife. They didn't seem to fit together. Suddenly he reached for the microphone. "Ladies and gentlemen, please register and get your buyer number. I'd like to see everybody registered so we can begin. Then we're gonna crank this thing off and get her sold."

Alison cast her eyes anxiously at Todd. He grinned and waved a numbered ticket at her. "Don't look so nervous, sis. It's nothing to sweat. Just keep in mind that we have to be highest bidder on one of the first four lots sold. That's the key. We'll have a crack at the whole parcel when Wiggins regroups the tracts for the second auction."

"I'm not sure I fully understand."

"Don't worry. Wiggins will explain in detail. He's starting."

Alison studied the map on the blackboard near the speaker's platform and compared it to a pamphlet she'd been handed when she entered the tent. On it the same map was diagramed, along with five photographs of various views of the property. She jumped when Wiggins's voice boomed through the microphone: "Ladies and gentlemen, welcome to Polk County. Welcome to Lake Ellen, to beautiful, clear Lake Ellen in the heart of Polk County, Florida. So nice to have you with us!"

She fidgeted, listening to the opening remarks as she went back over in her mind all Todd had drilled her on during the drive over from Grove Dale. She knew what Todd considered the land to be worth and approximately how much money she had to play with. She was eager to get on with it.

"Now, we'll be selling the property this way," Wiggins shouted.

"Okay," Todd said to her, "this is the important part. Listen."

"We'll begin with the four lots facing the lake. They will go for so many dollars per lot, the high bidder's choice of lot. The low bidders get only the right to bid again. When I say 'sold,' if you're the high bidder, you tell me which of the four lots you want. We reserve the right to regroup the property. We put the entire four tracts together, add up the bid price, divide it by four, and you're gonna need to add five percent to the total price in order to take out the small buyer. Then you'll be in for the whole parcel. Any questions?"

"Got it?" Todd asked.

"I think so."

"Any questions at all?" Wiggins hollered. "No? All right, let's have a sale! Here we go, ladies and gentlemen, here we go!"

Alison glanced nervously around the tent. Everyone looked so calm. They didn't even seem to be paying attention to a word Wiggins was saying. But Todd had warned her about these bidders. They might look like farmers, might act like hicks, but most of them had money in every bank in central Florida. They were shrewd, crafty businessmen, and they knew exactly what they were after.

The droning chant began, the garbled song of the auctioneer, with words spilling from his mouth in a running jumble that was barely intelligible. "How many dollars to sell this lot? How many dollars, your choice, come on in! Will you give me twenty thousand, how many give me twenty, anybody got twenty, anybody fifteen? Come on, give me twelve, give me twelve, ten, come on in folks, anybody give me ten? Anybody got four, give me four, how many give me four thousand?"

Alison watched as the two assistants roved through the crowd, punctuating Wiggins's teases in sharp, staccato echoes that filled the air. One was middle-aged and fat. The young one, dressed in black, looked like a preacher to her. The fat man pointed to the rear of the tent and held up four fingers.

"Four thousand, thank you, sir!" shouted Wiggins. "Four here, six there, how many give me six, how many six, how many five, five thousand, yes, thank you, ma'am. How many give me six?"

With her heart pounding in her throat Alison signaled six to the fat man in the aisle near her, her right hand held out low over her lap and the index finger of her left pointing horizontally beside it. Swiftly he signaled six with his fingers in the air and moved past her. Wiggins shouted, "I have six. Thank you, miss, six here. Who will give me seven, I need seven, I want seven, I need seven thousand, seven, who will give me seven? Yes, thank you, now who will give me eight? Eight, I need eight, who will give me eight, all right then seven-five, now I need seventy-five hundred, I want seven-five, who will give me seven-five?"

Again Alison signaled to the fat man, and again Wiggins shouted, "Thank you, yes, I have seven-five." Suddenly he broke away from his singsong chant and spoke slowly, seriously. "Ladies and gentlemen, now, we're talking about Lake Ellen. . . ."

Todd grinned and nudged Alison in the ribs. "Here comes the pitch. Listen to this huckster lay it on."

Wiggins spoke dramatically, emphasizing his words with flamboyant hand gestures. He reminded Alison of a preacher, too, except he was dressed in shirt sleeves and plaid pants. He *was* a preacher! This was his cause.

The chant began again, and the bids began to rise.

Alison spread her left hand wide and raised four fingers beside it, laterally over her knees. Faster than she could see him do it, the fat assistant held up nine fingers, and Wiggins said, "Thank you, little lady, I have nine, yes, I have nine, now I want ten."

She held her breath, not daring to look around. None of *them* were looking around. They were cool, these local yokels surrounding her, and from somewhere in the tent a bidder topped her price.

Alison stole a quick glance at Todd, then held both hands out in front of her with ten fingers spread wide.

Stuart stood in the rear of the tent with his arms folded across his chest, quietly watching and grinning. He'd had his eye on the main bidders from the start. There were three of them, Alison, a big lady in the third row over on the left, and a man in blue overalls and straw hat in the back row. He watched the lady drop out and leave only Alison and the farmer in the race. As Wiggins chanted on, Stuart noticed the farmer lean over to confer with his wife. The woman gave a little determined shake of her head. Stuart grinned. Alison was home-free. She didn't know it yet, but she was home-free on this one.

Turning abruptly to Alison, Wiggins pointed his finger at her and said, "Sold! The property goes to the little lady in the first row for ten thousand dollars. Which tract will it be?"

She leaned forward and spoke to his assistant. "Tract thirty-three!" he shouted. She watched the young man cross off the choice lot on the big diagram.

"Good girl," Todd said. "How're you doing?"

"Parched. I'm nervous."

"I'll get you a cold drink." Todd spotted Stuart the moment he turned around, smiling when Stuart quickly signaled silence. Todd pushed his way through the mob and joined him in the crowd around the boys who were selling cold drinks. "Stuart." He shook his hand warmly. "I didn't know you were here today. Did Alison—"

"No. I want to surprise her. Don't say anything, okay? Thought I'd take her for a late lunch somewhere."

"Sure. You'll have a bit of a wait though, buddy. This was just the first bid of eight, then Wiggins will regroup the property and open bidding on the entire acreage. We're staying till the last dog is hung. We're after the whole parcel."

"I understand. I don't mind waiting. I'm getting a kick out of watching your sister. How's she doing?"

Todd grinned. "She's a natural but doesn't know it. She's very nervous."

"That's one reason I don't want her to see me. It might make her worse." When Todd eyed him wisely, he quickly added, "Well, you know, since I'm in the real estate business and all, I thought it might make her self-conscious if she knew I was here."

"Sure." Todd popped open his can and took a sweeping glance around the room. "I'd better get back up there or she'll send out the troops. See you later."

Alison accepted the cold can gratefully. "I was all set to come after you. I think Wiggins is ready to start again. Don't you dare leave me to do this thing by myself!"

"I ran into some people I know." He patted her knee and reassured her. "You're doing fine. Really. It's going our way, I can feel it. It's going to move faster now. Getting hungry?"

Astounded, she said, "Is it lunchtime already?"

"Pushing noon."

"I'm fine, but I hope you brought your wallet. I'll be ready to eat a moose by the time we get out of here—if I live through it."

"You'll live through it."

Alison did live, and she liked the experience tremendously. With each new bid the pitch of excitement grew higher. She allowed the next two lots to go to other bidders but fought for the fourth one, that time in a five-way scramble for the property. Again she won high bid; it positioned her as high bidder on the entire lakefront tract. It had seemed an eternity reaching this point, but in actuality, within fifty minutes of the first chant of the auctioneer's song, the four lots bordering the lake, just under three acres altogether, were regrouped for bidding as a unit. And within ten minutes after that, for a total of $43,270, the parcel was hers, sold to Watson Properties. She drew a deep sigh of relief. It was half over now. Three acres in the bag; roughly four and a half more to go before the auction's end. She turned in her seat and gazed back up the hill, wondering how long the break would be before bidding would begin on the second parcel. She felt Todd's eyes on her and turned to smile at him. "How do you feel things have gone so far?" she asked.

"Couldn't have handled it better myself. Did you have fun?"

"Oh yes! I'm drained, but it was fun."

"Grab your second wind. He'll be opening bidding on the first hillside lot in about ten minutes. Are you game, or do you want me to take over?"

"No, I really want to do it. Just promise to feed me later."

"Hang in there, sis. I guarantee you you're going to have the nicest lunch you've had in years."

Everyone stood when it was over. Alison stretched her legs and looked around the crowd. Todd turned in a half circle, sweeping his eyes across their newly acquired property. "I am really pleased. I never dreamed we'd nail that second parcel for $31,000." Then he fixed his gaze in satisfaction on the rich green banks of the sleepy, still lake. "It's all ours now, and for under seventy-five grand. It's an excellent buy, Alison. Gordie will be ecstatic." Leaning closer to his sister he added confidentially, "It'll be worth three times that in no time. And that's unplanted. Just wait until you see that land up the slope filled with fruit trees."

"I'm excited about it."

Todd's eyes twinkled when he saw Stuart approaching. "Wait for me here, Alison. I'll take care of signing the contracts. It'll only take a few minutes." He edged through the crowd to the back of the tent.

Stuart waited until she was alone. "Congratulations, Alison."

She whirled around to face him. "Stuart! Where did you come from?"

"I've been here awhile. Almost from the start." He

grinned openly. "I couldn't wait till Monday to see you."

"It's fabulous to see you, but I think I'm glad I didn't know you were here while I was bidding. Did Todd see you?"

"A couple of times back at the concession stand. Speaking of which, are you thirsty? I'll get something for you."

"Oh, no. What I need is a cool restaurant somewhere. Todd said he'd only be a few minutes. Can you join us for lunch?"

"I've already told Todd I'd like to take you to lunch. He said for us to go on."

Inside the rustic restaurant Alison excused herself and hurried to the ladies' room, groaning when she saw her image. She'd perspired through most of her makeup, and her hair was a mess. Quickly she sponged cool water on her face, then ran a brush through her hair, letting it fall loosely around her collar. She smoothed on some blush and lipstick and squinted into the mirror. It was dark as a cave in the tiny rest room. Finally she gave up for lack of light. It would have to do.

At the table a tall Bloody Mary was waiting for her. Stuart was engrossed in the menu and didn't see her at first, then jumped to his feet to seat her. "Hello, gorgeous. Sit down with me and unwind."

"This is such a nice surprise."

"You're incredible, you know that? I enjoyed watching you back there. You were as smooth as glass, like you've been closing seventy-five-thousand-dollar deals for years."

"Todd made me look good. He drilled me for days."

"Whatever, I enjoyed it. I want you to relax now over a nice quiet lunch. Are you free to spend the afternoon with me?"

"I'd like that."

"I have a piece of property I need to check out over near Lakeland. I'm hoping you'll ride with me."

"Of course I will."

Alison settled back for the thirty-mile drive feeling beautifully drowsy. She was giddy from two drinks before lunch and the split of wine they had shared over the meal. She felt so good. She stole a glance at Stuart and smiled. How in love she was. He looked terrific to her. He was wearing jeans, too, his shirt open at the neck. It was a clear, light shade of blue, like the clear blue of his eyes. She laid her head back and closed her eyes, wrapped in the mood of the stereo sounds that filled the car.

"You going to sleep on me?"

"Maybe. It's your fault, plying a girl with drinks and wine and all that good food." When he took a gentle curve in the highway, she could feel the late-afternoon sun move across her face. Oh, yes, fall was here at last.

Stuart smiled to see her in repose. "Sleep if you like. I'll wake you when we get there."

"I'm only drifting in and out. I don't want to sleep. I might miss something."

She lost all track of time, drifting, daydreaming, wrapped in the mood of the moment, the closeness to him. When the car took a sharp curve, she opened her eyes and sat up. Stuart had turned down a narrow, shaded road, leaving the highway behind. "Are we almost there?"

"Yep. Just about a mile on ahead."

A clearing in the trees revealed a sapphire-blue lake, and around a curve, there it was! Nestled on a lovely, shaded lot was a cypress A-frame home, a house so like her place on Sunfish Key that it took her breath away. "Stuart! Is this it? Is this the property you're checking out?"

He rolled to a stop in the circular drive, then

turned in the seat to face her. "This is it. Will you come in with me? I have a key."

"I'm stunned," she said. "It reminds me so much of my place."

"Doesn't it? I thought that myself."

"Have you seen it before?"

"Yes."

Together they walked the few yards to the front door. "Honestly," she said, "if that were the Gulf of Mexico back there instead of that lovely lake, I'd swear this was 437 Sunfish Key Cove."

"But it is 121 Lake Madeline Lane."

"Lake Madeline. How lovely."

He slipped the key in the lock and pushed the door open wide. Leaning in, he kissed her gently on the lips. "Lovely, like you."

When she stepped into the center hall, she drew another excited sigh. "Stuart! The floor plan is even similar. Look, a center hall from front to back. And a deck beyond the French doors. It's so like mine. I can't believe this place. I wonder if the same architect possibly could have designed it. McIver commissioned him from over here someplace, I know that. His name was Irwin. Somebody or other Irwin."

"I wonder."

"How old is this place?"

"About six years, I understand. Come on. Let's look around."

She followed him up the hall past two bedrooms on the left, two bedrooms connected by a bath just as hers were on Sunfish Key. Then down, and facing the lakefront on the left of them was the living room. A huge picture window overlooked the water, and in the corner was a freestanding fireplace. "I don't believe this. It's giving me chills. I'm dying to know who designed it. Any way to find out?"

"Oh, sure. There's always a way to find out something you really want to know."

"And it's furnished," she exclaimed. "It looks as if someone is living here right now."

"Someone is. A bachelor. Hell of a nice guy."

"Why on earth would he want to sell? I can't imagine giving it up."

"He's getting married soon. He plans a big family."

"Oh." She followed him across the center hall, pausing to scan the view beyond the deck. At the water's edge was a small boat house and beyond it a *T*-shaped dock hung over the glassy water. It reminded her of their lake back home. "It's terrific, Stuart. I'll bet he wants a handsome price for this property."

"Yeah, a bundle. But I've found him a buyer."

"Really?"

"Uh-huh. Just wanted to show it to you first." He caught her hand. "Let's look on through."

She followed him through the dining room. It was smaller than hers on Sunfish Key, but a surprise was waiting in the kitchen. The room was much bigger than her kitchen and spilled into a wonderfully warm family room, big enough for a breakfast alcove with a view of the lake. It was inviting. "Oh, darling, I could move in." She sighed. "What's upstairs?"

"Only an upper deck and the loft. It's huge, though. And, of course, there's another bathroom. It's nice and big. Has a whirlpool. Want to go up?"

"I want to see it all. I'm jealous of the people who bought this house. I really didn't know there was anything like it over in lake country. Maybe there are places like this on every lake in central Florida."

"Well, no. This is special."

When Alison climbed the stairs, she could sense

Stuart's vibrant sensuality, could feel him close to her, his breath on her neck. A thrill of excitement rippled through her body.

She waited a moment for her eyes to adjust to the darkness. Stuart turned her gently by the shoulders to face him. "Alison, I want to hold you."

"Please," she said. "Please hold me."

Tenderly he gathered her in his arms, took her lips with his. She felt swept in a whirlwind of emotion, then passion, an all-consuming heat of bursting, blinding love. With every fiber of her being she returned his kisses, clinging to him, whispering soft words against his lips, eagerly offering promises of love.

Then she felt herself drawn over to a huge bed. "Will you love me, Alison? Will you make love with me here?"

"Yes. Oh, yes."

It was like that last heavenly time together, the night they had lain together in McIver's big bed, more than mere passion, more than simple desire. Her heart burst with love. She gave herself to him entirely, eagerly, longing to give back all the love she felt from him, and more.

Later, as they lay with bodies pressed together, clinging as one, she drifted, not wanting the afternoon to end. It was close to dark now. The late-afternoon sun's orange twilight rays slanted through the cracks in the shutters. She lay facing him, snuggling her nose against his neck. She basked in the moment, loving the touch of his gentle hands on her bare back. "When will he come home?" she asked.

"Who?"

"The bachelor. I don't want to be up here naked in his bed when he gets here." She giggled. "I have a hunch this isn't what he had in mind when he gave you the key."

"No problem. No one's coming today. It's ours for now."

"I wish . . ."

He drew back and gazed tenderly into her eyes. "What do you wish?"

"Oh, it's just a silly wish. I guess I wish we didn't have to leave here tonight."

"Do you?"

"Yes." She kissed the tip of his nose, then rolled over with her back against him. "But it's an impossible wish." She backed up, snuggling against his chest as she felt his arm circle under to cup her breasts against his forearm. "It's almost dark. Minnie will be pacing the floor if I don't get back there soon. She's fierce about serving dinner on time, Saturday nights in particular. She has a lot to do at home, you know, to get ready for Sunday. I'd never do anything to spoil Sunday for her."

"I love you, Alison Watson. We'll drive Minnie home tonight."

Smiling, she snuggled her back against his body and allowed herself to daydream a moment longer. Suddenly she spotted something, something that looked oddly familiar. Propped in the corner near the closet was a guitar. She sat straight up and stared at it. Then she reached over and turned on the lamp beside her. "Stuart Stratton, is that your guitar?"

He flopped back on the pillow and began to laugh.

"Stuart, tell me! Are you staying in this place? Have you been teasing me all along? You're renting the place, aren't you?"

"I've told you the truth. A bachelor owns it."

"I want the whole truth. Just whose place is this?"

He pulled her down against his chest, laughing still. Finally he caught his breath and said, "It's yours if you'll have it."

She struggled to pull away and got back on her

haunches to stare into his eyes for the truth. "What did you just say?"

He sat up and faced her, nose to nose. Taking his time, he cupped her cheek gently in his open palm, then traced the rim of her nose with his index finger, stopping to caress her lips before he circled the full outline of them with his finger. He leaned in and kissed her lightly, tenderly. Then he spoke. "Will you marry me, Alison Watson?"

For only a moment she looked into his eyes, then burst into tears, burying her face in her hands.

"Now wait a minute," he said, laughing again. He pulled her down with him to the pillow and took her hands from her face. With his thumb he wiped away her tears. "Were those happy tears, or sad?"

"Happy," she said.

"Then will you?"

"You know I will."

He gathered her against him and pressed her body to his chest in a giant bear hug. He could feel her tears against his shoulder. He leaned in to kiss them from her face.

"But how . . . I mean, why did you get this place over here? Your office is in Sarasota. You can't—"

"My new office is in Lakeland. We opened just over two weeks ago. I'm a three-location mogul now, with two more on the drawing board." He chuckled. "You'll have to start calling Stratton Real Estate, Inc. a multioffice operation if you ever get back into producing commercials for me, kid."

"Are you serious?"

"You bet."

"Then you're willing to move to central Florida?"

"I've already moved. I've been in this house going on five weeks."

She fell back on the pillow, astounded. "My God. You mean, when you came to the Grove the day of the storm, you were coming from . . ."

"From 121 Lake Madeline Lane."

"My God," she repeated. Suddenly she sat straight up in bed and eyed him haughtily. "Okay, smarty one. I want some other answers. I want to know about this A-frame. It just fell out of the sky and hit you right smack on the head, right?"

"No. As a matter of fact this house was the hardest part of the whole plan. It was a bitch. It didn't take a wizard to locate Irwin, but I thought I'd *never* get him to give it up. He was living here. He considered your Sunfish Key house the ultimate monument to his achievement, so he built this one in his neck of the woods for himself to retire in. They made a few changes to suit themselves, but essentially it was the same house as yours."

"They?"

"He and his wife. Their kids are grown. But she was some tough cookie when it came to wrenching this place away. I knew I didn't have time to have him build me one from scratch. The minute I saw it I knew I had to own this one. But, Jesus! That woman was as stubborn as a mule."

"How did you get them to sell?"

"Ultimately with a price they couldn't refuse. Plus I threw in a lot on a lake about five miles from here. Then I gave them the ol' Stratton Sales Pitch."

Alison rocked back and smiled. "So when I came over to Sarasota this week and you were gone you were . . ."

"I was working in my new office in Lakeland that day." He grinned. "And when I finally reached you that night I was phoning from this bed."

"You devil!"

He pulled her down close to him again, kissing her eyes, her cheeks, the tip of her nose. Against his neck she said, "But what will you do with your office in Sarasota?"

"I've hired a manager, just like I have in Kissimmee. I plan to travel to all three, Alison. It's one reason I'm settling in this location. It's central. I can easily get back home at night from any of them."

"Oh, my." Her voice was barely audible.

"But we'll live in the Big House during the week. I don't want to uproot Carrie and Wattie from school in Grove Dale. And God knows I don't want to do anything to upset Minnie's domain. Listen, lady, I want those people to like me." He grinned and pulled her closer. "But *this* place is going to be ours, darling, yours and mine. This will be our weekend hideaway. Here I can have you alone all to myself."

"Do you honestly mean you won't mind living that kind of life?"

"Mind? It's been my goal from the day you became free. I just had to give you a little time to yourself, that's all. But I intend to be inside your life from now on. I want to be a part of your world every day for the rest of my life." He bent in over her and smiled into her eyes. "But I've *had* it with your getting up and getting dressed and splitting the minute we finish making love. That's for the birds. Do you realize we've always missed out on one of the best parts, sleeping in each other's arms? You gave me a glimpse of that the two nights we spent in McIver's bed. It made me want more."

"Oh, yes."

"So, enough is enough. I'm through with this separation crap."

She laughed softly. "Anything else?"

"Yeah. A bunch else! I have a family, too. I have parents and two sisters and a brother-in-law and a nephew who's the neatest kid in the world. They're *all* neat. Terrific, in fact. Plus I have this wonderful little grandmother who's going to

charm the gold right out of your teeth when you
meet her. I've told all of them about you. I'm taking you home with me next weekend. I think I've
passed muster with your tribe. Now we'll see how
you do with mine."

"I'm scared."

"Don't be. One more thing, Alison Carrington
Watson Stratton. You're not through having babies.
My mother is dying to be a grandmother again, and
I'm ready to try my hand at being a father. I plan on
being a good stepfather with your two, but I want a
shot at starting from scratch, okay? I want two,
maybe three."

"Okay."

He looked surprised. "Okay? Really? You're
game?"

"I want it, too." Then she reached forward and
kissed him. His words stopped, and their lovemaking
began again.

The ride back was sweet. Alison felt a tingle, a special glow that prickled its warmth throughout her
body. She reached across the console to stroke his
thigh. "Damn bucket seats," she said. "I wanted to
be cuddled on the way home." He smiled and reached
out for her hand.

"Stuart?"

"Hmmm?"

"Should we tell them tonight?"

"Of course we should tell them. And we should set
a date. I plan to have our own private Christmas
party at 121 Lake Madeline Lane. You're going to
spend Christmas night in my arms, so if you want it
to be legal, you'd better decide on a wedding date before then."

"Then let's do it. Let's tell them all tonight. Will
you go with me in the back door when we get to the

Big House? I want to tell Minnie first." He smiled tenderly at her. "Minnie's been waiting such a long time for me to be happy." She paused, thinking it through. "Then my children next. I want to tell the children alone, just the two of them with us, okay? We'll go to my mother's sun room. That room is special to me. Everything important, somehow, has been decided in that room." She sat forward, pulling one leg up under her, and said excitedly, "Then we'll make Carrie and Wattie keep the secret until we announce it to the others. They will love it."

Stuart reached over and squeezed her hand. "Any way you wish."

"Then I want to tell all the rest at once. I'll invite them all over and we'll tell them together." Then, suddenly remembering, she said, "Oh, and Clair! I can't leave Clair out. I'll invite her, too." She fell back into the soft leather and closed her eyes. "It's all terribly exciting." Suddenly pensive, she gazed over at him. "Stuart?"

He glanced at her, smiling, admiring the rim of light that reflected along the contour of her exquisite cheekbones. "Yes?"

"McIver will be there, too. He would have been so happy. I can feel his happiness wrapping around us now." She drew a little sigh. "Oh, how I wish you two could have met. You'd have been such friends."

"I know."

"Darling, there's something else. There's something I've got to tell you. I-I'm not terribly proud of it, but it's there, and I have to say it now." She shook her head wearily and made a face. "God, it's hard. Especially since you've never been married."

"What in the world are you talking about?"

She took a deep breath, then blurted the words. "My marriage to Hunter wasn't my first. I've been married twice. I was married for two months, when I was seventeen years old, to Calvin Douglass, who lived next door."

He threw back his head and laughed.

"McIver kept telling me that it was over so fast, it didn't count, but he loved me no matter what, so I've always been afraid to believe that. I could cop out and say it was puppy love, but it wasn't even that. What it *was* was McIver caught Calvin and me having sex in the potting shed and—"

Stuart hooted with laughter, bending forward over the steering wheel.

She began to laugh, too. "Then it's all right?"

"Listen to me, beautiful. You're good and true, and I love you madly. It's marrying *me* that's important. *Now* is all that matters to me. We have the rest of our lives to be together. I can barely believe it yet. You've said yes, you've told me yes!" He sighed. "You've told me you want me, too."

"Oh, I do."

He felt for her hand in the darkness and lifted it to his lips. They drove silently for many minutes. When Stuart took the lazy turn off the highway and they passed the Little House, Alison spotted lights shining from the Big House up ahead. The moon in its final sliver was on the wane, yet it cast an incredibly lovely path across the lake through the clear air. She was filled with a feeling of love, of peace, a sort of inner peace that she had never known before.

Before they stepped from the car, Stuart turned to face her and took both of her hands in his. "May I hear it again? Will you marry me, Alison?"

"I'll marry you," she said. "Oh, yes, I'll marry you. I want our marriage to be forever."

"It will be, darling. Ours is the one that will last."

Together, arm in arm, they walked around the side of the house, down the wide pebble path that led to Minnie's kitchen.

A FAREWELL TO FRANCE
Noel Barber

"Exciting...suspenseful...Masterful Storytelling"
Washington Post

As war gathered to destroy their world, they
promised to love each other forever, though
their families were forced to become enemies.
He was the French-American heir to the famous
champagne vineyards of Chateau Douzy. She
was the breathtakingly sensuous daughter of
Italian aristocracy. Caught in the onslaught
of war's intrigues and horrors, they were
separated by the sacrifices demanded of them
by family and nation. Yet they were bound
across time and tragedy by a pledge sworn in
the passion of young love, when a beautiful
world seemed theirs forever.

"Involving and realistic...A journey to which
it's hard to say farewell...The backdrop of
World War II adds excitement and suspense."
Detroit News

**Now an Operation Prime Time
Television mini series starring
Deborah Kerr and Jenny Seagrove**

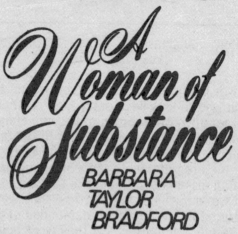

A Woman of Substance

BARBARA
TAYLOR
BRADFORD

THE IRRESISTIBLE NATIONWIDE BESTSELLER.
Set against the sweep of 20th-century history, it
tells the compelling story of Emma Harte, who rises
from servant girl to become an international corporate
power and one of the richest women in the world.

"A long, satisfying novel of money and power,
passion and revenge." *Los Angeles Times*

"A wonderfully entertaining novel."

The Denver Post

49163-X/$3.95

An **AVON** Paperback